4/16/12 **Officially Noted** PK
Pg. 125-137 light moisture
at outer right/left edge.

1/28/14 Moisture at bottom p. 219-280, MKS

River Road

Also by JoAnn Ross
in Large Print:

Blue Bayou

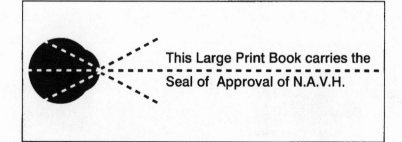

River Road

JoAnn Ross

WHEELER
PUBLISHING

Published in 2003 by arrangement with Pocket Books, a division of Simon & Schuster, Inc.

Wheeler Large Print Romance Series.

The text of this Large Print edition is unabridged. Other aspects of the book may vary from the original edition.

Set in 16 pt. Plantin by Myrna S. Raven.

Printed in the United States on permanent paper.

Library of Congress Cataloging-in-Publication Data

Ross, JoAnn.
    River road / JoAnn Ross.
      p. cm.
    Second book in the Callahan brothers trilogy.
    ISBN 1-58724-424-1 (lg. print : hc : alk. paper)
    1. Television actors and actresses — Fiction. 2. Soap operas — Fiction. 3. Louisiana — Fiction. 4. Large type books. I. Title.
PS3568.O843485R58 2003
  823′.914—dc21   2003042261

To Jay —
who never complains about living in a house
populated by imaginary people, taught himself to
cook so I don't have to live on cereal while I'm
deep in a book, and is always there to point
out the rainbow whenever I begin fussing
about storm clouds.
I love you.

1

Washington, D.C.

Finn Callahan hated bad guys, criminal lawyers, bureaucrats and cockroaches. At least the bad guys had provided him with a livelihood as an FBI Special Agent for the past thirteen years. Why the good Lord had created the other three remained one of those universal mysteries, like how the ancient Egyptians built the pyramids or why it always rained right after you washed your truck.

"It's not like I killed the guy," he muttered. The way Finn saw it, a broken nose, some bruises and a few broken ribs didn't begin to equal the crimes that scumbag serial killer had committed.

"Only because two agents, a Maryland state trooper and a court-appointed shrink managed to pull you off him before you could," the woman behind the wide desk said. There was enough ice in her tone to coat Jupiter. Her black suit was unadorned; her champagne blond hair, cut nearly as short as his, barely reached the collar, and her jaw thrust toward him like a spear. Put her in dress blues and she could have appeared on a U.S. Marine recruiting poster.

"I've spent the past hour on the phone with Lawson's lead attorney. Unsurprisingly, he wants to file assault and battery charges. And that's just for starters. I'm attempting to convince him to allow us to handle the matter internally."

Unpolished fingernails, trimmed short as a nun's, tapped an irritated tattoo on the gleaming desktop.

Finn had no problem with women in the Bureau; he'd worked with several and would have trusted his life to them any day. Hell, even James Bond had gotten a woman boss when Judi Dench took over as M. Finn didn't even have any problem with ice queens like Special Agent in Charge Lillian Jansen.

He did, however, have a Herculean problem with any SAC who wasn't a stand-up guy. From the day she'd arrived from the New York field office, Jansen had proven herself to be far more interested in the politics of the job than in locking up criminals.

"It's a helluva thing when an SAC takes the side of a sicko killer over one of her own men," he muttered.

"Christ, Callahan," the other man in the office warned. James Burke's ruddy cheeks were the hue of ripe cherries, suggesting that Finn's recent behavior hadn't been good for his blood pressure problem. A faint white ring around his mouth was evidence he'd been chugging Maalox directly from the bottle again.

"You're out of line, Special Agent," Jansen snapped. "Again."

Leaning back in the leather swivel chair, she dropped the sword that had been hanging over his head for the past forty-eight hours — ever since the killer it had taken Finn nearly three years to track through eight states had made the mistake of trying to escape from the hospital, just as Finn dropped by to see how the court-appointed psychiatric evaluation was going.

"I will, of course, have no choice but to turn this incident over to OPR."

The Office of Professional Responsibility was the equivalent of a police force's internal affairs bureau. Since many of its investigators possessed a guilty-until-proven-innocent attitude, a lot of agents tended to distrust the OPR right back.

The idea of being thrown to the wolves made Finn's gut churn, but unwilling to allow Jansen to know she'd gotten beneath his skin, he forced his shoulders to relax, schooled his expression to a mask, and although it wasn't easy, kept his mouth shut.

"You're scheduled to be questioned tomorrow afternoon at three o'clock. You are, of course, entitled to be represented by legal counsel."

"Now there's an idea. Maybe I can get one of those worms making up Lawson's legal dream team to represent me. Of course, the only problem with that idea is since Lawson's a gazillionaire sicko with bucks out the kazoo, I doubt any of those scumbags would want to take on the case of a middle income cop who got pissed off at their client for raping and killing coeds."

Ronald Lawson had murdered eight college women scattered across the country from California to Maryland. Finn's recurring nightmare was that there were still more missing women he hadn't yet discovered who could be linked to the guy.

"We would have had eleven victims if Callahan hadn't gotten to Lawson's house when he did and found those girls locked up in his basement." A chain-smoker, Burke's voice was as rough as a bad gravel road.

"That's part of my problem." Frustration sharpened the SAC's brisk voice. "The Georgetown girl's parents are close personal friends of the Attorney General. In fact, the AG and his wife are her godparents. They heard about Lawson's attempted escape on the nightly news and are pressuring the AG to allow Callahan's outrageous cowboy tactics to slide."

Finn shot a sideways look at Burke, whose expression told him they were thinking the same thing. That perhaps he just should have put his gun barrel into the guy's mouth and pulled the trigger in those midnight hours when they'd descended on Lawson's Pontiac mansion. Every cop in the place would have sworn on a stack of bibles that deadly force had been absolutely justified.

He'd always been a by-the-book kind of guy, the type of FBI agent Efrem Zimbalist, Jr. had played on TV, but sometimes the laws protecting the bad guys really sucked.

"How about we come up with a compromise?" Burke suggested.

"What type of compromise do you have in mind?" Jansen asked.

"Callahan takes a leave of absence until this blows over. Say, two weeks."

"That's not enough time for damage control. Four weeks suspension," she countered. "Without pay."

Finn had been staring up at the ceiling, pretending disinterest in the negotiation. When he realized Burke wasn't countering Jansen's proposal, he shot the SAC a savage look.

"Fuck that." He rubbed knuckles which had been bruised when they'd connected so satisfyingly with Lawson's jaw. *You are not,* he instructed his itchy fist, *going to screw this up worse by punching a hole through that damn trophy wall.* A wall covered with photographs of SAC Lillian Jansen with seemingly every politician in town. "I'll take my chances with OPR."

"Dammit, Finn, it's not that bad an offer." Burke plowed a hand through thinning hair the color of a rusty Brillo pad. "You haven't taken a real vacation in years. Go home, do some fishing, unwind, and when you come back all this shit will have blown over."

They both knew it'd probably take another Hurricane Andrew to blow this particular shit pile away.

"If I were you, I'd take your squad supervisor's advice." Jansen folded her arms across the front of a jacket as black as her heart.

Finn suspected that not only was she enjoying this, she was just waiting for him to squirm. *Not in this lifetime,* his expression said.

Want to bet? hers said right back. "If this goes any further, my recommendation will be to terminate you."

And she'd do it if it'd help her career. Hell, she'd probably run over her own dog if it'd get her a promotion to ADIC. Of course she didn't actually have a dog; that would take some kind of personal commitment — and from what he'd seen, the woman was only committed to her swift climb up the Bureau's political ladder.

"Two weeks." *Forget Hurricane Andrew.* Finn needed a tornado to come sweeping out of Kansas, swoop down over K Street, and drop a damn house on Lillian Jansen.

"Four." Her lips actually quirked a bit at the corners, hinting at the closest thing to a smile he'd witnessed since her heralded arrival from New York. She held out her hand, palm up. "And I'll take your weapon and shield."

Feeling Burke's gaze on him, the silent plea to make nice radiating off his squad commander like a physical presence, Finn swallowed the frustration that rose like bile in his mouth, took his .40mm Glock from his shoulder holster and resisted, just barely, the urge to throw it onto her desk.

When he failed to manage the same restraint with his shield, all three pairs of eyes watched the leather case slide off the highly polished surface onto the carpet. Finn hoped Jansen would ask him to pick it up, so he could suggest where she could plant those thin, pale lips.

"Do you know the trouble with you, Callahan?"

"No. But I have a feeling you're going to tell me."

"You've begun to believe your own press. There are those in the Bureau, including your former SAC, who may be impressed by your appearances on *Nightline* and your dinners at the White House. But as far as I'm concerned, you have a very bad attitude toward authority. You also take your work personally."

"And your point is?"

She glared at him with nearly as much contempt as he felt for her, then pressed a button on her intercom. "Please send in security to escort Special Agent Callahan out of the building."

"I'll do that," Burke offered quickly. It was obvious he wanted to get Finn out of the office before things got worse.

"It's not your job," Jansen said.

"A superior stands by his men." His tone clearly implied the SAC did not. If Jansen's eyes were frost, Burke's were flame.

Finn was willing to take the heat himself, but didn't want to cause a longtime friend any more problems. Especially since he knew Burke had put a second mortgage on his Arlington house to pay for his three kids' college tuition and couldn't afford a disciplinary suspension.

"Jim, it's okay."

"The hell it is," the older man shot back. "This whole mess stinks to high heaven." He pinned the SAC with a hard look.

Clearly unwounded, she merely shrugged in return. "You have ten minutes," she told Finn.

Finn turned on his heel with military precision, and had just opened the office door when she called his name. Glancing back over his shoulder, he imagined a black widow spider sitting in the center of her web.

"If I were you Callahan, I'd spend the next month sending out resumes. Because if and when you return, you'll be transferred to another field office, where — if I have anything to say about it, and believe me, I do — you'll be reassigned to desk duty."

Oh, she was good. Coldly efficient, deadly accurate, hitting right on target. She knew he'd rather be gut shot than spend the rest of his career stuck in some dreary outpost, shuffling papers. Finn would bet his last grade increase that, instead of playing Barbie dolls and having

14

pretend tea parties like other little girls, SAC Jansen had spent her childhood drowning kittens.

He heard Burke clear his throat, another less-than-subtle warning. But Finn refused to justify her threat with a response.

Since his work had always been his life, he didn't have any hobbies, nor had he bothered to accumulate any superfluous stuff that might clutter up either his desk or his life. He cleaned a few personal effects from his desk and was out of the building in just under eight minutes.

2

Los Angeles, California

The bedroom was bathed in a shimmering silver light. A sultry sax crooned from the stereo speakers hidden in the walls, a bottle of champagne nested in a sterling ice bucket beside the bed, and the warm glow of candles cast dancing shadows of a man and a woman against the walls.

"I dreamed about you," the woman said. She went up on her toes, her arms twining around his neck. "Hot, deliciously wicked dreams."

His hand fisted in her long auburn hair, pulling her head back to give his roving mouth access to her throat. "You're not alone there, darlin'," he drawled with the cadence of the Louisiana South. "I've been walking around with a hard-on since the moment you sashayed into that Vegas wedding chapel looking like a Hell's Angel's wet dream."

Her low, breathless laugh vibrated with sexual excitement. Amanda had known the black micro-skirt and studded, shaped jacket worn with nothing but perfumed and powdered flesh underneath had been an outrageous thing to wear to a wedding. Especially when you were the maid of honor. But it *had* been Las Vegas,

16

and the minister marrying this man to her half sister was a decidedly untalented Elvis impersonator.

Two hours later, after a surfeit of champagne cocktails blended with a little Valium, the bride had passed out in the honeymoon suite while the maid of honor and groom were two floors below, screwing each other's brains out.

Three weeks later, back in the mansion on River Road, they were still at it. "What is it about black leather that makes men so horny?" Amanda asked.

"It wasn't the leather. It was you. Christ, I've never seen a woman who looked more ready to be laid. You were wet and hot and in heat. I've never *wanted* a woman the way I wanted you. Hell, after banging you every chance we get, I still want you even more than I did that day."

"Then take me," she purred. "Now."

"Now," he agreed. Buttons scattered across the floor as he ripped open the scarlet-as-sin dress that fit as if it'd been sprayed onto her gleaming flesh, and dragged her down onto the bed.

Wrapping her legs around his hips, Amanda encouraged him with ragged gasps, breathless cries and earthy sexual suggestions. He peeled the dress off her slick body, revealing an ivory teddy that was a surprisingly innocent contrast to the dress lying in a crimson puddle on the carpet.

He left the bed only long enough to strip off

his trousers, then chuckled as Amanda's eyes widened at the huge bulge beneath his silk leopard printed bikini briefs. "See something you like, sweetheart?"

"There's definitely a great deal to like," she murmured.

He laughed appreciatively as he rolled her stockings down her legs, then used them to tie her wrists to the ebony bedposts.

Having recovered from her surprise, she gazed up at him, her green eyes limpid pools of desire. "There's nothing I won't do, Jared," she said, her voice throaty with sex and sin. "Nothing I'll say no to."

His hand stroked her, exploring, arousing. Kneeling over her, he followed the hot path with his lips. Engrossed in the moment, in each other, neither heard the French doors opening.

"Well, I'd hoped my husband and sister would get along." The icy British voice was like a splash of cold water on a blazing fire. "But don't you two think you're overdoing it a bit?"

"Vanessa!" The man leaped from the bed. "You weren't due back from Cornwall until next week."

"I found the country boring." The heat in the woman's eyes was a direct contrast to the chill in her voice. "Everyone tromping around in Wellies and shooting poor, defenseless birds out of the sky."

Amanda sighed. Obviously the fun was over

for tonight. "Well, I suppose I should be leaving." Scenes with betrayed wives were so utterly boring. "Unless," she suggested wickedly, "you'd care to join us, Van."

A flush rose like a fever in the betrayed woman's peaches-and-cream complexion. "You're an amoral slut. Just like your mother. It's no wonder Father divorced her and deserted you."

"Sticks and stones," Amanda drawled. "And for the record, our dear papa married your mother for the same reason your husband here married you. For your money."

Both sisters ignored Jared's stuttered attempt at a protest. Amanda's accusation was true and all three people in the bedroom knew it.

"Since it appears you're not going to take me up on my invitation, if one of you could just untie me —"

Jared Lee moved quickly to do just that, as if he couldn't wait to get her out of his house, out of his life. But before he could untie the stubborn knot in the first stocking, his wife pulled a small but potentially deadly pistol from her Coach bag.

"Vanessa, what in God's name do you think you're doing?" he gasped.

"Isn't it obvious, darling?" She pointed the gun at the most vulnerable part of his anatomy. "I'm going to ensure you never betray me with this cheap piece of trash again."

He flinched and went ghost white. His hands

instinctively dropped to his crotch. "You wouldn't."

"Jesus, Van," Amanda complained. "I can't believe you're being so middle-class uptight about a little infidelity."

Vanessa's chin lifted. "Perhaps if you were to actually marry that man whose ring you're wearing on your finger, sister dear, you'd understand my feelings better." She shot a scathing glance at her husband. "Quit trembling, Jared."

The injured wife was gone, replaced by the twenty-six-year-old CEO of Comfort Cottage Tea. "I believe, since I have use of them myself on occasion, I'll let you keep your testicles. For now. So long as you keep them at home. Where they belong."

"I promise, darling. This was just a small slip. I never planned to be unfaithful, but I was missing you so —"

"Don't embarrass yourself further by lying," she cut off his weak excuse.

He looked so desperate, Amanda was starting to feel sorrier for him than she did for herself. She, at least, was capable of standing on her own two feet. She couldn't remember the last time she'd been afraid of anyone or anything. Least of all this British bitch who'd bought herself an alcoholic Southern philanderer.

Finding the domestic drama increasingly tedious, she had just freed one wrist when the sound of a gunshot shattered the night and the smell of cordite overpowered the vanilla scent of the candle.

Pressing her hand against the lacy bodice of the bloodstained teddy, Amanda slumped back against the pillow.

Jared crumbled to the floor in a dead faint while his wife held the smoking pistol, a satisfied smile on her face as she looked down at her rival.

Silence descended. The candle sputtered out, plunging the room into darkness.

"Cut!" the director called out.

"Cut," the first assistant director called out.

"It's about time," Julia Summers complained. "There's a limit to how long a person can hold their breath, Randy."

"You're a professional, love." Randy Hogan's Australian strine bespoke outback roots. "I had every faith in you."

"I may be a professional, but I'm not Houdini." She tugged against the other stocking. "Could someone please untie me before my shoulder gives out?"

"Only if you'll agree to let me take you out to dinner," Shane Langley said.

A former baseball player who'd used his appearance as Mr. October on a Men of the Minor Leagues calendar to catapult him onto the cast of a daytime soap opera, he'd been asking Julia out since joining the cable network's prime time *River Road* cast three months ago. She'd been turning him down just as long.

"After what you did?"

"I have no idea what you're talking about."

"Springing that damn porn movie prosthesis you got from the props department on me without any warning."

"Surely you're not talking about Mr. Happy?"

She shook her head as one of the prop women loosened the stocking. "Mr. Happy?"

"He's aptly named." He retrieved his slacks and pulled them up his legs. "Come home with me tonight and I'll prove it."

"Shane, it's a good twelve inches long."

"A *very* good twelve inches." Boyish dimples flashed in cheeks tanned surfer bronze. "That's why women call him Mr. Happy."

"You're incorrigible." Along with a loyal audience, Shane had brought his penchant for obnoxious practical jokes with him to prime time. The *River Road* set hadn't been the same since his arrival.

Finally freed, Julia left the bed and slipped into the silk robe that Audrey, the wardrobe mistress, was holding out to her. "I hope you and Mr. Happy have a lovely evening, but I'm exhausted. Besides, I need to study my Bond script tonight."

As soon as this fifth season was wrapped up, she was going to Kathmandu to fulfill a childhood dream.

She'd been eight years old when her cousin had talked her into attending a 007 film festival in Santa Cruz. Watching Ursula Andress rise goddesslike from the sea in *Dr. No*, and having been taught by her parents that no dreams were impossible, Julia had decided, on the spot, to grow up to be a Bond Girl. After she'd gotten a little older and had actually read the novels the movies were based on and realized they were fiction, her goal shifted from *becoming* a Bond Girl to playing one in the movies.

Last month she'd beat out more than a hundred eager hopefuls, including Felissa Templeton, the actress who played Vanessa, for the role. Julia felt a little guilty about that, but Felissa had assured her that she was thrilled for Julia. When she'd added that she was far more interested in "serious work that will allow me to stretch as an actor," Julia hadn't bothered to take offense at the catty little dig.

"I've got an idea," Shane said. "How about I drop by your house with a pizza? We can run through your lines together over a bottle of wine. Then we'll take it from there and if you're suddenly moved to have your way with me, I sure as hell won't resist."

Before she could turn him down again, Randy clapped his hands. "Before you all rush off, I have a surprise for you, boys and girls." He paused for dramatic effect. "We're ending this season on a four-hour two-parter that'll be packaged as a TV miniseries and shown back-

23

to-back on consecutive nights. And the budget's been expanded to include a location shoot."

"Where?" Shane asked.

"For how long?" Julia followed up.

"This time next week, we'll be shooting in Blue Bayou, Louisiana."

"Where is that? I've never heard of it," Felissa Templeton said in a petulant tone far different from her character's upper-class British accent.

"It's a charming little hamlet in southern Louisiana. You'll love it," Randy assured her. "It's very romantic, with mysterious dark water, fireflies flitting through the hanging Spanish moss —"

"Mosquitos, alligators, tropical heat," Felissa cut him off, exchanging a look with Julia, who was equally unenthusiastic about this news.

"Don't be so pessimistic. Wait until you see the house we'll be using. As for how long," he addressed Julia's question, "depending on whether or not the weather cooperates, we'll be there two weeks. Three tops."

"Two weeks? But Amanda's going to die. Why do you need me to come along?"

"She's not exactly going to die."

"Please don't tell me we're reprising the vampire plot from the first season." It had taken two hours in makeup every day to prepare for her role as the lawyer-turned-vampire, until a mad scientist lover had invented a super sunscreen that allowed her to join the living once again.

"Don't worry, love, you won't be growing fangs again. But Warren's come up with an exciting new twist in the story line. You're going to love it." He patted her cheek as if she were a five-year-old, then framed his hands in front of him. "I can see another Emmy gracing your mantel for this one."

"I don't have a mantel. Has Kendall seen it?"

"You know we don't do anything without running it by the big guy. He loves it. Which is why he's authorized the extra spending. After the last sweeps ratings, Warren can probably do whatever the fuck he wants."

Warren Hyatt was a twenty-eight-year-old wunderkind who'd been lured away from the Sci-Fi channel. Julia liked him, even though his story lines tended to push the envelope even for the most fantastical soap opera. Since demographics had shown the off-the-wall stories had a huge appeal to younger viewers, his star was definitely on the rise.

"So what is this new story line?" she asked Warren who was leaning against a wall, clad in unpressed chinos and a polo shirt that had seen better days. He was madly scribbling on a yellow legal pad.

"It's a surprise," Randy broke in. "But don't worry, love. We'll get things wrapped up in time for you to take off for the dark side of the moon."

"Kathmandu."

He tipped down his Armani sunglasses and looked over the top of the dark lenses. "Do they get *Variety* there?"

"I strongly doubt it."

"Any Starbucks?"

"Probably not."

"How about Foster's?"

"That'd probably be a no, as well."

He shook his head and pushed the glasses back up. "Any place without Aussie beer, *Variety* or frappuchinos may as well be the dark side of the moon."

This from a man who'd grown up in a place where people were outnumbered by kangaroos and poisonous snakes. Although technically her contract had three weeks left to run, Julia had hoped to wrap up her part in the next two days, since Vanessa had just put a bullet through Amanda's heart.

"I don't get it. If Amanda's not going to die —"

"We'll discuss it in more detail later over pasta," Randy promised. "Kendall's corporate jet is landing as I speak, and he wants to meet with all of you tonight, at La Roma."

Julia rubbed at the headache that had just shot into her temples. Last year, Dwyers' Diapers, the conglomerate that had owned *River Road*, had been acquired in a hostile takeover by Atlantic Pharmaceuticals.

From day one, Charles Kendall, a senior vice

president of Atlantic, hadn't been able to resist sticking his unimaginative thumb into the series. After firing the show's producer, he'd declared himself the new executive producer.

He was also an ass pincher and an advocate for bringing back the casting couch. Neither of those qualities endeared him to the female cast members, though Audrey, in wardrobe, had told Damien, Julia's makeup man, that the script girl had seen one of the actors, Margot Madison, getting out of the back of Kendall's stretch limo the last time he'd visited the studio.

"Her blouse was fastened wrong," Damien had passed on with obvious relish. "And her hair looked as if she'd been in a wind tunnel."

"That's mildly intriguing. But none of our business." Having been on the hurting side of gossip too many times in the past, Julia was not going to help grow false rumors.

"Audrey said the knees of her stockings were ripped. I'll bet she'd been trying to blow her way into the bad girl slot that'll open up if you leave."

"*When* I leave," Julia corrected. After her futile admonishment not to pass on tales, the increasingly exaggerated story had added grist to the ever-grinding *River Road* gossip mill for days.

Three more weeks, Julia reminded herself. Then she'd be off this soap opera merry-go-round, on her way to Nepal.

3

After leaving his office, Finn stopped by his Crystal City apartment, which was as barren of personal effects as his desk, to pick up the suitcase he always kept packed and a stack of well-worn Ian Fleming paperbacks. Still fuming and wanting to get out of Dodge, he turned in his door and elevator keys to management, then left the building without a backward glance.

With Van Halen's "Sinner's Swing" screeching from the CD player, he headed his black Suburban southwest toward Louisiana, returning to the small bayou town he once couldn't wait to escape.

Because like it or not, the sorry truth was that Finn Callahan, the hotshot Special Agent who'd earned a medal for valor in the field from one president and had dined at the White House with another, had nowhere else to go.

Julia smelled them before she saw them. Dashing into her dressing room for a quick shower to wash off the fake blood, she was hit with a sweet, head-spinning scent. She stopped, stunned at the dozens of roses so darkly red as to be almost black, covering every flat surface, including the floor.

"Damn it, Shane, this is getting out of hand,"

she muttered. Just last week he'd filled her dressing room with heart-shaped helium balloons. The week before that, it had been a gorilla-gram that turned out to be a Chippendale dancer beneath the furry uniform. The other women on the set had throughly enjoyed the show. Julia, who resented any time taken away from work these days, did not.

"Shane?" a voice asked from behind a towering arrangement that would have been perfect for a Mafia don's funeral. "What makes you think it's him?"

"Graham!" Julia was nonplussed to see the man whose marriage proposal she'd turned down six months ago. "What are you doing here?"

"I felt we left things unsettled. We need to talk."

Be firm. You won't do either of you any good by going back on a decision you know is right. "I believe we're all talked out, Graham," she said gently.

At least she was. She hadn't ever intended to get involved with the British-born UCLA professor. Not seriously. And she still couldn't quite figure out how they'd gone from having a glass of wine to him proposing marriage.

It had begun innocently enough after she'd spoken to Graham Sheffield's class, when, surrounded by a subtle cloud of discreet aftershave, he'd walked her to her car — a snazzy BMW convertible Dwyers' Diapers had presented her with after *River Road* had led the ratings pack every week during its second successful season.

Accustomed to self-absorbed actor wannabes, Julia was flattered when Graham insisted on walking across an acre of melting parking lot asphalt to hear her opinion on why the bold strokes and rakish wit of the Bond films was only one of the reasons they'd led the marketplace during the 1960s and '70s.

"I enjoyed your presentation a great deal, Julia. I know my class certainly benefited from hearing an insider's view of the acting business." His voice had been part Sean Connery, part Pierce Brosnan and totally 007. Julia could have listened to it forever. "It seems a shame to say good-bye," he murmured.

When he casually plucked the door opener from her hand, she'd wondered if he was actually going to try to keep her from leaving. A moment later, she realized that he was merely intending to open the car door for her. He seemed to be a man of flawless manners.

Those manners didn't prevent him from moving closer, until she was close enough to smell coffee and wintergreen on his breath. "Are you doing anything this evening?"

Looking up into his eyes, which were the color of Hershey bars and possessed the adoring appeal of a cocker spaniel — two of her favorite things — Julia decided to forgo trying out the do-it-yourself bikini waxing kit she'd bought.

Over the next months he proved himself to be a man of taste, refinement and civility. Unfortunately, Julia had discovered that she was bored to tears by refinement and civility.

Their relationship hadn't been a total loss, though. She had learned to brew a decent cup of Earl Grey tea.

"I've belatedly come to the conclusion that your going to Kathmandu for a few weeks might be a good thing for us," he said now. "You know what they say about absence making the heart grow fonder."

Of course, there was another little saying about *out of sight, out of mind,* which she chose not to bring up.

"Oh, Graham." Julia sighed.

He was, beneath all that stuffy Oxford reserve, a nice man. And so sensitive. Too sensitive, she'd often thought, to succeed in the competitive world of Hollywood. He'd once admitted that he tended to take rejection too personally, which was why he'd opted to teach the craft of acting rather than attempt to establish a career of his own.

"Don't worry, darling, I'm not going to rehash all the old arguments about why we're perfect for one another." His smile was as infinitely reasonable and patient as the man himself. It was also, she thought with a flash of pique, just a tad condescending. "I just wanted to give you a little going-away gift before you left town."

"That's very sweet of you. But this is hardly a little gift." It looked as if a Rose Bowl float had blown up. Another thought occurred to her. "How did you get past security?"

"Bernie remembers we're a couple." *Even if you don't,* his tone implied.

"Not anymore," she tried again.

He appeared truly puzzled by her continued refusal to date a man many women would consider a great catch. Graham Sheffield was handsome, wealthy, worldly, and could, he'd informed her that first evening together, trace his family roots back to the English Tudors.

"Is there someone else? Shane Langley, perhaps? Is that why you assumed the roses were from him?"

"I only assumed that because he's got a thing for practical jokes." She told him about last week's balloon incident, then, after assuring him that the only man in her life right now was James Bond, managed to ease him out the door.

She was in and out of the shower in record time, threw on a pair of jeans and a T-shirt and ran to the parking lot, where her name, stenciled in white at her reserved slot, still gave her a secret thrill.

Bernie was in his usual spot in what was laughingly referred to as the guardhouse. At the sound of the BMW's engine, he glanced up from his paperback. He grinned at her, his missing teeth giving him the look of a cotton-haired jack-o'-lantern. Julia waved. He'd been sitting in this booth since the days when people thought television would be a passing fad, so there was no point in trying to explain that he shouldn't let anyone through the gates without the proper authority.

Besides, she knew how charmingly persuasive Graham could be, especially when he wanted something.

Her irritation about the upcoming location shoot and her discomfort at finding her former lover in her dressing room eased as Julia pulled into her driveway forty-five minutes later. Her robin's egg blue bungalow, located on Venice Beach, was cozy and bright and gave her a front row seat at the continually entertaining scenery right outside her door.

The purity and simplicity of the Craftsman style also appealed to her aesthetic sense and was immensely soothing, especially for someone who'd grown up with beaded curtains, velvet beanbag chairs, crystals hanging from all the windows, and furniture carved from grapevines which, while earning her father more money than a respectable hippie should possess during that stage of his artistic career, had also been incredibly uncomfortable. Hence the beanbags.

She'd bleached the pine floors herself and painted the walls a cheery yellow that brightened in the morning to the hue of freshly churned butter. Now, at the end of the day, it was deepening with the rich gold and bronze colors of the sunset streaming into the living room from the French doors leading out to the beach.

Toeing off her sneakers, she began leafing through the mail. There was a water bill, which seemed to get higher every month, which she found a bit ironic since an entire ocean lay just outside her front door, a postcard reminding her of an upcoming teeth cleaning, and an official looking envelope assuring her that either she or someone named Martin Stevenson from Salt Lake City may have won a million dollars.

She tossed another postcard, inviting her to a preview of the Fall Color Extravaganza at Elizabeth Arden's, onto the tile countertop. "Maybe I can get a makeover for when the Prize Patrol shows up at the door," she murmured as she retrieved a bottle of white wine from the refrigerator. After pouring herself a glass, she took the rest of the mail out onto the postage-stamp size patio.

She discarded an offer for a preapproved new credit card, and put aside a book club announcement she'd need to respond to before leaving the country.

An impossibly gorgeous blonde wearing a bikini skimmed by on Rollerblades, deftly avoiding a collision with a Lycra-clad bicyclist, who nearly twisted his head off his neck watching her skate away in the opposite direction.

Lovers strolled along the beach, arms wrapped around each other, seemingly oblivious to the outside world; joggers ran along the hard-packed sand at the water's edge. The tarot card readers were doing a brisk business, and the tide continued to ebb and flow as it had for eons.

But after pulling a photograph from the final envelope, Julia felt her world tilt on its axis.

The photo, computer printed onto inexpensive white copy paper, showed her lying against the pillows, a crimson bloodstain spreading across the bodice of an ivory silk teddy that clung to the tips of her breasts. Her eyes were closed.

Beneath the picture someone had typed: *You make a stunningly beautiful corpse, Amanda, darling. Love and kisses from your #1 fan.*

Puzzled how a photograph taken only a few hours ago could have gotten through the mail system so fast, Julia turned the envelope over. The blood drained from her head when she saw that it hadn't been postmarked.

Which meant the photographer had been at her house. Even worse, since the scene where Vanessa shot Amanda had been the final one of the day, if Graham hadn't held her up at the studio, she might have arrived home just as the photographer had been putting it through her mail slot.

She leaped to her feet. She scanned the beach, searching for . . . whom?

Several months ago, shortly after the beginning of the year, she'd begun receiving a flurry of letters from someone who declared himself her number-one fan. While they hadn't overtly threatened her, they'd become more and more possessive sounding. Enough that she'd begun to lose sleep, waiting for what, she hadn't really known. Which was what made the entire experience so unsettling.

Then, for some unfathomable reason, they'd suddenly stopped. Now, it looked like the letter writer was back.

There was a loud knock at her front door. Julia jumped and dropped her wine glass, which shattered into crystalline shards as it hit the stone patio.

4

Twenty hours and innumerable gallons of coffee after leaving D.C., Finn passed the blue and white sign welcoming visitors to Blue Bayou, Louisiana. Though the town and its people had changed dramatically since antebellum days, some things remained the same: according to the sign, the Rotary still met at Cajun Cal's Country Café on Wednesday evenings and the Daughters of the Confederacy at the Blue Bayou museum and bookstore on Saturday mornings.

Gaslights still glowed along oak-lined, cobblestoned Gramercy Boulevard, the planters edging the brick sidewalk overflowed with early fall color, and at one end of the lushly green town square, the twin Gothic spires of the Church of the Holy Assumption lanced high into the sky. At the other end of the square a majestic Italianate courthouse boasted tall stone steps, gracefully arched windows, and lacy cast-iron pilasters. The courthouse had served as a hospital during the War Between the States, and if one knew where to look, it was possible to find minié balls still lodged in the woodwork. A red, white, and blue Acadian flag waved beneath the U.S. and state flags on a towering pole in front of the courthouse, and a bronze statue of one of Finn's ancestors, war hero Captain Jackson Callahan, graced the lawn.

What had once been reported to be the largest flag in the state snapped in the breeze in front of the weathered, gray American Legion building, where military men had been shooting pool, sucking suds, and avoiding talking about the battles they'd fought since the War of 1812. Back when he'd been alive, Finn's father, Big Jake Callahan, had marched as flag bearer with the veterans in the annual Fourth of July parade.

Marching behind the honor guard in his Boy Scout uniform, Finn had watched his father with a young boy's pride and wondered how he'd ever measure up. Years later, there were still times when he secretly worried about that.

He turned the corner onto Royal Street, which boasted one of the state's best rows of single-story antebellum offices, and pulled the Suburban up to the curb in front of the office with *Callahan Construction* written on the window in black script. Below that, in a smaller font, was *Nate Callahan, mayor.*

Finn wasn't surprised his youngest brother had grown up to be a politician. Nate had, after all, been blessed with his *maman*'s good looks and his daddy's gregariousness. The combination had helped him win the award for selling the most Scoutarama tickets year after year.

Nor was it surprising he'd become a contractor. Back when they'd been kids, while his older big brothers were playing cops and robbers and having quick draw shootouts with cap pistols, Nate had been dragging home old boards he'd unearthed in the swamp, to build the jail.

Finn opened the door and walked inside.

"Well, look what the cat dragged in." A blonde wearing a pink-and-white striped spandex top looked up from painting her fingernails. "Hey, Finn. We didn't expect you back home so soon."

"I didn't expect to be back." He glanced into the adjoining office, which was empty. "Where's the tycoon?"

"Tycoon." She snorted. "That'll be the day. Your baby brother has always had this really warped idea that it's more important to be happy than rich."

Lorelei Fairchild and Nate had gone steady for a couple months back in high school; she'd strutted around in a sequined red, white and blue uniform and tasseled white boots, tossing her baton up in the air while his brother threw passes for the Blue Bayou Buccaneers football team.

She blew on her wet, glossy nails, then waggled them at him. "What do you think? It's Passionate Pink."

"It's sure bright enough." The color was like bubble gum blended into Pepto Bismol, but even Finn, who'd never claimed to understand the female mind, figured that wasn't the answer Lorelei was looking for.

She held her hand out at arm's length to observe it herself. "It is, isn't it?"

"Is Nate around?"

"Sorry, sugar, you just missed him. He's off gettin' some old bricks to use out at Beau Soleil before all those people descend on the house."

"I thought Jack and Dani were off on a belated honeymoon."

"Oh, they surely are. Jack finished his book and sent it off to New York City last week. So, as we speak, the newlyweds are in Hawaii, basking in the sun, lounging around on the beach, drinking mai tais and eating passion fruit." She sighed with dramatic envy and gazed out the window into the gathering darkness, as if imagining herself lying on some coral tropical beach.

"Why would people be coming to Beau Soleil if Jack and Dani aren't there?" His brother had spent the past several months restoring the magnificent Greek Revival mansion that had once belonged to Danielle Dupree's family.

"They're from Hollywood."

"So?"

"Didn't Jack tell you?"

"If he had, I wouldn't be asking, would I?"

Finn resisted the urge to grind his back molars. On the rare occasion he'd returned home over the years, he'd noticed with regretful nostalgia that the belles who'd wrapped themselves in clouds of floral femininity while flattering and flirting weren't nearly as common as they'd been when he'd been growing up. A clever belle could charm a man around her manicured little finger, but trying to carry on a conversation with this female named for a mythical siren was flat out exhausting.

Her peppermint pink lips, perfectly matched to her fingernails, which in turn matched the stripes in her top, curved upward, revealing sparkling white beauty queen teeth. "Remember when Jack's first book, *The Death Dealer*, was made into a movie?"

"Sure." He also remembered Jack and the production company had taken some hits for violence for that one.

"Well, seems he made friends with this Hollywood director who needs a plantation house for location shooting here in Louisiana, and since Beau Soleil's vacant, what with him and Dani in Kauai, and Holly and little Matt staying with Orèlia . . . he's such a darling little boy, isn't he? And Holly is just the sweetest thing."

"They're both great kids. Jack and Dani are lucky to have them." Finn figured Tolstoy could have written *War and Peace* in the time it was taking Lorelei to get around to letting him know where his other brother was. "So this Hollywood guy is filming a television show at Beau Soleil?"

"He surely is. And it's none other than *River*

Road. Mama and I were just tickled pink when we heard that, because it's our very favorite show. Why, we've never missed an episode. In fact, we have ourselves a bet about whose baby Amanda's carrying. I think it's Saxon's, which makes the most sense since he's her fiancé, but Mama insists she got pregnant the night her Jag broke down and she had to walk to that roadhouse to call for a tow truck, and ended up makin' love on the pool table with the sexy bartender after the place closed. Winner has to buy the other lunch at the Neiman Marcus Café in New Orleans."

She paused for a breath and eyed him speculatively. "You're a detective. Which do you think? I've lost the last three bets and I'd dearly love for Mama to have to be the one to spring for the chicken salad this time."

"Sorry. I can't help you since I've never heard of the show."

Morning glory blue eyes widened. "Gracious, darlin', where on earth have you been? Why, I thought everyone and their dog watched *River Road.* It does, after all, have international distribution. *TV Guide* says it's a huge hit in France and Japan."

"I've been a little busy." *Tracking down a stone cold killer.*

"Well, it's only been the hottest thing on television for the past five years. Shane Langley is even prettier than Brad Pitt. He plays the ne'er-do-well Southern rogue, Jared Jefferson Lee, who married Vanessa this season. Comfort Cottage Tea's been in her family forever. Her daddy — who's also Amanda's daddy — died when he keeled over while playing tennis at his club. Some say he was murdered, which I suspect is going to be another story line next season. Or maybe they killed him off because Keith Peters, the actor who played him, didn't get his contract renewed.

"Jared married Vanessa for her money. He used to be a lawyer, but lost his license to practice after he got caught embezzling funds from one of his clients to pay his gambling debts. Of course, he doesn't really love Vanessa, and started sniffing after her half sister Amanda ever since they met at their wedding — Vanessa's and Jared's, not Jared's and Amanda's — so I think they're going to have an affair.

"Which is really a good plot twist since, like I said, Amanda's showing signs that she's pregnant. She's engaged to Saxon Elliott, the town doctor, and he's a sweetheart, but he just isn't hunk material like Jared. Why, every time that man walks into a room, my heart just goes pitterpat." She tapped her fingers against her perky breasts.

"Havin' them all here is going to be the most exciting thing Blue Bayou's ever experienced. Mercy, everyone has just worked themselves into an absolute tizzy over it."

The idea of the entire town of Blue Bayou

worked into a tizzy was too much even for an FBI Special Agent to contemplate. Maybe he'd just lay in some groceries and hunker down out in the swamp until the Hollywood crew packed up and returned to Tinseltown.

"They're hiring local people to be extras," she continued breathlessly. "Mama and I are going to the tryouts. Mama's got herself a new hat that she's sure will help her get selected, but bless her heart, of course I'd never tell her to her face, but all those feathers make it look like a giant canary molted all over her head. I don't think that's exactly the look those TV people are going for.

"I'm hoping to get picked for one of the fancy dress ball scenes, but I can't decide whether I should wear my Miss Crawfish Days tiara, or the one I won for being crowned Sweetheart of the Shrimp Fleet last year. The crawfish one is taller and more ornate, but I am partial to the Shrimp sweetheart because it's more sparkly. Mama's lobbying for the Sweet Potato Princess crown. Which do you think I should choose?"

Finn was *so* in over his head here. "I haven't any idea." Inspiration struck. "What did Nate say?" If there was ever a man who knew the right thing to say to a woman, it was his baby brother.

"He suggested I go with the one that gave me the most confidence."

"Sounds good to me. And Nate is where?"

"Oh, didn't I tell you? Why, he's down in Houma."

"When do you expect him back?"

She shrugged. "Not for a couple days."

"Do you know where he's staying?"

Her pink lips turned down. "Sorry, hon."

"That's okay. Just give me his cell phone number."

"Sure." She glanced at a Post-it stuck on the monitor of her computer. As she read off the number, Finn wrote it down in the notebook he used for investigative notes. "But it's not going to do you any good to call."

"Why not?"

"Because he never turns it on. It frustrates folks no end, but he says if he turned it on, then people would call him."

Hell. That definitely sounded like his laid-back baby brother. "I don't suppose he happens to keep the keys to the camp here at the office?"

"You're in luck, sugar; there's an extra set in the top drawer of his desk."

She tilted her teased cloud of pastel blond hair toward the adjoining office. "I'd get them for you, but —" she wagged her pink-tipped fingers at him again — "my nails are wet."

Pressing a palm against her jack hammering heart, Julia went back inside the bungalow to answer the front door, locking the patio door behind her. Her breath escaped in a relieved whoosh as she viewed the familiar face on the other side of the peephole.

"Warren!" She flung open the door. "Come in! What a lovely surprise. Would you like some wine? I have a bottle of Chardonnay from that Sonoma Valley winery where we filmed the scene where Amanda pushed her grown step-daughter into a vat of grapes."

"I'd better not. I noticed this morning that I was looking a bit jaundiced, so I'm staying clear of alcohol until I can get a blood test to check for liver damage."

River Road's head writer was a card-carrying hypochondriac. Since his various life-threatening illnesses never impacted his work, everyone took his little neurosis in stride.

He'd been pitching film ideas to her for months, and been turned down each time, so he now seemed a bit puzzled by her enthusiasm. But apparently living by the *carpe diem* bumper sticker he'd stuck onto the lid of his laptop, he decided to seize the moment.

"I really believe I've come up with the perfect vehicle for you this time, Julia. I hoped you might get a chance to read it on the flight to Louisiana."

"Isn't that a good idea," she enthused, as if he'd just informed her he'd written both the Declaration of Independence and *The Great Gatsby* since she'd seen him last. Taking his arm, she pulled him into the bungalow, closed the door behind him, and double locked it.

"I'm dying to hear all about it!"

She flashed him her most delicious smile and hoped that this script would be a departure from his usual ideas, which invariably had her playing an exaggerated version of her *River Road* vixen role.

"I think you'll like it. I've been thinking a lot about what you said, about my last story being too over the top."

"Oh, I didn't mean that in a bad way. Why, I'm sure an actress with a wider range could have handled it wonderfully." She patted his arm. "I just didn't believe I had the range to play a bisexual prostitute serial killer possessed by Satan."

"You would have been terrific," he insisted again. "But I decided your suggestion of playing against your soap image was a good idea. So I went back to the drawing board and came up with this cool woman-in-jeopardy script."

"A woman in jeopardy?" Sirens sounded in her head as he held the slender stack of bound papers toward her.

"Yeah." He grinned his pleasure at having come up with a new story he thought she'd accept. "In this one you're a movie star being stalked by a crazy guy who's confused your movie roles with real life and keeps sending you threatening letters."

"A stalker?" This was not amusing.

"He's an obsessive fan." Since she still hadn't

47

taken the script from him, he turned to the first page. "It opens with the actress opening a letter and finding a photograph of herself in the shower."

It wasn't exactly the same as the "dead Amanda" shot, but close enough. Even as she told herself that she was overdramatizing a co-incidence, Julia tightened her fingers around the dead bolt key, the way she'd learned in her self-defense class, and tried to convince herself that she'd have no compunction gouging Warren Hyatt's smiling blue eyes out to save her life.

5

The sight of the weather-bleached cypress camp — built planters' style, on stilts — stirred long-forgotten memories. His father teaching him to check the traps, an uncle teaching him to cook, hanging out here with his brothers back in their teens, drooling over a stack of *Playboy* magazines and arguing whether they'd rather be stranded on a desert island with the pretty, peaches-and-cream sorority girls of the SEC, or the PAC 10's sun-gilded beach bunnies.

There were also memories not as sweet. Like sneaking out here the night before his father's funeral and getting tanked on the bottle of Jack Daniel's he'd filched from the bottom drawer of the oak desk in the sheriff's office.

Big Jake Callahan had kept the unopened bottle in the drawer as a reminder of his wild past and a daily test of the vow he'd made to quit drinking the day he'd proposed to Finn's mother.

The Jack Black was the first and only thing Finn had ever stolen in his life, and guilt had roiled in his gut along with the whiskey, sorrow, and most of all fear of how he, now the eldest Callahan male in the family, could even think of filling his father's size thirteen boots.

Finn pulled up next to the screened porch. Because of the constant conflict between water and land in this part of the country, there were times when the only way to the camp was by boat. Now there was a narrow, twisting road that Nate had recently graveled. Of course, one good storm and the road would turn right back into a waterway.

He unearthed the Spic and Span and spent the first thirty minutes cleaning the refrigerator, tossing out all the green mystery items he figured had been left behind after the bachelor party Jack had thrown for a friend a couple months ago. He put away the groceries he'd bought at the Cajun Market, where everyone had been eager to tell him all about the Hollywood people coming to town. Apparently Lorelei hadn't been exaggerating when she'd said folks were in a tizzy.

Next he unpacked. Swept the floor. Changed the sheets on the moss-stuffed mattress, then poured some vinegar into a pan and used the classified section of *The Times-Picayune* to wash the windows.

Finally running out of domestic chores, he pulled the tab on a can of RC Cola, went out onto the porch, propped his feet up on the railing, and settled down to watch the lightning bugs. Cicadas were singing their high-pitched night song; bullfrogs croaked a bass accompaniment.

"So," Finn said as night descended over the

bayou, "what the hell am I going to do for the next three weeks and six days?"

Warren appeared nearly as upset by the photograph as Julia.

"Ohmigod." His eyes darted around the room like nervous birds trying to escape. "Your stalker's back. But now he's threatening to kill you!"

Hearing it out loud made it sound incredibly far-fetched. Like a new plot twist on *River Road*. She watched him press the fingertips of his right hand against his left wrist and suspected he was checking his pulse rate.

If you're not careful, you're going to become as neurotic as Warren.

Six months ago, while working on a story line about Amanda's fifth husband dying of a heart attack — which may or may not have been poison induced — he'd been rushed to the UCLA Medical Center with palpitations he'd been convinced was angina.

Then there was last year's subplot which conveniently did away with her fourth husband, Helmut Heinz, the Swiss ski instructor she'd rashly married on a whim after sharing three bottles of après-ski champagne. Helmut had been blackmailing her, threatening to tell oil baron J. C. Honeycutt, husband number five, that she'd still been legally married when she'd walked down the aisle for the fifth time.

When Warren began writing the scenes

51

giving the ski instructor blinding headaches and attacks of vertigo, leading up to a fatal embolism, he began to suffer his own symptoms.

"I just know it's a brain tumor," he'd fretted to Julia, who'd driven him to the hospital and kept him company during the CAT scan which revealed nothing wrong.

He was lucky she was leaving the show; if Amanda wasn't scheduled to die from the gunshot wound Vanessa had inflicted on her, there was an outside chance Amanda would go through with her pregnancy — despite one abortion and two miscarriages, not to mention that fake pregnancy she'd used to nab husband number three. And Warren would undoubtedly suffer sympathetic morning sickness.

She didn't even want to think how he'd survive a subsequent fictional labor and delivery.

"Someone must have been on the set today, Julia."

"A lot of people were on the set today, Warren."

Whenever the script called for Amanda to strip down to her underwear, every male on the crew seemed to find a reason to show up for the taping. One of them must have brought a camera.

After the show had first launched five years ago, making Amanda a household name, a supposedly nude photograph of her ended up on the Internet, ratings soared into the stratosphere and she'd won the dubious honor of actually passing Pamela Anderson and Tommy Lee as the most downloaded photograph by males eighteen to thirty-four. Which, her agent had assured her when she'd complained about the invasion of her privacy, was a good thing.

"Surely you don't think one of the *River Road* family is your stalker?"

"No, I can't believe that." She took a deep breath and made herself sound calm. "I'll admit the thought flashed through my mind when I first opened the envelope. But I get all sorts of weird viewer mail." Just this week she'd received a half dozen proposals, three times as many propositions, and one warning, scrawled in the margin of a yellowed page torn from a bible, that God punished adulteresses.

"You only get your mail after it's been screened by all those people the network hired to answer it. When was the last time you got a viewer letter here at home?"

Good point. "It's probably just another stupid practical joke."

"If it is, it's not very funny."

"Practical jokes at the expense of others are never funny. I'm sure I haven't been threatened, Warren." The more she said it out loud, the more she began to believe it. "You have to promise me you won't say anything about this at dinner."

"But Julia —"

"Promise," she insisted. "It'll only stir things up unnecessarily and some waiter might overhear and call the *Enquirer* and it'll just give the tabloids more fodder." She hadn't been able to go into the grocery store for two weeks when the shower picture had shown up at supermarket checkout stands all over the country.

He nodded, but the worry in his eyes didn't give Julia a great deal of confidence.

Two hours later, in a private dining room in a trendy Melrose restaurant, Julia's concerns were justified.

"Someone sent Julia a death threat today," Warren announced.

The buzz of conversation up and down the table in the private dining room instantly went silent. Every eye turned toward her.

"I'm sure it was just a practical joke." Damn. They hadn't even gotten through the antipasto course. She explained about the photograph in as few words as possible, putting the most positive spin on it she could.

"If it is just a joke, it's sure not very funny," Shane responded to her theory.

"I hate to break this to you, Shane, but neither was Mr. Happy. And how about when you glued the silverware to the table at Margot's birthday party?"

The former Diva of Daytime frowned at the memory. "That was decidedly in poor taste."

Somewhere between forty and forty-five, Margot Madison was fast approaching the age when actresses tended to disappear from television and movie screens. And on those occasions they did get roles, their characters certainly didn't have the hot sex scenes Margot had built her early career on.

"Maybe it wasn't meant as a threat," Shane suggested. "You could have a secret admirer on the crew."

"That's probably it." Julia was grateful to have a new theory. And it made sense. Just last season, the head cameraman had taken to leaving little chocolate hearts and tapes of country songs he'd written about her in her dressing room. He'd quit the show and moved to Nashville when John Michael Montgomery actually bought one of his twangy ballads about a cowboy who'd lost his wife and house to another man, his truck to the bank, but thank God he still had his drinking buddies, his horse, and his good ole one-eyed hound dog, Duke. He'd been very sweet and Julia still missed him. She'd never been filmed as flatteringly as she had during the six months of that country boy's crush.

"No doubt Warren's just bein' a big neurotic sook again," Randy said. "But there's no use taking unnecessary chances."

"You're too important to the show," Charles Kendall weighed in from his power seat at the end of the long table. "We certainly can't afford to lose you."

Fortune magazine had reported the corporate vice president to be thirty-five years old, but his receding hairline made him appear older. His body, beneath the dark charcoal gray suit that stood out on Melrose Avenue like a blizzard in January, was pudgy and out of shape. His eyes tended to be a bit shifty and his manicured hands didn't look as if they'd ever done anything more physical than punch the buttons on his television remote.

When she'd first met him, Julia had been surprised such an unimpressive man had achieved so much power at such a relatively young age. Until Damien — who seemed to be tapped into every gossip line in Los Angeles — informed her Kendall was the son of the corporate founder's second wife by a previous marriage.

"I'm flattered. But I'm still leaving at the end of the season," Julia reminded him.

When she'd first announced her decision to quit the show, he'd assumed she was merely angling for more money, and had flown into town in his corporate jet, taken her out to dinner, and offered a fifty-percent increase per episode.

When she'd explained that her decision to leave wasn't based on income, but on a once-in-a-lifetime career opportunity, he'd doubled the first offer.

She'd politely but firmly turned that down, as well.

He'd tried reasoning. Cajoled. Then finally resorted to shouting, which certainly hadn't been any way to change her mind. Julia had remained resolute.

With visible reluctance, he'd finally accepted

her decision and assured her that she was welcome to return to the show if things didn't work out on the big screen. Then, as they'd left the restaurant, he'd pinched her butt.

"You're still under contract until the end of the season," he now reminded her. "We're launching a breakthrough new drug during the Louisiana story segment. We need your high visibility to ensure strong initial sales."

"What *is* the story?"

"You'll all be given the scripts on a day-to-day basis, the night before each day's taping," Randy informed them. "We'll be taping all four episodes over the next two weeks."

"That's two a week," Shane complained.

"Not only is he *People Magazine*'s sexiest man of the year, he can count, too," Margot murmured.

Shane gave her an uncharacteristically annoyed look. "My point was that it's not a great deal of time for me to get a handle on my character's motivation."

"This isn't *King Lear*, darling," Margot drawled as the busboy cleared away the now-forgotten plates. "You're playing a sleazy Southern alcoholic opportunist who's led around by his wandering cock. Surely that's not such a stretch."

The smile she flashed him over the rim of her martini glass was laced with acid. She and Shane had been an item three years ago, when they both worked on the soap *All My Tomor-*

rows. She'd been a fixture on daytime. An icon. He'd been the brash newcomer who'd figured out that if he had an affair with the actress who got the most screen time, she'd undoubtedly push the writers for meatier parts for her lover. Which was exactly what happened.

A flush rose from the collar of his body-hugging black silk T-shirt. "If anyone's an alcoholic —"

"Now, now, mate," Randy jumped in to smooth feathers before they became irreparably ruffled. "I'm sure Margot didn't mean anything personal. Did you, love?"

"I damn well did." The waiter had returned with the entrees. The older woman tapped the rim of her empty glass with a long fingernail, ordering her third drink of the evening.

"Can we stop the lovers' quarrel and get back to Julia's problem?" Warren asked peevishly. "I'm beginning to get a migraine." He paled. "Or perhaps this time I really do have a brain tumor."

"I'm sure that's not the case," Julia assured him. "It hasn't been that long since your CAT scan. And I really can't believe this is a serious threat."

"Nevertheless, there's no point in taking unnecessary chances," Charles Kendall said. "Perhaps we should notify the authorities."

That was the last thing Julia wanted. "Surely that's not necessary." Since police reports were public documents, there'd be no way she could

58

keep the disturbing photograph out of the news, which could inspire copycat threats.

"You don't want to call the cops." Randy immediately supported her case, and Julia could have kissed him. "Call them and the story will hit like a shower of shit, and the next thing you know, we'll be overrun by those supermarket jurnos. Why don't we just close the set and hire additional security?"

"Security costs money," Kendall muttered. As if realizing he'd made it sound as if money was more important than Julia's life, he added, "But a little extra expense shouldn't enter into the equation." He reached beneath the pink tablecloth and patted her thigh. "The important thing is to keep our star safe."

Julia was tempted to jab her fork into the soft hand that lingered on her leg. She didn't buy his concerned act for a moment; Charles Kendall would make Scrooge look downright generous.

He was constantly complaining about expenses, seeming unable or unwilling to understand that *River Road*'s glamorous style was a great part of the show's success. People might claim to be interested in simpler things these days, but if ratings were any indication, they continued to be fascinated by wealth. Particularly when those rich characters were behaving as badly as *River Road*'s inhabitants did. And Amanda was definitely the worst of the lot.

Outargued and outvoted, she ended up

59

spending the next two days with a former cop turned private detective and bodyguard. Julia suspected he probably didn't spend all that much time detecting; it would be a little difficult for a man with the girth of a sperm whale who'd adopted the 1980s *Miami Vice* pastel look to pull off surveillance without being noticed.

"There's no way he's coming to Louisiana with us," she informed Randy the night before the flight. "I doubt there's a seat on the plane wide enough for him, and that aftershave he bathes in is killing my sinuses." Apparently no one had informed him that not every woman was wild about an Aqua Velva man.

Realizing she wasn't going to budge on this point, Randy called Charles at his suite at the Beverly Hills Hotel. During a hastily called summit meeting, the powers-that-be of *River Road* unanimously agreed to leave the Hulk behind in Los Angeles.

That was the good news.

The bad news was that Julia was still going to be stuck with a bodyguard.

6

Finn felt like a guy who'd been shipwrecked on a desert island. When the bass boat that had been roaring up the channel cut its engine and began drifting toward the camp, he had to restrain himself from jumping into the water and pulling it the rest of the way into the dock. Bond Girl Pussy Galore, stripped down to suntan oil and a smile, could not have been more welcome than Nate.

"It's about time you got around to paying your big brother a visit." He put down the well-worn copy of *From Russia With Love* he'd first read in the eighth grade. 007 and the beautiful, Garbo-look-alike Russian corporal who'd been employed to seduce him had just boarded the Orient Express.

"It's only been three days." Nate tied up the boat.

"You and I must be living in different time zones, because it feels like I've been stuck out here for a month."

· "Time flies when you're having fun," Nate said agreeably. The sun was setting into the water in a blaze of red. "How's the fishing goin'?"

"Lousy." Finn hated fishing.

"You could always try shooting them out of the water."

"That's against the law."

Nate shook his head. "Christ, you can be literal. Well, no matter, because I brought dinner." He lifted some bags from the bottom of the boat. "I've got us some red beans, rice, a nice fat chicken, and some of the Cajun Market's spiciest boudin."

"Since when did you learn to cook?"

"Actually, anything 'sides burgers, grilled sausage or take-out pizza is a stretch," Nate admitted with a quick flash of his trademark grin. "But I figured you might like making one of Dad's old recipes while I spin you a tale. And make you an offer you won't be able to refuse."

Finn didn't trust his brother's offhanded tone. Years of dealing with criminals had him listening more to what Nate *wasn't* saying than his actual words. He was holding something back, which was totally out of character for his normally forthright brother.

Finn wondered all through supper what Nate was up to, but figuring that his brother would spill the beans when he was ready, he enjoyed the stories of small town life which sounded like an alien planet when compared to the world he'd been living in.

Three hours later, as the moon rose in the dark purple sky, Finn finally got his answer.

"You want to deputize me?" he asked incredulously.

"Just for a few days."

"I already have a job."

"Which you're currently on leave from."

"I'm going back." Finn was damned if he was going to let SAC Jansen banish him to the FBI's version of Siberia.

"Of course you are. But you've still got three and a half weeks in exile. I'm only asking for two of those weeks. Besides, you've already told me you're getting antsy out here."

Actually, he was on the verge of going stark raving mad. Still, Nate's offer wasn't any more appealing than drowning worms.

"I got stuck with one of those celebrity baby-sitting jobs years ago when I worked for the Manhattan office, and hated it. I swore I'd never do another one."

The Supermodel had been the daughter of the dictator of some obscure Carribean island. The guy had received death threats from a band of rebels, and rumors in the intelligence community said they might try to kidnap the daughter as a bargaining tool. So the local cops brought in the FBI as a CYA maneuver.

She'd run him ragged. It was bad enough that she'd insisted on going to seemingly every store and nightclub in the city; she'd also pulled every feminine trick in the book to seduce him. She'd only been in the city for five nights, but it had seemed like a year.

"Yeah, I remember. And I still doubt many guys would think spending twenty-four hours a day with a woman built for sin was much of a hardship," Nate said. "But this'll be different."

"Sure it will. And the Sox'll win the Series next year."

"Christ, you're a cynic." Nate shook his sun-streaked head. "Look, Jack's friend, this Hogan guy who's directed the movies made from his books, plans to shoot every day and into the evening. Since Blue Bayou doesn't have any nightlife to speak of, there'll be no reason for Julia Summers to leave the inn during her off hours. Besides, it pays damn well. Jack's not kidding when he says those Hollywood people throw money around like confetti."

"I've got all the money I need." Most of it tied up in stocks and bonds that continued to yield a nice little profit, making Finn glad he hadn't jumped on the tech and Internet band-wagon.

"Okay, let me put it this way." Nate ran a finger down the condensation on the neck of his Voodoo beer bottle. "I'm in a bind here. This isn't exactly the big city. Until I can find someone to replace Jimbo Lott as sheriff, the town's entire police force is down to two deputies, one who's pushing seventy and belongs on school crossing duty, the other who's fresh out of the police academy." He paused. "I don't suppose you'd consider taking the job."

Finn narrowed his eyes in what he'd been told was an intimidating glare. "Don't even think about it."

His brother shrugged. "That's what I figured you'd say. So, the thing is, the budget doesn't allow for me to hire extra private guys from out of town, but if I don't supply a bodyguard for Julia Summers, they'll have to take their dog and pony show somewhere else. And believe me, Finn, even if you don't need some of those bucks they'll be spending, Blue Bayou could sure as hell use them. If we don't get some additional funding, we may have to close down the after-school program at the Boys and Girls Club.

"Then there was last month's tropical storm, which turned the baseball diamonds at Heron Park back to bayou, so we've had to apply to the federal government for a loan to relocate them. Plus the prenatal nurse visitation program sure isn't cheap to run, and —"

"I get the picture." Having grown up in the remote bayou town, Finn knew how it had never entirely recovered after the oil bust. Jobs had been lost, people whose roots went back to the first Acadians had been forced to take jobs in the cities, and those who'd stayed had seen their income drop considerably. If Lorelei was right about them hiring local folks as extras, that could provide another much needed economic boost.

"So, who is this Julia Summers?"

"Obviously you've been spending too much time looking at Wanted posters. She's the hottest thing on the tube these days. Back when

Suzanne Bouchand and I were passing a good time together, before Suzanne got all carried away and started thinkin' about marriage, she used to make me watch it every Friday night with her."

Nate held out a glossy publicity photo of a modern-day Amazon lying in the surf wearing little more than two postage stamps and a Band-Aid. Her hair was a tawny red mane around shoulders that gleamed with glistening drops of sea spray and oil. Her glossy, kiss-me-big-boy lips were parted; her eyes, which were so green they had to be contacts, were darkly lined to emphasize their catlike tilt.

She had an old Hollywood sex appeal, like Rita Hayworth's Gilda who'd so sorely tempted poor old Glenn Ford. She also had *bimbo* written all over her.

"She looks like trouble." Only for family or country would Finn even consider spending the next two weeks with someone whose bra size was undoubtedly higher than her I.Q.

"Lorelei says she saw on *Entertainment Tonight* that Julia Summers is going to be the new Bond Girl."

"Well, shit, that impresses the hell out of me." She'd be perfect, he secretly allowed.

Ursula Andress had been the quintessential Bond Girl, the first of those beautiful women with the big breasts and double entendre names that were as integral to the stories as all the guns and gadgets. The actresses who'd followed had come close, though the more recent girls tended to be intelligent and athletic, as likely to exchange clever banter and engage in one-upmanship as they were to swoon in Bond's arms. While these women were definitely appealing, Finn took it as proof that political correctness had managed to get its tentacles even into the last true bastion of testosterone-driven fantasy.

"It's only fourteen days, *cher*," Nate coaxed. "If you won't do it for me, how 'bout doin' it for the little kids of Blue Bayou?"

"Jesus, you're shameless."

Nate grinned. "I'm a politician."

"So, how serious is everyone taking this so-called threat?"

"The producer seemed concerned enough, but I got the impression he was more worried about some crazy fan disrupting shooting before they finished the season finale."

"I suppose I could call the L.A. cops and get their take on things."

Nate shook his head. "Won't help, since she refused to bring the cops into it."

"Why?"

"Beats me. Maybe she's worried about the press getting hold of the story and blowing it out of proportion."

"If that's the case, why the hell is she agreeing to police protection while she's here?"

"I got the impression she's still not that eager about the idea, but since she refused to let the private guy they hired in L.A. come with her to Louisiana, we were a last-minute compromise."

"Terrific." An uncooperative Hollywood type was all he needed right now. Still, it wasn't as if he had a helluva lot to do until he returned to D.C.

Fourteen days. A guy could probably survive anything for fourteen days. Except fishing.

"When are they due to show up?"

"They're arriving in New Orleans the day after tomorrow, then coming down here by limo. They booked all the rooms at The Plantation Inn and I'll be throwing them a little welcome cocktail party. They'll begin shooting a couple days later out at Beau Soleil."

"If they bring out the drugs, I'm going to have to bust them," Finn warned.

Nate sighed. "I'd expect nothing less. Which is why I've already warned them that Blue Bayou has a zero-tolerance policy." He paused, eyeing his brother with a suspicious caution.

"What now?" Finn asked.

"I promised the director you'd meet their plane."

"That was ballsy. What would you have done if I'd turned you down?"

His brother shrugged. "Never happen. If there's one constant in life, it's the fact that I can always count on my big brother to come through for me." His expression sobered. "I really do owe you one, Finn."

"Believe me, Nate, I intend to collect."

Finn shook his head as he checked out the photo again. If the actress fell into the bayou, at least he wouldn't have to worry about rescuing her from drowning. Not with the set of water wings she'd managed to stuff into that teensy-weensy gold bikini.

7

As the airliner made its approach into New Orleans, Julia couldn't decide whether she was looking at bits of land surrounded by water, or water dotted with hundreds of tiny little islands.

She turned to Charles, who was seated across the aisle.

"Please tell me that you didn't hire the Incredible Hulk's Louisiana cousin."

"Large is good. It's intimidating. Keeps the crazies from trying anything in the first place."

"If a stalker *had* tried to get to me, I would have been on my own. I've seen glaciers on the Nature Channel move faster than that guy."

"I'm sure the Blue Bayou deputy will be more to your liking," he said, his tone letting her know he was still less than pleased with her demand to leave the L.A. bodyguard behind.

Julia wasn't so sure about that. Using voice mail to monitor her calls, she'd received three messages from the cop before leaving for the airport.

"We're probably just trading the human blimp for Barney Fife," she muttered.

Granted, he hadn't sounded much like Mayberry's inept deputy. His voice had been deep and gruff, his instruction that she call him back terse. He'd also sounded increasingly frustrated with the situation. Well, that made two of them.

"Callahan assured me he's just what we're looking for. Besides, it's a sensible solution. A local cop is bound to spot any strangers showing up on the set who don't belong there."

Julia allowed it made a bit of sense, and reminded herself that it was only two weeks. She could probably survive anyone for two weeks.

She changed her mind the moment she entered the terminal. It wasn't his height that gave him away. Nor his body, which while even more substantial than the *Miami Vice* wannabe, appeared to have not an ounce of excess flesh on it. His black hair was cut military short, another giveaway, and certainly too short for her personal taste.

But it was his alert ice blue eyes, which somehow managed to scan the terminal while not appearing to move, that screamed out Cop. With a capital C. This was no Barney Fife. And if he was a small town deputy, she'd eat her Emmy.

Damn. Though Julia understood, on an intellectual level, that the majority of police put their lives on the line on a daily basis to protect citizens, and she certainly appreciated their efforts on her behalf, she'd spent too many of her formative years watching cops drag her counterculture parents, Freedom and Peace, off to jail in paddy wagons to be comfortable around them. She'd even been arrested herself once, though the charges were dropped after she'd spent a night in jail.

"You didn't tell me Kendall brought in the FBI," she murmured to Randy.

"He didn't."

"Then you want to tell me who else would be wearing a suit and tie in this heat?"

The New Orleans humidity had hit like a steamy fist the instant she'd entered the jetway. Amazingly, the man's white shirt didn't appear to have a solitary wrinkle. The full Windsor knot of his dark blue tie was precisely centered beneath his starched collar.

Randy followed her gaze. "He certainly does stand out. But what makes you think he's your bodyguard? Perhaps he's picking up a prisoner. Or his wife."

"He doesn't have a wife."

"How would you know that?"

"Just call it a hunch." Surely a man with a loving woman in his life wouldn't look so hard. A man with a family — wife, kids, and a mutt who'd dig holes in the lawn and fetch sticks — wouldn't appear so unrelentingly rigid.

Definitely FBI, Julia decided as he squared his broad shoulders and began walking toward them.

"Welcome to Blue Bayou, Mr. Hogan," he greeted Randy. "I admire your work." He held out a huge bear paw of a hand. His nails were neatly trimmed, not manicured, but squared to precision that suggested a controlling nature. "I'm Finn Callahan. Nate apologizes for not coming to the airport to welcome you himself, but something came up."

"Nothing vital, I hope." Charles's brow furrowed at the idea that something might disrupt their shooting schedule.

"Just a little dispute over some traps," Finn assured him, then turned to Julia. "Ms. Summers. If you'll come with me, we'll get your bags."

She gave him a sweet, utterly false smile. "How lovely of you to offer. But that won't be necessary, Special Agent Callahan."

Those killer blue eyes hardened and his dark head dipped in a slight nod. "Good guess."

"Oh, it wasn't that difficult," she said with a careless shrug. There was no way she'd let him know that her stomach had taken off on a roller coaster the moment she'd spotted him. "You're obviously not a local cop, and since I'm neither visiting royalty nor a member of the presidential family, that rules out Secret Service. Which leaves FBI."

And there was no way she could spend the next two weeks in close proximity with this man. "I'm terribly sorry about wasting your time by bringing you out here today, but I won't be needing your services."

"Dammit, Julia," Randy complained. "You can't refuse a bodyguard."

"I don't know why not." She flicked her

tawny hair over her shoulder. "We are, after all, talking about *my* body."

Finn, who'd so far managed to keep his damn eyes out of trouble, couldn't quite resist this challenge to check out the body in question. Having rented a tape of last season's show last night — just to check out the cast of players he was going to be stuck with for the next two weeks — he'd admittedly been surprised by the woman now simply dressed in a waist-skimming white T-shirt and low-slung jeans.

That bikini picture, along with the over-the-top bad girl character she played and the news she was going to be the next Bond Girl, had given the impression that she was some larger than life sex goddess.

Even though he, more than most, knew appearances were deceiving — Lawson was Redford handsome, with a deceptively easy-going outward manner that had allowed him to lure the girls in the first place — Finn was having trouble picturing this slender woman as the voluptuous seductress he'd watched giving her pool guy the ride of his life in the shallow end.

The corporate honcho, Kendall, weighed in.

"It may be your body, but it's not your choice. Your contract with Atlantic Pharmaceuticals forbids any behavior that might jeopardize your ability to perform."

"That clause refers to off-the-set behavior," she argued. "It was only put in there by the insurance company lawyers to keep me from breaking my neck skiing or skydiving."

"Since the parameters aren't spelled out, the wording encompasses all dangerous behavior," he countered. "I've no doubt that the legal department would consider refusing protection after receiving threatening notes an unsatisfactory risk."

Finn had gotten her unlisted number from the director last night. Frustrated when all he'd gotten was her answering machine, he'd left his number so she could fill in the huge gaps Kendall had left out. When she hadn't bothered to return his calls, he'd spent the past eighteen hours getting more and more pissed. This conversation did nothing to improve his mood.

"If you don't want him, Julia, can I have him?"

When the Barbie doll blonde he recognized from the show's credits as Felissa Templeton put a French manicured talon on his arm and offered him a come-hither-big-boy smile, Finn decided Nate was going to owe him big time for this one.

They were beginning to draw attention. He turned to the others, who were watching the little battle of wills with undisguised interest.

"The limo's waiting to take you all on to Blue Bayou. Why don't you go ahead, and Ms. Summers and I will catch up with you at the inn."

It was not a suggestion, but an order. One

which not a single person questioned.

"That's very good," Julia murmured as they headed off like a herd of sheep. "You didn't even have to pull out your gun."

"I tend to save my gun for the bad guys. Along with the bright lights and rubber hoses."

She folded her arms, drawing his attention back to those breasts, which while not as full as they appeared on TV, were still pretty fine. "That isn't terribly reassuring, since I suspect you consider the entire population to be bad guys."

"Potential bad guys," he corrected as he took hold of her elbow and without utilizing force, began moving her forward. "And for the record, I was playing sandlot ball with my brothers when the Feds busted your parents. Which means there's no way I could have been involved."

While he may be on the SAC's shit list and in OPR's sights, Finn still had friends at the Bureau, who'd stayed late and pulled her hippie parents' thick FBI jackets.

"You've obviously been reading old files. But that doesn't mean you have the slightest idea what really happened back then."

"Our situations may have been different, Ms. Summers, but I do happen to know firsthand how it feels to be a kid and have your entire world pulled out from under you."

What in hell had him telling her that? He'd been sixteen years old when Jake Callahan,

Blue Bayou's sheriff, had heroically taken a bullet to save another man's life. His dad's death still hurt; Finn figured it always would.

A very strong part of him just wanted to let the woman have her own way. A stronger part, the sense of personal responsibility he'd learned from his father, knew that there was no way he was going to let her walk away with her life potentially in danger.

"Look." He reined in his frustration that she wasn't going along with the program. "It's obvious that we've got a problem here."

She tossed up her chin. A chin which, now that he was seeing it up close, was a bit too stubborn for classical beauty. "My only problem is that too many people seem to believe that just because I'm good at taking direction, I'll also take orders." A woven silver ring gleamed as she skimmed a slender hand through a wild riot of hair that looked as if she'd just gotten out of bed after a night of hot sex.

Finn told himself not to go there. 007 would know how to settle this: he'd toss off some sexy, witty line that would immediately charm the lace panties right off her. Or, even better, he'd just shut her up by hauling her against him and kissing her silly.

Finn momentarily wondered if those lush lips tasted as good as they looked, then ruthlessly shoved the forbidden idea back into a dark corner of his brain.

"I'm not real wild about our situation, either. But my brother's mayor of Blue Bayou and it just might hurt tourism if some nutcase decides to kill you while you're in town, which wouldn't bode real well for his reelection chances. So why don't we just lay our cards on the table and move on. I'll agree not to consider you an anarchist if you stop thinking of me as a storm trooper."

"I'm certainly no anarchist. And neither are my parents."

She did not acknowledge any willingness not to think of him as a storm trooper. The woman was really beginning to piss him off. Here he'd been willing to compromise, and she was still arguing. And, dammit, now she was marching away again.

"We obviously have different definitions." He fell into step beside her. "In my book, anyone who threatens to blow up a nuclear power plant isn't exactly into law and order."

"Did it ever occur to you that your so-called 'book' may be as fictional as my TV show? Besides, they were acquitted."

"Guilty people have been known to get acquitted."

Too damn often, to Finn's way of thinking. Unable to deny the strength of evidence against their client, which included three naked women locked in a dungeon in his basement, Lawson's damn dream team was now trying to ensure he'd end up in some cozy mental ward instead of the prison cell where he belonged.

"And sometimes innocent people are falsely arrested by overeager cops and prosecuted by ambitious politicians."

Finn rubbed at the boulder-size knot of tension at the nape of his neck. "Sort of like you were, when you were picked up for starting that riot in Sacramento last year?"

"It was hardly a riot. I'd merely joined a picket line of nurses demonstrating against losing more and more of their responsibilities to unlicensed hospital employees. It certainly wasn't our fault when some thugs hired by the other side started physically harassing us."

"You're the one who began the riot by wacking one of those so-called thugs with your protest sign."

"He knocked down a pregnant woman." She scowled at the memory. "After that, I'll admit things got a bit out of hand, but the case would have blown over if some overly ambitious district attorney hadn't been running for Congress on a law and order platform."

The newspaper articles he'd found on an Internet search stated the prosecutor had lost his election chances the moment the pictures of Julia Summers being loaded into a paddy wagon, along with a clutch of scrub-clad nurses — one who looked about to give birth to a ten pound basketball at any moment — showed up on the nightly news of every TV station in the state.

"We're not going to get anywhere arguing the United States judicial system," he tried to reason with her yet again.

Which was a joke. How the hell did you begin to reason with an actress who'd grown up on a hippie California dope farm, with parents who'd been too busy protesting the system and throwing red paint on army recruiters to ever get around to tying the knot like respectable people? And she appeared to be following in their protesting footsteps.

"The point I was trying to make was that I joined the FBI because I wanted to uphold the law. Not abuse it. But whether you believe that or not, given that clause in your contract, it appears you're stuck with a bodyguard until this production wraps up.

"As it happens, Blue Bayou's sheriff's department is currently shorthanded, so you can either take your chances with some Rent-a-Cop, or put up with me. Now, since I'm a straight-talking kind of guy, I'm going to admit that I'm not real wild about the deal either, since my lifetime goal was never to baby-sit some spoiled, argumentative Hollywood prima donna who never met a wacked-out cause she couldn't embrace."

Her chin shot up again. "Protecting nurses' jobs and patients' safety is not a wacked-out cause."

"Okay, I'll grant you that one." Finn's own maternal grandmother had been an LPN at the country's only remaining leprosarium in Carville. "But my point is that, just in case some nutcase out there has actually targeted you, your best bet to stay alive is with me. Because I'm the best there is."

"You're also more than a little arrogant."

"Thanks. I work at it."

"Oh, I think you're being overly modest, Special Agent. I doubt it takes any work at all."

She turned and began walking away again. Cursing beneath his breath, Finn reminded himself that he had two choices: Julia Summers or fishing. Which was no damn choice at all.

8

Julia had been raised in an atmosphere that celebrated the differences in people. Her parents had taught her at an early age not to stereotype and even without that early instruction, she'd witnessed the danger of such behavior firsthand when the government had painted her parents with that broad anarchist brush during her childhood.

Admittedly, they'd been social activists, embracing causes from saving the whales to stopping the war in Vietnam to the Equal Rights Amendment to reparations for American Japanese who'd been sent off to internment camps during the second world war. They'd also brought her up to fight for the rights of those who couldn't fight for themselves. But she'd always known that there was absolutely no way Peace or Freedom would have ever turned to violence.

"They don't even eat meat," she muttered to herself as they left the terminal in a black Suburban which, like his dark suit, screamed FBI.

When he slanted her a look, she realized she'd inadvertently spoken out loud. "My parents are vegetarians."

He nodded. "I know."

The simple acknowledgment only irritated

her all the more. "Doesn't it bother you at all?"

"What?"

"That you make your living invading the privacy of your fellow Americans?"

"No. Because I don't consider investigating the bad guys as invading privacy. And while it may be hard for you to fathom, from what I've been able to tell, most Americans don't feel that way, either."

"Maybe they're just afraid they'll be thrown in jail if they admit their real feelings."

His only response to the careless accusation, which Julia regretted the moment it came out of her mouth, was a slight tightening of his fingers on the steering wheel.

"I recently closed a case," he said in a mild, dry, just-the-facts-ma'am tone. "There was this rich computer software mogul who hop-skipped around the country, picking up coeds and slicing them up. That would've been bad enough, but since killing apparently didn't give him a big enough rush, he'd keep them prisoner first, sometimes for weeks. Rape was probably the easiest of the stuff he put them through."

"Ronald Lawson."

"I guess you've heard about the case."

"It would have been hard not to, since it was all over the headlines when he was arrested. But I didn't follow it very closely." The murderous sexual crime spree had been too horrendous to think about.

"Then you probably missed the part about him keeping trophies of the killings." His voice remained matter-of-fact, making her wish she could see his eyes behind the dark glasses he'd put on against the glare of the setting sun. "The night we raided his house, we found this walnut box in the safe behind a painting. The painting was from Picasso's Blue Period.

"One of the things in the box was a wedding veil and a yellow bikini. Seems his fourth victim had planned to get married the next day, then she and her groom were heading off to Bora Bora for their honeymoon. Needless to say, she missed both the wedding and the trip. We figure it took Lawson about a week to get bored with her."

As an actress, Julia was accustomed to putting herself in other people's skins. She shivered as she imagined the pain and terror the woman must have experienced. "Agent Callahan —"

"You might as well make it Finn. Since it looks like we're going to be spending a lot of time together."

"I'm sorry. I may have exaggerated." She'd never felt smaller.

He looked over at her, his eyes still hidden by those damn glasses. "*May* have?"

"All right." She threw up her hands. "I definitely overspoke. My only excuse is that I'm very uncomfortable with all this. And my early personal experience with your agency wasn't exactly positive."

He seemed to consider that idea. Then merely nodded and returned his attention back to driving.

When they drove past a cemetery, Julia's mind flashed back to a long-ago day. Rainbow's End Farm had been a warm and loving place where adults had gone out of their way to make the children feel loved. And safe.

Then, when she was five, she'd been throwing sticks for Taffy, her cocker spaniel, when one of the sticks had gone sailing across the dirt road leading to the milking barn. As she'd watched in horror, the dog, in enthusiastic pursuit, had gone racing after it and was hit by a truck delivering propane to the farm.

That was the day she'd learned firsthand about death. She'd been uncomfortable with the subject ever since, which made her wonder what kind of man could talk about such evils in such a matter-of-fact tone.

She turned toward him, taking in a profile that looked as if it'd been hacked from granite. He was not conventionally handsome, but many women would consider his rugged looks very appealing.

His heavily hooded eyes gave him a somewhat sleepy look that was deceptive, and his nose had a slight cant, suggesting it'd been broken. If his broad jaw was any indication, when they'd been handing out testosterone,

Special Agent Callahan had gone back for seconds. Oh yes, Julia could see the appeal — not that he was at all her type.

She'd always preferred artistic, sensitive men, fellow actors or musicians, and once, for a not-all-that memorable two months, she'd had an affair with a promising painter who'd called her his muse. Until he'd finished the last in a series of nude paintings.

Declaring himself creatively blocked, he'd moved on to greener, more stimulating pastures. But not before borrowing a hundred dollars she'd known at the time she'd never see again. She'd recently received an invitation to his one-man show at a gallery in Taos. But still no check.

Graham may have been boring. But at least he hadn't stiffed her.

As they crossed the Mississippi River, leaving New Orleans behind them, an unpalatable thought occurred to Julia.

"Are you carrying?"

He glanced over at her. "Carrying?"

"Isn't that what you call it? When you're armed?"

"Yeah." The corner of his mouth quirked. "That's what we call it. And I am. Carrying."

"I don't like guns." Even after having been mugged at the ATM last year, she hadn't considered buying a weapon, and had done a PSA with Tom Selleck about firearms safety. Ironically, it had drawn a firestorm of criticism from both the NRA and gun control advocates.

"Now, there's a news flash," he murmured. "You might find yourself changing your mind if your secret admirer decides to recreate that photo. But don't worry. I usually try to read people their rights before I shoot them."

"Did anyone ever tell you that you have a bad attitude, Special Agent Callahan?"

"Finn," he reminded her. "And yeah, it's been called to my attention — recently, as a matter of fact. But unlike my arrogance, the attitude comes naturally."

It was the first thing he'd said she found herself unable to argue with.

Since her parents believed that travel was broadening, Julia had been all over the world. She'd heard Big Ben strike the hour in London, marveled at the Renaissance beauty of Florence, listened to the hum of prayer wheels in Tibet, and had awakened to the sun rising over Mt. Kilimanjaro in Kenya. But the Louisiana bayou was a world apart, as foreign as anywhere she'd ever visited.

They drove past seemingly endless waterways, root-laced swamps, and rivulets ribboning the marshland. Sun glimmered over the bayou, backlighting the hanging Spanish moss in ghostly gold.

"Like a magician extended his golden wand over the landscape," she murmured.

"Twinkling vapors arose. Sky and water and

forest seemed all on fire at the touch, and melted and mingled together," Finn surprised her by quoting the following line.

"I hadn't realized they taught Longfellow at the FBI Academy."

"Sure they do. It's an elective, squeezed in between the course on how to beat up on suspects without leaving any bruises and the one on falsifying reports."

"The frightening thing is, I almost believe you."

"Even more frightening is that I almost believe you believe me. And now who's the one doing the stereotyping?"

Taking it as a rhetorical question, Julia didn't answer, though she secretly acknowledged his point.

"As for me knowing that poem, you can't grow up here in the swamp without knowing the story of those two star-crossed lovers," he said. "There's an oak tree in St. Martinville that's supposedly where Evangeline waited for her Gabriel."

"So you grew up here?"

At first, when her question was met by silence, she didn't think he was going to answer.

"My parents moved here from Chicago when I was seven," he said finally. "But my mother's people were part of the original group of Acadians expelled from Nova Scotia in *le Grand Derangement.*"

"That must have been quite a change for you."

He didn't respond.

"Well?"

"I'm sorry." The steel curtain had drawn closed again. "Was that a question?"

"Never mind." Julia refused to admit she was the least bit interested.

He sighed. "Sure, it was a change. But when you're a kid, your family's more important than where your house is located."

Remembering what he'd said about playing sandlot ball with his brothers, Julia was about to ask him about his family when he leaned forward and punched on the CD player. The down and dirty sound of Kiss's "Love Gun" came screaming out of the speakers, essentially cutting off any further conversation.

As unhappy as he was with this baby-sitting assignment, Finn was even more disgusted with himself for nearly sharing personal stuff he never discussed with anyone else. Despite being an actress, which wasn't exactly the most down-to-earth career in the world, and that episode with the nurses, she hadn't followed all that closely in her parents' hippie footsteps.

And although he'd throw himself off the Huey Long Bridge before admitting it, the fact that she was slated to be the next Bond Girl was pretty cool.

Out of the corner of his eye, he watched her drinking in scenery as different from L.A. or that bucolic commune she'd grown up on as Oz, and remembered how uprooted he'd felt when his father had brought his family to Louisiana, wanting to raise his children in a safe place, away from the mean and dangerous city streets.

Finn was a little surprised she'd so immediately honed in on what he'd been feeling when he'd first arrived in Blue Bayou. But an actress was undoubtedly accustomed to trying on different roles. Even that of a seven-year-old boy.

He wondered if such behavior had become second nature; wondered how a person would ever know whether or not they were seeing the "real" Julia Summers; wondered if she even knew herself who the real Julia Summers was — then reminded himself it didn't matter.

His job was to keep her safe. Which he had every intention of doing. Then, after sending her off to Kathmandu, he could return to the life he'd been forced to put on hold.

After all the miles of swamp and waving green fields of what Julia supposed was sugar cane, they drove across an iron bridge and came to a blue and white sign welcoming them to Blue Bayou.

"It's very different from the other towns we've passed," she volunteered over the ear-splitting music. The other communities had all stretched out on a narrow strip along the road, while Blue Bayou appeared to be laid out in squares, tree-lined cobblestone streets setting off pretty parks with bubbling fountains and lush gardens.

"That's because most of the other communities grew up along the road, to save valuable land for crops. Blue Bayou's patterned after Savannah."

They were driving through neighborhoods of brightly colored cottages and small, cozy white houses with wide front porches where people were sitting in wicker chairs beneath lazily circling ceiling fans. Several of them waved to Finn, who lifted a hand in response.

"A mix of Creole, Acadian and Native Americans had lived here for a long time, but they'd been scattered along the bayou like everywhere else. Then a rich Creole planter visited Savannah for a wedding and liked it so much, after he came home, he hooked up with an African-American architect and this is what they ended up with. They named it *Bayou Bleu,* after all the herons that nest on the banks, but over the years it became Anglicized."

"It's charming."

"I suppose it is." He seemed a bit surprised by that idea. "When I was a teenager, I thought it was about as dull as dirt."

Julia found herself unwillingly identifying with him. "It's hard at that age to live in a place where everyone knows your parents. Do yours still live here?"

"They died."

"I'm sorry."

"So was I," he said, putting a damper on any further attempt at conversation.

She'd already discovered that whenever a topic veered into the personal, he clammed up. Which was fine with her. Since she'd never see him again once shooting ended, she didn't need to know his life story. Though it was sad about his parents. Julia couldn't imagine a world without Freedom and Peace in it. She also wondered if the Callahans had died together, and whether their deaths might be what he'd been talking about when he'd said he knew what it was to be a kid and have the world pulled out from under you.

Not that she was all that interested. Just naturally curious.

They passed the VFW hall which, if all the trucks in the parking lot were any indication, was doing a bang-up business. The bumper stickers — *Thank a Vet For Your Freedom, I Don't Care How You Did It Up North, Coon Ass and Proud,* and *Real Men Don't Shoot Blanks* — were yet more proof that she was no longer in California.

He pulled up in front of The Plantation Inn, which reminded Julia of a scaled-down Twelve Oaks. "It's beautiful," she murmured appreciatively. "Like something from a movie set."

"The original inn, which housed troops during the Union occupation, blew away during a hurricane in the 1980s. It was a lot plainer, and the owners decided rebuilding in this style might appeal more to tourists."

As she entered the inn, Julia decided the owners were right. The lobby boasted huge bouquets of hothouse flowers, lots of rich wood, exquisite antique furniture, and leafy plants. Though she barely got a glimpse of it all on her rush to the elevator.

"Shouldn't we check in?" she asked as Finn put the coded card in the elevator slot and punched the button for the third floor.

"It's all taken care of."

The elevator door opened directly onto a corner suite which provided a view of the bayou in one direction and the flickering gaslights of what appeared to be the town's main street in the other.

"You know, I want very much to be annoyed at you." She walked over to the gold silk-framed windows and drank in the sight of the water, which was gleaming a brilliant copper in the final rays of the setting sun. "But if you had anything to do with me being booked into this suite, I'm willing to overlook your manhandling me through the lobby."

"There you go, exaggerating again."

"What would you call humiliating me by dragging me across the floor in front of the entire cast of *River Road*?"

"I'd call it doing my job. And I wouldn't think any woman who'd strip naked in front of the entire world could be that easily humiliated."

"The entire world doesn't show up on the set. I also always wear a bodysuit or flesh-colored bikini. Besides, I was brought up to believe the human body is nothing to be embarrassed about."

He gave her another of those slow looks that suggested he was recording her vital statistics for a Wanted poster. "I suppose that depends on the body in question."

The statement, coming from left field, left Julia at a loss for words. Finn Callahan was unlike anyone she'd ever met, and she couldn't quite figure out how to handle him.

But Amanda could. There wasn't a male alive who was a match for her feminine wiles. Julia had always left her character on the set, but as his slow, judicious scrutiny tangled her nerves, she decided to make an exception.

"Gracious, Special Agent," she purred. "Is that a compliment?"

"Merely an observation. You undoubtedly realize you're a stunningly beautiful woman. Otherwise you wouldn't have auditioned for that Bond Girl role."

"It's a great part. Even if it's a little intimidating following in the footsteps of Kim Basinger and Terri Hatcher."

Damn, why had she told him that? He was undoubtedly an expert at latching onto any little weakness and using it against a suspect. Not that she was a suspect. So why did she feel like one?

"I don't think you have anything to worry about," he said, his tone dry and matter-of-fact. "So what's your name going to be?"

"You'll laugh."

"No, I won't."

Julia supposed he was telling the truth. After all, the FBI wasn't known for its sense of humor. "Promise?"

"Look, if you don't want to tell me, fine. I was just making idle conversation."

"I doubt you've had an idle conversation in your life," she countered. "It's Carma Sutra."

He didn't laugh, but his chiseled lips quirked again in that way that softened the rugged planes of his face a bit. Julia was waiting for him to say something, anything, when the phone on a Queen Anne desk across the room rang.

He beat her to it, snatched up the receiver, barked out a brusque, "Callahan," listened a moment, then held it out to her. "It's for you."

"Why, what a coincidence. Considering this is, after all, my suite."

The call was from the director, reminding her of tonight's welcoming party in the inn's library. "Of course I remember," she assured Randy. "Yes. Seven-thirty." She stifled a sigh. "I'll be there."

Julia couldn't decide which she found more annoying: The idea of having to squeeze herself into a sexy, Amanda-style cocktail dress and toe-pinching shoes so she could chat up the natives, or Finn answering her phone.

"You're not going," he said after she'd hung up.

She lifted a brow. "I beg your pardon?"

"Nice take. It's the same duchess-to-peasant tone Amanda used with her yoga instructor, right before she got naked and taught him a new twist on the cobra pose."

That episode was from the beginning of last season, when *River Road* had been switched from its usual slot of Monday night to the supposedly dead zone of Friday. To hopefully keep their target audience at home on date night, Amanda had blazed through men like a brush fire in the Hollywood Hills.

"My, my, you *have* been doing your homework."

"I figured I should get a take on all the players." He rocked back on his heels. "So, which were you wearing in that scene? The nude bodysuit or the flesh-colored bikini?"

"Why don't I just leave that to your imagination? If you even have one."

He rubbed his jutting jaw. "Now that you mention it, I can't recall receiving one with my gun and shield when I graduated from the Academy."

Oh, he was a cool one. If they ever made a movie about that serial killer he'd tracked down, Tommy Lee Jones would be a shoo-in to play him. Jones might have a good fifteen years on Finn Callahan, but she couldn't think of any other actor who could portray so much rigidly controlled energy.

"Perhaps we can work on that imagination problem." Amanda rose from inside her and skimmed a fingernail down the front of his shirt.

Long dark fingers circled her wrist as he plucked her hand from his chest. "Just so we won't have any misunderstanding, as appealing as you admittedly are, for the next two weeks you're a case, like any other. Though you do smell better than most."

"Damned with faint praise." Even though she'd been attempting to jerk his chain, Julia was a bit miffed by his rejection. "Are you saying you're not interested?"

"I'm saying that I may be more selective than the men you're used to in L.A."

"Well, that's certainly to the point. And less than flattering."

Having always believed herself more like her calm, collected mother rather than her intense, passion-driven father, Julia was surprised to discover he'd tapped into a hidden temper.

"It wasn't meant to be flattering. Or an insult. I was merely explaining why, if you're expecting to ease small town boredom by having hot sex with your bodyguard every night, you're going to be disappointed."

"Believe me, Callahan, a woman would need a great deal more imagination than I possess to expect hot anything from you."

"Good shot." Even though he acknowledged the hit, it irked her that he didn't appear gravely wounded. Nor did he suggest proving her accusation wrong.

"Thank you." She tossed her head. "And while we're laying our cards on the table, you should know right off the bat that not only have I taken self-defense training, I also don't intend to allow anyone or anything to keep me from living my life. Which is why I'm going to that party tonight."

"Good idea." His tone said otherwise. He took hold of her chin, lifted her face to the lamp light, and skimmed a calloused finger beneath her eyes. "You look like someone's slugged you."

"Is that an example of your detecting skills?" She'd seen the shadows herself this morning, glaring evidence that unwilling concerns about her stalker's possible return had disturbed her sleep. Obviously the concealer she'd paid a small fortune for at Saks had worn off.

"I don't have to be a detective to see you haven't been sleeping. I'd think, since you have a busy day tomorrow, you'd want to go to bed early."

"I seem to recall suggesting something along those lines. But you turned me down." Because his touch was distracting her more than hers had appeared to affect him, she moved away. "And I don't really want to go, but it's part of the job description. The parish commissioners want to meet Amanda. How do you think it'd affect your brother's election chances if she doesn't show up?"

Good point, Finn thought reluctantly, torn between loyalty to his brother and his assignment. He also found it more than a little interesting that she referred to her character in the third person, as if she were making a mental distinction between them.

She tilted her head, studying him. "What are we going to tell people?"

"About what?"

"About what you're doing here with me."

"Why do you have to tell anyone anything?"

"Because for some reason, since I appear in their living rooms every week, people are unreasonably curious about my life and it's always best to have a story ready."

A story. It did not escape his attention that she didn't suggest telling the truth.

"Why don't you just say we're friends?"

"I don't know." She looked up at him. "That may be a bit beyond my acting ability, but I suppose I could try." She glanced down at a diamond-studded watch, yet another reminder to Finn that he and Julia Summers lived in entirely different worlds. "Now, if you're through throwing your weight around, Special Agent, I believe I'll unpack and get ready to dazzle."

As she left the room, even though he'd professed a lack of imagination, Finn had no difficulty hearing the bell signaling the end of round three.

9

She had to be out of her mind. She didn't even like Finn Callahan. So why had she thrown Amanda in front of him?

"Because you're not certain you can handle him," Julia decided as she wiggled out of her jeans. Even in Los Angeles, where you could throw a stick on Rodeo Drive and hit a dozen women more beautiful than she was, Julia was more accustomed to fighting men off than having to work to get their attention. "Amanda's tougher."

It wasn't as if he hadn't noticed her, she mused as she pulled the T-shirt over her head. A seamless flesh-hued bra followed. Stripped down to a pair of panties, she opened the suitcase some unseen bellman had delivered to her room, shook the wrinkles out of the dress she'd packed specifically for this party, then dashed into the adjoining bathroom to touch up her makeup.

A thought occurred to her as she was brushing on mascara. "What if he doesn't like women?"

She dismissed that idea the moment it entered her mind. He might be frustratingly remote, he might have ice water in his veins. But he was the least gay man she'd ever met.

Amanda could have him begging. On his knees. With that mental image providing some much needed amusement, Julia returned to the living room.

Finn had figured that since she seemed to view the party as yet another acting gig, she'd be dressed to kill. He'd definitely hit that one right on the money.

As she strolled out of the bedroom with a sultry, hip-swinging walk wearing — or not wearing was probably a more accurate description — a black outfit designed to make any male still alive below the waist swallow his tongue, Finn decided men were going to be walking into walls all over Blue Bayou.

The strapless top had been cut off just below her breasts and was connected to a hip-hugger skirt with two narrow black lace panels.

"Well?" she asked. Finn wondered how she managed to twirl on those ankle-breaking ice-pick high heels to show a mouthwatering expanse of bare back. "Do you think I'll help your brother's reelection chances?"

She wasn't going to get to him. She was a case, a favor for Nate. That was all. It was all he'd allow it to be.

As she completed the circle, Finn had to remind himself he'd outgrown thinking with his glands a very long time ago.

"If he claims credit for bringing you to town, he's definitely going to get all the male votes in the parish."

"Well, that's a start. Perhaps he can work on the women's votes himself."

"I don't think he'll have any problem with those. I do have one question."

"Oh?"

"How does that top stay up?"

"That's for me to know." She combed a hand through her hair, the gesture doing interesting things to her breasts, which Finn figured must be as bare as her back beneath that skimpy strip of material. When she smiled he felt a punch of something hot, lethal, and decidedly unwanted in his gut. "And you to find out."

"I guess some mysteries are destined to remain unsolved." Unreasonably tempted to touch, Finn slipped his hands into his slacks. "We need to talk before we go downstairs. I want you to give me a rundown on all the players."

She shook her head and sighed. "You really do have a one-track mind, Callahan." Silk swished against smooth, bare thighs as she sauntered over to the fruit basket on the desk. "It's been a long day and I skipped lunch. I'd better eat something so the alcohol won't go to my head."

She plucked out a Red Delicious apple and held it out to him. "Would you care for a bite?"

Because both the gesture and the throaty purr were so blatantly Amanda-suggestive, Finn laughed. "I think I'll pass."

"Suit yourself." She shrugged and exchanged

the apple for a ripe yellow banana, peeling the fruit with exaggerated slowness. "Where shall we begin?"

"With the photograph. Do you still have it?"

"No. I threw it away. And before you jump on my case about preserving evidence, I'd managed to convince myself it was only a practical joke."

"Yet it upset you enough not to want to keep it."

She shrugged her bare shoulders. "I don't keep junk mail, either."

When those perfect white teeth bit into the flesh of the banana, obscene thoughts ricocheted through his mind. Did she realize what she was doing to him? Hell, of course she did. The woman was a pro.

"What about the blonde?"

"Felissa?"

"Yeah. How do you two get along?"

"We don't run in the same circles — she's into the nightclub party scene — but we have a good working relationship."

"No professional jealousy?"

"Not on my part."

"How about hers?"

Julia considered that. "She's competitive, as everyone who lasts in this business has to be, but I don't think she stays awake nights counting lines to see which of us has more. And she's a very good actress."

"But she's not going to be the Bond Girl."

"True. And while I suspect she must have been disappointed about that, she says she never expected to win the role anyway."

"She was up for the part?"

"Yes."

"So you beat her?"

"It wasn't anything personal. They simply wanted another look."

"Hot, dangerous, black widow sex."

The director had used the same description. "There's always a measure of danger in a Bond film. I play a biophysicist who's an undercover *SPECTRE* agent assigned to assassinate 007, but falls in love with him instead. I think it also may have helped that I've had some martial arts training."

"Really." He sounded unconvinced.

"After I was mugged last year, I took a self-defense class at the gym. There was a woman there who introduced me to ninjitsu. I'm certainly not any expert, but I know some moves."

"Do your parents know their daughter's learning to be a ninja warrior?"

"Ninjitsu is far more about defense and spirituality," she countered. "Real ninjas, like in the movies, don't exist anymore. It may have helped me win the part, since they wrote it into the story. A stunt woman's going to be doing all the long shots, of course, since I'm not that proficient. But I believe what clinched my getting the role was the fact that I've not only seen all the movies, but read the books, as well. So, I know Bond's back story."

"You've read Ian Fleming?" He didn't bother to mask his surprise.

"There you go again, stereotyping."

"Profiling."

"Whatever. I'll bet you were guessing Jackie Collins."

"It fits. You're both part of the Hollywood scene."

"Please. I am as far from whatever people mean when they say the Hollywood scene as anyone in the business can possibly be, but actually I enjoy Collins. I also read Kafka. And Longfellow." She smiled sweetly. "I've very eclectic tastes."

"So it seems."

"I also realize some people consider James Bond merely a cartoon character, but that's only because there've been some bad movies made. The books are just filled with wonderful details about 007's spiritual and physical fluctuations. And *From Russia With Love* just happened to have been one of President Kennedy's top ten favorite books."

"How do you know that? You weren't even born when Kennedy was alive."

"You're not the only one who can do your homework. I know everything about the character and the stories."

"Okay, I'll bite," Finn said, amazed that he and this woman might have anything in common. "Who's the only man 007 answers to?"

"That's too easy. It's M, of course. Head of MI6. And it hasn't always been a man. Bernard Lee played M from *Dr. No* to *Moonraker*, then was replaced by Robert Brown. Their relationship was always a bit of a roller coaster, but things turned really ugly when Bond pushed him too far in *License to Kill*.

"The third M to play the part is Judith Dench, who's marvelous. She doesn't care for Bond's attitude, but thinks very highly of him. Is any of this pertinent?"

He shrugged broad shoulders more suited to an NFL linebacker than a federal agent. "You never know what's pertinent. Which is why it's best to cover all the bases."

"Felissa's no threat."

"I've heard that before. Had you gotten threats before winning the Bond role?"

"Of course I have. It comes with the territory, when you play a woman who'd seduce her stepsister's husband so she can claim he's the father of her child. Just last week, a woman in Blockbuster slapped me because Amanda had held her third husband's nitroglycerin pills out of reach when he was having his fatal heart attack."

"Does that happen a lot? People confusing you with your character?"

He wouldn't appreciate the charge that he seemed to fit in that category, as well. Though that wasn't surprising, since she kept throwing Amanda at him.

"Viewers occasionally blur the lines between fiction and reality."

"Terrific. So we're looking at several million potential suspects who'd like you dead."

"You have such a way with words, Callahan. If what I've seen so far is any indication, I've no doubt you have people lined up around the block to confess to crimes they haven't committed."

The accusation merely bounced off those wide shoulders. "Tell me about the pretty boy who plays Jared."

"Shane? He's definitely ambitious and wouldn't hesitate to sleep his way up the Hollywood ladder, but he's basically harmless and would never commit violence to get ahead. It also wouldn't make any sense for him to kill me, since his character's recent adultery with Amanda has really boosted his on-screen time."

"But you're leaving the show. He's probably not real keen on the idea."

"I wouldn't know. Why don't you ask him?"

"I will. What's your relationship with him?"

"I find him somewhat amusing, though I'm no fan of his practical jokes. But he shows up each day with his lines memorized, he doesn't eat garlic before a lovemaking scene, and our chemistry is good on-screen, which is important in a soap. And before you ask, I'm not sleeping with him, if that's what you're getting at."

"Have you ever?"

"No." She dared him to challenge that statement, but he merely shrugged again and seemed to take her at face value.

"How about the director? Ever sleep with him?"

"What are you? The morality police?"

"I wouldn't care if you and Hogan dress up like Tarzan and Jane and swing from the chandeliers. I'm just trying to get a handle on where the guy fits on a suspect list."

"He doesn't belong on it in the first place. Randy has a wife and six children."

"Some women might not be bothered by that."

"I'm not one of them." Julia felt the anger bubbling up and managed to control it. "Besides, he's not the type of man to commit adultery." Her eyes narrowed. "Or are you so suspicious of everyone, you're incapable of imagining someone staying true to wedding vows?"

"Sure, I believe in fidelity. But not everyone does."

"My relationship with Randy is strictly professional, Callahan."

"News flash. There's not a man on the planet who could keep his thoughts strictly professional around you."

"Really?" She tilted her head, intrigued by the idea she may have just found a chink in his armor after all. "Does that include you?"

"I said I wasn't interested. I didn't say I was

dead. So, let's talk about the actress who plays the former hooker."

"Margot." Realizing that he intended to work his way through the entire list of cast and crew, Julia let out a frustrated breath, leaned back in the chair, crossed her legs, and wished she'd just picked up the damn phone and gotten this interrogation over with last night.

10

Julia recognized Nate Callahan immediately. His eyes were a warm and inviting lake blue rather than Finn's lighter, chillier hue; his appealingly shaggy hair sun-tipped chestnut instead of black; his body, toned in a way that suggested physical work, lankier and more loose limbed than his brother. But there was no mistaking the resemblance in the masculine self-confidence surrounding him like an aura.

"You have a lovely town," she said after he'd welcomed her to Blue Bayou.

"We like it." His grin was quick and charming. "And the scenery's sure gotten a lot prettier in the past few hours."

"Aren't you sweet?" She smiled up at him. "And ever so much more agreeable than your brother."

"Handsomer, too."

She appeared to give that appropriate consideration, then fluttered her lashes in a blatantly flirtatious Scarlett O'Hara look that would have gotten her kicked off the most amateur middle school production of *Gone with the Wind*. "I do believe I ended up with the wrong brother."

"If you want to pass a good time, you probably did. But if you want to keep some nutcase from harassing you, you couldn't be in better hands, Ms. Summers."

"So Agent Callahan has already told me. And it's Julia." She glanced over at the clutch of people standing across the room, watching them with interest. She slipped her arm in his. "Since this is supposed to be a getting-acquainted party, why don't you introduce me to your parish council?" she suggested.

She was more than a little frustrated when Nate gave his brother a questioning look.

Even more irritated when Finn said, "Go ahead. Just don't leave the room."

Julia blew out a breath. "Why don't you go spread some of that Southern charm around, Callahan, while I mingle with the natives?

"Your brother," she fumed to Nate as they crossed the floor, "is, without a doubt, the bossiest man I've ever had the misfortune to meet."

"He can be a little heavy-handed, from time to time," Nate allowed. "But there's nobody better in a crunch. Once, when I was in the third grade, this gang of big kids kept stealing my lunch money. I didn't tell my parents be-cause it was so damn humiliating. But you can't get anything past Finn. He found out what was happening, went over to the park where they were playing a little after school one-on-one, and cleaned their clocks. They never bothered me again."

"Why am I not surprised he resorted to vio-lence?"

Obviously the man had possessed industrial-strength testosterone even as a schoolboy. She had never been the least bit attracted to men who opted for brawn over brains.

"That's the only thing those thugs would have understood. Hell, half of them later ended up in prison and I suspect it's just a matter of time before the others join them. I was damn lucky to have my big brother looking after me. You are, too."

Julia didn't want to be rude and argue with her host, but the only answer she could come up with was a muttered *humph.*

Finn was watching her ooze charm to the parish council, all of whom appeared appropriately starstruck, when a sloe-eyed brunette wearing a clingy red dress came up to him. Margot Madison, Finn mentally clicked through the *River Road* credits. The former madam of River Road's only brothel, turned romance writer.

"As hunky an addition as you are to our little family, Agent Callahan, you do realize, of course, that your presence is totally unnecessary," she said, dispensing with any polite opening conversation.

"Is it?"

"Of course. It's obvious Julia doesn't need a bodyguard. Because it's just as obvious that she sent that photograph to herself."

"Why would she want to do that?"

"To garner attention. We actors are outrageously egocentric. We can't bear not to be in the middle of the spotlight. God knows, Julia's certainly done whatever it takes to boost her career. Now that the buzz about her winning that Bond Girl role is beginning to die down, I've been expecting her to pull some stunt to get herself back in the news."

"It's a little difficult to take a picture of yourself from across the room without anyone noticing."

"She undoubtedly had an accomplice. Perhaps her agent. Or publicist. Or maybe even that stuffy acting professor she was dating for a time." She shrugged. "Julia's an actress. She wouldn't have had any trouble talking some man into helping her out."

Finn couldn't argue with that. "Is that what you'd do?"

"Absolutely." She smiled up at him. "Are you shocked?"

"I don't shock all that easily."

"I wouldn't guess you would. I saw the clip on the news after you apprehended that horrid serial killer." Her eyes glittered with avid interest. "I imagine you've seen a great many unsavory things in your career."

Her voice went up a little on the end, turning the comment into a question. Finn wasn't surprised; civilians seemed ghoulishly drawn to murder. And serial killers were the most fascinating of all.

"None suitable for cocktail party conversation. So, you were telling me about why Ms. Summers would send that photograph to herself?"

"Tell me, Special Agent, do you have to practice that just-the-facts-ma'am tone, or does it come naturally? Never mind." She waved her question away. "You'll have to forgive me. I have an unfortunate habit of being facetious when I'm excruciatingly bored. . . .

"Why would Julia fake a threat to herself? The answer is obvious, darling. Because it makes such juicy headlines. We all like to pretend that we hate the tabloids, but the truth is that we have a parasitic relationship with them. We need them to keep us in the public eye as much as they need us to fill their tacky little pages every day."

"I suppose a death threat might be the kind of story the *Enquirer* or *Star* could get their teeth into."

"Oh, they could masticate on it for months." Her crimson lips curved in a smile that was more predatory than friendly. "What our Julia lacks in acting ability, she definitely makes up for in imagination."

"I don't know anything about acting, but she seems pretty good."

The dress slid off a shoulder as she shrugged with calculated insouciance. "It's not that difficult if you're playing yourself. Believe me, Amanda and Julia could be twins separated at birth." She tossed back her champagne and snagged another glass from the tray of a passing waiter.

She swayed a little as she leaned toward him, worrying Finn that he might have to keep her from falling flat on her face. "Let me tell you a little shecret about television." She was beginning to slur her words, suggesting she'd had some warm-up drinks before coming downstairs to the party. "The schedule for an hour-long weekly series is so grinding, there's not a lot of room for an actor to stretch. If you're not playing yourself, you're going to make it a helluva lot harder than it need be."

Her words had Finn recalling a scene he'd watched where her character, who was being blackmailed by Amanda for some reason the tape hadn't made clear, had hired a buffed up, not-all-that-bright romance novel cover model to kill Amanda. The plan fell apart when the would-be assassin fell in love with his victim and refused to go through with the crime.

"I've been married five times," she revealed. "Six if you count Everett Channing, whom I made the dreadful mistake of marrying twice. Every one of those marriages has made it into the story line of the daytime soap I starred in before I moved to *River Road*. So have several of my affairs. As I told that officious little IRS man who audited me last year, that dalliance in Rome with the Italian shoe king was merely creative research, which I had every right to deduct."

Finn would have loved to have been present for that audit. "Thanks for your take on the situation, Ms. Madison. It's been very helpful talking with you."

"Any time, Agent Callahan." Her slow, blatantly sexual appraisal suggested she might be considering him a new research project. "You'll find I'm a very accommodating woman." With that gilt-edged invitation hanging in the air, she wove her way unsteadily through the crowd over to the open bar.

It was obvious that Margot Madison was jealous of Julia Summers.

However, Finn reminded himself as he watched Julia laugh appreciatively at something Nate had said, jealousy didn't necessary preclude the actress from being right.

"Welcome to Blue Bayou." The blonde holding the flute of champagne toward Warren had a beauty queen's smile and a cover girl's body shrink wrapped into a pink floral silk dress. A rhinestone-studded tiara rested atop a cloud of pale blond hair. "I'm Lorelei Fairchild. And I'll bet you're Warren Hyatt."

"That's right." Because it would have seemed rude to refuse, he accepted the champagne, deciding to dump it into one of those potted palms at the first opportunity. "How did you know?" People usually didn't pay attention to the writer. Especially in a room of actors.

"Because you're the most intelligent-looking

man here." Dimples deep enough to drown in flashed charmingly. She leaned toward him, as if about to share a deep secret. "I do so admire your work."

"You do?" He found himself holding his breath, waiting for those magnificent breasts to pop out of their scant covering.

"Of course. I'm all the time tellin' Mama, 'Mama, that Warren Hyatt is a literary genius.' "

"Really?"

"I surely do. Mama, of course, agrees. She's a huge fan, too. She absolutely adored the story line where you killed that Swiss ski instructor, but I think my favorite, until this latest triangle with Vanessa, Jared and Amanda, of course, was the one where that alien from outer space landed in River Road and snatched Amanda right out of her snazzy red convertible and beamed her up to his ship to take her back to his womanless planet to save their species."

That had been one of his personal favorites. "You didn't think the premise was too over the top?"

"Why, of course not!" She looked askance at the idea. Forgetting all about any potential damage to his liver, Warren took a sip of champagne. "I thought it was absolutely inspired. And sexy as all get out. I especially loved how you had her escape by pretending she was actually going to go through with having hot alien sex with him." She flashed another of those

117

smiles that caused him to go a little light-headed. "If you promise not to tell a single solitary soul, I'll share a little secret."

"I promise." The scent emanating from acres of creamy skin was making his head spin. At that moment, Warren would have agreed to anything.

"That's always been a personal sexual fantasy of mine."

"To be beamed aboard a spaceship?"

"No, silly." She skimmed a glossy pink fingernail down his sleeve. "To be taken against my will and ravished."

"Really?" he croaked.

"Well, not in actuality. I mean, I certainly wouldn't want some stranger to drag me into an alley, strip my clothes off and rape me in real life, but I do fantasize about a handsome masked man breaking into my bedroom at night and having his way with me. Why, just thinking about it gives me goose bumps all over, if you know what I mean."

Her light laugh flowed over him like warm honey as he imagined that lush body. All over.

"Well, of course you do. Since you're the one who wrote the story line in the first place. I haven't been able to sleep since I heard you were coming to town. I just kept lying all alone in bed, hoping that I'd get a chance to meet the one man who truly and deeply understands women's secret desires." She sighed and pressed her hand against a magnificent breast.

"You must be a purely wonderful lover."

That did it. He was definitely going to faint.

"Oh, dear. Are you all right?" Feminine speculation instantly turned to concern. "Gracious, sugar, you've gone as white as Stonewall Jackson's ghost."

"I'm fine." He took a deep breath. "The flight from L.A. was a bit bumpy. I think it's probably just a touch of lingering airsickness."

"Oh, don't you just hate that?" Glossy pink lips that matched her nails turned down in a sexy little moue. "I have a stomach like iron. Mama says it's as hard as my head, but she used to get butterflies something awful whenever we flew. They'd start flapping their wings even before she got on the plane. It got so she just couldn't travel anywhere, except on Amtrak, which really upset her because Mama does so love to visit new places, bless her heart.

"I swear, we tried everything: pills, hypnosis, those little wristbands with the magnets on them, why, we even got Nate to take us out in his boat, deep into the swamp where we paid this wonderful old juju woman to do a voodoo spell for her, but nothing worked.

"I can't tell you the despair we were in. Then, thank heavens, I found this miracle cure on the Internet and since we figured we didn't have anything to lose, we gave it a try." She smiled brilliantly. "It worked like a charm. Mama's never had a lick of trouble since."

"You found a miracle cure on the Internet?"

"Oh, it's just filled with the most interesting information, sugar. Why, you can't imagine. Anyway, the cure's as easy as pecan pie. You just splash some Southern Comfort into a glass of flat ginger ale and swallow it all down at once. The ginger ale settles your stomach while the whiskey calms you down."

She looked up at him through her lashes. "Maybe your wife or girlfriend can mix one for you before you fly next time."

A sledgehammer would have been more subtle. Warren began to worry that this was another of Shane's practical jokes. He quickly scanned the room, but the actor was busy charming a clutch of blue-haired old ladies, and didn't seem to be paying any attention to them.

"I guess I'll be mixing it myself, since I'm not married. And I don't have a girlfriend."

"Really?" Salome could not have looked more seductive when asking for John the Baptist's head than Lorelei Fairchild did as she nibbled speculatively on her glossy pink thumbnail. "You're still looking a tad pale," she diagnosed. "Perhaps we should get you back upstairs to your room so you can lie down."

Warren's first thought was that if he wasn't dead and in heaven, he must be hallucinating.

And even on the outside chance he was still breathing and this wasn't a joke, and this blond belle bombshell was actually suggesting what he thought she was suggesting, he reminded himself that energetic sex could kill you. He'd learned that firsthand when, a week before his twelfth birthday, his father keeled over from a heart attack at a mere forty years old while making love to his mistress in a suite at the Plaza on an alleged business trip to New York.

After the funeral, he'd heard his uncle Paul say that they'd been forced to go with a closed casket because the undertaker hadn't been able to wipe the smile from Warren Senior's face.

Deciding not to look a gift breast — horse, he corrected, dragging his wandering eyes from those lush white globes which, if they weren't real, were the best silicone job he'd ever seen — in the mouth, Warren reminded himself that life was filled with risks. Forgetting about his possible liver disease, he tossed back the champagne.

"You are," he said as the alcohol went straight to his head, replacing the blood rushing hot and thick to lower regions, "the most stunningly Southern woman I've ever met."

She flashed another of those beauty queen smiles that he decided would be the inspiration for the new character who'd replace Amanda as *River Road*'s vixen. "There you go, making my toes go as tingly as they did while I was watchin' Amanda being licked all over by that horny alien."

She was every sexual fantasy he'd ever had, all wrapped up into one luscious, sweet-smelling female body. Since he couldn't think of a single solitary line to fit this amazing occasion, Warren stole one he'd written for that womanizing Southern scoundrel, Jared Lee.

"Let's go upstairs, darlin'," he drawled, "and I'll make the rest of you tingle."

Carpe diem.

11

Finn was keeping an eye on Julia while scoping out all the players in this little drama he'd landed in, when Felissa Templeton sidled up to him. "Well? Have you figured out which of us is trying to kill Julia?"

"What makes you think it's someone from inside the show?"

"Oh, it's always someone the victim knows," she said airily. "I've made enough women-in-jeopardy movies to know that."

"Who do you think it is?"

"Margot, of course."

"That's interesting. Since she believes Ms. Summers is threatening herself to attract more publicity."

Felissa laughed. "Of course the old bitch would say that. She hates Julia's guts."

"Because Ms. Summers took over her bad girl role?"

"That's very perceptive of you."

"Thanks."

"So, you've watched the show?"

"I've seen a few episodes."

"Which ones?"

"One where your character and Amanda have a cat fight and fall into the fountain at Amanda's fourth wedding."

"Oh, that was fun." Remembered pleasure shone in her eyes. "Julia's just lucky Warren wrote that scene for me. Margot undoubtedly would have held her under."

"She hates her that much?"

"Mostly she just wants Julia off the show."

"How about you? Do you want her gone?"

"Well, of course I do, since playing the good girl is excruciatingly boring, and the bad girl gets the majority of lines each week and most of the press, besides. But there's no earthly point in trying to run her off since she's already going, isn't she?"

"I hear you tried out for the Bond Girl role."

"Every actress in Hollywood probably tried out for that role."

"But Julia got it. Does that bother you?"

"In the beginning, I suppose it did, just a little. But I've gotten over it. Especially since Warren's promised to give Vanessa an evil twin. Or better yet, multiple personalities. While those are admittedly getting a little overdone, I just know he'll be able to create a new twist that could earn me an Emmy when one of the personalities starts killing people and poor, suffering Vanessa goes on trial for murder."

As ludicrous a plotline as that might be, Finn decided it wasn't that different from Lawson's lawyers' attempt to pull an insanity defense out of their legal hats.

"There they go."

He followed her gaze across the room to

where Margot Madison and Charles Kendall were slipping out the French doors.

"They've been having a fling now for the past month," Felissa revealed. "It's my guess that she's doing a bit of horizontal lobbying to get him to reprise *her* old bad girl role. With the emphasis on *old*. Personally, I think she's wasting her time. Charles may write the checks and sit in the executive office, but Warren pretty much has carte blanche when it comes to *River Road*'s story line. So long as ratings stay as high as they are, he'll be allowed to write just about any plot he wants. Which is why, if Margot had any sense, she'd seduce him instead."

Her gaze shifted to the bespectacled writer who was standing on the edges of the crowd, appearing absolutely enthralled by Lorelei, who'd squeezed her voluptuous curves into a flowered dress that fit like a sausage casing. If she took an even halfway deep breath, she was definitely going to provide the entertainment for the evening.

"Damn," Felissa muttered.

"What?"

"It looks as if I'm about to lose a bet with Randy. I said it'd take at least an hour for Miss Gator Gulch over there to entice Warren to write her into the script. Randy bet she'd pull it off in under thirty minutes, which means I owe him a weekend at Las Costa."

As Finn watched Lorelei and Warren leave

the room together in a cloud of pheromones, he decided it was getting more and more difficult to tell real life from *River Road*.

"So, what do you think?" Nate asked an hour later.

"I think after this bash, you'll be elected mayor for life," Finn said.

"The parish council certainly seems happy enough. Of course, Mrs. Robicheaux's probably gonna have to go out and buy poor old Henri a Seeing Eye dog first thing in the morning, since his eyes seemed to have become detached from his head and glued to Julia Summers's very appealing body."

"I noticed. Unfortunately for him, so did Marie Robicheaux."

"Henri will be sleeping in the doghouse for sure, tonight . . . She really is something, isn't she? Julia, not Marie."

"Yeah. She's something all right. She's a pain in the ass."

Nate looked at him curiously. "I thought she seemed real nice. Not at all full of herself, like I figured some Hollywood star could be."

"She's an actress," Finn reminded his brother. "She can probably be anyone you want her to be. She's also on her good behavior with you."

"More's the pity. You sayin' she's being bad with you? And you're complaining? *Mon Dieu, cher,* I'm worried about you."

"Look, I watched the show. The woman can turn the charm off and on without missing a beat."

"You talking about the woman? Or the character she plays?"

"Both, since she seems to have been pretty well typecast. The lady's probably as phony as that two-headed coin you had back when you were seventeen and thought you might become a magician."

"I wasn't all that interested in magic. I was interested in Christy Marchand, who had herself a big old crush on David Copperfield. I convinced her I could make her float on air."

"And did you?"

"Hell, no. I never much got past palming quarters in the teach-yourself-magic book. But Christy didn't know that. And we sure passed a good time that summer. Lord, she looked good in that pretty harem magician assistant's outfit."

"You talked Christy Marchand, the class valedictorian who grew up to be a NASA scientist, into wearing a harem costume?"

"I billed myself as The Swamp Swami, so the costume fit the theme. And I didn't have to do all that much talking, since I was the closest thing to Copperfield in Blue Bayou. I'll admit, I didn't care whether she levitated or not. I just wanted to get past second base."

"So did the ploy work?"

"Far be it from me to besmirch the honor of

Southern womanhood, but since you're my brother and I know it won't go any further, I like to think back on that as the summer of my Grand Slam."

They shared a laugh.

"So," Nate said, "do you believe the lady's really in danger?"

"I've heard various theories tonight. But personally, if forced to take a guess, I'd say no."

"But you're not taking any chances."

Finn thought of those other women he hadn't been able to protect. "No," he said. "I'm not."

"Home sweet home." Julia stepped out of her heels the moment they entered the suite and padded over to the minibar. "Your brother's a nice man."

"Everyone's always said so."

"I'm going to have some juice. Would you . . ." Her voice trailed off as she glanced at him over her shoulder and saw he'd picked up the shoes. "Oh, great." She cast a frustrated glance up at the ceiling. "It's bad enough I'm stuck with Dudley Do-Right. Do you also have to be Felix Unger?"

"Do you have something against neatness?"

"No. But obsessive neatness is another entirely different matter. It's a definite sign of repression."

"I suppose you learned that on the commune?"

128

"No. Psych 101." Her pretty Manolo Blahniks looked oddly fragile in his big hands. She snatched them away.

"Ah." He nodded. "Well, that certainly makes you an expert."

"You're not that hard to read. Don't take this wrong, Callahan, but you're a bit of a walking cliché."

"That's one of the nicer things I've been accused of over the years. If you're trying to insult me, you're going to have to do better than that."

"How about you only view the world in black and white?"

"What's wrong with that?"

"In case you haven't noticed, the rest of the planet has moved on to Technicolor."

He shrugged. "Call me old-fashioned."

"That, too," she muttered. "I'll bet you even dream in black and white."

He wondered what she'd say if he told her that tonight he'd be dreaming of green eyes that could turn from a soft Southern moss to blazing emerald in a heartbeat. Of hair so bright it looked as if it'd burn his fingers if he gave into the urge to dip them into those lush fiery waves. Of creamy porcelain flesh he suspected felt a great deal warmer than it looked.

"Got me," he said easily. Because he was tempted, too tempted, he turned away, opened the closet by the suite's living room door, and took out a spare sheet and pillow.

"You're sleeping on the couch?" she asked as he tossed them onto the antique reproduction sofa. "Why? The suite has two bedrooms."

"They're too far apart."

Those remarkable eyes widened, just a little. "Surely you don't actually believe I'm in danger?"

"I don't know." There was no point in getting her overly concerned, but neither was he going to encourage her to shrug off a potential threat.

"Well, that's certainly honest."

"I may not always tell you what you want to hear, but if I say something, you can count on it being the truth. There's no way of knowing whether that picture was some guy's socially inept way of expressing admiration, or a threat against your life. But while you're stuck with me, as you so charmingly put it, I'm not taking any chances."

Their eyes met. And held, just a moment too long.

"Well. I don't exactly know what to say to that."

"How about good night?"

She looked prepared to argue. Finn figured she wasn't accustomed to taking orders. Tough.

"Good night, Callahan."

She put the shoes down in order to open the minibar, took out a bottle of orange juice, and disappeared into the larger of the two bedrooms.

As the door shut behind her, Finn let out a

130

long, weary breath. "Good night," he murmured. He was about to pick up the ridiculously spindly shoes when her words came back to him. What the hell, he decided. And left them where she'd dropped them.

Julia had just come out of the shower when her cell phone trilled. She threw on a robe, went into the adjoining bedroom, and located it in the bottom of her purse. Afraid it might be Graham, trying yet another shot at a reconciliation, she was relieved when the caller ID displayed her mother's cell phone number.

The door from the living room opened. During a long, mostly sleepless night, Julia had decided she'd exaggerated Finn's size. Now, looking at him taking up nearly the entire doorway, she realized he was actually even larger than the image that had tormented her sleep.

"So where are you, and how's the harmony and light tour going?" Although the thick terry cloth robe concealed far more than that dress she'd taunted him with last night, Julia felt vaguely uncomfortable. She turned her back on him.

"Oh, just wonderfully," the familiar rich, warm voice responded. "We're in Coldwater Cove. It's a charming little Victorian town on the Washington peninsula. People in the Northwest have always been more in tune with nature than some other parts of the country your father and I have visited over the years."

Julia's parents, Freedom and Peace, had been part of a group of flower children who'd drifted down the California coast when Haight-Ashbury had become too commercially artificial for their tastes. They pooled their funds to purchase a small dairy and, proving surprisingly entrepreneurial for hippies, they'd used the proceeds from milk and ice cream sales, along with ticket revenues to an annual summer solstice music festival, to fund their artistic projects.

For people who'd professed an aversion to private wealth, many had done quite well for themselves: among their ranks were a world-famous balladeer, two Pulitzer Prize winners — one a novelist, the other a poet — and a silver craftsman whose work was featured at Neiman Marcus and Saks.

Her parents had achieved their own measure of fame. One of her father's grapevine chairs had appeared in a retrospective of chairs as art at the Smithsonian, two of his paintings hung in New York's Museum of Modern Art, and a recent pictorial in *Vanity Fair* had shown one of her mother's woven blankets hanging on the wall of the President and First Lady's Texas ranch house.

Her mother gave a thumbnail sketch of their travels, then asked, "How are things in Louisiana?"

"So far, so good." Better now that Finn, apparently deciding her mother offered no threat, had returned to the living room.

"I'm glad to hear that." Julia could hear her mother's slight exhaled sigh. "You know I try not to interfere in your life, dear. But the reason I'm calling is that I'm worried about you."

"Me? Why?"

"I had a dream about you last night. Your aura was decidedly muddy."

"My aura's fine. All those mountains in the Northwest must be screwing up your signal."

"Laugh all you want," her mother said mildly. "But the vibrations coming from your way are decidedly unstable."

"I hadn't realized you'd begun predicting earthquakes." The smile in Julia's voice took the sting from her teasing words.

"Don't I wish. If I could, we would have been prepared for yesterday's tremor."

"Tremor?" Julia hadn't heard anything about a tremor in Washington state. "Are you all right?"

"We're fine. Though it was a bit exciting, since we were crossing the Evergreen Bridge at the time. . . . I was just about to get to that, dear," she said to someone Julia heard talking in the background. "Your father's unhappy because that troll candle you bought us the summer we sold my jewelry on the Grateful Dead tour fell off the dashboard. His head broke off. The troll's, not your father's."

Julia remembered the summer well. She'd been twelve and although she'd grown up surrounded by free love, it was the first time she'd ever been kissed. Woodstock McIntyre, whose mother sold tie-dyed T-shirts and Electric Kool-Aid from the back of a battered old Ford Econoline, had put his tongue in her mouth and touched her breast. Well, he'd touched her nipple, since she hadn't had anything resembling a breast at the time.

He'd then blabbed that fact to all his stupid friends, making her, for a brief time, consider joining a convent.

"Oh, you wouldn't want to become a nun," her mother had said when she'd found Julia crying her eyes out in the back of the VW minibus. "We're pagans. Although," she'd tacked on thoughtfully, "I believe Rainbow Seagull became a Buddhist nun for a time when she was living in Tibet. If you'd like, I could ask her —"

"What I want," Julia had wailed as only a girl whose life had been ruined could, "is breasts."

Charm bracelets had jingled as her mother had run a beringed hand down Julia's red hair. "And you'll have them. In their own time."

"Easy for you to say," she'd muttered into a pillow stuffed with organically grown cotton and lavender. Adding insult to injury, Woodstock had pointed out that Julia's mother — who'd be the last person to flaunt her sexuality — was really, really built.

"The candle's wax," she said, dragging her mind back from that day of adolescent humiliation that she could almost laugh about now. "Can't he just heat it up and shape it back together?"

"I suggested that. But he insists it wouldn't be the same, since he'd always know it was flawed."

Julia reminded herself that those idyllic families resurrected from television archives and given a new life on Nick at Nite had never existed. The Cleavers and the Brady Bunch were as fictitious as *River Road*. But even knowing that, there were times when she wondered what it would have been like to grow up in the suburbs with Donna Reed for a mother. What many now called New Age had been her parents' normal lifestyle for more than three decades, and despite their success, they mostly continued to live as they always had.

But these days, rather than driving the Volkswagen Julia remembered so fondly, they traveled in a luxurious bus that had been tricked out at the factory with all the comforts of home. Replacing the 70s perky-faced daisies, peace signs and anti-war slogans which had covered the original VW, her father had painted a mural of bearded wizards casting spells, fairies with shimmering wings who danced on sunbeams and slept amid petals of lush flowers, while fire-breathing dragons guarded the mouths of secret caves.

This wonderland was overseen by stunningly beautiful goddesses who floated above the scene in filmy, translucent pastel gowns and never suffered bad-hair days. Characteristically, when he'd bought this whimsical house on wheels, he'd written checks equal to the sticker price to local charities.

Her parents had been together thirty-five years, yet had never married. "Starhearts and soulmates don't need cold administrative documents to sanctify their love," Freedom had always proclaimed in his big, booming voice.

"And a piece of paper can't keep love alive," Peace always serenely pointed out.

The more Julia witnessed so many of her friends' marriages crash and burn, or even sadder yet, slowly, quietly fade into disinterest, the more she appreciated her parents' relationship. She'd never met two people more suited to one another, alike in every way, so bonded it was impossible to think of one without the other.

"You are keeping that malachite necklace I sent you close by, aren't you?"

"Yes, Mother," Julia said dutifully. The variegated green stone was supposed to break into two pieces to warn her of danger, which would admittedly be difficult to notice since she'd forgone wearing it around her neck and now carried it in her purse in a small black velvet bag.

"And the bloodstone?"

"Absolutely. Along with the obsidian, the turquoise, and the falcon's eye." There were nearly enough rocks in her purse to make up her own quarry. Remembering her mother's claim that the Danish blue falcon's eye would help her maintain control of her life, Julia idly wondered if she should dig it out.

After passing on her love to her father and promising to be extra careful, at least until the new moon, she hung up and returned to the bathroom to blow her hair dry and brace herself for whatever outrageous scenarios Warren had thought up for Amanda this time.

The morning cast meeting did not start out on a high note.

"What the hell is this?" Margot, looking a bit ragged around the edges, waved her copy of the revised script.

"It's the new story line I told you about, love," Randy said blithely. "Warren's come up with a ripper of an idea. Amanda's going to time travel back to the Civil War after Vanessa shoots her. We'll be a shoo-in to win our time slot in the sweeps."

"Fuck the sweeps." She stabbed the page with a long crimson fingernail. "Who is Fancy?"

"Fancy's who Amanda is in a past life."

"I'm going to be Amanda's *mother*? Do I have to remind you that it's stipulated in my contract that I won't play anyone's mother?"

"The mother's a bonzer part. She's wonderfully neurotic and needy. Gives you a chance to really chew the scenery."

"I'd like to chew Warren's fucking neurotic ass." She glared around the long table. "Where the hell is the little prick, anyway?"

"He called and said he's running a bit late. But he's on his way down."

"Sounds as if Warren's the one who may need protecting," Felissa drawled. "I do hope he didn't use up all his strength doing the nasty with that airhead blond bimbo last night."

"She's not an airhead." Warren entered the conference room, looking, Finn thought, more than a little smug. "Or a bimbo. And there's no need to be crude."

"Pots and kettles, darling," Felissa tossed back. "It was obvious that the overteased bleached blonde was just a small town slut looking for a fame fuck."

"She's not a slut." Finn wanted to remain as far out of the dynamics of the *River Road* cast as possible, but there was no way he was going to allow this woman to insult a friend. "She's just . . ." Shit. How the hell did you explain Lorelei to anyone who'd grown up north of the Mason-Dixon line?

"Southern," Warren supplied.

"Absolutely," Finn agreed.

"If we're through discussing Warren's sex life, I'd like to return to the subject of this new script." Margot pushed the pages away as if

138

they were contaminated. "There's no way the audience — and all my fans — are going to accept me as any grown woman's mother."

"People married younger in those days," Warren argued. "Your character was a child bride, forced by her father into a marriage of convenience with a much older cotton planter."

She muttered a short, rude curse and returned to skimming the pages. "Wait a goddamn minute! Amanda seduces my husband? Her own father? That's just sick, Warren."

"He's your second husband, which makes him her stepfather. And her name's Fancy," he reminded her.

"Whatever her name is, she's getting to sleep with *my* fiancé the night before he goes off to war," Felissa complained, leafing through the pages. "Why can't I seduce Margot's husband?"

"Because the audience would never believe it, since you're playing the Melanie Wilkes role."

"And Julia gets to be Scarlett?"

Felissa's tone was as much of a storm warning as the rumble of thunder out over the Gulf. Finn could tell the writer knew he'd made a tactical error with that comparison.

"Fancy's not at all like Scarlett," he backpedaled. "She's really a Confederate spy who has to determine if her mother's new riverboat gambler husband is secretly selling the plantation's cotton to the Northern army."

"So now I'm going to be married to a traitor?" Margot looked on the verge of going ballistic.

"I don't know if he's a traitor or not. I still haven't decided."

"Well, whichever, I absolutely refuse to compromise my character." She turned toward Kendall, who was seated on a sofa a few feet away from the table. "Tell him he has to change the script, Charles."

"I'll tell him no such thing." His eyes were hard as stone. "The story line stands as written."

"But my contract —"

"Has so many holes in it, it may as well have been written on Swiss cheese. Atlantic Pharmaceuticals' lawyers teethed on the *Art of War* and they love going into battle, so if I were you, I'd think twice about challenging this story line. And if you get it into your head to sulk in your dressing room, the way you did last month when you balked about that scene in the country club where Amanda threw champagne in your face, I'll fine you a thousand dollars for every minute you tie up shooting."

Fury drew her face into harsh, ugly lines. "You're an ungrateful bastard."

Kendall's face was just as hard. "You swore on your dear old granny's memory that you didn't have any ulterior motive in fucking me. I took you at your word. If you were lying, sweetheart, it's your problem, not mine."

Margot flung the bound pages across the room, shot Julia a white-hot look of hatred, then stormed out as dramatically as one might expect from a former daytime diva.

"Just another day in paradise," Julia murmured. "If you had any sense at all, Callahan, you'd escape now. While you still can."

12

"That was a nice thing to do," Julia said thirty minutes later after the story meeting ended.

Finn stepped back, allowing her to enter the elevator first. "What?"

"Standing up for that woman Warren left the party with last night."

"She's a friend," he said simply. He stuck the keycard in the slot that made the elevator bypass the lower floors. The doors closed.

"And that's important to you."

It didn't sound like a question, but Finn answered it anyway. "Yeah."

"That's nice."

"Is that a compliment?"

"Merely a statement."

They rode up in silence, side by side, both watching the numbers above the door light up.

"I lied," Julia said as they entered the suite.

"About what?" He wondered if she was going to confess she'd staged the threat.

"It *was* a compliment."

"Okay."

"Okay? That's it?" She folded her arms. "Perhaps spending all your time with police types and criminals may have left you a bit socially challenged, but it's customary, when one receives a compliment, to respond in kind."

"You want a compliment?"

"I didn't say that." Her answer was a bit too quick. It had sure sounded that way to Finn. "I merely pointed out that your answer was a bit curt."

"Just give me a minute to think of one."

Finn wondered if there were any words of praise this woman hadn't heard, and for some insane reason wanted to try to come up with something original. Which was one of the lamest ideas he'd ever had. Pretty words had always come trippingly off Nate's tongue and he figured Jack must do pretty well in that department, since the middle Callahan brother earned his living as a writer these days, but Finn had never been one to wax poetic.

"Forget it." She shook her head in disgust, stomped into the adjoining bedroom, and shut the door between them. It wasn't quite a slam, but it was damn close.

Finn shook his own head. Sighed heavily as he took his notebook from a suit jacket pocket.

No matter what else was going on in his life, he'd never had any trouble concentrating on a case. He'd developed the ability to shut out everything and everyone around him back when he'd been cramming for tests in a college dorm that made *Animal House* look tame by comparison.

But as he reviewed the details of the conversations he'd had downstairs last night, the words on the lined pages seemed to blur, replaced with an unbidden mental image of him and Julia Summers rolling around on the moss-stuffed mattress at the camp.

The moment Julia saw Beau Soleil, she was enthralled. "It's stunning."

"It looks just like Tara," Felissa said.

"I'll bet it's being eaten by termites," Margot said. Faced with being fired, she'd shown up for work this morning but it was obvious to everyone that she wasn't at all happy with her situation.

"It used to be," Nate, who'd come along to open the house for them, said. "But my brother thinks he's managed to run them off. He's been restoring the house for months, and though it's probably a lifetime project, if you'd seen the place when Jack started, you'd be amazed it looks this good."

Julia put the names together. "Your brother's Jack Callahan? *The* Jack Callahan? Who wrote *The Death Dealer*?"

"Yeah. That's him."

"I absolutely love his books. I cried when his DEA hero's wife was blown up in a car bombing meant for him, and I keep hoping he'll find a nice woman to fall in love with. Is it true the stories are autobiographical?"

"I honestly don't know. Jack doesn't talk all that much about his days in the DEA. You'd have to ask him."

144

"Is he going to be living in the house while we're here?"

"He's on a belated honeymoon. His wife's family owned Beau Soleil for generations before Jack bought it. Our *maman* was the housekeeper here when we were kids."

"Sounds as if there's a story there." A fairytale, she suspected.

"One with a happy ending." Nate's smile was quick and warm. Julia was a little unnerved that it didn't affect her nearly as much as a mere quirk of his older brother's harshly cut lips.

She wasn't sure what she was going to do about Finn Callahan, but since things between them had been silent and uncomfortable since she'd walked out on him yesterday morning, she didn't think she could stand to spend the next two weeks in a state of undeclared war.

She looked up at Finn. "You didn't tell me your brother was Jack Callahan."

"You didn't ask. And it's not germane to our situation."

Deciding that it was impossible to have a normal social conversation with this man, Julia gave up on any idea of a truce and turned back to Nate. "I love the double front stairs."

"Aren't they cool? The practical reason for the design is that because the women's hoop skirts were so wide, there wasn't room for two people to walk up them side by side. They also served to keep social order, since if a man saw a woman's ankles back in those days, he was duty bound to marry her. Having men go up one side and women the other prevented an escort from seeing a lady's legs when she lifted her hoop skirts to climb the steps."

"Hoop skirts." Felissa sighed happily, obviously pleased with the idea of wearing antebellum-era costumes.

Margot, on the other hand, seemed determined not to find anything positive about the experience. "Corsets," she muttered.

Julia sighed with resignation. The last time Margot had been in a snit, she'd disrupted not only the mood among the cast and crew, but the shooting schedule for over a week, as well. If this season-ending project ran late, she'd never make it to Kathmandu in time.

Things fell into a pattern over the next three days. Finn and Julia drove in silence to Beau Soleil each morning to meet the rest of the cast, who arrived by van from town. By the end of the first day, Finn had come to realize that acting involved a lot more than smiling pretty for the camera and shedding your clothes.

He sat nearby as Damien, the magenta-haired makeup man, chattered like a magpie while transforming Julia into *River Road*'s siren. Next her hair was brushed, teased, and sprayed into a sexy tangle of curls. Finally, while Finn waited outside her trailer, Audrey, the motherly wardrobe mistress, would dress her in period costumes that looked as if they weighed a ton and were probably even more uncomfortable than Damien's crotch binding leather pants, which had to feel like a sauna in this heat.

Then she'd spend hours waiting while people blocked scenes, arranged lighting, and myriad other things just to shoot a scene that maybe would last five or ten minutes. If things went well.

He began to recognize the transformation into Amanda. It wasn't that she turned from some ordinary person into Wonder Woman. Julia Summers was a naturally stunning creature, albeit with surprisingly uneven features — there was that feline slant to her eyes, her nose was a bit too pug, her lips too large, the chin too stubborn. But somehow they all fit together perfectly.

It was, he decided, watching Fancy flirt with her mother's husband, as if an already bright light inside her flared even hotter when the camera turned on her. Even on those occasions when she'd have to repeat the same lines again and again, she somehow managed to make them sound fresh each time.

At the end of each scene, Damien would leap to action with his brushes, powders and potions; the hairdresser would struggle to tame her curls, which were made even more wild by the unrelenting humidity; and the waiting would begin again.

And all the time, while Margot bitched about anything and everything, and Felissa fussed about the heat, Julia didn't utter a word of complaint.

That she was universally liked by the crew was obvious. It wasn't that surprising, since she appeared to take a genuine interest in them. Finn watched her ask a cameraman about his new son and ooh and aah over the snapshots the man proudly whipped out of his shirt pocket, commiserate with the script girl about her husband's infidelity, and encourage an electrician to adopt a puppy for his daughter's birthday from a Golden Retriever rescue group she'd made a fund-raising appearance for.

She was even gracious to the townspeople who'd been hired as extras, obligingly posing for pictures and signing autographs for the locals, who were openly enthralled. Finn recognized several of them and couldn't help noticing that not only did Lorelei show up in more than a few scenes, she also disappeared with the writer during the lunch break.

After they returned to the inn at the end of the day, Julia would order a light supper from room service and disappear into the bedroom, where he could hear her rehearsing her next day's lines aloud. Then, mere hours later, the process would begin again.

The third day of shooting dragged on, the final scene shot late at night in the plantation cemetery. Finn stood in the shadow of a broken-winged angel, watching her. Silvery moondust streamed over the bayou graveyard, illuminating tombs that stood like mute white ghosts in the ethereal glow. Julia/Fancy was wearing a clinging moss green dress which, though not entirely true to the period, could have been created from the mist that curled in clinging tendrils around her bare arms. She'd left her fiery hair loose, allowing it to curl over pearlescent shoulders.

"So you've come," a deep male voice echoed out of the thickening fog.

"I hadn't realized I had a choice." She tossed her head, and there was an adversarial edge to her honeyed Southern drawl. "Since you've put Belle Terre under Yankee occupation."

"Of course you have a choice." Captain James Farragut emerged from behind one of the tombs, wearing a uniform of Yankee blue. With his well-trimmed blond hair and beard, shiny brass buttons, and boots polished to a brilliant sheen, he could have stepped off a Union recruiting poster. Fancy O'Halloran had hated him on sight.

Thunder rumbled like Northern cannon fire in the distance. "During my stay here, you can meet me wherever I say, whenever I say, and I won't order my men to burn your beloved plantation house to the ground when we leave," he said matter-of-factly. "Or you can refuse, and I'll turn you and your sister over to my men, many of whom are rough farm boys who don't have any idea of how to treat a lady."

"And you do?" Her tone suggested that she

found it unlikely any man from New York City would have the faintest idea how to treat a genteel Southern woman.

His boots crunched on the crushed oyster shell gravel as he approached. "Absolutely."

They were standing face-to-face now, her skirt pressing against his thighs as he backed her up against a crypt, pinning her between the damp stone and his body.

Lightning flashed, brightening the scene to a daylight brilliance for a fleeting heartbeat of a second. Watching her closely as he was, Finn saw her faint shudder when the captain's fingers skimmed over her bare shoulders. With anticipation or fear, he couldn't tell.

"Of course," Farragut mused as his touch trailed lower, tracing the rounded curve of her upper breast, "one could argue that any woman who'd meet a man all alone in a deserted cemetery at midnight isn't really much of a lady."

The sky opened up. Rain fell in a torrent, as if being poured out of a bucket. Fancy cried out as he roughly tore the last of her pretty, prewar dresses down to her waist, but when he dragged her to the ground and began unfastening his wool trousers, she reached beneath her filmy skirt — exposing a mouthwatering length of stocking — and retrieved the derringer she'd stuck in a lacy garter.

"If you lay a hand on me again," she said, pointing the weapon directly at his groin, "or so much as touch a hair on the head of my sister or any other woman on this plantation, I swear, you'll be carrying your manhood back to New York in a basket."

If he hadn't known that this soap opera vixen had grown up on one of the last surviving flower child communes in northern California, Finn might have believed that Julia Summers was a true Steel Magnolia of the South.

They glared at each other for a long, tension-filled moment. The Union captain's eyes glittered with dangerous male intent. The rain had turned her dress nearly invisible; the thin wet material clung to her curves.

An instinctive male response to the provocative sight uncoiled in his loins; Finn ruthlessly reined it in.

"Rebel slut," Shane Langley, playing Captain Farragut, spat the words, then lunged at her again.

As the thunder boomed around them and the rain fell, Fancy pulled the trigger.

"Cut!" Randy's voice broke the night.

"Cut," echoed the assistant director.

The artificially generated storm abruptly ceased.

"Stone the bloody dingoes." The hard-driving Australian director bestowed the first compliment Finn had heard him hand out in three days of filming. "You pulled that scene off in one take."

"It was either that or let you rain on me for the rest of the night." Julia took hold of Shane's hand as he pulled her back onto her feet.

"I'll see you all back on the set at nine A.M. sharp. Julia, luv, you're due in makeup at seven."

"Dammit, Randy. That's only six hours from now. How do you expect me to get my beauty sleep?"

"I'd suggest you sleep quickly," the director responded.

"Don't worry, darlin'," her co-star said, his own natural Mississippi drawl more suited to a Confederate uniform than Union blue. "You're already drop-dead gorgeous."

"Flatterer," she muttered, slipping her arms into the robe Audrey held out to her.

"It's the God's own truth." He lifted his right hand.

"Isn't that sweet." She patted his cheek, her smile luminous. "But I'm still not sleeping with you."

He shrugged good-naturedly. "Can't blame a guy for trying."

No, Finn agreed silently. With the image of those long, firm legs replaying in his mind, he doubted there were many men who wouldn't attempt to parlay that scene into the real thing.

Julia didn't so much as spare him a glance as he followed her to her trailer; didn't say a word when he walked in right behind her as if he had every right to be there. Though he was grateful for her apparent change in attitude, Finn didn't trust her seeming acquiescence.

"God, I feel as if I've gone ten rounds with Mike Tyson," she complained. "In a mud pit. And I'm going to have bruises all over my butt tomorrow from that damn gravel."

Since he'd discovered that she had a habit of talking to herself, most often when she was preparing for a scene, Finn didn't respond.

She turned her back on him and shrugged off the robe, letting it slide down her body onto the floor. The wet, muddy dress that revealed more than it concealed followed, leaving her in a muddied corset and lacy silk pantaloons that might have come from a nineteenth-century Victoria's Secret store. "If you're going to insist on hovering over me like some oversize bullmastiff guard dog, you may as well make yourself useful and get me out of this damn straitjacket so I can breathe again."

The corset was white floral satin, heavily boned and laced up the back. It looked uncomfortable as hell, but winnowed her waist down to an unbelievably narrow size he figured he could span with his fingers. Fingers that were practically itching to touch her.

"Why don't I call Audrey?" he suggested.

"Because she's had a long day since Randy got it into his head to change costumes every two hours, and she still has tomorrow's wardrobe to get ready."

She flashed him a deliberately provocative look over her bare shoulder. "Which leaves you to undress me."

153

The pink ribbons tied at the back of her wasp-slender waist were wet and muddy. Deliberately testing his self-control, Finn drew them through the loops slowly, allowing his fingers to brush against perfumed flesh that felt like cool satin to the touch.

Neither spoke. But the higher he got, the more he sensed the tension that had been stretched nearly to the breaking point between them these past days begin to ease. When his knuckles brushed against her spine, not by accident, but design, he heard a slow languid sigh escape from between her lips.

"What did you think?" she murmured.

"About what? Lift up your hair so I can unlace these top ones."

She did as instructed, revealing a slender neck he found unreasonably erotic. "About the scene."

"I think it was getting pretty hot." He slipped the ribbon through the final loop. "Until you shot the guy's balls off."

"Did that make you wince? Want to grab your own?"

"Yeah."

"Good." There was a rasp of smooth silk against harsh denim as she leaned her nearly naked body back against him in a way that sent the last of the blood rushing straight from his head to his boxer shorts.

Finn knew the move was calculated when she looked up at him, her sexy come-and-kiss-me lips tilted up in the same smile he'd watched her use two days ago when her character had seduced her sister's Confederate Army fiancé before sending him off to fight for a losing cause.

"My gracious," she said in Fancy's slow magnolia drawl. "Is that your gun, Special Agent Callahan? Or are you just glad to see me?"

"What the hell do you think?" Because he suspected it was what she wanted, Finn refused to be embarrassed by his body's response and move away.

Buns of steel earned from daily yoga workouts wiggled against him in a way meant to test his resolve. Oh, she was good, Finn decided as he ground his teeth and forced his sex-crazed mind to run through the entire 1978 Yankees lineup. He was trying to remember who'd replaced the injured Willie Randolph at second base late in the season, when Julia gave him another smile, more wickedly seductive than the first.

"It's nice to know you're actually human, darling. I was beginning to wonder." With that less than flattering remark, she let her damp red hair fall back over her shoulders, held the corset against her breasts, and disappeared into the bathroom.

When he heard the shower turn on, Finn imagined her naked, imagined himself joining her in that compact shower, smoothing the fragrant soap that clung to her skin over her lush curves.

As his mind wandered into forbidden territory, flashing pictures that would make the old *Playboy* magazines his brothers used to snitch from him back in high school seem tame by comparison, Finn leaned his head against the wall and reminded himself that if he allowed his rampant hard-on to drag him into that shower with her, he'd undoubtedly be breaking every rule in the book. Along with some that hadn't even been written yet.

But that crack about not being human was pissing him off. What the hell did she think he was? Some sort of sexless android? Just because he didn't believe in giving in to temptation and mixing work and pleasure? Of course, he'd never been so tempted, either.

Finn had been threatened, shot at, and had even foiled an assassination plot that had earned him an ugly knife gash in the thigh and an invitation to the White House to have dinner with the President and First Lady. Unfortunately, he was beginning to fear that guarding the woman soap opera fans loved to hate might end up being the most dangerous assignment of his career.

He could protect Julia from her obsessed star-stalker.

But who the effing hell was going to protect *him* from *her*?

On the other side of the closed door, as the shower cubicle filled up with fragrant steam, Julia's reckless mind imagined Finn Callahan's broad, capable hands moving all over her wet slick body, touching her, doing all the erotic things he'd done in her dreams.

Leaning her head back against the shower wall, she lifted her face to the water and sighed. It was going to be a very long two weeks.

13

Julia woke feeling cranky and out of sorts after having spent the night tossing and turning, suffering unwanted erotic dreams about Finn, one of which had included a hoopskirt and a vat of warm honey.

The silent drive to Beau Soleil did nothing to ease her headache. When they arrived Margot looked hung over and was her typical acid self, deriding the room service waiter who'd taken all of ten minutes to bring her coffee to her suite, the van driver for "purposefully trying to hit every goddamn pothole in the goddamn road," and Warren for writing such "godawful drek."

Warren appeared unwounded by both her barbs and her stiletto sharp glares. He was deep in some creative zone, madly scribbling on a legal pad, undoubtedly changing the script yet again, Julia thought with a sigh.

Shane, who, if one could believe a barb Margot had thrown at him, had disappeared from the inn's bar last night with a cocktail waitress, caught up on missed sleep while Randy went over the script, blocking out scenes he intended to shoot today.

And all the time Finn remained beside Julia, as large and silent as the Sphinx.

Clouds were gathering out over the Gulf, dark portents of a possible storm, making Julia very glad Randy had decided to shoot the indoor ballroom scene, which flashed back to a time before the war, today. The light was an odd yellow, making Beau Soleil gleam more gold than alabaster. It truly was a stunning house, though Julia couldn't imagine ever thinking of it as home. To her it would be like living in a museum.

Dreading the prospect of another day laced up like a Christmas goose, she entered the trailer that served as a temporary dressing room. Someone had left a manila envelope with her name on the table. She sighed and opened what she took to be yet more revisions to the script. Blood rushed from her head in a dizzying rush when she saw the photograph. Sound roared in her head. Then everything went black.

The next thing she knew, she was lying on the couch.

"Wait here," she heard Finn say from what sounded like the bottom of the sea.

As if she were capable of getting anywhere without crawling. Julia looked up at him, but the way he was going in and out of focus only made her more dizzy, so she shut her eyes.

A moment later, a cold washcloth was laid on her forehead.

"Take a deep breath."

She managed a shallow, shuddering intake of

air that cleared away a few of the mental cob-
webs.

"Again." When she felt his fingertips against
her throat, Julia realized he was checking her
pulse.

She took another, more efficient breath.

"Good. Another." The deep, self-assured
voice, the reassuring stroke of his fingers as he
brushed her hair off her cheek, the coolness of
the damp cloth against her skin, all began to
calm her. "The color's coming back to your
cheeks."

She knew. She could feel it. Her heart, which
had been pounding against her ribs like an
angry fist, began to slow to something resembling a normal beat.

"I feel so foolish," she murmured. "I never
faint." She'd once gotten a little light-headed
when she'd stood up too fast after giving blood,
but had felt fine again after eating the cookie
the nurse had given her.

"There's a first time for everything. You're
going to have to start having something besides
coffee and half an orange for breakfast."

"Easy for you to say. You don't have to
squeeze into a spandex catsuit in a couple
weeks."

After winning the role, she'd belatedly realized the downside of becoming a Bond Girl.
Her body was going to be up on that huge
screen, inviting audiences all around the world
to criticize every blemish and lump. Which was

why she'd hired a personal trainer, a sadistic Russian immigrant she suspected must have run a gulag back in his homeland.

"Besides, I've skipped breakfast my entire life and never fainted before."

If her eyes hadn't been closed, forcing her to rely more on her other senses, if his hand hadn't still been on her face, she might have missed the way he stiffened ever so slightly.

"Never?" His voice was gritty, even for him.

"Never."

"Could you be pregnant?"

That made her open her eyes. "No."

"You sure?"

"Since I haven't been paid a visitation by some angel bringing glad tidings lately, I'd have to be six months pregnant, so yeah, I'm pretty sure I would have noticed by now. Besides, I'm on the pill."

"You haven't had sex for six months?"

"Gee, Callahan. Is that germane to our situation?"

"Touché." A flash of humor momentarily brightened his eyes, then just as quickly faded, replaced by concern. His lips had appeared to quirk, just a little, and thinking back on those disturbingly erotic dreams, Julia wondered what they would taste like.

Which was also not germane to the situation, she reminded herself.

"Maybe I'd better call a doctor." Her stomach fluttered when he brushed a wayward curl off her cheek.

"That's not necessary." She pointed toward the photograph lying face down on the carpet. "You might want to take a look at that."

Anger moved in waves across his face as he viewed the photograph, computer printed exactly as the first one had been. Having surreptitiously watched him nearly as carefully as he'd been watching her, Julia had looked beneath the stoicism he wore like a coat of armor, and begun to sense Finn Callahan could be dangerous. Now, taking in the muscle jerking in his dark cheek and the whiteness of his knuckles as he clenched and unclenched his right hand, she belatedly realized that if you were one of the bad guys, he could be deadly.

"How do you think he took it?" she asked, swallowing her fear. She would not allow some stalker to make her feel helpless or vulnerable. She sat up and pushed her hair back from her face with both hands.

He held the photograph by the edges. The better, she guessed, to protect any fingerprints that might be on the paper. "My best guess would be, since we were alone in here, he was outside the window."

That idea caused goose bumps to rise on her flesh. Despite an outside temperature in the low nineties, with a humidity nearly as high, Julia began to shiver. She wrapped her arms around herself, partly for warmth, partly in an unconscious gesture of protection.

"You probably think I'm acting like a ninny."

"Why would I think that?"

"Well, I do spend a great deal of my life performing for a camera, and, as you've already pointed out, I shed my clothes on a regular basis, so I suppose a single still shot shouldn't be so upsetting . . ."

"But this is different," Finn guessed. "Because those scenes were carefully scripted and professionally acted." He brushed his fingers along the top outline of her lips, which she was pressing together to keep from quivering. "Having some stranger filming your ordinary everyday private moments without any warning or permission would be enough to make anyone a little jumpy."

"I think what took me by surprise was that if someone on the cast isn't playing a very sick joke, my stalker's back."

"From last week, right?"

"No." She rubbed her eyes with the heels of her hands. "Before that."

"Before . . . When? And why the hell don't the police have a record of any stalker?"

"There wasn't any official report made, because he didn't quite fit the criteria for a stalker. He didn't make any threats, never tried to get too close to me. If he had, I'd know who he was.

"Since the photos were flattering, with equally flattering comments written beneath them, I decided it was merely a fan with a crush and not worth dragging the police into."

"That's what they're for, dammit. I can understand how you might be reluctant, given your background, to go into a police station, but believe it or not, cops do have other duties besides beating up civilians at traffic stops and setting up speeding traps to catch you when you're driving too fast to the airport."

"I went to traffic school," she muttered, irritated but unsurprised he knew about that. "Paid the fine and did my time."

"I know. The instructor said it was the only time in his memory that someone stuck all Saturday in the basement of a church brought home baked brownies to class."

"It was my birthday. My parents were at some jazzfest in Sedona — that's in Arizona —"

"Yeah. I've been there. Pretty little place."

"It's more than pretty. It's spectacular with all that red rock and impossibly blue sky. Did you know it's the red of the rocks that makes the sky look so blue over the canyons?"

"I've never heard the theory, but it makes sense . . . And you're changing the subject."

"I'm merely responding to your crack about the brownies. I didn't want to celebrate alone, so I baked some from my Mother's famous recipe and took them along for the class lunch break."

He lifted a dark brow. "I'll bet that made the second half of the day a lot more mellow for everyone."

164

"They weren't laced with anything. Geez, Callahan, even if I did drugs, which I never have, you must have a really bad opinion of me to think I'm that stupid."

"I don't think you're stupid. I also didn't think you'd actually done it. I was just —"

"Making a joke?"

Hell, Finn thought. What kind of opinion of him did she have if she found that idea so impossible? "Yeah. But not because I'm not taking this seriously."

"Of course you take it seriously. From what I've been able to tell, you're a textbook firstborn. You take everything seriously. And the only reason I didn't get the joke was that I wasn't expecting it."

Humor lit her remarkable eyes. "Perhaps we could work out some sort of system for you to warn me when one's coming up," she suggested. "Hold up a sign, perhaps. Or maybe a code word that'll serve as a clue."

When she smiled, Finn realized that despite what he'd said to Nate about her being a pain in the ass, he was actually starting to like — and admire — Julia Summers. "Clues never hurt," he murmured with a practiced casualness.

And speaking of clues . . .

He studied the picture more closely, seeking some small clue to the photographer. It had been taken by a digital camera, printed on the type of inexpensive white computer paper that could be bought at any office supply store.

"Is it like the others you've gotten? Either the first time or last week?" He didn't see any point in suggesting that having thrown the earlier one away hadn't been the most prudent thing to do.

"I'm no expert, but it looks like the same paper and the same printer. The flesh tones are off in the same way."

"You have a good eye." The skin above and between the corset laces was more pink than the pale ivory of a true redhead. More rosy than he knew hers to be.

Beneath the photograph her stalker had typed, *I'm very disappointed in you, Amanda. You should choose your lovers more carefully.*

"He thinks we're lovers," Finn said, more to himself than to her. A suspicion that had undoubtedly been fueled by this seemingly intimate moment which her stalker had frozen in time.

"It appears so."

"He — or she — is also jealous."

"Surely you don't think it's a woman?"

His gut told him it wasn't. But . . .

"I'm not ruling anyone out."

She tried to hold the shiver in, but accustomed to watching for the smallest of details, he caught it. Wanting to reassure, he took hold of her shoulders.

"It's going to be okay."

Hell. He'd known it was a mistake to touch

her. From the way her eyes widened, Finn knew she felt the same flash of heat, the sizzle of nerve endings.

"I'll keep you safe."

"I know." For a woman who had grown up surrounded by free love, an actress who could slip with silky ease into the skin of a siren, her green eyes were surprisingly innocent. "You may not be the easiest man in the world, Callahan. And I'm not even sure I like you. But I do trust you."

It would be against every tenet he believed in if he gave into the temptation to take that wide, generous mouth. The safest thing to do would be to take his hands off her. Unfortunately, if he'd been a fan of safe, he would have made his mother happy and become a corporate lawyer instead of a cop.

His fingers stroked, soothing the knots at the base of her neck. His eyes delved deeply into hers, hoping he'd find the refusal that would stop him before he stepped over the line.

"Callahan . . ." He knew he was lost when she lifted a hand to his cheek. Knew the same smoke that was clouding his mind was billowing in hers.

The hard-won control Finn had forced himself to take on so many years ago deserted him. Knowing what he was about to do was wrong, knowing it would create even more problems, he lowered his mouth to hers, stopping just a breath before contact.

Her eyes were deep green pools. A man could drown in them, if he wasn't careful.

She recklessly wrapped her arm around his neck and closed the distance.

14

The first touch of lips was like being punched in the gut with a velvet fist. The way she drew her head back just enough to stare up at him assured him that she'd felt it, too.

The little voice of caution, of conscience, he was usually able to count on deserted him. All Finn could think about was how much he wanted to strip that T-shirt and tight, low-slung jeans off her body and touch her. All over. Taste her. Everywhere.

As dangerous as that idea was, even worse was the realization that she wanted him to do exactly that.

Since he'd already broken his rule about getting involved on the job, Finn decided to deal with the consequences later — when his body wasn't throbbing, his blood had cooled to something below the boiling point, and his brain wasn't clogged with her scent.

She shivered, not from cold, not from fear, but anticipation. And that was his undoing.

This time he dove headlong into the kiss, dragging her right along with him. Tongues tangled, teeth scraped, arousal flared. His hands streaked over her, desperate to touch. Melting against him like heated wax, she encouraged him with soft sighs, low moans and dazed whimpers.

He tangled a hand in her hair and pulled her head back, allowing his mouth access to her smooth white throat. When he touched his tongue to the hollow where her pulse was pounding hot and hard and fast, Finn imagined he heard a hiss of steam.

Dark desires drummed in his head. Erotic images of all the things he wanted to do to her, with her, flashed through his mind like strobe lights, blinding him to anything and everything but her.

He wanted her. He wanted to press her back against the cushions, wanted to feel those long, slender legs around him; he wanted to bury himself deep within her, taking, possessing, claiming. That was just for starters.

Battered by hunger, by need, Finn forced himself to back away now, while he still could.

A little cry of protest escaped her lips as he broke the heated contact. Ruthlessly reining in his runaway desire, he nearly groaned as he took in the sight of her — eyes still a little soft-focused from lust, wine-sweet lips parted, her face flushed the soft hue of the late summer roses his mother had loved to tend in Beau Soleil's gardens.

"Wow." She pressed her fingers against her lips as she stared up at him. Her voice was ragged, her breathing hard.

She wasn't the only one. His chest was heaving like a man who'd been on the verge of drowning and pulled to safety just in time. Which was pretty much the case.

Finn pushed himself off the couch and put a safety zone of about five feet between them.

"I owe you an apology."

"You tell me you're sorry you kissed me, Callahan, and I'll forget I'm a pacifist and slug you." Her chin tilted up in that way he was beginning to enjoy. Her voice and her breathing steadied. "You liked it while it was happening. A lot."

Despite having just caused himself one helluva problem, her spark of spirit made him want to grin. Which was odd. He couldn't recall the last time he'd grinned.

Nate, of course, was well known for his lady-killing boyish grin, and Finn had heard more than one woman describe Jack's bold, cocky one to be a pirate's, dark and wickedly appealing. But to Finn's knowledge, no one ever mentioned his smile when describing him.

In fact, one frustrated former lover had, just before their brief affair ended, accused him of hiding all his feelings — if he even had any — behind a damn impenetrable stone face. He hadn't challenged her accusation since she was pretty much right. Any FBI Special Agent who revealed emotion wouldn't last long on the street, or in the Bureau. If there was a way to compartmentalize his feelings, Finn hadn't found it. Not that he'd ever looked all that hard; his life, both professionally and personally, had always suited him just fine.

So how was it that both seemed to be spinning out of control at the same time?

The thing to do now was to prioritize. First he'd regain control of this immediate situation with Julia. Then he could tackle the problem of how the hell he was going to get through the next week and a half.

"Sure, I enjoyed it." He might not volunteer information, but neither did he lie. "You're a dynamite kisser." Because it was too tempting to kiss her again, Finn sought something, anything, to say to cool things down. "Of course, I suppose I shouldn't be surprised. Since you've had a lot of practice."

Fuck. Finn could have taken out his Glock and shot himself the minute he heard the words coming out of his mouth. If either Nate or Jack had heard him screw up like that, they'd probably be on the floor howling with laughter.

Instead of crumbling into a little puddle of hurt feelings, she fired right back at him. "Correction: *Amanda's* had a lot of practice. If you can't tell the difference by now, you're even more clueless about the opposite sex than you let on."

"Okay." *You can defuse this situation,* Finn assured himself. *Hell, you aced hostage negotiation and terrorist training. Handling one woman, even one who was as pissed off as this one seemed to be, should be a piece of cake.* "You're right. I misspoke."

"Now there's a governmental bureaucratic word for you," she muttered.

"I may be clueless when it comes to women —"

"*May* be?"

Finn forged on. "I may be one of the most socially inept guys you've ever met —"

"Oh, believe me, Callahan," she interrupted him again, "you win the crown."

He ground his teeth. "The thing is, you're understandably upset right now. And probably, although you've been doing a bang-up job of hiding it, a little scared. I had no right to take advantage of you that way."

"You weren't taking advantage of me. I wanted you to kiss me. Are you going to try to tell me that you haven't wondered what it would be like? That you haven't been at all curious?"

Truth warred with the desire to get out of these treacherous waters, he was already in way over his head. "Sure. But I shouldn't have allowed it to happen."

"Allowed?" That had her on her feet in a flash. "You *allowed*? Listen, you insufferable, arrogant —"

"Dammit, you've got a short fuse."

"Only when I'm forced to be locked up in close quarters with a bossy, humorless control freak." Her finger jabbed against the front of his shirt; Finn grasped her hand and held it against his chest.

He sighed heavily, then tried again. "Look,

I'm probably all you've accused me of and a lot more. I also think you're gorgeous, sexy as hell, not to mention being a very nice woman."

"Nice," she muttered. Finn was encouraged when she didn't yank her hand away. "A glass of wine with a shrimp salad at the beach is nice. TV weather forecasters are nice. The guy who greets you at Wal-Mart is paid to be nice. Excuse me if I don't find *nice* that huge a compliment. As for being gorgeous, I honestly don't see it, though others seem to. But I can't take credit for great genes. My mother's stunningly beautiful."

"I know." Once again, Finn could have bit his tongue off. For someone who *never* spoke without thinking first, he was definitely bypassing his brain today.

"That's right." She shot him a frustrated look. "You've been busy digging up dirt on me and my family, so you've undoubtedly seen all our mug shots."

"As a matter of fact, I have. Are you going to slug me if I say yours looked pretty damn good?"

"For a woman with a number across her chest." A reluctant smile teased at the corner of her lips. "Damn it, Callahan, you really do know how to sweet-talk a girl, don't you?" It was her turn to sigh. "I can't believe we're even having this conversation. I can't believe I kissed an FBI agent. I especially can't believe that even as irritated as I am at you right now, I

174

want to do it again."

That made two of them.

Kissing her had been a huge mistake. Instead of easing his hunger, now that he knew she tasted every bit as good as she looked, he was starving for more. Forbidden fruit was always the most appealing.

"Probably not as much as I do." In a gesture more suited to Nate, one he would have groaned at only a few days ago, Finn lifted their joined hands and skimmed a light kiss over her knuckles. "The thing is, it can't go anywhere."

"What makes you think I want it to? We're just talking a kiss here, Callahan. Basic physical attraction. Did you hear me say anything about needing orange blossoms or ever-afters?"

"No. But don't most women want them?" Frustrated, he rubbed the bridge of his nose. If he fucked up his work as badly as he had this, he wouldn't be able to get a job as a meter maid.

"A woman doesn't necessarily need marriage these days to be fulfilled."

"I know that." He had women friends in the Bureau who'd drilled that into him. "What's your favorite *Fleming* novel?"

"What?" She blinked at the apparent sudden change in subject.

"Your favorite Bond book. Which is it?"

"That's easy. *On Her Majesty's Service*. Why? And what's yours?"

"It changes. I suppose right now I'd have to

say *Thunderball*." Finn could definitely identify with the disgraced spy who was sent off to a health farm for two weeks to get his act together. "And it's interesting that yours just happens to be the one book in which the guy gets married."

"His wife also gets killed in the end. Which blows any theory you might try to be formulating about my reading tastes and my own personal feelings about matrimony."

"Okay, maybe you'll follow in your parents' footsteps and skip taking the vows, but I'm pretty good at profiling and I'd peg you as the type of woman who believes in the happily-ever-after kind of storybook love."

"Don't you?"

"I believe in it for some people."

His parents came instantly to mind. Jake Callahan had doted on his dark-eyed Marie and she'd openly adored him. In fact, there'd been times when their penchant for public displays of affection had embarrassed the hell out of their three sons.

"Now you have me curious." She tilted her head. "Are you saying you've never thought about spending the rest of your life with one special woman?"

"Not really."

He wasn't like Nate, who was open about his desire to go to his grave playing the field, but Finn's work precluded any sustained relationship. His last had been in the early days of his hunt for Lawson. He'd been dating a bright, ambitious senatorial aide who, while her work might keep her up on the Hill until all hours of the night, was not at all pleased when he stood her up for one of the inaugural balls.

He'd been notified that another girl's body had been found in the desert outside Las Vegas, the MO too close to the first murder in San Diego to be ignored. In his rush to catch the first plane out of National, he'd forgotten to call the aide, which had resulted in a blistering message on his voice mail, complete with sexual suggestions that were as physically impossible as they were graphic.

Since then his relationships had been kept to brief, no-strings affairs with women he knew well enough not to risk playing sexual Russian roulette. Sometimes they'd go out to dinner, have a few drinks, then return to her place for some hot steamy sex, after which, more often than not, he'd return to his own apartment before morning.

Other times they'd skip the preliminaries and go straight to the sex. Since the women were every bit as career driven and no more interested in a long-term relationship than he was, everyone stayed happy.

After his brother Jack's wedding a couple months ago, there were times when Finn had tried to imagine himself settling down with a wife and kids. He could see himself possibly getting married. Someday. Years from now, when he was retired, settled down, and wanted companionship for his old age.

"So, how about you?" he asked, partly because he wanted to move the focus away from him and partly because he was curious. "Is there some special guy in your life these days?"

She seemed to be living alone in her Venice house, but that didn't necessarily mean she wasn't involved with someone. He hadn't had time to do an in-depth investigation.

"Do you honestly believe that if I was in an intimate relationship, I would have kissed you like that?" She shot him a seething look. "You're the hotshot profiler. Do you think I'm the kind of woman who'd cheat on anyone I cared about?"

"I take it that's a *no.*"

Julia folded her arms. "One thing I love about you, Callahan, is how good you are at reading subtleties."

The bitch of it was, he'd always been good at picking up nuances. But it was difficult to think clearly when his body craved her and his mind was so full of her all there was room for was hunger. He'd spent the past nights twisted into a pretzel on that hard, too-short couch, unable to get his mind off the woman sleeping just on the other side of the bedroom door.

Did she sleep in the nude? Or in some slinky bit of Hollywood siren's satin? Right before dawn this morning, he'd imagined her in a brief bit of lace and silk designed to make a man's mouth water.

He'd envisioned skimming his hands over her slender curves, thought about how he'd nudge the thin straps down with his teeth. A mental picture of her sitting in the middle of that king-size bed, amid tousled sheets, the bit of froth clinging provocatively to the rosy tips of her breasts, had filled his mind.

Two hundred push-ups later, he'd still been edgy, itchy, and, although it wasn't her fault he couldn't keep his mind reined in, a little angry at her for his inability to do so.

He shook his head. "It would be a mistake."

She didn't need to ask what he meant. "Perhaps. But I've always believed that we regret most the things we don't do. Things we're left wondering about after the opportunity has passed."

Finn didn't have to wonder what being with her would be like. Even before he'd made the mistake of kissing her, he'd known that sex with this woman would be hot and explosive. And dangerous. A need this strong could make a man weak. Vulnerable.

"Point taken. But we're talking about more than just sex. Even if I didn't have a rule about mixing my personal life with my professional one —"

"This isn't exactly professional. Despite what you keep saying, I'm not an official FBI case you've been assigned to. You told me that you agreed to baby-sit me as a favor to your brother. That, to me, seems to move it into the personal arena."

He blew out a breath. "Do you have to argue every little point?"

"When something's important to me. I was brought up to question the status quo and never take things at face value. And in case you haven't dug up a copy of my yearbook, I also happened to be captain of my high school debating team."

"Now why doesn't that surprise me?" Finn's brain was finally beginning to clear. "Yeah, I want you. Any man in his right mind would. I haven't felt this way about a woman since I fell for Jaclyn Smith when she was one of the Angels."

Her eyes narrowed. "I have difficulty picturing you watching *Charlie's Angels.*"

What did she think? That he'd spent his adolescence glued to PBS? "Hey, I wanted to be a cop. So I watched a lot of crime shows." When she arched a challenging eyebrow, he grinned again. "Actually that one was a lot better with the sound off."

Her light laughter touched her eyes and made them sparkle appealingly. "There may be hope for you yet, Special Agent."

"That's debatable."

"You're a hard man, Callahan."

"I'm a realist."

"A pessimist," she shot back without heat.

She'd splayed her hands on her hips, drawing his attention to bare flesh as smooth and tasty-looking as cream. All-too-familiar smoke clouds began billowing again in his mind.

"Dammit, don't you own anything big and baggy and ugly?"

The humor in her gaze brightened to delight.

Finn saw the exact moment she remembered. The light in her eyes went out, like a candle snuffed out by an icy winter's wind.

"Well, at least I can't say you're not a distraction," she said on a soft, exhaled breath. "For a minute I'd almost forgotten what you're doing here."

She pressed her fingers against her eyes. "Okay, I admit it. Whoever he is, he's got me scared."

He hesitated, reason warring with the need to comfort. This time when he took her in his arms, it was to soothe rather than arouse.

15

Two hours later, while he watched Julia flutter around the ballroom dance floor in a scandalous scarlet gown, flirting outrageously with the men and scandalizing the women, Finn decided that while she may look as delicate as a magnolia blossom, the lady definitely had a steel core. Not a single person would ever guess that she'd received another threat this morning.

Except, of course, the person who'd slipped it into her trailer.

They'd pulled out all the stops today. The room, which Jack had restored to its original glory earlier in the year, was crowded with the cast and extras from as far away as Lafayette.

The women's hoopskirts swayed like colorful tulips as they danced in the arms of formally dressed men to the sounds of a string ensemble hired from New Orleans.

Finn was standing on the sidelines, watching her take advantage of a break in shooting to get her picture taken with one of the extras, an elderly woman dressed in mourning, when Nate came up to him.

"She looks good."

"She always looks good." Finn frowned at the scores of Blue Bayou parish residents who had come out to Beau Soleil to watch the goings-on, as they'd been doing every day. Even knowing that having a movie company come to town was on a par with waking up one morning and finding Disney World had moved its magic kingdom to your front yard, he wasn't comfortable with the crowds.

Unfortunately, his arguments to Kendall and Hogan to close the set had been rejected. Making matters worse, a crew from *Entertainment Tonight* was scheduled to arrive this week. Apparently showing stars mingling with local folks made for good TV.

"You thinking of calling in reinforcements, now that she's gotten that second photograph?"

"I don't know."

"With so many people on the cast knowing about that first photograph, it's going to be hard to keep it under wraps." Nate said what Finn had already been telling himself.

"It's just Kendall, Hogan and the primary cast. At least it's supposed to be. To everyone else, we're sticking to the friends story."

"Looks like you're getting to be pretty close friends." Nate's quick grin belied the seriousness of the topic. "I watched the two of you earlier, between takes. You probably had a dozen people between you, but you could have been the only two people in the room."

"I'm just doing my job."

"Come on, Finn. You're talking to your brother here. A man who's pretty damn good at picking up women's signals. And she's broadcasting at 100,000 watts." His gaze skimmed over Finn's face, taking in the bags beneath his eyes, his unshaved jaw. "She's not the only one."

"Sleeping with her would mean putting aside my personal code of ethics."

"I've always admired you, big brother. But I hadn't realized you'd become a monk since leaving home."

"I'm supposed to protect her. Not take advantage of her vulnerability."

"I can understand that." Nate nodded. "And it's a good excuse. But why do I get the feeling that it's not just Julia you're trying to protect?"

The woman had not only disturbed his life, she'd unsettled his entire universe. For as long as Finn could remember, he'd been the rock. The big brother Jack and Nate could turn to when they'd had problems, or fucked up, which Jack had done a lot more often than Nate. Though Finn had always suspected that his youngest brother had had his own way of dealing with their father's death.

He'd become the responsible one; Jack had turned rebel. Nate, who was the most gregarious of the three, seemed to decide that it was his duty to ease those horrendous days with unrelenting smiles, easy humor and charm.

Nate had been the only one of the Callahan boys who could make their mother smile through her tears. And less than a decade later, when she'd been dying of breast cancer, it had been Nate who, despite her protests, immediately dropped out of college and moved back home to be with her. Marie Callahan had died with her eldest and youngest sons at her side, smiling at some foolish joke Nate had made.

Finn figured he'd always owe Nate for that one. He also knew that, like all of them, Nate had inherited Big Jake's Irish tenacity and could, in his own cheerful way, be as unrelenting as water carving away at a stone.

"My life's fucked up enough right now," he said. "I've got the Wicked Witch of the West back in D.C. to contend with, and even if Jansen wasn't in the picture, my career takes up all my time and energy. Besides, there's no future in getting involved."

"Who's saying anything about a future? Ever think about just loosening up and enjoying the moment, *cher?*"

Nate was smiling but Finn thought he heard a hint of friendly censure in the mild tone.

"No." As if sensing his gaze on her, Julia looked up from a discussion of the script with the writer and director. When her lips curved in a luscious Bond Girl smile, Finn nearly forgot he knew how to breathe.

Oh, God. He was so getting to her, Julia thought. Having become attuned to Finn in the few days that they'd been forced together, it had seemed perfectly natural to feel his gaze from across the room. He stirred her senses, warming her blood as if he was touching her with those big wide hands, instead of his eyes.

Did he know what he did to her? How he made her feel? Most men had a strong sense of their seductive powers. The majority, at least in Los Angeles, seemed to possess an inflated opinion of their ability to charm a woman into their beds.

But Finn was a different breed entirely. Julia was beginning to come to the conclusion that he didn't have any idea how he could turn her to mush with one of those hot, hungry looks. Beneath the uptight suit and tightly controlled, Joe Friday attitude, she sensed untapped passions. He was not an easy man to know. He'd be a difficult man to love.

Love? She shook her head. What a ninny she was. She'd obviously been working on a soap opera too long; if she didn't watch out, she'd become as susceptible to suggestion as Warren.

Dragging her gaze from Finn's, Julia was trying to focus on what the writer was saying — something about adding lines to one of the nonspeaking extra's parts — when she heard a sudden buzz move through the group of Civil War–costumed extras, sounding like a swarm of hungry bees.

Eyes turned toward her. A few at a time, then more, until she felt as if she were in the cross-hair of some hunter's rifle.

When she saw the tabloid paper being passed around, a cold chill skidded up her spine.

"I think it's a lovely idea," she assured

Warren. "And yes, it'd be great PR. Small town beauty queen 'discovered' in the steamy Louisiana bayou." The locals were now studying her with the fascination an entomologist might observe a new and rare type of beetle. "Would you do me a favor?"

"Sure," he said, looking a bit puzzled by her sudden shift in topic.

"Would you go get that paper that seems to be causing such a stir among the extras?"

"Sure," he repeated. She watched him exchange a few words with a middle-aged woman who was currently reading the tabloid. When his eyebrows sketched up like blond wings and he shot her a surprised — no, make that shocked — look, Julia prepared herself for whatever pack of lies the paper had printed this time. Even braced as she was, she was stunned by the tabloid Warren reluctantly handed to her.

There, on the front page, was the photograph of Finn unfastening her corset.

River Road's Vixen in Ghostly Bayou Tryst With Rebel Lover From a Past Life! the headline screamed.

"Oh, God." She turned the page, skimming down the text. "This is preposterous."

There was another photograph of her taken in the plantation's cemetery, with the mist swirling around her legs, Shane's hand — just his hand, no other identifying features — on her breast. The implication, of course, being that the same man who was unlacing her corset on page one was caressing her in a graveyard in the photo on page two.

"Finn's supposed to be the ghost of a Confederate soldier who's been waiting for me to return to Beau Soleil for more than two hundred years?"

"It's quite creative," Warren allowed. "I wish I'd thought of it."

"Oh, God," Julia repeated. Surely people wouldn't take such an outrageous story seriously?

Well, she'd wanted to tap Finn's deep-seated passions. As she cautiously lifted her gaze and found him continuing to watch her in that steady, unblinking way of his, Julia feared he'd probably hit the roof. Anyone would resent such lies, especially someone who'd neither asked nor wanted to be thrust into the public spotlight.

As he'd been doing from the beginning, he surprised her.

"Well," he drawled as he scanned the pages she'd reluctantly shown him, "at least they're not saying I'm Big Foot."

Her relief at having dodged that bullet was short-lived. Five minutes later, during another break in shooting while Finn tried to track down the tabloid's source, Julia was sitting on a stool in the plantation house's kitchen, having her makeup touched up, when Randy came into the room and held out his cell phone.

"It's your mother."

"My mother? What's she doing calling on your phone?"

"She tracked me down. Apparently there's an emergency."

Julia's blood chilled. "Hello, Mom?"

"Julia, darling, I'm so relieved to have found you."

"What's wrong? Is it Dad?"

"Oh, no, dear. I'm sorry, I didn't mean to frighten you. No, it's just that your father and I were passing the market on the way to this wonderful little crystal store that has the most spectacular selection of rose quartz I've seen in a very long time, when I felt this strong urge to go inside."

"You've seen the paper," Julia guessed.

"Yes. They're actually quite flattering photographs, for a tabloid. Of course you've always had a lovely back. . . . Is it true? About the ghost?"

"Of course not!" She'd no sooner scoffed than Julia remembered her mother believed in ghosts. Along with fairies and Druids and all sorts of spirits that went bump in the night.

"Oh." Peace sounded vaguely disappointed. "What about the man?"

"Believe me, Mom, I'm not having a location affair."

"That's not what I asked. I was merely inquiring about him."

"The photo's from a scene we shot in the

plantation cemetery. It's Shane's hand. He's playing a Yankee captain."

"A Yankee as in a Civil War Yankee?"

"That's it. Warren added a time travel thread to the story line."

"What a wonderful idea!" Pleasure shimmered in Peace's warm voice. "How does this OBE occur?"

Julia had never believed in out-of-body experiences. Until this morning, when Finn had kissed her and she'd felt herself capable of floating right up into the sky. "Amanda gets shot and goes into a coma."

"Comas are a common way for people to use astral projection to work out karmic structures in their physical lifetime," her mother said matter-of-factly. "I'm pleased Warren did his homework. Who's the other man?"

"What other man?"

"The one unlacing your corset."

Julia's breath caught. Her mind whirled as she struggled to decide how much, exactly, she could admit to this woman who'd always been able to know when she was lying.

"He's just a man."

"That's not what I sensed. There's something very intimate about the photograph, darling."

"Of course it's intimate. I was in my underwear. Finn was just helping me with my costume."

"Finn. He's Irish?"

"Half Irish. The other half is Cajun."

"My goodness." Peace exhaled a breath. "That's quite a passionate combination."

"If you met him, you certainly wouldn't think so," Julia hedged, desperately hoping her mother couldn't read her mind as the memory of that kiss flooded into it.

"I don't want to argue, dear, but I believe you're wrong. Why, the paper nearly singed my fingertips . . . Just a minute. Your father's speaking to me."

Julia strained to hear the conversation, but all she could catch was Peace's usual smooth tone being overridden by her father's louder, stronger one.

"Julia, this is your father," a deep bass boomed out.

"Hi, Daddy. How's the harmony tour going?"

"It's probably our most successful yet. The mood's been contagious; I even caught one of the sheriff's deputies who'd been assigned to the festival singing along to 'White Rabbit.'"

"I wouldn't have expected a cop would be a Jefferson Airplane fan."

"That's exactly what I thought at the time. But don't change the subject. I want to know about this man who's laying hands on my daughter in front of the entire world."

"It wasn't the entire world. We were all alone in my trailer and —"

"That's even worse. Your mother says it's serious."

"No offense, but I think Mom's crystal ball

must have gotten cloudy. Finn's just a friend, Daddy."

"Finn? He's Irish?"

"Half," Julia repeated what she'd told her mother.

"Your great-grandfather was Irish."

"I know, Daddy."

She vaguely remembered her parents taking her to Galway to meet her father's maternal grandfather when she was five. He'd had lush white hair, a smile that could charm the fairies, and a sweet tenor voice that sounded like music on the Irish breeze. During their month-long visit he was never without peppermints in his scratchy wool shirt pocket, just for her.

"Emotional people, the Irish." This from a man who lived on the edge of his own bold emotions. A man whose paternal grandfather was a Russian cossack.

"He's a friend," she said again. "I think you'd like him." And pigs would sprout gossamer wings and start soaring over the bayou.

"That remains to be seen."

"What?" Every atom in Julia's body went on red alert.

"We're coming to Louisiana."

"Why on earth would you want to do that?"

"To meet your friend, of course. And make sure he's good enough for my little girl. I've got to run, sweetheart, this damn cell phone signal's breaking up." It sounded perfectly clear to her. "See you in a few days."

He ended the call, leaving Julia listening to dead air.

"What on earth was that all about?" Wondering what they put in the water up in Coldwater Cove, Washington, Julia had the strongest feeling that her father was actually coming here to grill Finn.

It couldn't be. Could it?

Just last week, she'd been wishing that her parents had been a bit more like the Cleavers or Jim Anderson, that unrelentingly calm, utterly sane sitcom father who always knew best.

Of course in those old sitcoms, even the adults didn't appear to have sex lives. As for their children . . . She could just imagine how Jim Anderson would have responded to his Princess rolling around with some boy in the back seat of a '55 Chevy. Or on a couch in a trailer.

Be careful what you wish for.

Right on the heels of that idea came another more unsettling one. How Freedom, the former political radical who'd been arrested innumerable times for protesting the system Finn Callahan had sworn to uphold, would respond to his daughter's relationship with an FBI Special Agent.

"What happened?" Her makeup man, Damien, brushed color into her right cheek with deft strokes of his sable brush. "This morning you were absolutely glowing. Now you look as if you're coming down with some nasty tropical bayou fever."

Julia scowled into the lighted mirror. "Well, that's certainly flattering."

"If you want flattery, call the president of your fan club. My job is to make you beautiful. Which usually isn't such a chore."

"It's been a long day."

"True." He performed the same magic on her left cheek. "But you've had long days before. You worked twenty hours last year when that idiot editor's assistant managed to erase half the week's work. But even then you didn't look so washed out." He squeezed a little concealer from a tube and began dabbing it beneath her eyes. "My guess is that it's got something to do with Mr. Tall, Dark and Grim."

"He's not grim." It was the third time in the past two hours she'd felt the need to defend Finn. "Just serious."

"Seriously grim. Close your eyes."

Julia did as instructed. He set the concealer cream with powder, then skimmed a little mascara onto the ends of her lashes. "Don't furrow your brow that way, darling. It'll give you premature wrinkles. You've been licking your lips again," he scolded as he touched up the color.

"My mouth keeps getting dry." Every time she looked at Finn, who was currently waiting outside.

"So does mine. Big macho brutes do that to me." He stood back and studied her. "Apparently they affect you the same way. At least this one does."

"He's just a friend."

"Really, Julia." He huffed out a breath. "How long have we been together?"

"Nearly five years."

"Which is probably longer than most Hollywood marriages. And haven't I agreed to go traipsing off to Kathmandu with you?"

"It's not exactly a sacrifice. You're being very well paid."

"Money isn't anything. There's no way I'd spend three months of my life in a country where such a large percentage of the eligible males are Buddist monks, if I didn't adore you to pieces. Is your boyfriend coming with us?"

"He's not my . . ." She sighed as his knowing gaze met hers in the mirror. "I don't know what Finn is, exactly." That was definitely the truth.

"He's gorgeous, is what he is. In a supersize, rough-hewn cop sort of way. He reminds me of what you might get if you took Tommy Lee Jones's DNA and stirred in some Hulk Hogan. Don't worry, you'll be able to decipher your feelings a lot better after you sleep with him."

"What makes you think I haven't?"

"Because the pheromones in the air are nearly lethal. You're exuding so much sex on the set, it's a wonder the fire marshal hasn't shut us down for endangering a historical site." He fanned himself with the sable powder brush. "And your incredible hulk is a walking testosterone bomb waiting to explode."

"He's not my hulk. Besides, it would be a mistake," she repeated Finn's analysis of their situation.

"That failed playwright you were seeing when you first came to *River Road* was a mistake. Along with the last three artists and that pudgy, out-of-shape Welsh folk singer who sang naked."

"Ian sang about stripping away the trappings of our lives. About getting back to our natural selves."

"If *my* natural self looked like Humpty Dumpty, I sure as hell wouldn't go stripping off my clothes in public. I'd also like to see him try to pull that act off back home on those Welsh moors. Believe me, once Mr. Stiffy got frostbite, the guy would change his act faster than I can say Ricky Martin."

"Mr. Stiffy?" She lifted a brow at him in the mirror. "You've been talking to Shane, haven't you?"

"We haven't exchanged two words since I told him he ought to lighten up on the Botox because he's starting to look like a Ken doll. Personally, I think he's homophobic, but it could be he's just narcissistic."

She suspected Damien might just be right. She also wondered if all men named their penis. Then she thought of Finn. *Not in this lifetime.*

"And to get back to my point about your

having lousy taste in men," Damien said, pursing his own lips as he dipped into a pot and brushed some gloss onto her mouth, "let's not forget the deadbeat married poet —"

"Let's also not forget that I did not know he had a wife," she interjected firmly.

"I seem to recall three wives, actually. There was the art dealer in Paris, the editor in Stockholm, along with the heir to that silver fortune in Guadalajara. And it was obvious he had you pegged for number four, so you could help continue to support him in the style to which he'd become accustomed. And I don't even want to think about the time you wasted with that English professor."

"He reminded me of Cary Grant playing Henry Higgins." She'd always been a sucker for *My Fair Lady.* "Or Connery's James Bond."

"The man was definitely no 007. What he was, dear heart, was a mistake. Just like the others. On the other hand, the guy who fills out that size forty-eight long suit so deliciously is more along the lines of riding a boat over the edge of Niagara Falls."

"That sounds like a huge mistake." A dangerous mistake, she reminded herself.

"It could well be." He brushed a bit of iridescent powder over the crest of her breasts, which were plumped up to spill over the deeply cut neckline of her ball gown by a heavily padded bra that made her feel as if she was wearing the Golden Gate Bridge on her chest. "But think of the rush on the way down."

"Think of crashing on the rocks and breaking to smithereens."

Now that she'd had more time to think about it, Julia had decided Finn was right about not taking things further. After all, using Damien's boat analogy, they were two ships passing in the night. The *Titanic* and the *Lusitania*. "My life's too complicated right now. I don't need a man making it worse."

"Everyone needs a man, sweetcheeks. They're the cherry on top of the hot fudge sundae, the whipped cream atop the crème brûlée —"

"Crème brûlée doesn't have whipped cream."

"You make it your way, I'll make it mine." He began to put away his pots and jars. "Besides, if you're telling the truth about not wanting to get involved with the big guy, it looks as if you may be off the hook."

Julia followed his gaze out the window, to where Felissa was looking up at Finn as if she was a sleek Siamese cat and he was a giant bowl of cream.

It took her a minute to recognize the emotion that shot through her. And when she did, it was staggering. She, who could not recall ever feeling jealousy toward anyone for anything, suddenly felt like scratching the actress's hyacinth blue contacts out.

And that was just for starters.

16

"What took so damn long?" Finn demanded when Julia came out of the trailer.

"Should I be flattered I was missed?" He recognized her smile. It was the same one Amanda pulled out whenever she was about to screw someone. Literally or figuratively.

He folded his arms. "I'm being paid to guard your body. Which is a little difficult to do when you won't light anywhere."

"I wasn't in there that long."

"It seemed like a lifetime." He glanced across the room and groaned as Felissa met his eyes and licked her lips.

Julia laughed. "What's the matter, Callahan? Can't you handle a little flirtation?"

"That's more than flirting. The woman's like that rabbit in the commercials. She just keeps on coming."

"Perhaps you can take out your gun and shoot her. I'll bet that'd do the job."

"Bullets would just bounce right off. She's got a steel exterior."

"I can't believe she's that much of a problem." She shrugged. "After all, as a cop, you're undoubtedly used to throwing your weight around from time to time. And you're a lot bigger than she is."

"So she pointed out."

He still couldn't believe she'd shared that sordid little story about having made a porno flick back when she'd been a struggling actress. The director, apparently, had assured her she was a natural at giving blow jobs. If that hadn't been bad enough, she'd actually come right out and assured him that if Julia couldn't handle his "obvious endowment," she'd love to help him out.

Julia tilted her head at the muttered comment he'd meant to keep to himself. Then gave him a slow, speculative gaze that followed the same path that earlier female appraisal had taken. The difference was that the blond barracuda's hadn't stirred any feelings. That was definitely not the case this time.

"So?"

"So what?"

"Are you? Larger than the average bear, so to speak?"

"That's for me to know." He tossed her own words back at her. "And you to find out."

"Don't look now, Special Agent, but you just made another joke." Her eyes laughed up at him. "If you're not careful, people may just figure out there's a human being beneath that suit. And speaking of suits . . ."

She laced his fingers with hers in a casual, uncalculated gesture. "I have this teensy little problem I need you to help me out with."

Her hands were slender and soft as she led

him up the metal steps into the trailer. He'd watched them pouring tea for the Yankee captain and been struck by their natural grace. He'd also wanted them on his body.

A mistake, he warned himself yet again. As he breathed in her seductive scent hanging in the air, he forced himself to remember that.

"Let me get this straight," he said, five minutes later. You want to take me shopping."

"That's right." She smiled encouragingly.

"For new clothes." He didn't bother blocking off the scowl.

"Not an entire new wardrobe. Just something a bit less imposing."

"I would have thought imposing would be a good look for a bodyguard."

"It's a great look for a bodyguard," she agreed quickly. Too quickly. Her smile was bright and decidedly forced. "I know I'd certainly think twice — more than twice — before trying to get by you."

"So what's the problem?"

"While it's a great look for a bodyguard, it's not exactly the right look for my lover."

"I'm not your lover."

"Well, I know that, and you know that. But, well . . ." She began twisting her fingers together.

"Well?"

"My parents don't know that. They think we're —"

She paused, seeking the right word — "involved."

Ah. "The tabloid," Finn guessed.

"Yes." She let out a long breath. "They called me earlier. From Washington. The state, not the capital."

"I see." Actually, Finn didn't see anything at all, but wanted to get to the bottom of whatever had rattled her.

"They wanted to know who it was undressing me on the front page of the *Enquirer*."

"I wouldn't think that would matter to them."

"Not matter?" Color that had nothing to do with the makeup guy's work flooded into her cheeks. "They're my parents. Wouldn't you be interested in some man who was unfastening your daughter's corset?"

"It's a moot point since I don't have a daughter."

Her frustrated sigh ruffled a lock of hair that had fallen over her eyes and she shoved it back with an impatient hand. "Don't play word games with me, Callahan. You might be bigger than I am. And armed, but I just happen to have been seventh-grade regional Scrabble champion."

"I'm impressed."

"You should be. Though Woodstock, the former champion, wasn't," she admitted.

"His name was Woodstock?"

"It seemed normal at the time. His mother,

Enlightenment, was friends with my parents. We grew up together."

"It figures. So how come you don't have a goofy name?"

She lifted a brow. "Excuse me?"

"I wouldn't think two people named Peace and Freedom, who had a friend named Enlightenment, would have settled for an ordinary name for their daughter who is anything but ordinary."

Julia smiled a little, deciding to take that a good way. "Thank you."

"You're welcome."

"And while I hate to burst your little stereotyping-profiling bubble, I happen to have been named for my grandmother," she informed him loftily. "Who also wasn't the least bit ordinary. She was a jazz singer. My father practically grew up on the band's tour bus."

"Why does that not surprise me? What was her name?"

"Julia Rose Summers."

"You're kidding." He looked suitably impressed. "I've got all her songs on CD and a handful of vinyls I can't play because I don't have a turntable, but I still like taking them out of the jackets and looking at them. Holding them. They're a lot more substantial feeling and the jackets are large enough to show off the art."

"That's what Daddy always says," she murmured, a bit surprised that this man would have anything in common with Freedom.

"God, your grandmother was The Monterey Rose. Wow." He skimmed his palm over his hair. "Her cover of 'They Can't Take That Away from Me' is even better than Lady Day's, which was pretty damn great itself."

"I'll tell her you said so. She toured with Billie Holiday for a while in Europe."

"I know. I paid a small fortune for some bootleg studio cuts from when the two of them were just fooling around, doing riffs together. So, she's still alive?"

"She owns a club in Carmel."

"I'll have to try to get there one of these days. Does she still sing?"

"On special occasions."

"Hey, any time The Rose sings is a special occasion."

It was the most enthusiasm she'd witnessed from him thus far. It also made him seem far more human. In fact, he reminded her of her paternal grandfather, Rose's second husband, a steady, solid, easy-going man who didn't say much and had spent much of their marriage driving the tour bus back and forth across the country. The Rose's first husband had been a sax player who'd abandoned her as soon as she told him that they'd made more than just music together. Seven months later, Julia's father had been born.

"So tell me about Woodstock," Finn said, returning the conversation to its original track.

"Why? He's not my stalker."

"Maybe not, but I'm curious."

"Why?"

He shrugged. "Why don't you just humor me?"

"And here I thought I'd been doing that all along," she said dryly. "He was just a boy I had a huge crush on. The only reason I entered the competition was because he was in it. He'd been sixth grade champion the year before and I figured if we practiced together he'd finally notice me."

She sighed. "It was not one of the highlights of my life. It was also where I learned boys don't like girls to beat them."

"Maybe boys feel that way, but I'm perfectly willing to admit you can probably beat me at Scrabble. But I'd leave you in the dust at Clue."

"I should hope so, since you're a detective. I doubt if it would have made a difference even if I had let him win by pretending I didn't see that triple word score. Because the only thing he was interested in at the time were breasts. And I didn't have any."

Enjoying her tale, Finn tried to remember the last time he'd been amused by anything. Three years ago, he decided. Before Ronald Lawson had decided to take up a new hobby.

"He's probably eating his heart out now."

She laughed softly at that. "Actually, he moved to L.A. and became a plastic surgeon. He's very popular; a lot of the breasts you see in the movies are his."

"But not yours."

"No." She looked down at the front of her nineteenth-century gown. "If they'd only had Wonderbras when I was growing up, my entire life could have been different. Woodstock might have fallen madly in love with me, we might have gotten married, had children —"

"And set up housekeeping on Sunnybrook Farm."

"You don't have to make fun of me. Just because you don't want marriage and a family."

How the hell did they get from shopping to Scrabble to talking about marriage again? "So what was this favor you wanted from me?"

"It's just a small one. Teensy, actually. My parents, like any loving, caring parents, are understandably interested in knowing more about the man they think I'm in love with."

"Love?" Finn blinked.

"Yes." Her chin popped up in that way he recognized all too well. "And you don't have to behave as if I'd just exposed you to plague. I didn't say I *was* in love with you. I merely said they *believe* I'm in love with you."

"Because of some tabloid piece of crap?"

"No. That would be ridiculous."

To Finn's mind, the fact he was even having this discussion was ridiculous.

"I suppose the picture didn't help," she allowed. "But it's mostly my mother's vibes."

"Vibes."

"Yes. My mother's an intuitive." Her look dared him to challenge that remark.

"Okay."

"You're laughing."

"Do I look like I'm laughing?"

"No. But since nobody can possibly be as serious as you appear to be, I've decided that you must keep your laughter on the inside."

"How did you guess?" His tone was dry as dust. "It's dancing a happy jig right now with my inner child."

She crossed her arms beneath those breasts he thought were just about perfect. More than a handful was overkill, anyway. "I find it difficult to believe you even have an inner child. I have the feeling you were born thirty. And grim."

Well, that was certainly flattering. Finn was on the verge of being pissed, when he remembered that they'd be a lot better off if she didn't like him. That would prevent a repeat of that kiss he never should have allowed to happen.

"Nailed that one," he said mildly. "And for the record, I wasn't laughing about your mother. In fact, I've used psychics before in my investigations."

"You? Mr. Just-the-facts-ma'am Callahan?"

"I'll try whatever it takes to bring the bad guys to justice." So it sounded corny. It was the truth. "Some of the psychics have been obvious frauds, with others it's a toss-up whether they were right or just lucky. Then there's that third group who can't quite be defined, but seem to have something going for them. I'm willing to accept that your mother might fit into that third category. So, what did you tell them about me?"

"I told them the truth. That we're not in a romantic relationship."

"Then what's the problem? And what does all this have to do with your wanting to go shopping?"

"They didn't believe me."

Finn could see this one coming, like a bullet headed straight toward him in slow motion.

"So they're coming here," she said when he didn't respond.

"Here?" Everything inside him stilled. "To Blue Bayou?"

"Here," she confirmed. "To Blue Bayou. To meet you."

Jesus H. Christ. Finn knew his feelings about this little bombshell must have shown on his face when her tawny brows drew together.

"I realize that socializing with hippies is not exactly something you'd normally do —"

"Try never." He'd never bought into the concept of reincarnation, but if those mantra chanters really were on to something about making redemption for past sins, he must have been a real prick in his previous life.

She exhaled a long, frustrated breath that once again drew his eyes to her breasts. "Believe me, Callahan, when my father finds out you're an FBI agent, he's going to hit the roof. Which is why we're going to have to give you a makeover."

"A makeover?" Her words jerked him out of a fantasy of spreading whipped cream over that creamy flesh revealed by the low neckline and taking a very long time to lick it off. Finn folded his arms. "Guys don't get makeovers."

"Of course they do. I've seen it on *Oprah*."

He rolled his eyes. "The woman could do an entire week around transvestites, but I still wouldn't put on pantyhose and a dress."

"You really do have a rotten attitude." When she tossed her head, the sun streaming through the blinds of the trailer turned her hair to flame. "Look, why don't we just call this entire bodyguard thing off? It's not like those photographs were specific. I'll admit they had me a little unnerved, but when I think about it more clearly, I realize I'm undoubtedly just over-reacting.

"So, why don't you just get back in that Suburban and go back to Washington? When my parents arrive, I'll tell them we broke up. Which they'd undoubtedly believe since I'm sure the idea of my getting involved with a cop, let alone an FBI agent, has never entered their realm of possibility."

Here's your out. Finn felt like a guy teetering on the edge of a pit of quicksand. One false move and he'd be stuck.

"My going back to D.C.'s not an option." He

209

wasn't about to reveal why he couldn't return to work. Yet. *Damn.* "Look, I have clothes out at the camp I own with my brother. Why can't I just wear those?"

"Are they casual?"

"Even I don't fish in a suit."

"I have trouble picturing you fishing."

That made two of them. "I've got T-shirts. And jeans."

"Let me guess. The T-shirts have FBI lettering on them and the jeans are creased to a knife edge."

He couldn't believe he'd been forced into a situation where he had to defend his wardrobe. "I happen to work for the FBI —"

"A fact I'm attempting not to wave in my parents' faces. Besides, has it ever occurred to you that working for the FBI is what you do? Not who you are?"

"No. It hasn't." He'd always defined himself by his work; Finn wasn't certain he could separate the man from the agent, which was a moot point since he didn't want to try. "As for the jeans, that's the way they come back from the cleaners."

She sighed dramatically. "Come on, Callahan. Be a sport. Don't tell me a big, strapping man like yourself is afraid of a little shopping trip. Or would you rather I just go into the city alone and pick up some things?"

Short of tying her up, he doubted he could keep her from doing exactly that. Not wanting to let her out of his sight, and afraid of what kind of clothes she might choose just for spite, with eyes wide open, he took that fatal step. "Let's just get it the hell over with."

As if never expecting any other outcome, she smiled. Not an Amanda hit-you-in-the-groin smile, but a quick, pleased Julia one that aimed directly at the heart. As it hit the bull's-eye, Finn imagined the huge sucking sound he heard was the quicksand closing in around him.

17

Since there was no way he was going to let her drag him around like a trained pup in his own hometown, after the shooting wrapped up for the day, and she'd changed into a short denim skirt and a striped knit top that left one shoulder bare in a way that made him want to bite it, Finn drove them to the city.

"I adore New Orleans," she said as the lights of the skyline grew closer. "The food, the music, the atmosphere —"

"We're not here to play tourist," he warned as they crossed the Mississippi.

"Spoilsport."

"I believe we've already determined that. And for the record, it's one of the things I do best. So, here's the plan. We're going to go into the store, snag what we need, and get the hell out and back to Blue Bayou."

"Whatever you say." Lord, he could be bossy. Along with a whole new sartorial look, they were going to have to work on his attitude. Because right now the coiled, controlled male energy radiating from him just screamed FBI. "Of course, your ordeal will be over far more quickly if you promise not to argue about every little thing I pick out."

Seconds passed. He was looking straight

ahead and for a moment she thought he hadn't heard her over the Van Halen screeching from the speakers.

"You're not going to try to put me in a Grateful Dead T-shirt are you?"

"Of course not. Unless you're prepared to discuss the significance of their concert posters on the seventies pop art scene."

His sideways stare set her straight on that.

"I didn't think so," she said. She'd never met a more unlikely Deadhead. Though the pounding seventies metal rock hinted at possibilities. She would have pegged him more as a Sinatra guy.

"There is no way I'm going to let you dress me up like some throwback from Haight-Ashbury. I'm willing to make some concessions to the situation, but the clothes have to be conservative."

"Absolutely."

"And regular guy sneaks. None of those sissy Birkenstocks."

"I wouldn't think of it."

"Okay." He nodded, apparently satisfied.

"And I'd suggest you not mention to my father you think Birkenstocks are for sissies. You may consider him a throwback to the sixties, but even those critics who don't like his art have always raved about the primal male power of his work."

"Believe me, if there's one thing I have no intention of discussing with your father, it's primal male instincts."

"Good." It was her turn to nod.

With his attention turned back to his driving, Finn missed seeing Julia's lips curve in a faint smile of anticipation.

His internal radar went off the scale as they entered the trendy boutique in the lobby of the five star hotel she'd had him drive to on Canal Street. When she plucked a shirt from a rack, Finn decided the time had come to stand his ground.

"No way."

"You said you wanted something conservative."

"The frigging shirt is pink!" he hissed. How conservative was that?

"Actually, it's Tropical Rose," the saleswoman, a sleek blond forty-something said. "A preppy favorite."

"It's lovely," Julia said. The smile she bestowed upon the woman suggested *What can you expect from an uncivilized barbarian?* "But not quite what we're looking for."

She held a polo shirt up against Finn's chest. "Oh, I like this one."

"Good choice." The woman nodded. "Bastille Purple. It's one of our more popular colors this season." Finn had the feeling it was the same thing she'd say whatever a prospective customer selected.

"I can see why," Julia said. "It's very attractive. A bit like crushed merlot grapes. And the name is so evocative, don't you think?" she asked Finn.

"Oh yeah, Bastille has a real nice ring to it. If you like thinking about filthy mobs and public beheadings."

"Don't be sarcastic. Come over to a mirror and see how well the deep color contrasts with your eyes. Perhaps if you were to just try it on . . ."

The speculative look in Julia's gaze was almost as terrifying as the idea of showing up in Blue Bayou in a preppy pink or purple polo shirt. Finn grabbed her elbow and dragged her behind a nearby display of mannequins that looked as if they were posing for a *GQ* cover. "There is no way in hell I'm wearing anything on that rack."

"I thought we had an agreement."

"Our agreement was for you to pick out something conservative."

"I doubt if there's a more conservative store in all of New Orleans. Why, I have it on good authority that Republicans love these shirts, Finn."

"I find it hard to believe you even know a Republican."

"I know you."

"Apparently you didn't inherit your mother's intuitive talents. I'm an Independent." He folded his arms across the white dress shirt that had always suited him just fine.

"What a surprise." Her sweet smile couldn't

quite conceal her own sarcasm. She exhaled a resigned breath. "All right. They may not exactly be you."

He'd learned not to trust her easy acquiescence.

She began rifling through a rack right next to them and pulled out a pair of tweed pants with suede inserts on the inside of the thighs. "How about these?"

"I categorically refuse to wear the same pants Elizabeth Taylor wore in *National Velvet*." Those were even worse than the prissy pink shirt.

"It's the Equestrian look. I saw a report about it on *Fashion Emergency*. It's predicted to be a very popular trend this fall."

He folded his arms. "Do I look like a trendy sort of guy to you?"

"No," she admitted. "You look like a cop."

"I am a cop. And I'm willing to play along, within limits, but from here on in, I'm picking out my own clothes."

"Nothing that requires a tie. And those wing tips have to go."

Did every damn thing have to be up for negotiation? "I can live with that. But I don't do tassels." He'd seen her eyeing the tasseled cordovan loafers when they'd first come in the store.

"No tassels," she agreed.

That settled, Finn went hunting at a midprice department store down the street.

"Don't you want to try them on?" Julia asked as he grabbed a pair of jeans from the first rack they came upon.

"No need." He scooped up a pair of black T-shirts, then headed over to the shoe department. Although Julia hadn't put a stopwatch on him, she guessed he'd managed to gather up a new wardrobe, including crew sox, in under five minutes.

"They'll fit."

"Why don't you humor me?"

"What the hell do you think I've been doing since you got this cockamamie idea?"

"Please? You're not exactly average size. What if we get back to Blue Bayou and discover they need alterations?"

He cursed without heat. "I don't want to leave you alone."

"I could come in the dressing room with you."

"Yeah, you and me together in an enclosed place with me taking off my clothes. That's about the worst idea you've had yet."

"Haven't you ever heard of restraint, Callahan?"

"Yeah. But it's not a word I'd use in regard to you. Let's go."

She was beginning to learn to recognize when she'd hit the stone wall of Finn Callahan's resistance.

"I'll pay for them," she said when he pulled out his credit card and put it on the sales counter.

"The hell you will."

"You're only buying them because I wanted you to wear something other than that suit." She picked up the AmEx card and put her own down in its place. "So, it's only fair I should pay."

"I've been buying my own clothes for some time." He snatched the green card from her hand, slapped it onto the counter again, and held her platinum one out to her. His expression could have been hacked from granite.

"Oh, do whatever you want." She snatched her card back with a huff. "Though it's ridiculous, since you won't even be wearing them that long."

The salesman's head jerked up like a puppet's, making Julia realize how he'd misinterpreted her statement.

She couldn't resist.

"It's not as if you haven't earned them, sugar," she drawled in the same voice Fancy had used to lure her sister's long-time fiancé into that one-night stand before he headed off to war in his newly woven Confederate gray uniform with the snazzy epaulets. "Why, you've already exceeded the money-back satisfaction guarantee Madame Beauregard promised me when I booked your services. It's just amazing what a girl can find in the Yellow Pages these days."

Her finger trailed up the back of his hand, slipping beneath that starched cuff that was still, after an excruciatingly long day, amazingly white and stiff. Nearly as stiff as he'd just gone. "And just think, the night's still young."

From the way Finn signed the charge slip, in a bold, rough scrawl as black as his expression, Julia suspected that she wasn't exactly going to receive a standing ovation for this performance.

"That was real cute," he ground out from between gritted teeth as they left the store.

"I'm sorry." Julia was already regretting her actions, but if only he hadn't been so damn autocratic! "It was just a spur-of-the-moment thing."

Silence.

"You have to admit that clerk's expression was priceless. Who would have guessed that anyone in a town where strippers dance in club windows, women flash their breasts to get Mardi Gras beads tossed to them from a float, and one of the most popular tourist spots is a voodoo museum, could be shocked by anything?"

Thunderheads of frustration darkened his face. "You let the guy think I was a damn . . . gigolo."

"I know. And that was terrible of me." Her smile encouraged him to see the bright side. "But at least he thinks you're a very good gigolo."

18

Undeterred by the anger radiating from him in waves, Julia put her arm through his as they walked toward the parked SUV. A green trolley headed toward the Garden District rumbled past, bell clanging. "It's getting late," she said with studied casualness. "What would you say to having dinner before we go back to Blue Bayou?"

Finn assured himself that the only reason he was willing to go along with this obvious stalling tactic was that he was hungry. Also, as good as the inn's fare was, he was getting sick and tired of room service every night. "I suppose you've already made reservations?"

"Of course not. And I'm disappointed you'd even think me capable of such subterfuge, when we both know you're the one in charge."

"Yeah, right." As he watched her curvy butt climb into the Suburban, Finn knew he was getting closer and closer to a line he'd sworn not to cross. A line which, once he was on the other side, he would never be able to go back across.

The damn thing about it, he thought as he twisted the key in the ignition, was that he was having a harder and harder time remembering why that would be such a bad thing.

"I do have a suggestion where we might eat," she said.

"Now there's a surprise," he said dryly.

As her perfume bloomed around them on the warm, sultry air, Finn ignored the little voice in his mind asking if he really thought he was in charge of anything in his life these days. He didn't want to know the answer.

He'd expected her to choose some fancy place with snowy tablecloths, formally dressed condescending waiters, tasseled menus written in French, and ridiculously inflated prices. Instead, they ended up at a crowded, noisy place above a strip joint. The lack of any outdoor sign suggested it catered to locals, and while he didn't do a head count, one glance told him that the place was undoubtedly violating fire department occupancy limits.

The tables crowded together were covered in white butcher paper, the spices in the best gumbo he'd tasted since his mother's were hot, the jazz cool. If he wasn't still so pissed off about the gigolo thing Finn would have been enjoying himself.

"Are you intending to speak to me anytime soon?" Julia asked as the waiter — an African-American who appeared to be at least in his nineties, who'd greeted her with open affection which suggested this was not her first time here — took away their bowls and delivered their entrees: shrimp rémoulade for her, a huge platter of étouffée for him.

"I'm not sure you want me to."

"Don't you ever give in to impulse?"

He put his fork down, leaned back in his chair, and looked straight at her mouth. "More often than I'd like lately."

Before she could question that, a female tourist dressed in shorts, a T-shirt in Mardi Gras colors of purple, green and gold that read LET THE GOOD TIMES ROLL and sporting a bright yellow perm that made it look as if she'd put a wet finger in a light socket, pushed her way through the crowd to their table.

"I knew it was you!" she crowed. "Why, the minute you came in, I told my husband, that's Amanda from *River Road*. Didn't I, Leon? Didn't I say it was Amanda?"

"Sure as heck did," the beanpole thin man agreed in a West Texas twang. "Howdy, Miz Amanda." If he'd been wearing a cowboy hat, he would have tipped it. "We don't want to be interrupting your supper —"

"Don't be silly, Leon," his wife waved away his apology with a plump hand laden down with turquoise and silver rings. "Why, everyone knows Amanda doesn't eat. I think she's suffering from anorexia," she confided to Finn. "She's been getting skinnier and skinnier ever since she started taking those energy booster pills Dr. Wilder got her hooked on.

"Dr. Wilder used to be married to Amanda's best friend Hope, whose career as a fashion designer was destroyed when Amanda seduced that professor at River Road College into inventing a formula that made that stuck-up Hope's fashions disintegrate during her big important runway show in Paris, which left her so embarrassed and depressed she drowned herself in the Seine, which opened the way for the doctor to marry Amanda. But then he got murdered, leaving Amanda the chief suspect, since they'd been playing doctor themselves for months."

She beamed at Julia. "That suit you wore for your testimony at the trial was just the prettiest thing, and you were so clever to wear pink because it made you look a lot more soft and vulnerable than you are.

"Why, by the time you finished telling your story, you had even the district attorney in tears. And I was bawling my head off. Wasn't I, Leon?"

"She was crying so hard she couldn't cook supper that night," the man confirmed. "We had to eat out at The Chat and Chew."

The woman shoved a cardboard disposable camera toward Finn. "Would you make our picture with Amanda? The girls back home at the bunco babes' club in Rattler's Roost will never believe I actually met her, otherwise."

Finn exchanged a quick glance with Julia, who seemed to repress a sigh, then smiled. Unlike the other ones he'd witnessed, this did not quite reach her remarkable eyes. She stood up beside the woman.

"Not here. Between us . . . Leon, move aside so Amanda can squeeze in." She bumped an ample hip against her husband, nearly pushing him into a waiter carrying a tray of Hurricanes. The waiter's deft steps, as he dodged just in time, saved them all from a rum and passion fruit shower.

"Okay, honey." She flung an arm around Julia's shoulder, as if they'd been best friends since childhood. A woman seated alone at a nearby table obligingly leaned out of the picture frame. "On the count of three, everyone say *fromage*."

Finn shot the picture, then another, "just in case," the woman instructed. She'd taken back the camera and was on her way toward the door — probably to take it to the nearest Fotomat, Finn figured, when she turned back toward the table.

"Are you anyone?" she demanded on afterthought.

"Non," Finn said, borrowing from his mother's bayou French. "I'm jus' Miz Amanda's Cajun gigolo, doin' my best to make sure she passes herself a good time in our Big Easy."

The woman's eyes widened. "Did you hear that, Leon?" she asked as they waded back through the crowd to the door. "Didn't I tell you that girl was nothing but poor white trash? What sort of woman would hire herself a

224

gigolo? And what kind of man would service women for money?"

If Leon had been given an opportunity to respond, his answer was droned out by the band.

Alone again, those damn pouty lips that had been tormenting him since before he'd been stupid enough to kiss her, curved in a brilliant smile. "Why Agent Callahan, I do believe you shocked her."

"I didn't plan to. It just came out."

"Did you see her face?" Julia laughed. "Maybe you should give into impulse more often."

He considered that. "I don't think so."

"How do you know if you don't try?" The legs of her chair scraped on the wooden floor covered in sawdust as she stood up and held out a hand. "Do you have any idea how long it's been since I've gone dancing?"

Those long legs were close enough he could bite her thigh. Since he was sorely tempted to do exactly that, Finn settled for the lesser of the two evils. Besides, the piano man was pounding away on a raucous Jerry Lee Lewis song that wasn't the least bit conducive to romance. Not that the impulses bombarding his body had anything to do with romance.

It was only sex. A man could live indefinitely without sex. Look at the Dalai Lama. And the pope, though he might not really count since how much temptation could there be when a guy spent all his time in a city pretty much devoid of women?

There had to be other males who managed it, though.

Somewhere in the world.

The dance floor made the rest of the place seem downright roomy. Naturally, instead of staying on the perimeter of the crowd, like any sensible person, she headed straight toward the very center, where bodies were packed together like a tangle of the night crawlers he and his dad used to hunt for bait with a flashlight.

She'd no sooner stopped and turned back toward him when "Great Balls of Fire" segued into a slow, plaintive soul sound.

Terrific. If he hadn't been sitting knee to knee with her since they'd arrived, Finn might have suspected she'd bribed the band just to torture him a little more.

Determined to prove that it didn't take a religious calling to control his dick, Finn yanked her against his chest.

She twined her bare arms around his neck and melted against him like she had during that mind-blowing kiss.

"Mmmm. Nice."

Impossibly, more couples crowded onto the dance floor. Hell, if they got any closer together, she'd be inside his suit. Her nipples felt like little berries against his chest and her stomach pressed against his erection. When desire twisted in his gut and caused a painful tightening in his groin, Finn gritted his teeth and fell back on the mental trick to control rampant teenage lust that Father Dupree had taught his varsity baseball team.

Her fingers absently stroked his neck as she hummed along to the bluesy ballad about love gone wrong. Trying to concentrate on the batting order of the 1975 World Champion Cincinnati Reds wasn't working a damn bit better than it had when he was sixteen.

"Favorite Bond line," he said, seeking something, anything to keep his mind off how perfect she felt against him.

"That's hard. There are so many . . . Perhaps when Dimitri Mishkin asks 007 how he wants to be executed, and he complains about there being no chitchat or small talk and says that's the trouble with the world. 'No one takes the time to do a really sinister interrogation anymore. It's a lost art.' I love his dry wit under pressure." She twined her arms more closely around his neck. "How about yours?"

Finn decided this had been a bad idea, as he envisioned the command center getting audio-visual with Bond and Holly Goodhead in the nose cone of the spaceshuttle in *Moonraker*. The final scene, where Q, when asked what Bond was doing, responded, "I think he's attempting reentry, sir."

"You're right, there's too many to choose."

She continued to sway, humming along with the music and driving him crazy.

"Finn?"

It was the first time she'd called him by his name, and the way it sounded, all soft and breathy, affected him more powerfully than raunchy sexual words cried out in the heat of passion ever had.

"What?"

"I really am sorry I embarrassed you back at that store."

"Forget it." He slid his hands down her back, allowing them to settle against the warm, bare skin at her waist. "It's no big deal. Besides, I got even."

"It's not the same thing. I'm used to people confusing me with Amanda and thinking the worst. But you were upset. You probably won't believe me, but I'm usually much more circumspect. Especially in public, among strangers.

"When I'm with friends, that's different. But even then I can't remember another time when I purposefully set out to make anyone uncomfortable. I mean, one of the things that drives me crazy about Shane's penchant for practical jokes is that they're at the deliberate expense of others, which is one of the few good things about my possible stalker, since it's made him give them up for the time being, but —"

"Would you do something for me?" Finn broke in.

She looked up at him. "What?"

"Shut up."

Assuring himself that he couldn't get into that much trouble on a public dance floor, even in the Big Easy where hedonistic pleasures had been turned into a profitable tourist industry, Finn lowered his mouth to hers.

Unlike his first kiss, which had swept through her like a tropical storm, this was like sliding into a warm lagoon. He took his time, the tip of his tongue skimming along the seam of her lips, encouraging hers to part. Which they did. Willingly. Eagerly.

His clever mouth was devastatingly controlled. And tormentingly slow.

Hurry, she wanted to beg him as he tilted his head, changing the angle of the kiss. *Before I remember all the reasons why this would be a mistake.*

There'd been so many times over the past days Julia had gotten the feeling Finn could read her mind. But now, if he sensed her need, intuited her impatience, he didn't reveal it. Instead, with slow, sure hands he stroked her back, sending her floating on rising tides of sweet desire.

The smoky room seemed to dissolve, like sea foam beneath a warm sun. She was lost to him. Absolutely, utterly lost. Time stopped; they could have been the only people on the dance floor, on the planet as they swayed together, breaths mingling in a slow, undemanding meeting.

When he began to hum along with the sultry, sad sound of the tenor sax, vibrations thrummed from his mouth deep into her moist, needy core. The heat of his body warmed her from breast to thigh; his mouth continued to seduce her until they seemed of one shared breath as he took her deeper, then deeper still. Then, just when she was on the verge of drowning, he retreated.

She pressed her fingertips against her tingling lips. "Does this mean you forgive me?" she asked when the power of speech returned.

"I've never been one to hold a grudge." He took hold of her hand and kissed her fingertips. "Life's too short. And you taste too damn good."

She shouldn't have had that glass of wine after such a long day. The way he was looking at her made her head reel, her throat go dry, and her knees turn all wobbly.

They'd stopped any pretense at dancing.

He wanted her. Julia didn't need Amanda's extensive experience to know when a man's mind was on sex. And Finn Callahan wasn't just any man.

When the band broke into a drum-banging rockabilly, he put his hand on her back and began walking off the dance floor. "You've got an early call and you've already had a long day. We'd better get back to town." Julia was a bit surprised when his tone suggested he was no more eager to call it a night than she was.

They were back out on the sidewalk again and Finn had just unlocked the passenger door when a biker, clad in skintight black leather pants, a Harley-Davidson T-shirt, and enough chains to stretch from here to the Moonwalk, called out to her.

"Hey, Amanda, I gotta know, are you gonna get an abortion?"

Julia flashed one of her professional smiles. "Now, I'd just love to tell you, darlin'," she answered in Amanda's smoke and honey drawl. "But if I breathed so much as a single solitary word about the plotline, those mean old producers would have to kill me."

He laughed at that and blew her a kiss.

Their attention on the biker, neither Finn nor Julia noticed the woman who'd kept herself out of the photograph exiting the restaurant. She was in the shadows, watching them intently as Finn opened the Suburban's door. She failed to smile at Julia's little joke; indeed her expression was murderous.

"It must get old," Finn said as they drove away from the restaurant. "Losing your privacy."

"I've gotten used to living in a fishbowl. Besides, it's a trade-off."

"It'll probably get worse after the Bond movie comes out." Finn figured even a minor royalty from her Bond Girl poster profits could be enough to set a person up for life.

"Perhaps. But I'm hoping people's attitudes might change a bit since a 'movie star' —" she made little quote marks in the air with her fingers — "is viewed a lot differently than a TV actor. Viewers invite us into their homes every week. They invest a lot of time — sometimes years — and emotional energy into the characters. So, I think they get to feel like part of the family."

"A dysfunctional family."

"True. But that's what keeps people tuning in every week."

"That, and you wearing those bodysuits and taking all those steamy showers."

"That, too." She laughed, clearly not apologetic of what some strident feminists had blasted as a role that exploited female sexuality and demeaned the strides women had made in the workplace.

Once they left the bright lights of the city behind, night closed in on them. Clouds had drifted in from the Gulf, concealing the moon. The fields of sugar cane and forests of cypress stretched outward from both sides of the road like ghostly shadows.

"It really is like another world," she murmured as an owl swooped silently down from a snag, flashing across the fog-softened yellow beam of the headlights. It snatched up a field mouse that hadn't quite managed to make it across the pavement to the safety of the cane field, before being swallowed up again by the dark. "Like from a movie. The world time forgot." She turned toward him. "Do you miss it?"

"It's impossible to miss something you're

never really away from. The land may not look all that substantial, but roots grow deep here. Once the bayou's in your blood, it never lets go."

"But you don't live here. Is it because there's not enough challenge?"

"There're a lot of challenges that comes with living in the swamp. But I guess I just felt too confined."

"Plus it's difficult to get people to view you as an adult in the town where you grew up," she suggested. "Even when I go home to the farm, I'm still Peace and Freedom's little girl."

He shrugged, deciding that they might actually have this in common. "It's not that I mind being regarded by everyone as my father's son —"

"But you wanted more. More autonomy. More excitement. And sometimes you feel a little guilty about that," she guessed, "even though it's as perfectly natural as the tide flowing out to sea, or a flower reaching for the sun."

"Are you actually comparing me to some daisy?"

"Are you always so damn literal?" She exhaled a long sigh. "Okay, like a tree reaching for the sun. A giant sequoia. Is that better?"

Despite her teasing, he sensed she was genuinely interested. "It's not the excitement." He'd never been particularly introspective, but took a moment to consider her suggestion.

"If I wanted excitement, I would've been a street cop. Or joined a SWAT team. I always knew I'd be in law enforcement, but I also knew I wasn't an adrenaline junkie. I suppose I chose the FBI because I enjoy solving puzzles."

"And because you're a red, white and blue patriot —"

"Anything wrong with that?"

"Of course not. There you go, jumping to conclusions, trying to pigeonhole me into some neat and tidy counterculture box."

"Nothing neat or tidy about you, sweetheart."

"Since I've had such a lovely evening, I'm going to pretend that's a compliment. And for the record, my parents brought me up to love my country."

"Sure they did. That's why they spent so much of the seventies bucking the system and promoting anarchy."

"Anarchists do not create working, cooperative societies. Rainbow's End Farm was not only financially successful, it's as close as you can get to a pure democracy. It's because they love this country that they felt the need to speak out when they believed things were going in the wrong direction. But this isn't about them."

"Could have fooled me. I thought our little shopping trip was about pulling the wool over their eyes."

"Maybe I just wanted to go dancing. And it's

not that I'm trying to hide that you work for the FBI, I just don't see any point in rubbing it in their faces."

"I don't see why that'd be any big deal. Since if they do think there's anything going on between us, instead of setting the record straight, you're going to lie and say we broke up."

"I don't want them to worry about me, which they'd do if they knew why we're really together. Besides, it'd only be a little white lie."

"Black, white" — he shrugged — "it's still not the truth, the whole truth, and nothing but the truth."

"That may work fine in court, but this is a personal matter."

"Maybe you're not giving them enough credit. Let's say, for argument's sake, that we were involved —"

"Involved like sleeping together?"

"Involved like involved. We're talking hypothetical here. My point is that, even if they were to believe we're in an intimate relationship, they shouldn't get all uptight about what I do for a living. Aren't flower children supposed to be open-minded when they're not smoking dope or having free sex?"

"It's been a very long time since my parents dabbled in illegal drugs, and while you probably won't believe this, they've always been monogamous."

"How would you know?"

She folded her arms. "Because they told me.

And we've always been absolutely honest with each other."

"Until now."

She shot him a look. "Touché."

"For some reason I can't figure out — except for the possibility I've gone nuts and don't realize it — I'm willing to go along with this little charade of yours," he said. "To a point. But I'm still convinced it's a waste of time." Looking out into the well of darkness, Finn broke another rule and shared a thought with her. "I can understand and even admire your desire to protect your parents from worrying about you because you love them —"

"Unequivocally."

He believed that. This was not a woman who did — or felt — anything by half measures. "But there's still one thing we have to get clear. If it comes down to a choice between your safety or protecting their feelings, there's not going to be a choice. Is that understood?"

"You're one of the few men I've ever met who says precisely what he means."

"Perhaps you need to meet a different type of man."

"I have." The smile she bestowed on him was designed to dazzle. And did. "And with that we come full circle, back to why you became an agent in the first place. Deep down inside that gruff exterior is a man who cares, Finn. Sometimes too much."

She turned toward him, her eyes skimming

over his face. "This last case was hard on you."

"Yeah."

"Because you feel you should have caught the killer sooner?"

"Most cops would feel the same way."

"But it ate at you. You lived the case day and night for three years. You lived in Lawson's head. Every woman you saw on the street, in a bar or a restaurant, riding on a bus or across the aisle in a plane, all became potential victims. You looked at them the way he would. Thought of why he might pick out any one of them, imagined what he'd do. And then you found them when he was finished with them, and you were the one who became their voice. You were the one who spoke for those dead women, but even that didn't quite ease your conscience."

"They wouldn't have been dead if I'd caught the guy sooner."

"True. But did you ever consider how many you saved? Not after you captured him, but during that time? I looked the case up on the Internet last night. You were right on his trail nearly the entire time."

"Not close enough."

"You can't know that. The two of you obviously became close, in a fashion. If you were in his head, he was undoubtedly in yours. And if that's the case, there could have been times you don't even know about when you were close enough that he sensed you following him, and didn't dare make his move. Nights the women who might have ended up his victims got home safely. Because of you."

Even the shrink Burke had sent him to after his little blowup hadn't suggested that.

"I never thought of it that way."

"Perhaps you should."

Finn didn't respond as they drove through the night in silence. But he did wonder.

19

Several of the cast and crew were still in the bar and called out to Julia to join them when they returned to the inn, but she begged off, claiming she still had lines to memorize before morning.

Warren was sitting at a table in the far corner, deeply engrossed in conversation.

"Well, they certainly seem to be getting along well," Julia murmured in the elevator, more to herself than to Finn. She liked Warren a great deal and worried about his being hurt by someone who might only view him as her ticket out of the bayou.

"Who?"

"Warren and that local blond cheerleader-type belle he's been spending his evenings with. The one with the mother who wears that horrid hat that looks as if a bird died on it."

"The belle is Lorelei. Her mama with the hat is Miss Melanie."

"You're kidding."

"Nope. And not only that, Miss Melanie's sister is Miss Scarlett."

"Well, fiddle-dee-dee. And I thought folks on the commune saddled their kids with tough names."

"Lorelei and Miss Melanie are loyal fans."

"So they tell me. Mercy, I didn't think I was going to be able to get a word in edgewise between the two of them." She nailed Lorelei's breathless accent as she fanned herself with her hand. "Lorelei's certainly doing all right for herself. After Warren was so obviously smitten with her the night of the welcome party, he started writing her lines, which just goes to show that the casting couch hasn't entirely been tossed out with the old studio system. Though in this case, I suspect it's the actress who's manipulating things."

"Lorelei isn't like that. She may play the belle, but that's because she actually is one. What you see is pretty much what you get, and if she sleeps with a guy it's because she likes him."

"She seems to like you well enough."

"We go back to high school. She knows Nate better."

"So I gathered. If the hat lady can be believed, their wedding's in the planning stages."

He laughed at that idea. "Miss Melanie's been writing out the guest list and choosing the songs and flowers since Lorelei was five and Nate was six. For a lady with a cotton candy exterior, she's your quintessential steel magnolia. I can't see her giving up until her daughter's safely married off."

"Safely. What an odd way to put it."

"You weren't around when Lorelei got herself engaged to some Baton Rouge banker with a gambling problem, who got himself in debt to the mob. Her Shih Tzu got kidnapped. The thugs left a letter in his little wicker bed suggesting she was next if her rat of a fiancé didn't cough up the bucks."

"What happened?"

"Nate calmed her down, found where they were keeping the dog, and brought him back home."

"What happened to the fiancé?"

"That's not so clear. Some folks say he's in the Witness Protection program, working as a caddy at a country club in Tucson. Others say he ran off with one of the mobster's daughters and is hiding out in Little Rock working as a hospital orderly. There's also another theory that he's had plastic surgery and is selling bibles door to door in Kansas."

"Who says small towns are boring?" she said with a smile as they entered the suite, which seemed to have shrunk in the past few days. It was nearly claustrophobic tonight, the tension rising as thick as morning fog over the bayou.

"Would you like a nightcap?" she asked.

"Thanks, but I don't drink."

"I noticed that at dinner, but thought perhaps it was because you were on duty."

"No. I don't drink, period."

She tilted her head and studied him. "Is there a story there?"

"Not really."

"Then I'd guess it's because you don't want

to risk giving up control."

"Don't you think you've done enough psychoanalyzing for one night?" There was no humor in his half smile.

"Sorry. Professional hazard." She took two bottles of mineral water from the minibar and held one out to him. "I enjoy tinkering with characters, taking them apart, getting beneath the surface to see how they work."

"I'm not a character."

"Of course you are." She took a long drink and told herself that her dry throat was only due to the heat. "As much as I detest putting people into neat little boxes, everyone does pretty much fit an archetype. You're a classic romantic and literary staple: tall, dark and silent."

"And yours would be?"

She didn't stop to ponder the question. "Artistic. A bit unconventional. Occasionally given to flights of fantasy. But grounded, in my own way."

"This from someone with a purse full of rocks."

Was there anything he didn't notice? "They're crystals. From my mother. And it's not that I actually believe in them."

"No?"

"No. It's more like I don't disbelieve." She shrugged as she tossed the bag in question onto the sofa. "Besides, what harm can they do?"

"How about give you a very sore shoulder

from lugging them around?"

"Good point." She rubbed the shoulder in question. "I don't suppose you know anyone who'd be able to work the kinks out?"

"Why don't you try sleeping it off? If it's still sore in the morning, have Hogan call a masseuse."

"I could do that. But mornings are so hectic, what with hair and makeup, script changes, dry-blocking, and beginning to tape the scenes. Perhaps it'd be easier if you could give it a try for me tonight. I know I'd sleep ever so much better if my body were more relaxed."

"I'm not a masseuse."

"How hard can it be? All you have to do is put your hands on me. And begin rubbing."

He looked at her long enough to make her blood pulse with expectation. Julia could tell he was definitely tempted. "I'll get you an aspirin."

Foiled again. "Dudley Do-Right lives," she murmured. "Have you ever considered moving across the border and joining the Mounties?"

"Nah. The uniform sucks."

"Some women like a man in uniform." He'd look fabulous.

"Maybe. And the Mounties are good enough cops —"

"They always get their man."

"It's a catchy motto. But their uniform reminds me of an operetta."

"*Indian Love Call.* Nelson Eddy and Jeanette

MacDonald." She grinned when he looked surprised. "My parents used to act out those old musicals with friends in the farm's theater."

"Why do I have difficulty picturing your parents as Mickey Rooney and Judy Garland putting on a show in the barn?"

Because they'd been getting along so well, the sarcasm grated more than it would have before. "If you'd seen Mama Cass and Jerry Garcia in *Take Me to St. Louis*, you might change your mind. Maybe you can't imagine it because you're a snob.

"Yes, you are," she said when he arched a challenging brow. "A cop snob. You think that just because you carry a badge and arrest bad guys, you're better than the rest of us flawed civilians."

"That's bullshit."

"I don't think so. And you know what, Callahan? You're also the male version of a cock tease."

He went very still. "What the hell are you talking about?" His shoulders were stone, his eyes fierce and narrowed.

"You kissed me the other day. And again, tonight in the restaurant. Kissed me like you wanted me."

"What man wouldn't want you? Besides, you're the one who keeps telling me I ought to give in to impulse once in a while."

"That's all it was? An impulse?"

"Sure. You're a sexy woman, and I've spent

the better part of a week watching you shed your clothes and get down and dirty with enough guys to make up a basketball team."

"Surely a hotshot detective like you ought to be able to tell the difference between real life and fantasy."

"Sure. But playacting or not, it's still hot. It gets a guy to thinking about things."

"A guy? Or you?"

"Me. Ever since you got off that damn plane, I've been thinking about all the things I wanted to do with you. To you."

She watched his mouth draw into a grim line and remembered the way it tasted. Tantalized. Tormented.

"But I've been working overtime to keep things professional. Then you flutter those Scarlett O'Hara eyelashes and wheedle me into taking you into the city —"

She couldn't deny it. "Is it so wrong to want to escape another evening locked in protective custody?"

That wasn't the whole story. The truth was that she'd wanted to be alone with him away from Blue Bayou and *River Road*. She'd wanted him to hold her again. Kiss her again. And that was just for starters.

"This suite isn't exactly Angola Prison. Then you drag me to that club —"

"I was hungry."

"Sure you were. But you'd hardly taken a bite when the next thing I know, I'm out on the dance floor and you've wrapped yourself around me like some damn Bourbon Street hooker —"

His mouth slammed shut. But it was too late. Julia felt the color drain from her face. The sharp pain in her heart.

"Well." She drew in a shaky breath and fought against the tears. She hadn't wept over a male since Woodstock. Then again, she couldn't remember being both so hurt and furious as she was now. "You've certainly made yourself very clear."

"I didn't mean it." He caught her arm as she tried to escape into the bedroom with some pride intact. "Dammit, Julia, you've just got me frustrated and angry at myself and —"

"You're frustrated?" Her voice rose a full octave, like Jeanette MacDonald's had when singing those duets with Nelson Eddy. "*You're* frustrated?" she repeated. "What about me? Do you think it's easy for me to have a man keep acting like he wants me —"

"That wasn't acting. I did. I do."

"Shut up and stop interrupting me. You keep coming on to me, Callahan, then you back away, hiding behind your shiny gold badge. Some people might consider you a hero, but I think you're a coward. You're afraid of your own feelings. You're afraid to take a chance."

She glared at him when he didn't respond. "Well? Don't you have anything to say to that?"

"You told me to shut up."

The sound that came from deep in her throat was somewhere between a growl and a scream. "I've had it with you, Callahan. First thing tomorrow, I'm going to insist that you be fired. Then I'm going to refuse to show up on the set if you're anywhere in the vicinity."

"That's stupid."

"Not as stupid as some of the things I've been doing lately." Like letting a stiff, stuffed shirt Neanderthal creep past her defenses into her mind. And, dammit, heart.

"I'm going to go to bed now. Alone. And don't worry, you're off the hook where my parents are concerned, too." She dragged a hand through her hair, appalled that it was trembling. "You know the ridiculous thing about all this?"

"What?"

"Ever since they called, I've been worried about how you'd view them. Concerned that they wouldn't measure up enough to overcome your obvious prejudice against them. But the truth is, I had it all backward.

"No matter what you may think, my mother and father are good people. Caring people who might not show up at the Episcopal Church on Sunday mornings, or vote a straight Republican ticket, or have dinner at the country club, but they're real and honest and neither one of them has a prejudiced bone in their body. Which is why they're too good to even waste their time with a rigid, controlling, inconsiderate jerk like you."

Didn't anything get to him? He was standing there, as rigid as the statue of the soldier she'd seen in front of the courthouse down the street. Could he really be so unfeeling? "I'm going to bed."

"That's a good idea."

"And tomorrow you're going to be gone."

When he didn't respond, Julia swept from the room, threw herself onto the bed, and squeezed her eyes tightly shut to close off the hot tears brimming at the back of her lids.

There was a loud thud from the other side of the wall. Then nothing but the sound of cicadas singing their lonely songs out in the bayou.

She wasn't going to talk to him. During the night, while Julia had been tossing and turning, she'd vowed that if Finn was still there in the morning, she'd simply walk off the show. Let Kendall the ass-pinching executive producer deal with that, she decided.

Until she came out of the bedroom and saw Finn sitting at the table, wearing his stark FBI suit, looking even worse than she felt. His eyes were heavily lidded, his uncharacteristically unshaven jaw shadowed, and his shirt, wonder of wonders, was actually rumpled, as if he'd spent the night in it.

Sympathy stirred. Just a little.

He didn't look up from the laptop computer he was tapping on. An incredible aroma wafted from a waxed bag on the table beside the computer. "What do you know about Atlantic Pharmaceuticals?"

As she sat down across from him, Julia reminded herself that she'd always considered the silent treatment more than a little juvenile. "Not much. Only that it bought out Dwyers' Diapers last year, which made it owner of *River Road*. And that Charles Kendall could be the poster boy for nepotism. Why?"

He poured her a cup of coffee from the carafe, added the perfect amount of cream and two sugars, and handed it to her. His knuckles were bruised, explaining that hole in the wall that hadn't been there yesterday. "Did you know they're about to launch a new drug?"

"Now that you mention it, that's what this on-location shoot is all about. The episodes are airing during sweeps, at the same time Atlantic's launching the drug."

"Providing a huge built-in audience for its advertising blitz," Finn guessed.

"That'd be my guess." She took a sip of the chicory coffee she was becoming accustomed to. "For someone who didn't earn his own wealth, Charles is terribly tightfisted. The only reason I can imagine him springing for this end-of-the-season increase in budget is because Atlantic's got a real winner on their hands this time."

"Or a real loser."

She thought about that for a minute, then

shook her head. "If it were possible to sell a loser product with an advertising blitz, we'd all be drinking New Coke and driving Edsels."

"Maybe he doesn't have a choice."

Now he'd piqued her curiosity. "Why do you say that?"

"There's a rumor on the street that Kendall's ass is on the line, because it looks as if Atlantic Pharmaceuticals' new wonder drug is going to tank, big time."

"Street as in Wall Street?"

"Yeah. Atlantic's hoping a huge promotional campaign during your two-night season special will prevent a stock free fall."

"That's quite a lot to expect from a soap opera."

"True. But it turns out Kendall also promised his stepfather, who happens to be CEO, that he can get you back for another season to help keep the hype up for the product's first year. It appears you're a commodity, sweetheart."

"Like potatoes and pork futures," she muttered. "I've already informed him that there's no way I'm returning to the show."

"If the rumors are true, you could probably name your own price."

"I'm not leaving for money," she told him the same thing she'd already told Charles Kendall innumerable times. "I'm leaving for a role I've dreamed of since I was eight years old. I'm also moving on because I'd enjoy the chance for a role where I actually got to keep my clothes on for an entire scene. . . . So what's this drug that's going to tank?"

"An antidepressant."

"Atlantic already produces an antidepressant. You can't turn on the television without seeing the commercials."

"Yeah, but this is different, because it's for animals."

"Animals?"

"Yeah. Specifically cats."

Abandoning the last of her irritation, Julia laughed. "How on earth do you diagnose a depressed cat when they mostly lie in sunbeams, feel superior to their owners, eat and sleep?"

Finn's grin was slow and, perhaps because he shared it so seldom, unreasonably appealing. "That's pretty much what the focus groups said."

"I'm impressed you were able to find that out," she allowed. Something occurred to her. She looked at the computer. "You didn't do anything illegal, did you?"

The smile turned to a scowl. "Hell, no."

"Good."

A strained silence settled over them, broken only by the tapping of the keys and the cheerful chirps of a bird outside the window. Having been brought up in an environment that believed in clearing the air, Julia was uncomfortable with this lingering, silent conflict.

"I've been thinking about what you said,"

Julia carefully waded into the dangerous conversational waters. "About us sleeping together."

"And?"

"And I've decided that you're right . . . Are those donuts?"

"Yeah. Nate brought them by while you were in the shower."

"I think I've just fallen in love with your brother."

"You and at least half the women in the Western world."

"He's sweet and sexy and considerate. Women find those traits appealing."

"As opposed to rigid, controlling and inconsiderate?"

"I may have exaggerated just a bit, because you made me so angry. But the fact remains that we're too different, that our worlds are too far apart, and we'd never be able to make a relationship work outside of bed. Maybe not even there."

"Want to bet?"

"All right. Maybe we'd be compatible in bed. Maybe you'd be the best lover I've ever had and maybe I'd make you forget any other woman you'd ever slept with. Maybe we'd set the sheets on fire and burn this place down. But what if things got complicated?"

"There's no 'what if' about it. Sex complicates things."

"That's exactly my point. We only have a few

more days here, then we'll be going our separate ways, so why risk any messy entanglements?"

"Why indeed?" he murmured, reaching into the bag for a glazed bear claw.

"Then we're agreed?" As he took a huge bite, Julia reminded herself that Carma Sutra's wardrobe did not allow for an extra ounce. "That if I allow you to stay, there'll be no more kissing?"

"If you allow it?"

Interesting how he could intimidate with a mere lift of a brow; he was probably a crackerjack interrogator. She took another sip of coffee. "Well, you are working for me. Technically."

"Technically, I'm not working for anyone."

"You're being paid to be my bodyguard."

"As it happens, I had the check from the production company made out to the Blue Bayou after-school recreation program. If I don't stick it out, the kids are going to be the ones who pay the price."

"Stick it out. Well, that's certainly a flattering way to state it. So, you're putting up with me to help some kids?"

"No. I'm putting up with you because my brother asked for my help, and I don't believe in letting family down. I'm putting up with you because despite the fact that you can be a pain in the ass, I don't take threats lightly and I want to keep you alive long enough to watch you wear that catsuit in the new Bond flick.

"But the number one reason I'm putting up with you is because I'm discovering that you're not anything like the prima donna television star I was expecting."

"Gracious, Special Agent, that comes awfully close to flattery."

"Take it any way you like it. It's a fact."

"I believe I'll take it as a compliment, then, since you're so stingy with them. I'll also admit that for a rigid, controlling, blue-suited government storm trooper, you can be rather nice. At times. Which is the only reason I'm putting up with you. Well, that and the fact that you're a dynamite kisser."

"You're not so bad yourself."

"So, are we friends?" Like Finn, she'd never been able to hold a grudge. It took too much emotional energy and was a waste of time.

"Sure." He shrugged. "Why not?"

"Now there's a ringing endorsement." She rested her elbows on the table, cupped her chin in her palms, and looked at him over the bag of doughnuts. "Want to seal it with a kiss?"

"Nope." He brushed the crumbs into his palm and dumped them back into the bag.

"Surely you're not afraid of a friendly little kiss between friends?"

"No. But you might want to be. Because if I touch you right now, I'm going to have you."

It was neither threat nor promise. Merely, Julia realized, like so many other things Finn said, a statement of fact.

"What if I touch you?"

"Same thing goes. My libido's hanging by a ragged thread, which is not a good thing, since I need to stay coolheaded until the film wraps and you're safely off to Kathmandu."

"Still, it seems we should celebrate this new stage in our relationship somehow."

"Have a Krispy Kreme." He pushed the bag toward her.

Drawn by the aroma of forbidden warm fat and sugar, she gave up trying to fight temptation, chose a chocolate-filled donut, bit into it, and nearly wept with pleasure. "Oh, God. . . . Okay, you're safe. Because I think I may just ask your brother to marry me."

"If anyone could make him tumble, it'd probably be you. But he's vowed to play the field until they bury him in the Callahan family tomb. Nate views commitment as something that happens when the guys show up with a straitjacket and a one-way ticket to a rubber room."

"He'll change his mind," she predicted blithely. "When the right woman comes along."

"She'd better bring a length of rope to hogtie him. Because he won't go down easily." He leaned toward her. "You've got chocolate on your mouth." A long finger set her skin to sizzling as he touched the corner of her lips.

When he sucked the chocolate he'd gathered off his fingertip, she felt herself melting. Bone by bone. Atom by atom. "You're doing it again." Her voice was uncharacteristically fractured.

"Yeah." He skimmed a thumb along her jaw. "It'd help if you told me to keep my damn hands to myself."

"It'd help if I *wanted* you to keep your hands to yourself." She drew in a deep, painful breath. "But I don't. I want them on me. Everywhere. All the time."

"Damn." He slowly shook his head. "Don't you have any natural defenses?"

"Of course. At least I did. Until you came storming into my life."

This time his curse was rough, and as ragged as her nerves. A tension as heavy as the rain falling outside the silk-draped windows rose to hover between them.

He leaned closer.

So did she.

His lips were a mere whisper away from hers, which parted on a slow sigh that was half surrender, half anticipation.

His eyes darkened, like molten obsidian flowing over cobalt.

They both jumped apart as the shrill demand of the phone shattered the expectant silence.

"Saved by the bell," he muttered as he scooped up the receiver.

"That's not funny."

"I wasn't trying to be funny. . . . Yeah, she's here with me. Yeah, we'll be right down." He hung up without any polite good-byes. "The shooting schedule's been changed again."

"There's a surprise."

"Instead of the Confederate attack scene, they're going to shoot some more footage inside Beau Soleil." He paused. "It's the scene Hyatt added yesterday. The one where the Yankee captain rapes Fancy."

Upping the sexual content of the movie one more notch, Kendall and Warren had decided to inject the scene into the early part of the time-travel story at the editing stage, so it'd occur before the confrontation in the cemetery when Fancy pulled the gun on him.

It was just another scene. Just acting. But Finn knew he was in trouble when he hated the idea of any other man putting his hands on this woman.

20

Damn. Her lipstick was smeared. Oh well, a little smeared Max Factor was definitely worth the kiss that had smeared it. Lorelei smiled to herself as she repaired the damage in the mirror of the rest room assigned to the extras.

"Isn't this just the most fun?" she asked the elderly woman standing next to her. "I cannot believe I'm actually going to be in a movie."

The woman, seeming intent on tucking wayward strands of gray hair beneath a bonnet, ignored her.

"Are you from around here? I don't recognize you."

"New Orleans." The woman's voice was deep and sounded as if she'd spent decades smoking. Her hands, on the other hand, didn't appear nearly as old as her face, which Lorelei took to be the work of the makeup people. She thanked her good fortune — and *River Road*'s writer — that she hadn't been assigned the role of this elderly widow.

"Oh, then you probably don't find this nearly so exciting, since New Orleans is pretty lively itself. Out here in the sticks, watching paint dry can be considered entertainment. Of course, there was that little flap a few months ago when the sheriff got arrested, but everyone knew he was a crook, so it was more a case of him finally getting his comeuppance rather than a surprise. Then, of course, Jack Callahan moved back to town and bought Beau Soleil. You've probably heard of him. The famous writer?"

That earned a muffled grunt.

Undeterred by her listener's seeming lack of interest, buoyed by a night of lovemaking and the prospect of actually getting to speak real lines today, Lorelei chattered on.

"His stories are horribly dark, and not at all what I'd usually read. I tend to like books with happy endings. But Jack's are very well written and exciting, though I'd certainly recommend reading them with the lights on. Why, after I read The Death Dealer, every time I heard a little noise outside the house at night, I was sure it was a Colombian drug kingpin coming to murder me in my bed."

She trilled a laugh at the absurdity of that idea. "As if any drug kingpin would bother coming to Blue Bayou. As I said, the only real criminal to set foot in town for ages was the sheriff, who's doing time in Angola right now. I hear they have him in solitary, which isn't surprising since even though he was a bad cop, he was still technically a member of law enforcement, which I'm sure didn't exactly endear him to the rest of the inmates."

As she paused to take a breath, the woman, apparently satisfied with her hair, turned and walked out of the rest room, closing the door behind her.

"Well." Lorelei's breath ruffled the blond fringe of curls tumbling over her forehead. "Some people just have no manners." She couldn't imagine anyone, even someone from the city, being so rude. "Obviously a transplanted Yankee," she decided. Thanking her lucky stars that her mama hadn't given birth to her north of the Mason-Dixon line, Lorelei patted her own hair, flashed her best beauty queen's smile at her reflection, then satisfied, followed the woman out of the rest room.

Julia did not take the sight of Warren waiting at the steps of her trailer when they arrived at Beau Soleil as a good sign. She was right.

"We're adding a scene," he announced.

"I know. The rape one."

"No, another."

Her stomach sank. "Dammit, Warren, if we keep this up, we're going to run over schedule."

"Maybe just a bit," he allowed.

"More than a bit. At this rate I'll be lucky to get to Kathmandu before the wrap party. In fact, I'm probably in danger of being the only support hose–wearing septuagenarian Bond Girl in history."

"Now you're exaggerating."

"Gee, with perception like that I'm surprised you're not a writer."

"Snapping at me isn't going to speed things

up," he said, clearly wounded. "It's not my fault Kendall keeps tinkering with the script."

"I suppose there's a good reason?"

"Sure. He decided he wanted more outdoor footage for visuals, so I came up with a scene where Fancy drives out into the swamp to meet with her mother's husband, the blockade runner."

"I can't keep track. Is the husband working for the Blue or the Gray now?"

"Both. He's a double spy, mostly working for himself. Both sides are paying him for information. Fancy's going to seduce him into giving her some of his ill-gotten gains to save Beau Soleil."

Julia rubbed her temple, where a headache warned. "Please tell me she's at least not going to be wearing curtains."

"And have people accuse us of stealing from *Gone With the Wind*?"

"Why on earth would anyone think that?" Julia glanced over at the buggy that looked suspiciously like the one Scarlett had been driving when she'd gone out to the sawmill and nearly gotten herself raped, which had, in turn, resulted in her husband's getting shot when the men had been duty bound to defend her honor. "What makes you think I even know how to drive a carriage?"

"I thought you told me you'd grown up on some kind of farm."

"I did. And I had a pony cart, but I'm not at

all sure it's the same thing."

"Don't worry," Randy, who'd arrived to join in the conversation, assured her. "We'll use one of the stunt doubles for the actual driving. That way we can shoot your shapely arse climbing into the carriage and your knockers as you climb back out."

"You have such a way with words." Julia could feel the irritation simmering just beneath Finn's impassive exterior and realized once again how alien all this must be to him. She'd never met a man less suited to the Hollywood life.

"I'm no writer, but I do know how to frame the bloody shots that helped get you that Bond Girl gig," Randy countered without heat. "The carriage scene'll be great. The big guy was all for it when Warren thought it up."

Julia shot Warren a look. "Thanks a lot."

"It actually makes more sense this way," he argued. "When she comes back from the drive, all mussed and smelling of sex, the Yankee will decide to take some for himself."

"Why don't we just let Amanda return to the twenty-first century?" Which would allow *her* to leave for Nepal.

"We're not sure she's going to go back to the present."

"What?" Julia stared at him.

"Kendall's considering keeping her in the coma for the rest of next season."

"How are you going to explain that a different actress is lying in the hospital bed?"

"We might not have to. After all, *Bewitched* didn't make a big deal of switching Darrens. Or we'll write something in about her being horribly disfigured — perhaps Vanessa shot her twice, once in the heart, then her face — and when the bandages come off, voila, all the reconstructive surgery has left her looking different."

"That's not very realistic."

"If viewers wanted real life they could tune into CNN or C-Span, rather than visiting River Road," Randy pointed out.

Kendall came out of Margot's trailer just in time to hear that statement. There was a tell-tale lipstick stain on his collar.

"I agree that it'd be better if we didn't have to resort to such tactics, Julia. But I talked with Atlantic's board of directors this morning. There's already a huge buzz about the film out there. They've authorized me to make you an offer that would more than make it worth your while to return for a sixth season."

"I promised Dwyers' Diapers, when I signed my first contract, that I'd stay until there were enough episodes in the can for syndication," Julia reminded him. "We're finishing up our fifth year. So, I'm leaving." Her tone was mild, but firm. "It's not that I haven't enjoyed playing Amanda, but —"

"I know, I know." He threw up hands she didn't like to think about having been all over

263

Margot's surgery-enhanced body only moments earlier. "You need to stretch creatively."

Julia refused to take offense at his voice, heavily laced with sarcasm. "Yes." She refused to back down from his challenging gaze. "I do."

"A Bond movie is not exactly *Sophie's Choice*."

Julia smiled sweetly. "Neither is *River Road*. At least in the Bond film, the only man I'm going to bed with is 007."

"She's got you there, mate," Randy said on a bark of a laugh while Kendall glowered.

Warren lingered after the others left to begin getting ready for the day's shooting. "I know you've got to start hair and makeup, but may I have a couple minutes of your time? It's kind of important."

"Sure. What's up?"

"I was hoping we could talk. Privately." He glanced up at Finn, with a wariness he might have approaching a snarling rottweiler. Clearly uncomfortable, he cleared his throat. "It's personal."

Julia wondered what fatal disease he was coming down with now. If she were a betting woman, she'd put her money on malaria or yellow fever. "All right. We can talk in the trailer."

She turned to Finn. "Why don't you go get some coffee? I'll be fine."

"Of course you will," he agreed mildly. "And I'm staying here."

Now, there was a surprise. She sighed as he checked out the inside of the trailer, as he had every day before letting her enter. It might have bothered her, had it not been for the all too vivid memory of opening that envelope and knowing her stalker had been there. She hadn't noticed anything missing, but remembering what Finn had told her about Lawson keeping souvenirs, she wondered if she should take a more careful look around. Had he roamed the two rooms, touching her things? The idea made her skin crawl.

"What's the problem?" she asked the writer, after he'd turned down her offer of iced tea or soda.

"What do you know about spontaneous combustion?"

"Not all that much." She didn't mention she'd experienced it the first time Finn had kissed her. "Why?" Suspicion stirred. "Please tell me you're not going to write it into the script?"

"No. Like I said, this is personal." He took a deep breath. Dragged his fingers through his hair. "Sometimes I think it's going to happen to me."

"Spontaneous combustion?"

"Yeah. I realize that it's not all that common for people to burst into flame —"

"I don't believe it's ever happened." It took a

herculean effort not to laugh. "Though Ripley might correct me on that."

"I wouldn't want to get in the record books that way."

"Warren." She patted his hand. "I was joking."

"Oh." The problem was, he didn't seem to be. "It's whenever I'm with Lorelei. My skin gets all hot and though I haven't taken my temperature, I'm sure it must be around five hundred degrees. And when she touches me . . ." He blushed fire-engine red. "I swear, Julia, I nearly burst into flame right on the spot."

"Oh, Warren." Julia lifted her hand to his hot cheek. "You don't have to worry. It's not possible to actually burn up from being in love. Though sometimes it can feel like it," she allowed.

"That's what Lorelei says. But I was worried. More about her than myself. I really care for her. If she caught on fire because I'd burst into flame, I'd never forgive myself."

"I honestly don't think you have a problem. Actually, you sound pretty lucky."

"I am." The broad smile cleared the concern from his freckled face. "I can't believe a woman like that would be interested in a guy like me."

"Don't be silly. She's the lucky one," Julia said, meaning it.

While Julia was busy reassuring Warren, Finn was standing at the base of the steps, monitoring the stopwatch feature on his watch when

Lorelei came up to him, looking like a strawberry ice cream cone in her pink hoopskirted dress.

"Hi, sugar. Someone told me Warren came over this way."

"Yeah. He's inside, talking to Julia."

"Oh. I guess I'll just have to wait, then. He's promised me more lines, and I have to admit I'm anxious to see if he got them approved. He thinks I have a good chance at a real future in television."

"That's nice."

"Mama and I are thinkin' of moving out to Hollywood so I can focus on my career."

"Good for you." He cast a glance at his watch. Two minutes, Hyatt had said. They were now approaching six. And counting.

"Of course, if that fails, I can always become an astronaut and go into outer space and walk naked on the moon."

"Works for me." Okay, that was it. Sixty more seconds and . . . "What did you say?"

Lorelei pouted prettily. "If you'd been paying attention, you wouldn't have to ask that."

"Sorry. My mind's on other things."

"*One* other thing, anyway. And it's okay that you didn't hear me. I understand." She smiled up at him. "I think it's wonderful about you and Julia."

Finn narrowed his eyes. "What about Julia and me?"

"That you're an item, of course. Why, it's as

obvious to everyone as the nose on your face."
She fanned herself with the lace-trimmed fan
looped around her wrist. "Gracious, there's so
much energy bouncing around when you two
are in a room together, it's like being inside a
pinball machine. . . .

"This is turning out to be such a wonderful
thing for everyone, isn't it?" she said when Finn
didn't immediately respond to the pinball machine comment. "Not only in the romance department, but mercy, it's amazing how
everyone's gotten a job. Even people who'd
probably never, in a million years, get work in
Hollywood. Like that woman over there." She
pointed her fan toward an elderly woman
dressed in mourning. She frowned thoughtfully.
"I wonder who she is. It's obvious that she's not
from around here."

That got Finn's attention. "You sure?"

"Of course. She hasn't spoken a word to
anyone since the first day. And she's always off
by herself during breaks. I tried to have a conversation with her earlier and she just cut me
off cold. I don't know why she's even here in
the first place, unless it's because she's obviously such a Julia Summers fan."

"Why would you say that?"

"Because I noticed her yesterday. She's always watching her."

Finn studied the woman closer. The fixated
way she was staring at the trailer reminded him
of the way Jack's dog, Turnip, stared at a steak

bone. The intensity in her gaze made the hair on the back of his neck stand up in a way he hadn't felt since he'd approached Lawson's suburban torture chamber.

"You don't recognize her?"

"That's what I've been telling you," Lorelei said in a huff. "For pity's sake, Finn Callahan. If you'd just pay a little attention. . . ."

He could tell she was just winding up when the metal door opened and Julia came out, followed by Warren.

"You've got the extra lines," he told Lorelei.

Her eyes filled and she beamed like a beauty contestant who'd just been crowned Miss America. "Oh, you are so sweet, sugar, I don't know how I'll ever make it up to you."

He blushed beneath his freckles. "Maybe if we put our heads together we can think of something."

"I'll just bet we can," she chirped.

It was all Finn could do not to roll his eyes as they walked off together, seemingly joined at the hip.

"They seem happy," Julia murmured.

"Seems Hyatt's promised to make her a star."

"It's an old story. There are certainly still men who misuse their power in Hollywood, but he's not one of them. Of course, she'll need more than looks to succeed, but she's very beautiful, in an ultra spun-sugar sort of way. I can almost hear little hearts over her *i*'s when she talks."

"She's been that way as long as I've known her. Which, thinking about it, was back about the same time she won her first Blue Bayou title when in the second grade."

"That young." Julia didn't envy the other woman at all. She couldn't imagine trading a moment of her childhood for a tiara and satin sash. When she was seven, she'd been running barefoot through meadows, wading in crystal creeks, and riding her sweet old mare, Buttermilk, bareback.

"Her mother got her started on the pageant trail when she was just a baby in Georgia, then they kept it up when they moved here. She's got a photograph on the office desk of Nate crowning her. I can't remember how, exactly, he got roped into it, but if the sappy, puppy dog I'm-in-love look on his face was any indication, he didn't consider it a hardship. In fact, it was sort of like the one he's got now."

Her gaze shifted to where Finn's brother was deep in what appeared to be an intimate conversation with the continuity girl.

"He's not in love," Julia determined. "It's more like friendly lust." She looked up at Finn. They both felt the jolt as the atmosphere became charged. "Not that there's anything wrong with lust, of course."

"Not at all." Pheromones. He was being battered by them, just like being inside that pinball machine Lorelei had mentioned. "Anyone ever tell you that you've got one helluva sexy mouth?"

"All the time." Those lips that had been tormenting his sleep curved in a slow, sexy Amanda/Fancy smile designed to hit a man between the eyes. And lower. "But I can't really take credit since I inherited it from my mother."

"Sounds like your dad's a lucky man." He was surprised he could still speak, being bombarded from within as he was.

"He is. My mother's a very special person. Would you stop looking at me like that?"

"How am I looking at you?"

"Like you want to ravish me."

"I do. How about you? Would you like to be ravished?"

"Absolutely." She tipped her face up in feminine invitation. "And that's just for starters."

He dragged his hands down his face to keep from putting them on her. Then reminded his scorched brain why he was here at Beau Soleil, with her, in the first place.

"Keep that thought. Meanwhile, see that woman over there? The one dressed all in black?"

She scanned the group of extras. "Yes."

"Do you know her?"

"I can't tell. She's turned away. Should I go over —"

"No." He suspected he was being overly cautious. But better that, than putting Julia in harm's way and finding out the hard way that the woman was carrying a weapon. "It's just something Lorelei said." He shook his head, deciding that his detecting skills were getting rusty if he was finding clues in Lorelei's breathless monologues. "Apparently she's been watching you."

The woman began moving away toward the cemetery. "Although technically we're an ensemble cast, Amanda's pretty much the star of the show." Julia shrugged. "A lot of people watch her."

The first assistant director, who was in charge of keeping all the planned scenes shot on time, called for the extras to gather on the *gallerie*. The old woman moved slowly, almost painfully, her back hunched, her head down, as if carefully watching her step as she crossed the shell gravel. She sure didn't look like much of a threat. But then Finn thought of those blazing eyes.

"Do me a favor."

"All right," she said without pause.

"Don't you want to hear what it is?"

"Not particularly, since I can't think of anything you might suggest I wouldn't say yes to."

"Damn, you're not making this easy."

"It hasn't been easy from the beginning."

"No," he agreed in a deep sigh. "It hasn't. Keep away from her, okay?"

"You're kidding." She glanced over at the group of extras, then back up at Finn. "You're not, are you?"

He shrugged. "It's probably nothing. But there's no point in taking chances."

Obviously she thought he was being overly cautious. He could read the doubt in her gaze. But then her attention drifted back to the extras and, as if sensing her appraisal, the woman raised her head. When their gazes met, Finn could practically hear the sizzle of heat.

"Ouch." Julia breathed, after the woman looked away, breaking contact.

"Yeah," Finn said.

"I don't think she likes me."

"You don't have to be a detective to see that."

"She's probably just another one who confuses me with Amanda, like the woman who hit me in the video store. Then there was a heavyset black-haired woman who looked as if she was about to murder her husband and throw him in the bayou the night of the welcome party."

"Marie Robicheaux. She's always been jealous and obviously didn't like the way her Henri was looking at you. Nate and I were thinking that we sure wouldn't want to be in that car on the drive home."

"That's too bad." She sighed. "Amanda's such a dual-edged sword. People always want to meet her. She is, after all, far more interesting than me."

"Not from where I'm standing."

She smiled at that. "Ah, but as you've already

pointed out, you're a man of discriminating tastes."

"You've got that right."

The morning air was lush with perfume and promise. That same promise was echoed in Julia's eyes as she looked up into Finn's. The world paused as the planet seemed to cease spinning.

"What were we talking about?"

"I don't remember." If she didn't stop looking at his mouth that way, he wasn't going to be responsible for his actions.

Hell, there was no point in lying to himself. Whatever happened, he damn well would be responsible. There were lines to draw, barricades to keep up, and since he wasn't getting any help from her, he'd have to keep things from getting out of control himself.

"Amanda," he remembered, feeling a flash of relief as his brain kicked back in. "We were talking about her. And that old woman."

"That's right." She looked downright disappointed that he'd forced the change in mood. And while he didn't like being the one to put those shadows in Julia's eyes, she'd be a whole lot better off disappointed than dead.

He called out to Nate, who was leaning a hand against one of Beau Soleil's white pillars while his other toyed with the ends of the woman's dark hair.

After saying something that earned a smile from her, Nate strolled across the yard to join them. He was whistling.

"Would you stay here with Julia?" Finn asked his brother. "There's something I want to check out."

"Sure. Anything I can do?"

"Just don't let her out of your sight."

He flashed a grin down at Julia. "That's sure no hardship."

Julia smiled back up at him, wishing just a little that if she had to fall for one of the Callahan brothers, it would've been this friendly, uncomplex one.

21

"I've never met a man quite like your brother," Julia said to Nate as she watched Finn walk away. "Has he always considered himself responsible for the entire world?"

"Pretty much," Nate said. "Even before our dad was killed."

"He was killed?" She remembered Finn telling her his parents had died, but when he'd refused to offer specifics, she'd opted not to push. "In an accident?"

"No." For the first time since she'd met him, his expression turned sober. When his eyes shadowed and his mouth grew into an uncharacteristically tight line, Julia sensed that there was more to Nate Callahan than the easygoing, smooth talking Southern male she'd first taken him for.

"He was murdered. I was twelve, Jack was thirteen, and Finn was sixteen when it happened. Dad was Blue Bayou's sheriff."

"Finn said you'd moved here from Chicago."

"Yeah. The ironic thing was, Dad had brought us here because he thought it'd be safer than Chicago. Even before that day, Finn was the big brother Jack and I could always depend on. I couldn't count the number of kites he retrieved from trees or fishing lines he untangled. He was also the one with the stash of *Playboy* magazines that pretty much defined our adolescence."

She smiled at that, as he'd meant her to, then watched Finn disappear around the corner of the house.

"He'll be okay," Nate promised, picking up on her tension. "If there's one guy who can take care of himself, it's Finn. Like I said, he was probably born responsible, but after Dad was gone, he stepped into the role of man of the house as if it were the most natural thing in the world."

"It must have been difficult for him."

"Probably was. But he's never uttered a word of complaint. Not then, or anytime since. At the time, I'm not sure any of us realized how hard it must have been on him, trying to become a father when he was still really a boy himself, he."

His Cajun accent had deepened and the subtle, seemingly unconscious change in syntax told Julia it was an emotional topic for him. Which was probably why Finn, who was the least open individual she'd ever met, had refused to discuss it.

Julia's heart ached for the boy Finn had been as she pictured him doing his best to fill what must have been an enormous void in the Callahan family.

"What happened? How was your father killed?"

"Oh, *mon Dieu,* that was a bad day." He dragged a nicked and calloused hand through his sun-tipped hair. His gaze momentarily grew distant, giving her the impression he was re-living it. Then he sighed and shook his head, as if to rid it of painful old memories. "He was at the courthouse testifying in a domestic abuse case, when this crazed, drunk swamp dweller with a beef about his family situation came storming into the courthouse to murder the judge.

"Dad threw himself in front of the bullet. The judge lived. Dad died. And our lives changed forever."

She couldn't imagine how she'd feel if it had been her own father. She'd certainly watched Freedom put himself in danger enough times, including that occasion he and a group of Greenpeace activists had piloted their small boats back and forth in front of a Japanese fishing fleet working the waters outside San Diego. Two boats had been swamped. The Coast Guard, called in to rescue the protestors, had not been at all pleased.

"That must have been horrendously hard on all of you."

"*Mais,* yeah. At least I had two big brothers I could talk to and count on, but Finn, who'd al-ways been steady as a rock, just seemed to get tougher. And quieter.

"I'm not tellin' tales, since everyone 'round here knows it, but Jack started rebelling pretty bad then; these days they'd probably call it acting out. In some ways he had it the roughest since he'd been there when it happened, and while it doesn't make a lick of sense, I've always had the feeling he blamed himself for not having done something to stop it."

"That's sad. That a boy would think such a thing."

"Even sadder that he'd continue to think it as a man. He's moved on these days, though. Looking back on it, I guess I was pretty much in denial. *Maman,* who'd never worked a day in her life for wages, went to work as the judge's housekeeper right after Dad's death.

"It's his daughter Jack married. They had a fling one summer when they were kids, her father and my mother broke them up, then they got back together this year after her marriage fell apart and her husband died. Anyone can see they belong together."

"That's sweet. I suppose, in a small town like this, people's lives are probably pretty connected." Not so unlike Rainbow's End Farm, she thought.

"They tend to be."

"I imagine Finn has a lot of old friends who still live here."

"Sure." He shrugged, then got her drift. "Finn never dated anyone seriously, Jules. At least none that I know about. And I sure as hell never saw him get as close to any other woman the way he is with you."

279

"Perhaps no one else in Blue Bayou has needed a bodyguard."

"I don't have to tell you that it's more than that."

"Perhaps." It was going too fast, she thought. Too fast and to where? That was the question she couldn't answer. "It's complicated."

"Now you sound just like Finn. It doesn't have to be complicated, *chère*. Not unless you let it." He linked their fingers together in a casual, friendly sort of way. "You like him, he likes you, neither one of you is married, or engaged, or even going steady." He paused. "You're not, are you?"

"No."

"Then there's no reason for you not to just quit fighting it and pass a good time."

He made it sound so easy, Julia thought, and a rush of relief flooded through her as she watched Finn walking back toward them.

"She's gone."

"Gone?"

"Yeah." Frustration was etched onto the rugged planes of his face. "Like into thin air. There's something else."

Julia was almost afraid to ask. "What?"

"Kendall's going to check more carefully, but she doesn't appear to be on payroll."

"I don't like this," Finn muttered as he and Nate watched Julia climb into the black, single-horse carriage.

Today's dress was rich green and trimmed in dark gold. It might not be made of drapes from the plantation house, it might be satin rather than velvet, but it would be hard for anyone watching not to think of *Gone With the Wind*. Despite Warren Hyatt's denials, even Finn could tell they were trying to tap into that viewership.

Like the scarlet ballgown, the low, round neckline displayed the crest of her creamy breasts; the upsweep the hairdresser had spent nearly an hour creating, only to cover it with a forest green bonnet, showed off a long, slender neck adorned with an emerald ribbon.

As clouds, pregnant with rain began to darken the sky, Finn dragged his hand down his cheek and realized he'd forgotten to shave. What the hell was the woman doing to his mind?

"They're going to get a stunt woman to do the actual driving," Nate reminded him. "And you're going to be right here. What could happen?"

"If there's one thing I've learned over the past thirteen years, it's that anything can happen." Thunder rumbled; lightning forked on the horizon. "And usually does."

He'd no sooner spoken when another thunderclap shook the air with the roar of a cannon. The dappled gray gelding suddenly reared up, front hooves pawing at the air. Before the wrangler could grab the bridle, the horse took off like a bullet, dragging the carriage behind him.

"I fucking knew it!" The reins were dragging ineffectually on the ground. Wishing he'd gone with his gut, which had been screaming that the new scene was not a good idea, Finn took off running, Nate right behind him.

Hoping to cut the horse off before he got to the bayou, Finn caught up with the carriage about fifty yards from the water. Lunging forward, powered by a mighty burst of adrenaline, he managed — just barely — to grab the streaming mane. Using every bit of strength he possessed, he pulled himself up onto the horse's back just as the sky overhead opened up.

"Whoa, dammit!" Mindless of his own safety, he leaned down and gathered up the dragging reins, then yanked on them. Hard.

The damn horse, tearing toward the still water as if trying to outrun the devil himself, didn't stop.

More adrenaline flooded Finn's mind, causing time to seem to crawl to the speed of a televised NFL replay. Hooves hammered into the ground, throwing up clods of soggy turf.

"Goddammit, I said whoa!" No longer caring whether he broke the damn animal's neck, Finn yanked on the reins even harder.

They were less than a yard from the edge of the bayou. An alligator began moving with surprising speed out of the way, sliding into the water like a log that had rolled down the slope.

Two feet.

One.

The muscles in Finn's arms and shoulders were burning. They were down to mere inches when the horse attempted to jump a fallen snag. He cleared it with room to spare, but the axle broke as the carriage bumped jerkily over it. When one of the front yellow wheels fell off, both horse and carriage came to a sudden, bone-rattling stop.

"Thank God." Finn threw the reins to Nate — who'd amazingly stayed right behind them, revealing the lightning speed that had once made him one helluva base stealer. He slid off the broad back and pulled himself into the carriage.

"It's okay," he assured Julia, who had somehow stayed on the seat. Her fingers were gripping the sides of the carriage with such strength Finn had trouble uncurling her fingers. "You're okay."

She was trembling as Finn drew her into his arms.

Nate whistled. "Well, that was certainly close."

"Too damn close." Finn ran his hands, which were none too steady, over her shoulders, down her arms.

"Would you do me a favor?" Julia asked in a ragged voice.

"Anything." With his blood pounding furiously in his ears and his lungs feeling as if they were on fire, Finn would have moved heaven and earth to get her anything her heart desired.

"When I get my voice back enough to grovel, would you please not rub in the fact that I ever complained about you being here in the first place?"

"I won't say a word about it. But I am going to tell Hogan that you're through for the day."

"Oh, you can't do that!" Color returned to her too-pale cheeks, like red roses blooming in a field of snow. "We're already so behind schedule. If we break off shooting, it'll add at least another day before we can wrap."

"In case you didn't notice, you were nearly killed." The bonnet had fallen off during her wild ride. Finn pushed her tumbled hair back from her face, which he framed between his hands. "I'd say that calls for an afternoon off."

"He's right," Randy, who'd caught up to them, said. "You've got a real emotional rape scene coming up, Jules. I need you in top form."

"I'm a professional." She lifted her chin in that way Finn was deciding was more effective than the loudest shout. "I'm not going to fall apart just because of a little accident. Just give me some time to get my hair redone and —"

"Dammit, Julia. We all know you're a bloody trooper," the director complained. "So I'm ordering you to take the rest of the day off."

"My flight leaves for Kathmandu in less than

a week, and I intend to be on it. I also intend to complete all my scenes. Which means there's no time for any days off."

They both looked at Kendall for confirmation.

"We'll resume shooting first thing tomorrow morning," he decreed.

"You realize, of course," Finn muttered as he helped Julia into the Suburban, "that you're all flat out nuts."

"And your point is?"

He shook his head, then touched his fingers to her cheek, skimming them along her jaw, down her throat, and over her shoulders. "You're all scratched up."

"I suppose it's from the tree branches the horse ran beneath."

"Probably." She flinched as he lightly pressed a deepening bruise at the soft flesh where her shoulder connected with her neck. "We should have the ER doc check you out."

"I don't want to go to the hospital."

"Dammit, I don't want to argue with you about this."

"I don't want to argue, either. Because quite honestly, I don't think I have the strength for it. It'll take twenty minutes to get to town, but news travels a lot faster and I'm really not up to running the gauntlet of reporters who'd show up at the ER. Besides, I'm sure all I've got is a few scratches."

He turned the key in the ignition. "I didn't

realize you had a medical license."

"I'm not a doctor," Julia allowed. "But I did play one on TV. A guest spot on *ER* last season," she elaborated at his sideways glance.

Concerned for her well-being, he refused to smile. "Cute. Real cute."

"Please? Surely you learned basic first aid training in the FBI?"

"That was Boy Scouts."

"Let me guess. You were an Eagle Scout."

"Yeah, I was. Want to come up to my place and see my merit badges?"

Her light laughter at one of his rare attempts at humor was warm and rich. He owed Nate big time for bringing her into his life, if only for this brief, fleeting time.

"Unless we try sneaking in through the kitchen, we're not going to get past any reporters staking out the inn," she pointed out as they drove away from Beau Soleil.

Hell. And she really didn't seem all that badly injured.

"You've got a point. I'll take you out to the camp."

"The camp?"

"Where I was staying before Nate brought me back to town to be with you. It's been in my family for generations. It won't be easy for anyone unfamiliar with the area to find, so I doubt we'll be bothered by the press. But if you've got any wound that can't be cleaned with soap and water, the deal's off."

"That sounds wonderful."

Better than wonderful, Julia thought. The chance to be alone with Finn all night long was sublime.

Understanding why Tess Trueheart fell in love with Mountie Dudley Do-Right, she leaned her head against the back of the seat, closed her eyes, listened to the rain pinging on the roof, the swish, swish, swish of the windshield wipers, and smiled with anticipation.

22

Because her velvet carriage shoes were too impractical for walking across the boggy land, Finn carried her to the cabin, the full satin skirt flowing over his arms. Although it was only a few yards from the oyster gravel driveway to the door, they got drenched again on the dash from the Suburban.

He carried her into the bathroom. "Give me a call when you're out of those wet clothes and we'll take care of any cuts."

After he'd left her alone, she'd managed to strip out of the heavy green dress before being stymied.

"Finn?"

"Ready?" He opened the door.

"Almost. But I could use some help again with the wet laces."

Julia was accustomed to wearing far less than the corset and lacy white pantaloons on a set surrounded by men. But this was so, so different. The way Finn was looking at her caused her breath to back up in her lungs.

She had the feeling the same desire was written all over her face. He'd changed into a gray T-shirt and jeans and looked so good. Better than good. He looked big and tough and sexy as hell. If he'd chosen to be an actor instead of an FBI Special Agent, he would have had producers willing to run over their grandmothers to cast him in their films.

"So you do own something else besides that suit."

"It's a little hard to drown worms while wearing a suit."

"Why do I have trouble picturing you fishing?" she murmured with a half smile, proving yet again that she could hit pretty close with those characterizations of hers. "Why did you let me drag you shopping?"

He shrugged. "You'd been working damn hard. So far, Hyatt's written you into every scene. I figured you deserved a break. An evening on the town."

"Our first date."

"I guess you might call it that."

At least it wasn't a total denial. He didn't smile enough, she mused. She'd have to work on that.

"You've taken over my mind." His voice was rough and husky with need, a shared need she felt all the way to the marrow of her bones. He began plucking the pins from her hair, allowing the curls that hadn't escaped during her wild ride to tumble over her shoulders. "I can't stop thinking about all the things I want to do with you."

"I'm having trouble coming up with a reason why that isn't a good thing." She drew in a quick, unsteady breath that revealed he wasn't the only one unsettled by all this.

"That makes two of us." Finn's stomach was tying itself into tight knots. "I want to give you fair warning before this goes any further."

"This?" Seeming amused, she arched a brow.

"You. And me." He put his arms on her shoulders and turned her around, giving him access to the corset ribbons. "And sex."

"Ah. Well, that's certainly laying your cards on the table."

"I'm a straight-talking guy. If you want hearts and flowers and pretty speeches, you'd be better off with Nate." Though if his silver-tongued playboy brother laid one of his clever hands on this woman, he'd have to shoot him.

"I like Nate. He's probably the most naturally charming man I've ever met, but nice, too — which is a bit of a surprise, since most men who are women-magnets are insufferably egotistical." She glanced back over her shoulder, her eyes as green as a tropical lagoon and just as inviting. "But I don't want Nate. I want his big brother."

"It can't go anywhere."

"You think not?"

"I know not."

"Because we're too different?"

"Yeah. For starters."

"Sounds as if I've got a lot of strikes against me," she murmured.

"Not you." How could she think that? "Us. Together."

"You may be right." She sighed. "I've always thought the reason my parents get along so well is that they're so much alike. They share so many things in common."

"Which we don't."

"No, we don't." She brushed some wayward curls away from her face with an uncharacteristically nervous hand. Her breath hitched. "But it doesn't seem to matter all that much right now, does it?"

"No." There was no point in lying. Finn reminded himself that they were both adults. They knew how the game was played. "It doesn't." He drew in a deep breath. "There's something you should probably know about me."

"I know everything I need to know."

"Not everything. You don't know why I'm here. In Blue Bayou."

She glanced back over her bare shoulder. "You didn't come home to go fishing?"

"I hate fishing. I came home because I didn't have a choice. I'm working off four weeks suspension, for beating the shit out of Ronald Lawson."

He could tell she was surprised by that. "When you arrested him?"

"No. When he tried to escape from the hospital where he's being mentally evaluated. It admittedly wasn't the right thing to do, but it was damn satisfying. Then things got political and —" he shrugged — "here I am."

"That's not right." He assumed she was referring to his lapse in control. But it was her turn to surprise him. "That you were suspended for keeping a killer off the streets. Personally, if I were the Director of the FBI, I would have given you a commendation."

"I suppose that's only one of the reasons why you'll never be FBI Director."

"It's just as well," she said on a slight sigh. "Since I can't imagining explaining such a career change to my parents . . . So, is that all? No confessions about beating little old ladies with rubber hoses for operating unlicensed bingo games in nursing homes? Or hauling in people for not paying library fines?"

"The FBI doesn't arrest citizens for overdue library books. And I don't believe I've bludgeoned any old ladies in, oh, at least six, maybe eight months."

"I'm ever so glad to hear that." As the last lace was undone, she turned around. "And now that we've cleared the air, I certainly wouldn't object to your kissing me."

He gathered up a handful of fiery hair as soft as thistledown and felt himself growing hard when he imagined it skimming over his thighs.

He'd been walking around in a constant state of arousal since she'd landed in Louisiana. Need was eating away at his insides. The sensible thing to do would be to shut up and satisfy both their lust and curiosity, so they could move on.

"No strings," he said, wondering which of them he was warning.

"No strings," she agreed, her voice as breathless as his was roughened. "We'll keep things physical. Enjoy this time together and each other; then when it's over, we'll both move on."

"The Bureau makes us get yearly physicals," he volunteered. "I had mine a couple months ago. Everything was okay. So you don't have to worry about any sexually transmitted diseases."

"I had to get one for the studio insurance. Same here."

"Okay. So, now that we've taken care of the health disclosure issue, let me make absolutely sure we're both on the same page, here."

"For heaven's sake, Finn." Her frustrated sigh ruffled a curl that had fallen over her eye. "If you make every woman jump through hoops like this, I'm amazed you get any sex at all."

"Not every woman is looking for a long-term relationship."

"I'm off to Kathmandu in a few days. How long-term can this be?"

Good point. "Okay, so what you're saying is that you're willing to have hot, steamy sex with me for as long as you're here in Blue Bayou, then when the film wraps, we'll just shake hands and you'll trot off to Nepal. No harm, no foul."

"Did anyone ever explain that not every conversation has to be an interrogation? Yes, that's exactly what I'm saying. Except for one point."

"I knew it." Here came the *but,* the loophole in her argument.

"If we're going to be having all that hot, steamy sex, I think a good-bye kiss would be more appropriate than a handshake. We're both adults, Finn. We're unattached, I want you, and you want me. I may be an actress, and I might have grown up on a commune, but inside this Bond Girl body is a very levelheaded woman."

"The Bond Girl body is dynamite." He touched his lips to hers and drew forth a sigh. "But it's the woman inside it that's been driving me crazy." After all, it was the damn wondering that was causing the tension between them. Since sex could never quite equal the fantasy, it was only logical to get it behind them. "I'm going to have you, Julia. And when we're done, your head is going to be anything but level."

She grinned at that. "Promises, promises." Touched her hand to his face. "Does this mean we're finished negotiating the terms of our brief, hot, sexual affair now?"

"Yeah. I guess so." She was making him feel a little foolish for trying to do the right thing.

"Good. And since we don't have any Krispy Kremes handy, how about sealing this deal with a kiss?"

Since he was only human, and male, Finn finally surrendered, deciding to take Nate's advice and just take what he'd been craving for too long.

He covered her mouth with his as he carried her into the bedroom, then stood her beside the same bed in which his grandmother had been born. The bed his mother had been conceived in. The bed a horny teenage Finn had brought girls to, where they'd enthusiastically rolled over the mattress, eagerly learning the basics of sex, but none of the subtleties.

He'd gotten better over the years, more skilled, less selfish, more caring of his partner's needs and desires. But never had anything felt so perfect, so right, as being in this place at this time with this woman.

Instead of the usual fumbling of zippers and buttons, and shirts that got caught up on eager arms, their undressing was like something from the movies, all soft fades and slow dissolves.

"It smells like a garden," she murmured as he laid her down on the mattress.

"That's because it's stuffed with moss and herbs."

She smiled up at him. Sweetly. Endearingly. Looking, he thought, almost like the young girl he imagined must have driven all those farm boys to distraction. "I like it."

"I'm glad."

Since he'd been standing on the edge of this towering cliff for too long, Finn had imagined whenever he'd pictured this moment — which he had, too many times to count — that he'd just dive in headfirst.

But now that the moment he'd tried like hell

to avoid was finally upon him, Finn found that he didn't want to hurry. He wanted to draw things out, to pleasure them both.

He drew her to him, stroking her hair with one hand, while the other cupped her exquisitely lovely face. His lips brushed feathery kisses against her lids, which fluttered shut at his touch, then against her cheeks, and that soft, fragrant place behind her ear.

He touched his mouth to hers, moving back and forth, tasting, teasing. All his edgy hunger faded as he allowed himself to bask in this gentle, undemanding meeting of lips, mingling of breaths.

Time slowed. Then seemed to stop. The past spun away, back into the mists; the future seemed a lifetime away. There was only now. Only her. Only him.

Julia lifted her fingertips to his mouth, tenderly touching his lips. Exploring the harsh lines of his face, skimming over his hair.

Outside the wind moaned, the rain hammered on the tin roof, and thunder grumbled. Inside there were soft sighs, low moans and murmured words.

He nuzzled at her ear and wondered that any skin could be so silky. Nibbled his way across her smooth bare shoulders, then licked a wet path down to her breasts and brought the blood simmering to the surface.

"I want to know what you want." His words vibrated against soft skin. She was so soft. So sexy. So impossibly tempting. "What you need."

"You." She slid her hands down his chest, her fingers skimming though the scattering of dark hair that arrowed down to his cock, which felt as if it might erupt at any moment. "Oh, God, Finn, I want, I need, you."

"We'll have each other soon enough, *chère*." Determined to maintain control, he caught her hand and continued on his leisurely, erotic journey. His mouth grew hot, his hands possessive. "But meanwhile . . ."

Having been ready for fast, flaming sex, Julia found herself falling under the spell of his slow, sensual exploration. He was scattering kisses over her stomach, the inside of her thigh, the back of her knee, which, amazingly, seemed to be directly connected to other, more vital body parts.

She should have known a man like Finn, who focused on the smallest detail, would be thorough. His hands and mouth were everywhere, caressing, feasting, an agonizingly slow journey from her lips to her toes, discovering hidden, secret flashpoints of pleasure. And everywhere his lips touched, he left tormenting trails of fire and ice.

She couldn't bear it much longer. Julia's body craved; her heart hungered. When he pressed his mouth against the heat between her legs, the keen edge of his teeth scraping against the ultra-sensitive flesh, his tongue diving deep, she felt a flood of hot moisture and moaned.

Hungry for him, desperate to taste him as he was her, with a greedy sense of wonder, Julia pulled away, just long enough to shift position on the soft fragrant mattress so they mirrored each other, hands shaping the swell of hips, hungry mouths closing over straining shaft and bud.

His thumb parted the sensitive pink folds, and pressed down at the same time he thrust his fingers deep inside her.

Her eyes flew open and she cried out his name as she shattered.

She was limp. Boneless. A hurricane could have swept through Blue Bayou and she couldn't have moved a muscle to save herself.

"I need to . . ." She couldn't think. Couldn't talk. Her fingers stroked his sex which was, like the rest of him, decidedly oversized. If her mind wasn't scattered into little pieces all over the floor, she might have been concerned about how on earth she was ever going to handle that. "*You* need to . . ."

When she lifted her head off his thigh and pressed her dry lips against the nobbed tip of his penis, gathering in the wet gleaming evidence of his readiness with her tongue, Finn fisted his hand in her hair.

"Don't worry about me. For now, just relax. And take."

How did he expect her to relax when he was creating such havoc in every atom of her body?

He shifted their positions yet again so she was lying on her back, looking up at him, wondering if she'd ever seen a more perfect male specimen. He was a large man, but had not allowed himself to soften. She couldn't detect an ounce of superfluous flesh on his body; he reminded her of Michelangelo's *David* that she'd seen in the Accadamia in Florence.

But this man was not marble. He was strong, hard muscle, dark skin that smelled of musk, rain, vaguely of horse, and male power. And for this stolen time together in Blue Bayou, he was hers.

He braced himself on his elbows and, looking into Julia's eyes, slowly lowered himself onto her, the weight of that magnificent body pressing her into the mattress. Julia loved the strength of his long legs, the beguiling power emanating from his every pore, the taste of herself on his lips as he kissed her — hard and long and deep.

He slid his fingers into her again, widening her, preparing her. Then he rubbed his penis against her still tingling clitoris, first back and forth, then in tiny circles, refusing to stop even when she whimpered and begged for release. She twisted beneath him, hands gathering up fistfuls of sheet, inarticulate pleas falling from lips he was bruising with his kisses.

But there was no need for words. A Trappist monk, cloistered for a century, would have had no trouble hearing the need in her ragged voice.

Her climax lasted longer this time, like waves rolling onto the shore, crashing against granite cliffs.

"Beautiful," he said in a rough sound that was half groan, half sigh. "I could watch you like that forever." He bent his head, brushed his lips against hers as he took his cock in his hand and guided it into her welcoming warmth. The first touch of flesh against flesh was like an electrical shock.

"Please don't stop," she murmured when he paused. Her hair looked like tongues of flame as she tossed her head on the pillow. "I want you to take me, Finn." As lovely as those earlier climaxes were, and they had taken a bit of the edge off her hunger, she still wanted all of him. And now.

She closed her eyes and bit her lip as the broad flare of his penis pushed past the opening.

"Hell. I'm hurting you."

"Never." She exhaled a breath and pressed a palm against his lower back to prevent him from pulling out. "I love it." She arched her back, lifting her hips even higher and exhaled another deep, soothing breath. "May I please have some more, sir?"

He laughed, the sound rumbling from his chest like friendly thunder. "Since you ask so politely, how can I refuse?"

He pressed on, inch by solid inch, filling her, stretching her.

"Ah," he breathed as her body responded, wrapping around him like a greedy fist to draw him in even deeper. "You feel so good, baby. All hot and wet . . . Hold on."

His mouth covered hers in a hard, mind-blinding kiss as he thrust the rest of the way into her, all the way to the hilt. He was thick and full and vital, filling her body as he'd already filled her heart.

Finn stilled for a moment, giving her body time to adjust to the erotic invasion. "You okay?"

"Better than okay," she said in a pleased little sigh. "I've never felt so good in my life."

He smiled at that, against her mouth, and said, "How about going for a personal best?"

He began to move, rocking against her, slowly at first, then faster, harder, deeper, punctuating each thrust with her name.

This time they came together. Julia cried out against his neck; her legs tightened around his hips. She could feel his thighs go rigid, the contractions that convulsed inside her, his release, the spasms racking his body in a vigorous series of pulses.

She didn't know how long they lay there, chest to chest, legs and arms entwined, hearts beating in unison, her body sparking with sharp spasms of aftershocks, listening to the rain on the roof and Finn's labored breathing against her neck.

If the world came to an end this very minute, she couldn't complain. Because she'd already been to Paradise.

"I didn't know you spoke French."

"I don't." He touched his lips to hers with a gentleness that belied the power he'd just brought to their lovemaking.

"My parents believed in widening horizons," she said against his mouth as he amazingly, started things stirring inside her all over again. "I could speak three languages before my tenth birthday."

"Good for you."

"My point is . . . oh, God, I can't believe what you do to me," she sighed when his hand trailed up her inner thigh. "Anyway, I know French. And you were speaking it."

"It's Cajun French." He gave her a surprisingly playful nip on the chin. "I was nearly eight when I started learning it, so it doesn't come as naturally to me as it does to Jack and Nate."

Then there were all the years at the Bureau when he'd worked to rid his voice of any trace of his bayou roots, wanting, needing to fit the FBI's All-American prototype. Finn closed his mind to his work; determined that this stolen night be only about them. "It only comes out when I disengage my brain."

"You ought to disengage your brain more often, because I like it. It's sexy. And all those other things you said you were planning to do to me were pretty good, too." She ran a finger down the side of his face, dipping into the cleft in his chin. "Tell me some more."

"Why don't I just show you?" he suggested.

"Oh, good idea." Her arms wrapped around his neck, surrendering to the fantasy, to Finn.

23

Although the idea had originally bothered him, Finn had wanted her from the beginning. And now he'd had her — again and again, and it had been better than he could have imagined. The problem was, as he lay with her in his arms this morning, listening to the bayou come awake outside, Finn idly wondered what it would be like to keep her.

Dangerous thinking, that. Impossible thoughts. The deal they'd made was for no strings. No commitments. And he was a man of his word.

"Well," she murmured as the bedroom began to light up with a rosy glow, "that certainly should have done it."

"Yeah." He touched his lips to the top of her head.

"These next days should be much easier, don't you think? Without all that sexual tension between us?"

"Yeah." She had a little birthmark, shaped almost like a heart, at the back of her neck. Finn bent his head and kissed it.

"Where did you get that scar?" she asked.

"Scar?" He nuzzled his face against her breasts.

"The long, dangerous-looking one on the

inside of your thigh."

"Oh, that." Since it wasn't his favorite subject, he skimmed the tip of his tongue across her nipple in an attempt to distract. "It's nothing."

"Finn." She arched her back, offering that creamy flesh to him even as she refused to drop the question. "I want to know."

"It wasn't anything." He switched to the other breast and felt her shiver beneath his mouth. "I just got in the way of a knife." He didn't mention that knife had been intended for the president, and he'd managed to get the would-be assassin before the guy could get to the protective ring of Secret Service guys.

She leaned back to look at him, breaking the warm contact. "You said you joined the FBI because you didn't need the adrenaline rush of being a cop, so I haven't thought about your work as dangerous."

"It's usually not." Neither was he about to bring up the Bureau's Hall of Honor for agents lost in the line of duty. "Sometimes things just happen."

"Things like being stabbed."

"Yeah." The mood had definitely changed, and not for the better. Sighing, Finn picked up his watch, which was lying on the bedside table. "It's getting late. I'd better shower."

"Would you like some company? After all, I was brought up to be an environmentalist, and saving the world's resources — like water — is very high on our agenda."

Finn was amazed at how little it took to make him want her all over again. "Well, if we're saving the world . . ." He scooped her from the bed and carried her into the bathroom. As the room filled with steam and his head filled with her, Finn decided there was a lot to be said for environmentalism.

The rape scene Finn had not been looking forward to watching was filmed just before they were to break for lunch.

Langley, in his role of the Yankee captain, caught Fancy's arm as she entered the front hall, which boasted a mural depicting the story of the Acadians being driven from Nova Scotia and ending up in the Louisiana swamp. It was one of the hallmarks of the house, which Jack and Nate had gone to a lot of trouble and expense to restore.

"Where the hell have you been?" the actor demanded.

She pulled free, removed her bonnet, and tossed it onto a table. "Out."

When Langley's eyes, filled with scorn and lust, crawled over her, Finn, who wasn't wild about the fact the guy kept getting to put his hands all over Julia, begrudgingly admired his acting talent. It was hard to believe that the edgy, dangerous army officer was actually a flirtatious ex-baseball player from Tupelo.

"You were with a man," the Yankee accused.

"Don't be silly." She brushed by him and headed toward the stairs. "Perhaps Yankee women are different, but we Southern ladies are quite content with our own company. We don't always need to have a man around, telling us what to do."

"You don't quite understand, do you, Fancy?" He snagged her arm again and jerked her back toward him. "So long as I'm here, you damn *will* have a man telling you what to do. Because you're under house arrest."

"Why fiddle-dee-dee," she tossed the words Finn had watched her fight against saying at him. "That little old detail must have just slipped my silly female mind."

"Don't waste your time playing the fluttery Southern belle. Your mind's a damn steel trap," he countered. He pulled her against him, hard. "As for your body . . ." He trailed his fingers down her throat, over the crest of her breasts. "It gives a man ideas."

Even knowing it was coming, Finn flinched when she slapped the actor. "Take your ideas and your filthy Yankee hands somewhere else, Captain."

She lifted her skirts and was nearly to the first landing when he caught up with her. When he hit her and Julia/Fancy fell crumbled at the Yankee's feet, Finn's jaw tightened, even knowing that the actor had pulled the punch.

"*Mon Dieu,* that looked real," Nate murmured.

"Yeah."

His brother slanted him a look. "You okay?"

"Sure," he lied through his teeth. "Why wouldn't I be?"

"I sure as hell would have a hard time watching someone mistreat any woman. 'Specially one I had feelings for."

"They're just acting." Finn unclenched his hands, which had fisted.

When the damn Yankee ripped the front of the dress — which had been designed to tear away — down to her waist, he heard a low snarl and realized it had come from him.

"Down boy," Nate warned. "They're just acting."

"Yeah." Finn exhaled a breath and forced himself to stay where he was.

But damn, it was difficult as he watched one of the Yankee's hands grasp her breast. When the other reached beneath her skirt, he knew he'd never be able to look at Beau Soleil's staircase the same way again.

She was fighting him, kicking her firm, smooth legs, pounding her fists against his back, twisting her head to avoid the harsh demands of his mouth. He backhanded her again, once, twice, a third time, knocking the fight out of her long enough to clamp both her wrists in one hand and yank them high above her head. She tugged helplessly, but could not free herself.

"That's it, keep fighting, love," Finn heard Hogan saying. "You may be a slut, but you've always chosen who you give it away to. You've too much Southern pride to allow yourself to be taken without your consent."

Knowing the director could give instructions without worrying about the boom microphone picking up the sound because this part of the scene would be scored, Finn wondered what the hell kind of music went with rape. Lawson had favored chants and Japanese drummers. The search of his mansion had uncovered the CDs in the stereo in his media room, and speakers in the walls and ceiling of his dungeon.

Finn felt the rage rising up again. Rage and despair, which were a goddamn pisspoor, not to mention dangerous, combination.

"You shoot this guy and you'll kill my reelection chances." Nate's words might suggest a joke, but the low, serious voice was nothing like his usual easy tone.

"Shit," Finn muttered as the camera went in for a close-up of her lovely, tortured face. He shoved his left hand, which had instinctively gone to the grip of the Glock at the back of his jeans, deep into his pocket, rattling change. "I fucking hate this."

"You're not responsible for those girls' deaths, *cher.*"

Not at all happy that anyone, even his brother, could read his thoughts and his heart so well, Finn shot Nate a hard, sideways look.

"I wasn't talking about them."

It was the sympathy in those unusually sober eyes that got to Finn. "Weren't you?"

"No." He jammed his right hand deep into the other pocket and was grateful when Nate didn't challenge his lie.

"Are you sure you're all right?" Julia asked for the third time.

"Of course." Or he would be, if people quit harping on it. "And shouldn't I be asking that of you?" Finn took hold of her hand and felt another low surge of anger rumbling through him. "Your wrist is bruised."

She shrugged. "I'm a redhead. I bruise easily."

"I was on the verge of shooting Langley," he surprised himself by admitting.

"You're not serious." Her wide eyes scanned his face.

Finn shrugged, wondering grimly why the hell his brain disengaged whenever he was around this woman. "No." He wasn't totally convinced himself that he wasn't serious, and that worried him. Just a little. "Besides, as Nate so succinctly pointed out, I'd ruin my brother's chances for a second term if I murdered some hotshot Hollywood actor."

"Well, that's certainly a good reason not to commit homicide." She managed a smile at that, even though her eyes continued to hold little seeds of worry.

"Look, I have something to say to you," Finn said awkwardly. "But I don't want you to get the wrong idea. Because it doesn't have anything to do with that scene you just finished." The scene that had taken sixteen goddamn takes and ground his nerves to dust. "Well, not in any prurient way."

"There's something to be said for prurient. Under the right circumstances. With the right person."

"Remember what I said about wanting to ravish you?"

"I do and you did. A woman would be unlikely to forget the most memorable night of her life, Finn."

"It *was* good, wasn't it?" He allowed himself to get momentarily sidetracked by his own memories.

"The best. And you know what? I'm discovering I'm insatiable. Because I want to do it again."

"That's sort of along the lines I was thinking." He paused. "I want to be alone with you. Now."

"Thank God." A half laugh tumbled out in a shuddering breath of shared need. "But we don't have time."

"Not to do it right." He closed his hand overs hers. "But I at least want to kiss you. Hard and deep and long. And while you might be used to public performances, I'd prefer not to have an audience."

When he lifted her hand and kissed her palm, a dark and dangerous thrill skimmed through Julia. "I left my script in the trailer," she said breathlessly. "I need it to rehearse my lines for the next scene, whatever it turns out to be." The way Warren and Charles kept switching anything around, it could be any one of the handful still left to film, and endless ones yet unwritten.

As they crossed the yard to where the trailers were parked, Julia was aware they were being observed by most of the crew and a great many of the extras.

She also realized they were undoubtedly fueling the tabloid coverage of their relationship. But right now, with need battering away at her, she decided that since they were already so blatantly ripping off Margaret Mitchell's classic novel, she might as well take yet another page from Scarlett O'Hara's book, and worry about the consequences tomorrow.

They'd no sooner entered the trailer when Finn grasped her waist, lifted her off her feet, pressed her back against the door, and captured her mouth.

Staggered by his heat and speed, Julia put her hands on his shoulders, wrapped her legs around his hips and hung on for dear life. His mouth was hot and thrillingly greedy, his fingers dug deeply, possessively into the flesh beneath her dress. Flesh that was burning so furnace hot as she slid down his hard, aroused body, willing her legs to hold her, she was amazed the material hadn't burst into flame.

Her head spun, her heart hammered as her mouth opened to his; when he thrust a hand beneath the yards of billowy emerald material, her blood began flowing molten in her veins.

"God, I love how hot you get," he ground out as he cupped her with one of his large hands. "And wet."

Needing to touch Finn as he was touching her, Julia reached between them, but the hand that wasn't creating havoc between her trembling thighs caught hold of her wrist.

"It's not that I'm trying to recreate that scene on the stairs, but if I let you touch me, *chère,* you're never going to make it back to the set," he warned. His deep voice, harsh with hunger, vibrated through her like a tuning fork.

He captured the other wrist and lifted them both above her head, effectively holding her prisoner. "You know that, don't you? That I'd never force you. And that watching you act that scene with Langley wasn't what made me hot."

"Of course I know that," she managed to say as his free hand coursed up her inner thighs, only the thin layer of her ruffled pantaloons between them.

She drew in a sharp, expectant breath as his hand dipped beneath the waistband. "Because I know you," she managed in a weak, thready voice that sounded nothing at all like her usual strong, confident one.

She'd been so, so wrong when she'd accused him of being clueless about women. The way he'd driven her to more orgasms than she'd ever had in one night, along with the way he was skimming gathered moisture over her outer lips, making her burn, making her ache, proved that this was a man who knew how to please.

A jolt of lightning shot through her when he skimmed a fingertip over her clitoris. When he began moving it up and down, the slight abrasion feeling like the finest grade sandpaper, she arched her body toward him, needing more.

"Finn . . . Please . . ."

"Just relax, *chère*." His mouth took hers again. When he rubbed the heel of his hand against her, her body began to throb, drenching the cotton beneath his stroking touch. "Let it come."

As if she had any choice, Julia thought as he pressed harder, faster, causing her breath to clog in her lungs. When he slid first one, then a second finger deep within her, she choked out a whimpering little sound of need.

Her body clenched at him, ripping a groan from deep in his chest, assuring her that despite his seemingly enormous control, Finn was every bit as needy as her.

She closed her eyes, surrendering to the erotic sensations ricocheting through her. Those treacherous fingers were deep inside her, moving in and out. In and out. In. Out.

All it took was a final, wicked skim of a fingertip to send her into the void. Arching against him, clinging to him like a drowning woman. Julia sobbed out Finn's name as the climax shuddered through her.

Drained, she sagged against him; if he hadn't released her hands to catch her, she would have fallen to the floor.

"Oh, my God. That was definitely one of the best ideas you've had yet. You know the only thing that bothers me about this?"

"What?"

"We wasted so much time trying to pretend we weren't attracted to each other. Do you realize how many more times we could have done this?"

"We'll just have to make up for quantity with quality."

She laughed as she framed his face with her hands and lifted her lips to his lightly, more promise than proper kiss. "Absolutely."

24

After making some quick repairs to her hair and makeup, and ensuring that her legs would indeed hold her, Julia went back to work, only to learn that Charles had called yet another meeting in Beau Soleil's magnificent library.

"Julia's right about us running late," the producer announced from behind a wide cherry desk Julia suspected was a genuine period antique. "We're too far behind. We're going to have to return to the original script."

As Julia tried to recall which one that was, Warren bristled. "You're the one who keeps demanding major changes and new scenes."

"You'll just have to make the scenes we've got left more layered, so they reveal more changes in the plot and character arcs. There's no reason why we need all these characters. Like that blond housemaid you've written in, who's going to be serving Fancy breakfast in bed tomorrow. Why the hell do we need that scene? Other than the fact that you're fucking the actress?"

"My personal relationship with Lorelei Fairchild has nothing to do with this," Warren argued, a hot flush rising from his collar. His eyes, behind the thick lenses of his glasses, were uncharacteristically hard and resolute. "Lorelei just happens to be a natural-born actress and I think she could add a lot to the story line. But the main reason I wrote that scene was to give us a chance to actually show Fancy in bed with her stepfather. So far we've only alluded to it."

"The audience isn't dense, mate. They've got the picture," Randy said.

"True," Kendall said. "Still . . ." He rubbed his double chin and turned toward Warren. "I suppose it would be stronger if we actually show her willing to do whatever it takes to save Belle Terre. Including sleeping with a man she detests."

"A man who's feeding information and supplies to the Yankees," Warren reminded him. "A man she's plotting to kill."

"I don't buy it," Julia complained. "Okay, maybe the audience can understand her need to save not only the home that's been in her family for generations, but her way of life, as well. But you're making her horribly unsympathetic having her sleep with a man she despises and intends to murder."

"Ah, but that's her dilemma," Kendall said. "She doesn't despise him anymore. She loves him. Which makes her more conflicted about her intention to do murder."

"She loves him? Since when?" Julia snatched a script from the desk and began leafing through it, trying to find some part she might have missed. That's what she got for being so distracted. She'd never had a problem concentrating until now. Until Finn.

"Since I just decided it," Kendall said, looking more than a little pleased with himself. "The war's winding to an inglorious end, her stepfather's been promised land and property, but he's wily enough to realize that he's already suspected of dealing with the other side. Which is why he's going to have to start winning people over. Beginning with Fancy."

"Why Fancy?" Margot said a little petulantly. "His wife was important in society before he married her. Why doesn't he just stay faithful? That will still allow him to end up with her property when the war's over."

"Because it's becoming more and more obvious that the North's going to win the war. Which means she'll no longer own any property," the producer said patiently. "It'll become the spoils of war."

Julia wondered if she should be worried when she could actually, almost, follow his line of reasoning. "But he can still end up with it because the victorious U.S. government is going to give Belle Terre to him for services rendered?" she asked.

"That's it." Warren beamed at her as if she'd just correctly answered the million dollar question.

"But his wife's blood runs Confederate gray," Felissa argued. "Once *she* discovers he's been dealing with the enemy, why won't she rally their neighbors against him? I may not have a college degree, but even I know lynchings were not uncommon after the war."

"She won't be able to rally anyone, because he and Fancy are going to make sure she isn't going to be alive."

"You're going to kill the wife?" Margot looked less than pleased by this latest twist.

"Oh, it's a crackerjack of a death scene," Randy assured her. "You're going to love it."

"Are you saying Fancy's turned traitor now, too?" Julia scowled at that new twist.

"It's a soap," the producer reminded her. "Which means no one is who they seem and the plot can turn on a dime."

"Wait just a damn minute!" Margot said as an unpalatable thought occurred to her. "If the wife is going to be murdered, does that mean my modern day character will be killed off, too?"

"Of course not," the producer said, not quite convincingly. "You're vital to the show. Especially if Julia insists on leaving."

"I *am* leaving," Julia said under her breath. What did she have to do? Have the words tattooed on her forehead?

"What about *my* character?" Felissa demanded. "What's she supposed to be doing while all this is going on?"

"She's going to almost die in childbirth. But fortunately for her, Fancy saves her life by delivering the baby."

"How am I going to have a baby? I haven't been pregnant."

"No problem." The producer waved her complaint away with a pudgy hand. "We'll simply tweak the time line, to allow more months to have passed."

"She hasn't seen her fiancé since the beginning of the war," Julia said, backing Felissa up. "And there's been no indication she's slept with any other man. Soap or not, it would be nice to have some semblance of continuity. If the war's almost over, this has to be the world's longest pregnancy. Whose baby is it? And what's she carrying? A baby elephant?"

"Sarcasm doesn't suit you, love," Randy chided. "As to who the father is, we'll just keep the audience guessing."

"Which means you don't know," Felissa accused.

"It's Warren's job to figure it out." A pinky ring flashed gold in the sunlight streaming through the French doors as Charles waved away her complaint. "My job is to come up with plot devices that resonate with an audience. And childbirth is right up there with weddings and death scenes."

"I'll grant you that," Julia said. "But I thought you wanted to cut back on scenes. What you're suggesting will only add more." She was never going to get to Kathmandu at this rate.

"Not that many. We'll just work a little later each day. You said you wanted Fancy to be more sympathetic," he reminded her. "What's more sympathetic than delivering a baby in the middle of a battle outside the plantation house?"

"Reviewers are going to think we've gone flat out nuts," Julia complained.

"It's the audience that counts. And they've proven over the years they'll buy anything where your character's concerned. Besides, what do you care? You keep saying you're not going to be here."

"I'm not."

"Then it's none of your concern. All you have to worry about is showing up on time and knowing your part. Because the better you've memorized your lines, the faster the shoot will go and the sooner you'll be on the way to your new life."

Ten minutes later Julia was still fuming, walking off her frustration, muttering about the ridiculousness.

"Thank you," she said to Finn as she stopped at the water's edge several hundred yards from Beau Soleil.

"For what?"

"For not offering advice."

"Are you kidding? All I know about your business is that you have to be nuts to want to do it. No offense intended," he tacked on quickly.

"None taken. Because it's true." She folded her arms and sighed as she watched a trio of blue herons walking along on their stilted legs.

One ducked his feathered head into the water and speared a small striped water snake, which disappeared into his long beak.

"It's just so frustrating." She sighed and willed the anger to drain out of her. He was standing behind her; when she leaned back against him, he looped his arms lightly around her waist and leaned his cheek against the top of her head.

"I might not be an expert on show business, but I do think I'm getting a handle on how to take your mind off it."

Her lips quirked. He'd loosened up so much since they'd met. Or perhaps she'd quit expecting the worst from him.

"Think so, huh?"

He turned her toward him, drew her against his chest. "I know so." His lips nibbled at hers, tasting, teasing. She'd just gone up on her toes, twining her arms around his neck, when the distant roar of a diesel engine captured her reluctant attention.

"Oh, no."

"What now?" She felt him tense, as if prepared to protect her against invading vandals.

"They're here. Freedom and Peace." How could her parents' impending visit have slipped her mind? Because, she thought, as the huge fancifully painted bus drove into view, her mind was filled with Finn. "My parents."

After exchanging greetings and kisses and being enveloped in her father's arms like a cub embraced by papa bear, Julia said a silent little prayer and introduced her parents to Finn, and him to them. Her father was dressed in his usual black shirt and jeans. Like country singer Johnny Cash, who owned one of his paintings, Freedom had sworn to wear the color until no American lived in poverty. He'd added a touch of color since Julia saw him last: a small red, white and blue Stars-and-Stripes patch over his chest pocket.

His hair, which he'd tied back with a leather thong, was long and beginning to be streaked with gray, which was also a surprise since she'd never actually thought of her father as a grown-up. He was a long way from being old yet, but it was odd to think of him no longer being young.

Peace, on the other hand, could have been Julia's slightly older sister. Her hair was still a burnished auburn, her body, beneath the flowing sunset color tunic and skirt, as shapely as ever. The faint lines extending out from her soft, moss-hued eyes were evidence that she smiled easily and often.

"Mr. Callahan." She extended a slender hand. "We've so been looking forward to meeting you."

"It's good to meet you, too, Mrs. Summers."

"Oh, please, call me Peace," she said, her melodious voice singing like a silver bell. "All our friends do." She tilted her head. "You're an earth sign."

"So I've been told."

"And Julia's air."

"Is that so?"

"Yes. Everything's individualistic, of course, and I'd have to do your chart, but they can often balance each other beautifully."

"Earth signs can also tether airs to the ground," Freedom growled. He extended his hand, which was scarred and nicked from years of chiseling his famous chairs before turning to paint and canvas. "Callahan." His tone was frankly skeptical, his eagle-sharp dark eyes openly appraising this man he wasn't yet prepared to welcome into his daughter's life. "So, you've known our Julia long, have you?"

"Daddy," Julia murmured.

"Not as long as I'd like," Finn said, surprising Julia by lacing their fingers together at his side in a show of solidarity.

"Isn't that lovely, dear." Peace's soft eyes pleaded with her husband to make nice. "I remember you saying much the same thing to my father."

"I don't recall anything like that." He didn't take his gaze from Finn.

"Oh, you did." Julia thought it was the first time in her entire life she'd heard her mother fudge the truth. "The day I brought you home to meet my parents."

Family lore had Julia's maternal grandfather, a San Francisco investment banker, less than thrilled when his daughter, Katherine, broke

324

off her marriage to a corporate lawyer for Jonathon Summers, a love-bead–wearing, pot-smoking, long-haired hippie Deadhead Berkeley war protestor who had the nerve to claim he was going to support the two of them by carving furniture from discarded grapevines.

The older man had hit the roof, thrown them out of his Pacific Heights mansion, cut off Katherine's trust funds, and refused all contact with the couple until Julia's birth melted the ice he'd encased himself in since that day he'd stubbornly let his daughter walk out of his home and his life.

"No." Freedom had never been one to shade the truth. Not even for social niceties. "What I told him was that he was an uptight, pampered Republican establishment capitalist crook living in the lap of luxury off the backs of honest, hard-working laborers."

"Well, there was that," Peace allowed, sharing a faint smile with Julia. "But you did inform him that we were going to spend the rest of our lives together, whether he liked it or not."

"And I meant every word. Including the crook part, but especially the part about the rest of our lives." Julia watched the male antagonism he'd been radiating toward Finn soften as he looked down at his partner of more than thirty years.

Then he returned his attention to Finn, who appeared respectful, but not a bit intimidated. "I think the bus may have a leak in its air hose.

I don't suppose you'd know anything about engines."

"A bit." It wasn't exactly a lie. Finn had helped his brother change the spark plugs on Jack's old GTO back when they'd been kids.

"Then let's go take a look at it." Freedom turned and walked toward the fancifully painted home on wheels, clearly expecting Finn to follow.

"It'll be all right," Finn assured Julia, easily reading her concern. He touched his hand to her cheek, bent his head, and brushed a quick kiss against her lips, which had the power to curl her toes.

"Your Finn seems nice," Peace murmured. "His aura is very intense, but that can be a good thing. So long as all that force is directed toward good."

"Oh, it is," Julia assured her.

"Of course it is. That would be obvious to someone without any intuition." She combed her hand through the slide of hair that fell to her waist in the same style she'd worn as a young girl handing her heart to a man who'd bring his own brand of force into her life. "I'm also relieved to see that you've given up dating weak, undependable men."

"They were artists. Creative men. Like Daddy."

"Whether they were creative is for others to judge. But believe me, darling, they were nothing like your father. It's possible for a man

326

to be artistic and strong. Your father is. They were not."

Good point. "So how come you never mentioned that before?"

"Because we all have to make our own choices and mistakes. I'm also finding it amusing that you'd follow in my footsteps when you decided to fall in love."

"I'm hardly following in your footsteps, since I'm certainly not in love with Finn." Julia might have grown up in an open environment, but she wasn't prepared to discuss her lustful feelings for Finn with her mother.

"Whatever you say, dear," Peace said mildly. She ran her graceful hand down Julia's riot of curls. "My father was less than pleased I'd fallen in love with a bohemian spirit. I doubt yours is thrilled with the idea of his only daughter giving her heart to an FBI agent."

"I haven't given anyone my heart," she insisted. "And how could you tell he's FBI? The tabloid didn't mention him being a Special Agent. And besides, he isn't wearing a suit."

Peace laughed at that. "Darling, the man doesn't have to wear a suit to reveal who he is. It's as plain as those riveting ice blue eyes."

"Damn. Finn said it wouldn't work," Julia muttered.

"Is everything all right?" Her mother's smile faded as she looked at Julia with maternal concern. "Is your stalker back? Is that how you and Finn happen to be together?"

"I don't know." She was not surprised that her mother had put two and two together. "I've received a couple of strange notes, so Finn's watching out for me as a favor to his brother, who's the mayor. But I can't believe it's anything really serious." She glanced warily over toward the back of the bus, where both men appeared intrigued by the engine. "What do you think Daddy will do?"

"I have no idea. Which is one of the more interesting things about living with him. However, there are two things I do know."

"What are those?" Julia asked apprehensively. A crew from *Entertainment Tonight* was arriving in Blue Bayou this afternoon, so a fistfight between her father and her lover was not what she needed right now.

"Your father has never been anything but fair. And," Peace's speculative gaze skimmed over the men, "your Finn can certainly handle anything Freedom plans to dish out."

"Oh, God," Julia moaned.

Freedom had never minced words. He did not now. "You realize you're not fooling anyone."

"I'm not trying to," Finn said mildly.

"I'm assuming my daughter knows you're a Special Agent."

"Yessir. She does."

"So, she's in on the subterfuge, too?"

"It's not exactly subterfuge," Finn hedged.

"She wanted to protect you and your wife."

"Us? How?"

"She's received some letters that may or may not be threatening."

"Her stalker's back?"

"I don't know," Finn said honestly. "But I promise you, sir, if that's the case, I won't let anything happen to your daughter."

Freedom gave him a long hard look. "I suppose I'll have to trust your word on that. At least you look up to the job of keeping Julia safe." He rubbed his jaw, his gaze still on the engine. "Are you sleeping with her?"

"I don't want to be rude, sir, but I believe that would be between Julia and me."

"She's just a baby."

"Your baby, perhaps," Finn allowed. "But she's a grown woman. Capable of making her own choices."

"Like sleeping with an FBI agent." Freedom dragged his hands down his face. "Christ. If I was a religious man, I'd believe this was divine retribution."

"For past crimes?" Finn hoped they weren't going to get into that. He really wasn't up to a lecture on the excesses of the government against free-thinkers.

"In a way." Freedom finally glanced over at Finn. "Peace's father was Winston Stanford. As in Stanford, Worthington, Madison, Young and Moore."

Finn exhaled a slight whistle. The man was

one of the most prestigious names in investment banking and well known for his philanthropy. "As well as Stanford University."

"None other, though he's a distant relative several times removed from Leland Stanford. Julia's mother was a student at the university when she met me at a peace rally."

"I'll bet the guy was tickled pink when she brought you home to dinner."

"We didn't make it through the cocktail hour." Because it had been decades since he'd spent a miserable week drying her tears and assuring her that everything would be all right, Freedom smiled a bit at the memory. "He mellowed once Julia was born." That brought up another thought. "Are you planning to get my daughter pregnant?"

"Not intentionally."

"Not intentionally," Freedom murmured. "Do you have any intentions at all where my daughter's concerned?"

"I intend to keep her safe until she leaves for Kathmandu. If you're talking about any future between us, I care about your daughter a great deal, but I doubt that's in the cards."

They were too different, their lives worlds apart. Even if he was prepared to settle down, which he wasn't, Julia Summers would be the last person he could imagine leading a life of comfortable domesticity. Especially just when her already strong career was about to take off.

"Well." Freedom thought on that for a long, silent moment as they both went back to studying the diesel engine with all its belts and wires and hoses. "At least I'll have to give you points for honesty."

"I don't lie, sir. And I'd never lie to Julia."

"Dammit, don't call me sir." Freedom shot him his most irritated look yet. "The name's Freedom." He shook his head and made a disgusted sound. "FBI," he muttered.

Another silence settled over them.

"So," Finn said finally, "did you really bring me over here to talk about the engine?"

"Hell, no."

"Good. Because I don't know a damn thing about it."

"Neither do I." Freedom slammed down the fire-breathing-dragon–painted hood. "It's been ages since I had a good Cajun meal. You know any place around here that's decent?"

"Cajun Cal's is as close as you're going to find to my *maman*'s cooking."

"That may not be saying much. How good a cook was your mother?"

"The best, sir. Freedom," Finn corrected at the pointed look, managing to get the name out without choking.

"Then let's go."

They were headed back to the women when Freedom stopped and shot Finn a look that would have made any FBI interrogating agent proud. "Let's get one thing straight, Special

Agent Callahan. You hurt my baby girl and I'll track you down, wherever the hell you are, and rip your miserable cop heart out with my bare hands."

"Sounds reasonable to me," Finn agreed.

25

For Julia, who'd been so anxious for her time in Louisiana to hurry up and end, it was as if the final days of shooting had grown unwanted wings. They were working longer hours, starting at dawn and working long after sundown, after which she'd return to the suite, take a bubble bath Finn would run for her, then lie moaning on the bed while he massaged the day's tension out of her, which usually turned into an entirely different kind of tension reliever.

The nights were also far too short. Although they shared a bed, nestled like spoons, Julia feeling warm and happy and secure in his arms, she came to resent the time she had to waste sleeping.

Peace and Freedom had remained in Louisiana, but didn't spend much time at Beau Soleil. Her father, declaring that the bayou had stimulated his muse, took his easel out into the swamp each day, capturing the rich wealth of nature of the mysterious moss-draped land and in his own bold strokes way, revealing the deep currents that ran beneath seemingly still dark waters.

While Julia's father painted, her mother talked herbs and potions with local traiteurs, whose magical healing ways went back centuries.

Besides the dinner at Cajun Cal's, which was every bit as good as promised, they'd had lunch together once, and dinner twice. Julia was relieved that Freedom and Finn had forged some sort of truce. The energy surrounding them reminded her a bit of how her childhood marmalade cat, Pussy Galore, had responded when she'd brought home a mangy stray that seemed to be part Pekinese, part Dachshund, and, her detractors had said, part drowned rat. After a bit of hissing and snarling, Pussy had reluctantly allowed the dog into the fold but usually kept one eye on her. Just in case.

They were coming down to the final wire. Unless Charles changed his mind yet again, there was only one more scene to shoot. Then came the wrap party, which everyone really needed after such a grinding schedule, then at last she'd be going back to L.A. And finally, Kathmandu.

"I'm going to miss this," she murmured as she and Finn sat facing one another in the tub.

"They don't have bathtubs in Nepal?" Her legs were stretched out between his. He lifted her foot and began doing some clever magic with his thumbs against her arch.

"I'm sure they do." She leaned her head back and closed her eyes, her mind drifting, her body melting as he switched to her other foot. "But I doubt they come so well accessorized. If you ever decide to leave the FBI, you could definitely have a career turning women to mush."

"Nah," he decided as he abandoned her feet to trace the contours of her breasts with his fingertips. "As appealing as I may have found that idea in my twenties, I guess I've just become a one-woman gigolo."

"I meant you could give massages for a living." Her senses were pleasantly fogging.

"I'm not sure it'd be as much fun, getting paid. Besides," desire sparked as his thumbs skimmed over her nipples, "you're the only woman I want to put my hands on."

He'd changed so much, she mused as her mind floated and her body warmed beneath those large, wickedly clever hands that had learned all her sensual secrets and discovered more she hadn't even known were possible.

At first, the only time he'd seemed to lower his barricades had been in bed. It was the one place he'd allowed his emotions free rein, making Julia occasionally wonder what her chances were of keeping him in bed forever.

Still, although the walls would go back up again each morning, they didn't seem as high or as thick as they'd initially been. He'd never be as gregarious as his brother Nate. Or as devilish as his brother Jack was said to be. But he'd begun to loosen up, laughing easily and often; touching her hair, her face, holding hands with her in front of the crew, even in front of the *En-*

tertainment Tonight crew, which resulted in a breathless Mary Hart advising the world that even as she was set to play super spy James Bond's latest lover, Carma Sutra, it appeared Julia Summers had found a real-life hero of her own.

"And you're the only man whose hands I want on me," she said now, sucking in her stomach as he trailed a fingertip between her breasts, over her stomach to lightly tug the curls between her thighs.

"Good." He scooped up some bubbles with the hand that wasn't creating such havoc beneath the water, and began spreading them over her breasts. "God, you're gorgeous."

"You're pretty gorgeous yourself," she murmured as she sank lower into the water. Into seduction.

"How can you tell? Your eyes are closed."

"Believe me, I've memorized every glorious inch." No wonder Warren had been concerned about self-combustion. If she wasn't a level-headed woman, she might worry about it herself.

"Open your eyes."

It took an effort, but she managed to do as he asked.

"Look at this." Her breasts were draped in iridescent lather, but he'd left her ruby-hard nipples bare. The sight of his wide, dark hand against those snowy bubbles, against her fair skin, was the most erotic thing she'd ever seen.

"Did I ever tell you that I was a soda jerk for a while?"

"I don't believe it came up," she said raggedly, as those fingers inside her began seductively moving in and out.

"Breaux's Drugstore had a fountain. Before I was old enough to get my driver's license, I used to build hot fudge sundaes for pretty girls." He skimmed a thumb over first one taut peak, then the other. "That's what you remind me of, two scoops of French vanilla with whipped cream and red cherries topping them off. Sweet and indulgent and very, very tasty."

His lips closed over her nipple, battering her senses with the tug of his mouth, which connected directly to the dark sensation between her legs. Not wanting to come alone, needing to share everything, she rolled over on top of him, taking him deep inside her, embracing him as they both slid under the water.

They were on their way to Beau Soleil for the final day's shoot when Finn's cell phone rang. He flipped it open and tensed when he saw the caller had blocked his identity. "Callahan."

"Finn?"

"Jim? What's up?" Figuring Jansen had been busy trying to get rid of him while he'd been away, Finn braced himself for the worst.

"I've got some good news and some bad news," his superior told him.

"Give me the good news first."

"Jansen's gone."

"What do you mean, gone? Wait a minute, let me guess. Someone threw water on her and she melted?"

"She's been transferred. Well, more like demoted to desk duty out in the hinterlands. So far out, I figure it'll take her about fifty years to crawl her way back up to Boise."

She'd come from Idaho on her rocket ride up the Bureau's ranks. It appeared her rocket had crashed and burned.

"Why? What did she do?"

"It was more a case of what she didn't do. She didn't pay enough attention when Lawson fired his counsel and hired himself a female lawyer."

"He's entitled." Finn had thought it had been a stupid move when he'd heard about it the other night on the news, but if dumping the dream team weakened Lawson's defense enough to ensure his conviction, he was all for it.

"Sure, but then she stalled when brass told her to move the guy out of the hospital to a more secure facility."

"Because she wanted to keep him in her jurisdiction." And garner all the press that would entail, Finn supposed.

"It'd be my guess she didn't want to lose the headlines," Jim Burke said. One of the reasons they'd always worked so well together was that they often thought alike. "But she miscalculated badly."

Finn felt everything in him still. "You're not telling me he tried to escape again?"

"No." The drawn breath was easily heard across the miles. "I'm telling you he *did* escape."

"Fuck," Finn ground out, causing Julia, who'd been studying her script, to look over at him. "Anyone know where he's gone?"

"He seems to have gone to ground. Remember that house he had in North Carolina?"

"In the mountains around where he grew up." They'd found his fourth victim in the well in the back yard.

"We tracked him to a truck stop at the North Carolina–Virginia border. We're guessing he's headed home."

"Hell, the ground there is riddled with limestone caves." If Lawson stayed put, it could take years to find him. The Bureau still hadn't found the Atlanta Olympic bombing suspect who'd supposedly been hiding away in those same caves; Finn had come to the conclusion that guy had died long ago. But he wouldn't believe Lawson was dead until he saw the body for himself.

"We've got agents headed there now. And the state cops have brought out dog teams. I'm trying to get your suspension overturned so you can get in on the hunt, but you know the red tape involved. Jansen built up a pretty strong political base, which seems to be lobbying to shift the blame to the guys who were assigned to guard Lawson, so it may take a day or so."

"They might have screwed up, letting him get away. But it was her command." Which meant the SAC should have been prepared to accept responsibility.

"Standing by her men wasn't in her playbook," Burke said, telling Finn nothing he hadn't thought for himself innumerable times. "Since you know Lawson best, the director's bound to want you on the case."

"Yeah. I want me on the case, too." After his supervisor promised to keep him up to date, Finn flipped the phone closed again.

"Was that about Lawson?" Julia asked.

"Yeah. He escaped."

"So I gathered. And you're going after him."

"Yeah. After you're safe on the plane for Kathmandu."

He could sense she was prepared to argue, and appreciated when she didn't challenge his choices.

"You'll get him," she said calmly.

"Yeah." Finn couldn't allow himself to consider the alternative. He worried momentarily that Lawson might actually come after him, then decided that he wouldn't go to the trouble of escaping only to risk showing up here in the media spotlight.

Hell. The guy was turning out to be just like the killer in all those Halloween movies: just when you thought for sure he was a goner, he'd leap up, knife in hand, for another sequel.

He'd find him, Finn vowed. And this time, if he was lucky, Lawson would give him the excuse to end things once and for all.

"All right, everyone," Randy said as everyone gathered to shoot the kidnapping scene. "Since time is money, and I know everyone's eager to take off on holiday, we're going to attempt the impossible and pull this off in one take. Julia, you'll be in the cemetery, digging up the silver you'd hidden there at the beginning of the war.

"The Yankees are holding your stepfather prisoner. You plan to buy his freedom with some of the sterling, then use the rest to finance a new start in Texas, where you've heard people don't ask questions regarding others' backgrounds.

"With the cannons booming, you don't hear the men creeping up behind you in the fog. When you do become aware of them, it's too late. You're captured by a group of rebel deserters who've concocted a plan to kidnap you and finance their own trip west by selling you to a brothel in New Orleans."

"A brothel?"

"A brothel," he agreed. "Worn out by the trials and tribulations you've undergone, on the brink of starvation because the Yankees have burned your fields and taken all your livestock for their army, you can't bear the idea of further degradation. So instead of fighting for your freedom, you pull the derringer from your garter and shoot yourself through the heart."

"I don't believe that."

The director shot Julia a frustrated look. "You don't believe what?"

"That Fancy wouldn't fight. This is a woman who's done whatever it took for survival. She's within days — perhaps even hours — of this nightmare being over. And now she's giving up?"

"You've never heard of metaphors?" Charles challenged in that bull-like way Julia hated. "She's been defeated. Like the South. She's a woman in ruins. Like Belle Terre. Fancy symbolizes the excesses of the antebellum era finally brought to its knees."

"I agree with Julia," Warren spoke up, as he had been doing more and more. Julia wondered if he was merely starting to understand his power, or if perhaps his relationship with Lorelei Fairchild had boosted his self-confidence. "Which is why I wrote Fancy fighting like a wildcat."

"That's the way I see it," Randy seconded. "Not only do we get another Fancy fight scene, which audiences will love, but since we need to get the story line back to modern times, it'll be more dramatic if the renegade soldiers take her hostage. Then, when she escapes, she can make that leap back to the twenty-first century."

"I don't like it." Kendall folded his arms in a show of the Golden Rule: he who owns the gold, rules. "Since Julia insists on leaving *River*

Road, there's no point in having her return. We'll still get back to the twenty-first century by killing her off in the Belle Terre cemetery, which will result in her dying while lingering in that coma."

It was the first time the producer had actually acknowledged she was leaving the show. Julia was relieved he'd finally seen the light. But Amanda had been good for her and she intended to remain true to character, flawed though it might be, until the end.

Warren insisted, "Neither Fancy nor Amanda would kill themselves. They're survivors. Fancy has survived a war; certainly she isn't going to view being kidnapped by a bunch of thugs as the end of the world. Particularly since she has a way of getting men to do what she wants. She'd probably seduce each and every one of them, or at least promise them sex, then hold them at gunpoint with their own weapons and escape."

"Viewers want retribution," Kendall said stubbornly. "Fancy has betrayed everyone in her life. She deserves comeuppance."

"Why don't we try it this way first, mates?" Randy suggested. "Then if it doesn't work, suicide's still on the table. The extra riders we've pulled in for the kidnapping are already here, so we might as well shoot the scene for insurance. Because if it turns out you're wrong, Kendall, and the suicide scene doesn't work, it'd cost us a bloody fortune on wasted days while we rounded everyone up again."

"All right." Charles was obviously less than pleased with this suggestion. Julia suspected the only reason he was willing to concede to even try the scene her way was that time was money and they were wasting too much of it standing around here arguing. "When you put it that way, it seems only cost effective to give it a try."

Not even attempting to conceal his satisfaction with having won that argument, Randy turned toward Julia. "All right, love, here's the setup. You're in the cemetery, placing flowers on the grave of your sister's fiancé, having realized too late that it's him, not your stepfather, you love. Will ever love. You throw yourself on his grave —"

"Isn't that a bit overly dramatic?"

"You're bleeping right it is. Which is why it works. So, because you're weeping, you don't hear the thunder of the horses' hooves at first. When you do, you look up — wiping your tears from your face — expecting it to be those hated Yankees soldiers returning to Belle Terre after the battle.

"Instead, you're thrilled to see the group of men in tattered gray uniforms who you believe have broken through the battle lines. The cannon fire is growing closer; you realize that the war is finally coming to an end and you're looking forward to a new start.

"But that's not to be. They've already

planned to kidnap you. Both sides think you've been spying on the other, but these are blokes without principles or scruples, so they're just going to hold you hostage until the war ends, then hand you over to the victors. For a price, of course."

"Of course," Julia murmured.

Randy and Warren then began arguing that it might be a good idea to have Fancy seduce her captors. Fortunately, they finally opted for the cliff-hanger ending of just having her kidnapped. As patient as Finn had been, Julia knew he would have been less than thrilled watching the seduction scenario played out.

26

Watching Julia being kidnapped by Confederate thugs might not be as bad as watching the rape scene on Beau Soleil's stairs, and definitely not as heart wrenching as when the horse and carriage had been tearing toward the water, but Finn sure couldn't call it entertainment.

"All this is starting to make whatever she's going to go through on that Bond movie look like kiddie's play," Nate observed as one of the rebels dressed in tattered and bloodied gray yanked her off the mound of dirt that had been brought in to look like a freshly covered grave, and pulled her astride his horse.

"We've always ended each episode with a bit of a cliff-hanger," Warren, who was standing nearby, said. "And a big one at the end of the season. Viewers have come to expect it."

"Well, they're definitely not going to be disappointed with this one then," Nate said.

Finn didn't say anything. His eyes remained riveted on the riders and horses as they raced away into the fog, which was even thicker than usual this morning. He could barely see his hand in front of his face. That hadn't deterred Hogan, who'd declared it only heightened the suspense and besides, if it did prove a problem, computers could take care of it in editing.

"Cut," Hogan called out.

"Cut," the assistant director echoed.

"And that's finally a wrap," the director said, making Finn all too aware of the fact that Julia would be leaving tomorrow.

In the beginning, he'd been looking forward to that day. When things had been different. When he hadn't known how much more satisfying his days were when he began them with her smile, how much more pleasurable his nights were when he spent them making love to her. And how much enjoyment she brought to all those hours in between.

She did more than just rile up his glands; she filled his senses, balanced him in a way he hadn't felt in a very long time. Since a young woman had been found murdered in San Diego's Griffith Park and had set off the thirty-month nearly round-the-clock chase for Lawson that had consumed not just his every waking hour and most of those he should have been sleeping, but his mind. She'd been right about them becoming linked in some eerie way. Somehow Lawson's thoughts had become his, writhing in his brain and before his mind's eye like poisonous snakes.

Finn had dreamed of the women, all young and pretty and filled with life when the killer had picked them up at the local watering spots around the universities, and taken them to whatever home he'd been living in at the time. Julia had once accused him of only viewing the

347

world in black and white. What he hadn't told her, hadn't told anyone, was that whenever he'd look down at one of Lawson's victim's bodies, discarded like old rags onto a trash heap, he'd pictured her last days of life in vivid, blinding Technicolor, down to the last horrendous detail.

He'd forced himself to watch every minute of their autopsies, acknowledging that they were more than mere files that were piling higher and higher on his metal desk. Although it was by far the most difficult thing he'd ever done, and hoped it was the most painful thing he'd ever have to do, he'd attended their funerals and assured their weeping mothers and shell-shocked fathers, whose suffering made his own inconsequential by comparison, that the monster who'd brought so much misery to so many, would be brought to justice.

"Justice," he scoffed now. The only real justice would be to put Lawson in a cage with all those grieving parents and sisters and brothers, and walk away.

Nate glanced over at him. "Did you say something?"

"No," Finn responded brusquely, as he always did when this subject came up. But somehow, when he hadn't been paying close attention, his internal walls had begun to crumble. "I was just wondering at what point vengeance becomes justice. And vice versa."

"I suppose it depends on your point of view."

"Yeah. I suppose so."

"You got him once," Nate said. Finn had told him, and only him, about Burke's call. "You'll get him again."

"I fully intend to." The riders had returned. At least four of them had. But hadn't there originally been six? "How long has she been gone?"

Nate blinked at the sudden shift in topic, then followed Finn's gaze to the wrangler, who was unsaddling the horses. "I don't know. Five minutes, maybe. Six?"

The short hairs at the back of Finn's neck prickled. Never a good sign. "However long it's been," he said, "it's been too damn long."

Julia blinked her eyes, attempting to focus through the shadows. She had no idea where she was or any memory of how she'd gotten here. The last thing she remembered, she'd been flung over the back of a horse that was thundering through fog as thick as a gray velvet theater curtain.

"It's about time you woke up," an unfamiliar voice said. "I was getting afraid you'd overdosed."

Was she awake? Or dreaming? Had she fallen off the horse? That might explain the maniac who was pounding away with a sledgehammer inside her head.

He mentioned an overdose. Which was impossible, since she'd never done drugs. But maybe she'd been given drugs? Was she in a hospital? She tried to focus through the dark shadows, but everything was blurry, as if viewed through dirty glass.

It didn't feel like a hospital. Or smell, sound, or look like one. There were no bright lights, no busy activity out in the hallway, no disembodied voices paging doctors over the intercom, no low, steady beeping of monitors or distant sound of televisions from adjoining rooms.

There was no rattle of metal trays outside her door, which made her realize she was hungry. And instead of the smell of antiseptic, the air, drenched with moisture, was thick with the rank odor of mildew.

Her arms and shoulders felt as if they'd been yanked out of their sockets. Had she fallen off the horse during that kidnap scene? She tried to ease the ache, only to discover that she couldn't move. Someone had tied her wrists to the rusted iron headboard of a narrow bed, in much the same way Amanda had been tied to the bedposts in that scene they'd shot before leaving Los Angeles.

Julia struggled to steady her breath. Tried to concentrate. She seemed to be in a cabin that was nothing like Finn's cozy camp. The mold and musty smell suggested it had been deserted for a very long time. If there were windows, they must have been painted black, because the only light coming into the room was a stuttering thin sliver that managed to shine through a gap in the rotting boards.

How long ago had she been unconscious? Minutes? Hours? Days?

"I know this is a cliché. But where am I?" Her throat was sore and raspy. "And who are you?"

"You don't need to know either of those things," said a gruffer male voice coming from the shadows. "You just need to know that if you follow the program and don't try anything funny, everything will be okay."

Julia found nothing funny about her situation.

"Are you my stalker?"

"I've never had to stalk a woman in my life." He sounded honestly affronted. Terrific. An overly sensitive kidnapper, who was undoubtedly armed. That's all she needed.

"If you're after ransom, you're never going to get away with this," Julia warned. "In case no one has informed you, kidnapping is a federal offense. You're going to have the FBI after you. And believe me, those guys take their jobs very seriously." Oh, God. Finn. He must be going crazy.

"The FBI? Is she right, Jimmy?" the first voice asked. "I don't want the Feds after me. I thought we were just gonna pick up some extra dough."

"I told you not to use names," the first man snapped back. "And hell no, she's not right."

Julia heard the strike of a match. The acrid scent of burning sulfur stung her nostrils.

"She's just trying to do a number on you."

"It's not like we're *really* kidnapping her."

Julia wondered who he was trying to convince: her, or himself. She could read the lack of conviction in his voice. At least one of her abductors was concerned about what he might have gotten himself into. Surely she could talk her way out of this. And if not her, Amanda.

The deep purple shadows kept her from being able to see them. "What would you call this?" she asked. "If not a kidnapping?"

"Think of yourself as our guest," the second man suggested.

"Gee, I was certain I'd sent in my RSVP declining this fun party."

Stall. Even without windows, it was dark enough in the cabin that she suspected it might be approaching twilight. Surely Finn would be showing up to rescue her at any moment.

"If it's just money you want, perhaps we can work out some sort of deal."

"Are you saying the TV network will pay to get you back?" the man who was not Jimmy asked.

"I don't know about them." This was no time to get herself into deeper trouble by telling a lie they could prove false. *Stall.* "But my parents would be willing to pay whatever you're asking."

"Your parents are fucking hippies," Jimmy

scoffed. He exhaled a thick stream of smoke into the humidity-laden air as he laughed. His cigarette was not the kind you could buy in any store.

"We saw them when you all came into Cajun Cal's," the first man volunteered.

Another clue. They'd been at the Cajun restaurant. They didn't sound as if they were locals. Then again, neither did Finn. Except when they were making love and he allowed his control to slip.

"They may be hippies, but they're rich hippies," she said. "One of my father's chairs was in the Smithsonian and Harrison Ford owns one of my mother's weavings."

"Big deal," Jimmy scoffed, but she could tell he was interested. Now she just needed to get him to nibble a bit on the bait.

"I think so. Not everyone gets in the Smithsonian."

Hard heels that sounded a bit like cowboy boots hammered on the floor as he came out of the shadows to stand over her. Along with the pot, she breathed in male sweat and an acrid scent that could have been nerves. "If you don't shut up, I'm gonna put a gag in your mouth."

He was obviously edgy, and Amanda had been in jeopardy enough times for Julia to know that even the best laid plans often blew up in your face. He was obviously not comfortable with this situation, which made her suspect he was not your everyday garden variety criminal, out for a fast buck before moving on.

And that made him all the more dangerous.

Think, she told herself. *There's a way out of this. All you have to do is think of it.* She closed her eyes again and narrowed her whirling thoughts down to one succinct question: *What would a Bond Girl do?*

Where the hell was she? A trio of Jim Lafite's hounds were baying in the woods. A helicopter donated by the Louisiana Fish and Game Department swept back and forth over the bayou, rotors churning. Half the town of Blue Bayou was out searching for her; the other half was hovering around Beau Soleil, watching. And waiting.

"This is even more interestin' than watchin' them shoot that movie," Jean Boudreaux said as he sat on a log and watched the beehive of activity.

"A whole bunch more," Frenchie Hebert, his best friend for more than seventy years, agreed. "That was pretty much stop and go, stop and go, all day long. I've decided I don' want to ever be no movie star, me."

Jean shot him a look. "Like you'd have a chance in hell to be a movie star."

Frenchie spat a stream of tobacco juice, hitting an RC can one of the searchers had dropped onto the ground. "Maybe I could. Maybe I couldn't. But 'at's beside the point, since I'd never do it. Hell, makin' a movie's more damn boring than sitting on a rock waiting for your trap to fill up."

"*Mais*, yeah," Jean agreed. His attention drifted from the sixties model cherry-red GTO that had just pulled up in front of Beau Soleil with a squeal of brakes, to that blond actress who was built like a brick shithouse. "But all the women you get would probably make it worthwhile."

Frenchie considered that for a minute as he zeroed in on Felissa Templeton's ass when she bent over to take a Dr. Pepper can out of an ice-filled trash can and hand it to a sheriff's deputy from Point Coupée parish. "Guess it would, at that," he said as he pulled a pouch from his shirt pocket and stuck another plug of Apple Jack chew between cheek and gum.

Jack Callahan was in a hurry, but took the time to open the GTO's door for his wife before heading across the yard on long, purposeful strides.

"I heard on the radio driving here from the airport," the middle Callahan brother told Finn. "What can I do?"

Finn shook his head in frustration. Hours had passed without a sign of her. The horses had returned of their own accord, giving no clue as to where they'd been.

"Just what everyone else is doin', I guess. Sign up for a quadrant and start covering ground." He glared out over the miles of low land and water. It was going to be dark soon; he didn't want to think of her somewhere out there with gators and snakes and God knows what kind of two-legged animal.

"How was the honeymoon?" he thought to ask.

"Pretty damn great. 'Specially since I never thought I'd ever be havin' one, and if anyone had asked my opinion even a few months ago, I'd have said the whole concept was a chick thing." Despite the seriousness of their situation, Jack flashed one of his trademark killer smiles. "Turns out they're not bad for guys, either. When this is over and we get Julia Summers back safe and sound, you might want to give it a try."

Finn shot a look at Nate. "What have you been telling him?"

"Not a thing." Nate held up his hands. "I swear. Do you really think I'd interrupt a guy on his honeymoon just to tell him you'd fallen hard for the newest Bond Girl?"

"It wasn't Nate," Dani Dupree Callahan offered as she joined the brothers. "It was Ed Pitre down at the gas station. And I think it's wonderful. Jack and I are so happy, I want everyone to feel the same way, and it's high time you found someone to love."

"Find being the definite concept," Finn muttered, deciding this wasn't the time or place to argue about his feelings. Especially when he hadn't sorted them out for himself.

"I'm so sorry." Dani hugged him. "But it'll be okay."

Finn had always liked Dani, from the time she'd been a skinny little thing with braces and blond hair down to her waist who'd follow after Jack like an adoring little puppy dog. Both of them had been through some tough times, which was why Finn was real glad things had worked out for them.

"It's my fucking fault," Finn repeated as he had for hours. "Sorry about the language, Dani."

"Don't worry about it. It's a stressful situation." Finn appreciated her not bringing up the fact that Julia's disappearance was eerily similar to the case he'd devoted three years of his life to.

"You had no way of knowing this was going to happen," Nate said yet again. Unfortunately, his family role of comforter wasn't working today.

"It was my job to know." Finn's lips were pressed in a grim line, his thoughts even darker than his expression. "I was supposed to be protecting her, dammit."

Julia's mother joined them, having just completed a live interview with WGNO News out of New Orleans. "She's all right," Peace said. "A little frightened, as anyone would be under the circumstances, but she's keeping her head."

"See that in your crystal ball, did you?" Finn immediately regretted his rash words. She'd been incredibly calm and supportive, proving that when she'd decided to take on a new name, she'd chosen well. "Hell, I'm sorry." He raked a hand over his hair. "That was out of line."

"It's an upsetting situation. You're right to be a little unnerved. Heaven knows, I hate to think what Julia's father would be doing if he couldn't be out walking off his anger." Freedom was out with Jim Lafite and his bloodhounds.

Something occurred to Finn. "If you can read her mind —"

"Actually, I can't. It's more a case of sensing her feelings."

"Close enough. Can you get a sense of where she is?"

"I'm sorry, it doesn't work that way," Peace said regretfully. "Besides, I'm so unfamiliar with Blue Bayou, anything I'm picking up probably wouldn't mean anything to you."

"Why don't you give it a shot?"

She sighed, then ran her hand through her hair in a gesture Finn had seen Julia make a thousand times. "It's dark." She closed her eyes and went into what seemed to be a slight trance. "There are trees. And dark water all around." She opened her eyes again and looked up at him. "That's not much help, is it?"

No. Not when the sun was slowing sinking into the bayou and everything around them for miles was all trees and water.

"That's okay." It was his turn to try to reassure her. "I figured it was worth a shot."

"There is something else," Peace ventured.

"What's that?"

"She's not alone."

Fuck. Since he had no idea what he was dealing with, Finn had no way of knowing whether that was a positive thing, or negative. It could be incredibly dangerous for anyone, especially someone who had no swamp experience, to be alone at night on the bayou. On the other hand, depending on what her kidnappers had planned, Julia might be better off taking her chances with the gators.

27

Unsurprisingly, for this part of the country, there was no electricity in the cabin. A kerosene lantern on a rough wooden table added a petroleum stench to the muggy air and cast spooky shadows on the wall. The light also drew moths that beat their wings against the glass panes and mosquitoes that seemed to think she was an all-you-can-eat buffet.

The two men were playing cards. After that brief conversation when she'd regained consciousness, they hadn't said a word to her. But the younger man, the one who wasn't Jimmy, kept casting nervous glances her way. Nervous, and, Julia thought, familiar. It was the way men looked at Amanda.

The unmistakable chords of the *William Tell* Overture suddenly overcame the frogs and cicadas from outside. Jimmy snatched a cell phone off his belt. Julia found it a bit ironic that a kidnapper would choose the Lone Ranger's theme song for his customized ring.

"It's about time you called," he barked out. "Yeah, we've got her."

"What?" She watched him frown. "A week? How the fuck do you expect us to keep her under wraps for a week with everybody but the nationalfuckingguard out looking for her?"

A week? Julia bit down her panic; it wouldn't help. *Think, dammit!* While she didn't have a single doubt that Finn would find her, the idea of being out here in the middle of nowhere with these two men for a week was impossible. Her captors had said they wouldn't hurt her, but since they'd already proven themselves capable of criminal behavior by obviously drugging her, bringing her here, tying her up and holding her hostage, she didn't put a great deal of faith in either one of them to tell the truth. The man named Jimmy let out a long, harsh string of curses.

"Dammit, I can't hear you," he complained. "The reception's shit here. We must be too fucking far from a cell tower. Let me go out-side."

Without giving her so much as a glance, he left the cabin.

With Jimmy gone, Julia's odds for escape had just gotten fifty percent better. *You can do this.* Between Amanda and Carma Sutra, escape was not only possible, it was almost guaranteed. She hoped.

"Excuse me?" Julia hated the way her voice sounded so frail. So vulnerable. Never let your opponent sense your fear, her ninjitsu in-structor had drilled into his students. Easy for him to say. She doubted he'd ever been tied up in some remote bayou cabin with the *Deliver-ance* twins.

When the other man didn't appear to hear

her, reminding her that there was a delicate balance between making herself heard and speaking loud enough to bring Jimmy back into the cabin, she cleared her throat and tried again. "Excuse me?"

"What?" He cast a quick, nervous look at the door. Obviously she wasn't the only one concerned about the other man returning to find them talking.

"I'm thirsty." Although her eyes were burning from the smoke, she looked up at him the way Amanda did whenever she was luring a hapless male victim into her sticky, dangerous web. "I don't suppose you have any water?"

"I'm not supposed to talk to you."

"It must get old." She shook her head regretfully on the bare mattress that was undoubtedly crawling with all sorts of creepy disgusting things she didn't want to think about. "Having Jimmy tell you what to do."

"He isn't the boss of me."

"Isn't he?" she asked sweetly. "He certainly seems to be running the show. You're not the one taking the important phone call right now, are you?"

"That's because someone has to be in charge."

"Of course." She suspected he was parroting Jimmy and hoped that somewhere, perhaps deep inside him, he'd harbor a bit of resentment. "But why can't it be you?"

"Because it's always Jimmy."

"Why?"

"Why what?" He looked confused.

"Why has Jimmy always been the one in charge?"

"Because I'm dumb. Jimmy's the smart one. He even goes to college."

"Really." She couldn't quite keep the skepticism from her voice.

"He does," he insisted. "UCLA."

Even as she realized he'd just given her a clue, Julia's mind whirled. Could these men have actually followed her here from Los Angeles? Was one of them her stalker? That didn't make sense, since Jimmy was obviously working for someone. Maybe her stalker? Since when did stalkers hire accomplices?

Perhaps she was being held for ransom. It wasn't an impossible idea. Considering all the press her movie contract had gotten, perhaps someone had decided the studio would be willing to pay big bucks to get her back. Which just went to show what they knew about Hollywood. If she wasn't in Kathmandu on time, the producer would replace her quicker than you could say "Bond. James Bond."

She thought back on what Finn had told her about Charles assuring his father that he'd have her on board for a sixth season. Surely he wouldn't risk prison just to keep her from getting on that plane so she'd lose the Carma Sutra role and, in his mind, have to return to *River Road.* Would he?

Deciding to sort all this out later, once she was free, she turned her thoughts back to escaping. "Well, he might go to college, but you're definitely the handsome one," she purred, drawing forth a blush that shone like hot coals in the dim sooty light. "Besides, I think you're selling yourself short in the brains department."

"You do?"

"Oh, I certainly do, sugar. Personally, it seems to me that you're every bit as smart as Jimmy. Even smarter."

"He's always been the smart one," he said doggedly. "And I've always been dumb. In school he could figure out the letters in the books, but they always looked screwed up to me."

"That doesn't make you dumb." Obviously this man was not her letter writer. "Only dyslexic."

He frowned. "What's that?"

"It's a disorder that makes it difficult to read. Didn't anyone ever test you?"

"Got tests," he muttered. "Failed 'em all, which is why I dropped out in the eighth grade. It just got to be a bummer, you know?"

"I can imagine," she said, her voice oozing with sympathy. "But it really is a very real condition that interferes with the ability to recognize written words. We did an episode on the subject just last season."

"Hey, I saw that." She could practically see the cartoon lightbulb flash on over his head. "You had a one-night fling with that guy you met when your Jag crunched his minivan. The one who taught special ed classes."

Julia didn't point out that it had been her character who'd had the steamy one-night stand. If he was blurring the lines, so much the better.

"You know," she said conversationally, "this situation reminds me of an episode we did two seasons ago. Maybe you saw it — the one where I was kidnapped aboard an alien's mothership?"

"Yeah. Wow. You were really sexy when you were showing that outer space guy where to touch a woman."

"Thank you." She shifted a bit on the mattress, arching her back as best she could, drawing attention to her breasts which, thanks to the corset Audrey had lashed her into this morning, appeared nearly as lush as a Playmate's.

"My arms are getting so horribly sore," she complained. "Can't you untie me just for a minute so I can get my circulation back?"

"Jimmy said you had to stay tied up until we get the order to let you go."

Her spirits took a nosedive at the thought of staying tied up for days. Julia resolutely pulled them back up. "So Jimmy isn't the one giving the orders? Does this other man have a name?"

"Well, sure he does. Everyone has a name."

"Would you happen to know what it is?"

"Jimmy didn't tell me. And I didn't ask, since it's none of my business. Knowing stuff gets you in trouble, like when my pals Sam and Matt decided to hit that 7-11 and shot the clerk. I wasn't even there when they did it, but because I'm the one who bought Sam the damn gun, the DA sent me to prison as a co-conspirator. So now I'm out and all I want is enough money to buy me a car. The bus service in L.A. really sucks. I've got my eye on a lime green Charger I figure I can fix up and run at the drags."

Terrific. She was being held hostage for a nineteen seventies muscle car. "Why would anyone hire you and Jimmy to kidnap me and keep me here?"

"I don't know. I just do what Jimmy tells me to do. Then I can't get arrested, 'cause I don't know nothing."

"Surely you must have overheard something. Perhaps I can help out your memory," Amanda suggested silkily.

"Nah. I don't think so."

"Oh, I think I could, sugar," she drawled, tossing in a little Lorelei Fairchild. That belle routine had worked gangbusters with Warren, who was so far beyond this man in intelligence they could have been born on different planets.

"How do you figure to help my memory when I don't got one in the first place?" He was clearly tempted. He also knew something he wasn't saying. Every time he lied to her, his eyes went darting all over the room like nervous birds trying to escape.

"Sometimes we have things in our minds, but we just have to know the way to get them out. Why don't we play a little game?" Her lush tone and come-and-get-me-big-boy gaze returned his attention to her.

His broad brow furrowed. "What kinda game?"

"It's like Truth or Dare, but with a twist. We ask each other questions, and if you guess the answer, I have to give you a kiss. If I answer yours, you get to kiss me."

He folded his arms across his chest. "That's all we're talkin' about?" His eyes narrowed to slits. "Just a kiss?"

Deciding he might not be quite as dumb as she'd first suspected, Amanda smiled her most dazzling smile. "Just for starters. It's like *Jeopardy*."

"Don't watch *Jeopardy*. I like that millionaire show, 'cause you got more time to answer the questions."

"We'll play like that one, then," she assured him. "The more questions you answer, the more you win."

She was looking up at him through the fringe of lashes Damien had darkened with several layers of mascara. Had that been only this morning?

"Guess that sounds like an okay deal."

More than okay; she could see the anticipation glowing in his lust-filled eyes.

"Doesn't it?" Amanda could be slick, aggressive, shrewd and decidedly mercenary. Even, on occasion, under the right circumstances and the proper motivation, kittenish. But she was definitely at her best when she turned meltingly, implicitly sexual. "So, if you'll just be a sweetheart and untie me —"

"Maybe I don't want to. I've never fucked a woman when she was tied up before. It'd be just like bein' one of them porn stars. Sometimes I think I could be real good at that. Mr. Timex is just as big as them on the videos."

Julia categorically refused to ask.

"Don't you wanna know why I call my johnson Mr. Timex?" he asked slyly.

If there was any bit of information she could go her entire life without learning, it was why this swamp creature had named his penis. Damn. "Only if you want to tell me, sugar," Amanda cooed.

" 'Cause it takes a lickin' and keeps on tickin'." He winked and put his hand on the crotch of the filthy jeans he must have changed into after discarding that scratchy wool uniform. "Which you're about to find out."

"Now, doesn't that sound like fun?" It was all she could do not to throw up at the idea. "But this bed is awful narrow and I'll bet the springs just squeak to beat the band, which doesn't bother me all that much, since all my attention's going to be on giving you a good time. But you might not want Jimmy to hear what's goin' on in here."

She watched the wheels grind exceedingly slowly as he followed that thought to its logical conclusion. If she couldn't get this idiot to untie her soon, Jimmy would finish his conversation with whoever had hatched this plot and she'd lose her chance to escape.

"If I untie you, you gotta promise me you won't try to escape," he finally decided.

"Oh, I surely do," she said. "In fact, I'd cross my heart, if my hand was free." She forced an Amanda smile she had never felt less like in her life.

She nearly wept with relief when it turned out that whoever had tied her had used a basic slip knot, which allowed the rope to loosen swiftly. She took a breath that was meant to calm, tried to remember what her ninjitsu master had taught her about staying centered, then stood up on legs that were decidedly wobbly.

She skimmed her fingers over his prickly jaw, around his chin, managing to dodge the mouth that had been aimed for hers. The idea of this man kissing her nearly made her gag, but Julia reminded herself that it was only acting, something she did every day.

Her hands continued down his chest. She toyed teasingly with his belt buckle, then knelt in front of him. He was watching her with a fixed, unblinking look that reminded her of an alligator watching a nutria.

She could do this. It was only acting.

She unfastened the buckle, and slid the stiff, stained denim down his thin legs. Mr. Timex stirred beneath the yellowed white cotton briefs. Drawing in a calming breath, Julia drew the briefs down his legs.

She cast a cautious glance up at him. He'd closed his eyes, waiting. Anticipating. His pants were down around his ankles, like shackles.

It was now or never. She took another deep breath, then found her center, aligning herself as she'd been taught — mind, heart, will, and intention. Then she jerked on his ankles, pulling him off his feet in a move that might not be textbook ninjitsu, but effective.

He landed flat on his back with a thud, causing Julia to cringe when the back of his head connected with the cypress planks, and she hoped she hadn't killed him. She was relieved when she pressed her fingers against his throat and found a pulse, then used his belt to hog-tie him. It was nearly the same ploy Amanda had used to escape that horny alien. When she got out of here, Julia was going to kiss Warren for having written it.

She opened the door gingerly, relieved when it didn't squeak. She couldn't see Jimmy, but could hear his voice coming from the shadows around the corner of the cabin. He was arguing loudly, and from his tone, she suspected he was not coming out on the winning side.

"If you're not going to get out here and take the bitch off our hands, I'll just fucking take care of the problem myself," he shouted.

Julia suspected that his method of taking care of "the problem" would not be a good thing.

She'd practiced the ancient act of silent walking in her classes, though she'd never expected to use it, and she was extremely grateful for her training as she slipped through the shadows away from the cabin. Whenever she stepped on a branch or accidently splashed through water, she reminded herself that her instructor had taught her that some noise was all right. After all, nature was not entirely still.

While she had no way of knowing where she was or where she was going, she did know that she didn't want to be out here all alone when the sun, which was a great deal lower in the sky now, went down.

Her actions might be considered foolhardy, but taking her chances with the bayou seemed far preferable to trusting Jimmy to release her.

Once she was about a hundred yards from the cabin, she began to move slowly, cautiously, down the narrow road, cringing at the crunching sound of her nineteenth-century slippers on the clamshell gravel. But to leave the road would be risking sinking into the swamp.

"It'll be okay," she assured herself, stifling a

scream as a gator floated past her in the dark, silent water. They definitely looked less threatening out at Beau Soleil, when she was surrounded by people. And, of course, when she was with Finn, who had his gun and could shoot one dead if it decided to eat her.

Finn — he was going to be frantic. And, she feared, furious at himself. Then there were her parents. She'd wanted to save them from worrying; now they had something far worse to be concerned about.

She'd have to make it up to them when she got back to Blue Bayou safe and sound. And she would be all right, Julia insisted. Because the alternative was unthinkable.

28

"There's something funny going on," Finn said to his brothers when they'd gathered to devise a new plan. There were miles of swamp; locating Julia once it turned dark would be like finding the proverbial needle in the haystack.

"What's that?" Nate glugged from a plastic bottle of water, then wiped his mouth with the back of his hand. Despite the ominous dark clouds gathering overhead, searching was hot, sweaty work.

"Nearly every guy, and a lot of the women, too, have been dragging their asses all over this place today." Even that magenta-haired makeup guy had stripped off today's skintight purple leather pants, changed into some uniform trousers Audrey had given him, and had hardly stopped long enough to take a piss.

"It's not surprising that we'd have so many volunteers. It's obvious everyone likes Jules," Nate said. "With good reason."

"Kendall hasn't joined the search." Finn said what had been nagging at his mind for the past couple hours. Nate and Jack glanced over at the producer, who was away from the others, talking into a cell phone. Which wasn't unusual; his ear had been practically glued to the thing since he'd arrived in Blue Bayou. Nor was his obvious irritation with whoever was on the other end of the line unusual; he'd already demonstrated himself to be impatient and unpleasant.

"He's not in real good shape," Jack said. "I'm not sure he'd last five minutes."

"And he hasn't seemed like the type to put himself out for anyone else," Nate said.

"True enough. But you'd still think he'd at least pretend to show some concern."

"Are you suggesting he has something to do with this?" Nate asked. "That doesn't make any sense. She's too important to the show."

"The show just wrapped for the season," Finn pointed out. "And she's not coming back."

Nate frowned. "All the more reason why he's not a real strong suspect. He doesn't have a dog in this fight anymore."

"How about insurance?" Jack asked. "Does the show carry a policy on her?"

"Yeah." Finn had already looked it up the night he'd found out about the cat pills. "A million dollars, which is chicken feed for a place like Atlantic Pharmaceuticals. It runs out the same time her contract does. Tomorrow."

Jack blew out a breath. "I've seen people killed for a lot less back when I was workin' DEA."

They both had.

We'll find her, Finn vowed. As they resumed searching, he found himself desperately praying to a God he'd thought he'd stopped believing in sometime between Lawson's fifth and sixth victims.

The sun was blood red and going down as Julia came around a corner and saw the building. It was weathered, the paint was peeling, the metal roof rusted, and the plank door had been faded by time and sun to a dingy rust color. It was the most beautiful thing she'd ever seen.

She muttered a heartfelt "damn" when her skirt caught on a bush, causing her to fall to her knees. Again. Fighting back tears — she couldn't waste energy on anything that wasn't going to get her back to Blue Bayou, to Finn — she pushed herself to her feet and resumed stumbling toward it.

The interior of the building was dark and cheerless, smelling of sawdust and despair. A tall, lean African-American man who didn't look at all suited to such a depressing place stood behind the bar. Behind him on the wall were dark bottles, dim lamps and dusty bottles of wine. And a baseball bat, which she assumed he must use to keep order.

Not that it appeared any of the bar's clientele was capable of causing any trouble. Hunched over their drinks, they looked as if life had defeated them and they were just waiting for the final bell. There were a few muttered complaints as the sun entered with her, then most went back to contemplating the universe in their glasses, as if answers could be found in the brown depths of whiskey.

Strangely, now that she was reasonably safe, fright came crashing down on her. The whippet-slender man came out from behind the bar in seconds, catching her shoulders with firm, capable hands as she swayed.

"Please," she managed. She'd put her teeth through her bottom lip during one of her many falls, and suspected it must be terribly swollen by the way she had trouble getting the single word out. She swallowed and tried again. "May I use your phone?"

Finn found her safe, thank God, in the tiny room the bartender of the No Name called an office. She was sitting on a cracked vinyl couch that looked as ancient and abused as the men who were sitting on stools out in the bar, cradling a cup of tea in her hands. Her hair was a wild, matted tangle around her shoulders, her dress was torn and muddy, and more mud and bruises darkened her face and arms. She'd never looked more beautiful to him.

"Carma Sutra, I presume?" he asked with a calm that belied his pounding heart.

"It's about time you showed up, Special Agent," she said with the same feigned casualness. There'd been no disguising the joy and relief that had flooded into her eyes, the same joy and relief that had swept over him.

"Are you all right?" He sat down beside her and cupped his hands over her shoulders. Her face was scratched and a large bruise in the shape of a handprint darkened her cheek, infuriating him.

"I am now." She lifted a hand to the cheek of this man she loved. "Because you're here."

She managed to give him an edited version of events. There was no point in bringing up the details about her undressing her captor; it wasn't germane to their situation.

He called the state police on his cell phone, gave them the new location to search, then tipped her face back, a finger under her chin. "I should have been there for you." His touch was tender, but a fury hot enough to melt glass blazed in his eyes. "In the swamp."

"You're here now." She curled her fingers around his wrist, and lay her throbbing cheek against his palm. "That's all that matters." She sighed. "I don't suppose they're at the cabin anymore."

"Probably not. But it doesn't matter: they're not going to be able to get away with every cop in the state looking for them. And when we find them, I'll get them to tell me who hired them."

Looking at his face, Julia didn't want to think about how he'd conduct that interrogation. "I know you're angry —"

"That's putting it mildly."

"— but you have to promise me you won't bring out the rubber hoses." She was kidding.

Mostly. "If not for me, for your own career. You're just coming off suspension, Callahan. I'd hate to be responsible for your losing your shield for good."

"I'll try to restrain myself. For you."

He kissed her on the brow. Julia could feel the anger in him slowly fading away, just as the fear that had left her feeling so shaky began to dissolve. It was so good to be with him. Amazingly, and as impossible as she would have thought it a mere two weeks ago, they were good together.

The sight of her being carried out of the office and across the floor garnered the attention of every grizzled barfly in the place.

"You don't have to do this," she insisted. "I can walk."

"Of course you can. But maybe I like the idea of sweeping you off your feet."

"Why, gracious, Special Agent, are you suggesting that there's a romantic lurking inside that big, manly body?"

"I guess there is now."

He paused just long enough to introduce her to the man behind the bar, Alcèe Bonaparte, who was a childhood friend of all the Callahan brothers. Then took her outside to the Suburban and buckled her up with the tenderness and care one might expect for a precious child.

"By the way," he said mildly, "I had Nate move your stuff from the inn to Beau Soleil. I want to keep you under wraps until it's time to put you on the plane."

There'd been a time when Julia might have considered his behavior highhanded. No longer. "Are you sure it'll be okay with your brother and his wife?"

"Actually, it was Jack's idea, and Dani was all for it. They just got back this afternoon." He twisted the key in the ignition. Then turned toward her. "Damn."

"What's wrong?"

"I forgot something."

He was looking at her that way again. That hot, bone-melting way she knew would still possess the power to thrill her in her nineties, when the only Bond Girl role she'd be able to win would be 007's grandmother.

"What?" she asked in a whisper as her mouth went dry.

"This." He bent his head and kissed her with the slow, deep reassurance they both needed.

Peace wept openly when Finn returned her daughter to her, safe and sound. Freedom's eyes gleamed with moisture.

"I owe you, man." He held out his hand and in the handshake that followed, both men knew their previously cautious relationship had just been cemented.

Julia's own eyes stung with hot tears as Finn introduced her to the rest of his family. She could see both Nate and Finn in Jack, but this middle brother was edgier, his eyes darker, cheekbones sharper, his personality seemingly roughly honed. His flowing black hair had been pulled back into a ponytail which, along with his gleaming gold earring and rakish grin, had her thinking of the pirates that had once hidden out in this bayou after raiding Spanish ships on the Gulf.

His embrace was so easy, so natural, that Julia suspected he was a toucher. There was nothing sexual in the gesture, and as he introduced her to his wife, it was obvious that Danielle Dupree Callahan was the only woman in the world for him. Love, devotion, and pride radiated from every male pore.

Dani was slender, with warm hazel eyes and a slide of blond hair that stopped at her shoulders. "I'm so pleased you'll be staying with us," she said with a welcoming smile. "Jack and I thought you'd like our room." When Julia started to protest, she held up her hand. "I insist. As you no doubt noticed while you were filming in the house, the upstairs is still in what will undoubtedly be a lifetime renovation, and the guest room is filled with paint cans. Besides, my clever husband installed a bathtub I suspect would be considered decadent even in Hollywood."

Julia was filthy, sore, and felt like something that had been dragged out of the swamp. The tub clinched it. "That sounds wonderful."

While Julia, Peace, and Dani chatted about house renovations, Finn checked out the group who'd gathered for her return. They all seemed openly and honestly relieved, including Kendall. Which left Finn without a suspect.

Even as he assured himself that Julia would be safe once she was on the way to Kathmandu, Finn knew he wouldn't feel comfortable until whoever had orchestrated the kidnapping was behind bars. But meanwhile, Lawson was out there . . .

Once again he was forced to wonder if Lawson had come after him, and decided to use Julia as a pawn. That idea was gaining more credence when a slight movement behind one of the tombs got his attention.

"Shit! I knew it," he shouted. "Take Julia into the house and stay with her," he instructed Nate as he sprinted toward the cemetery, Jack right on his heels.

"What on earth?" Julia stared after them.

"I guess he just cracked the case," Nate said with what Julia found to be amazing aplomb under the circumstances.

When he put his hand beneath her elbow to usher her into Beau Soleil, she shook off the light touch. "Whatever's happening, I want to watch."

"The back upstairs windows look out onto the cemetery," Dani said. "You can watch from there, so Finn won't be distracted worrying about you."

Remembering that wicked looking scar on his thigh, Julia allowed herself to be convinced.

She'd no sooner entered the house when the threatening sky opened up.

"What if whoever it is has a gun?" Julia fretted.

"If he tries to use it, he's in trouble. Finn's a crack shot," Nate assured her. "He and Jack used to have quick draw shootouts with cap pistols when they were kids. Jack was fast, but Finn was like lightning."

Real guns were a long way from cap pistols. Dear God, surely they weren't going to have a shootout in Blue Bayou's cemetery? Even Warren wouldn't have come up with such a thing.

Julia dragged her hands down her wet face, then leaned forward, trying to see him through the thick gray curtain of falling rain.

29

Where the hell was she? Finn ran through the cemetery, rain blinding his vision, knowing that if he failed, the hunter who'd been stalking Julia and arranged to have her kidnapped would return another day, more determined than ever. Even more focused on his prey.

When he caught a glimpse of a bit of black dodging around a marble obelisk, he lifted the Glock, prepared to shoot, when a chip of marble blew off the wing of the angel atop the tomb behind him. Finn dodged behind it.

"Nothing like an old-fashioned gunfight to get the blood racing," Jack said conversationally as he joined his brother behind the tomb. "Do we know who we're chasing?"

"No. But if she's really an old lady, I'll eat my shield." He took a deep breath. "On the count of three."

"Got it," Jack agreed.

"One . . . two . . . three." Finn darted out, bending low as he charged the obelisk, Jack right beside him, just like back when they'd been kids.

The extra who was once again dressed in widow's mourning lifted her heavy skirts and began running across the sodden turf, past the tomb of Andre Dupree, who'd won Beau Soleil in a bourré game before the War Between the States. The two Callahan brothers chased after him, beginning to close the gap.

"FBI," Finn shouted. "Stop or I'll shoot." It might sound like a television show cliché, but once in a blue moon it worked. He also wanted to be sure he identified himself as a law officer if he ended up shooting the guy. Which seemed like a damn good idea right about now.

He was close enough he could hear the shooter's labored breathing. It was down to inches. Finn reached out the hand that wasn't holding the pistol, his fingers brushing black taffeta. The guy tried to dodge a low black iron fence around a pair of gravestones and slipped on the wet ground. As he struggled for his footing, Finn launched himself airborne, the same way he had gone over the opposing team's defensive line for a touchdown back at LSU.

They went down together. When the shooter's gun skittered across the gravel, Finn kicked it out of reach. Then he put the barrel of his own Glock, the backup piece to the one he'd had to hand over to Jansen, against the attacker's temple.

"Maybe you didn't hear me," he said. "I said to fucking stop."

"Fuck you," the male voice shot back.

"I think I'll pass," Finn ripped off the jet bonnet and the gray wig, grabbed hold of the short hair, and slammed the shooter's face against the ground. "But I bet there'll be lots of guys up at Angola who'll be more than happy to take you up on the invitation."

He pulled a pair of the handcuffs he was never without from his pocket, yanked the man's hands behind his back, and captured his wrists.

"Nothing like the satisfying click of metal on metal," Jack said approvingly.

"You can say that again. Now, here's what we're going to do," Finn told the man lying beneath him. "I'm going to read you your rights. Then we're going to get up. And if I were you, I wouldn't try anything funny, because I'm really pissed off at bad guys in general these days, super pissed at cretins who get their rocks off hurting women, and you can't even imagine, in your worst and darkest nightmares, how pissed I am at you in particular, and how I'd love an excuse to blow your fucking head off."

"You wouldn't dare," the man said. "Not with all these witnesses."

"Want to bet?" Finn countered. "Maybe you aren't tapped into the Blue Bayou gossip line, 'cause if you were, you would have heard that I'm on disciplinary suspension for beating up a perp. I probably would have killed him, but two FBI agents, a Maryland State trooper, and a court-appointed shrink managed to pull me off him before I could."

Finn's emotions, usually so steady, were on a hair trigger. "Get up." He jerked his prisoner to his feet, aimed the pistol directly at the center of his back, and pushed him forward.

As frightened as Julia had been to find herself tied up in that cabin, it was nothing compared to hearing the sound of gunshots from Blue Bayou's cemetery. Despite Nate's assurance that his brother would be all right, Julia was flooded with relief when she saw the trio headed toward the house. She flew down the stairs and out the door, heedless of the rain.

"Are you all right?" She raced to Finn, intending to throw her arms around his neck, but was stopped by the sight of the treacherous pistol in his hand.

"I'm fine. But I'll be a lot better when this creep's behind bars."

She took a closer look at the woman clad in black mourning. "Graham? Is that really you?" With the wig and bonnet off, it certainly looked like him. "What on earth are you doing here?"

"What do you think I was doing?" Graham Sheffield asked peevishly. "I was protecting my property."

"Property?" Julia stared at his face and wondered why she hadn't seen through the makeup and women's clothing to the man who'd proposed on their first date. Perhaps because her mind had been so filled with Finn.

"You're mine, Julia. You've always been mine. And you knew it, too, or you wouldn't have slept with me."

Hell. If she'd known he was going to bring that up, Julia might have wished for Finn to shoot him back in the cemetery.

"I knew we were meant to be together the first time I tuned into *River Road* and saw you making love to that ski instructor in the hot tub at the resort. I knew he wasn't good enough for you. Which he proved by blackmailing you a few months later."

"Graham, that was Amanda."

"Well, of course it was," he huffed. "I can tell the difference. I am, after all, your number one fan."

Her heart hitched as the reality hit home. "It was you who sent me those letters?" Something else clicked in. "That's why they stopped coming after I came and talked to your class."

"Of course. I didn't have to write anymore, because you were in my life. Where you belonged." His eyes narrowed. "Where you still belong. I love you, and although you may have problems with commitment, you know you love me. I want us to spend the rest of our lives together."

"Great way you had of showing it," Finn said as a pair of cop cars arrived, lights flashing, sirens screaming. "Having a woman kidnapped and held hostage in some filthy cabin is not the way to get her to fall in love with you."

"I needed time alone with Julia, away from distractions. So I could convince her that we're soulmates." Despite the fact he was covered in mud, despite his hands being handcuffed behind his back, his voice slid back into that patronizing royal tone that she suspected his British ancestors had used with their serfs. "And, of course, I couldn't let her leave for Kathmandu."

"Because you'd stand out like a sore thumb if you tried to stalk her there," Jack said.

"Watch over her," Graham corrected stiffly. "I am not a common stalker."

"Who were those men?" Julia asked.

"James was one of my students. The other one was his brother."

"A brother who'd served prison time for conspiracy in an armed robbery and shooting." Julia's temper flared.

"James didn't mention that," he said defensively.

"Did it ever occur to you that you were putting me at a terrible risk?"

"Of course I realized there was an outside chance of your being injured, but then I could have taken you back to L.A. and cared for you."

"And if I'd died?" How had she not noticed how mentally disturbed Graham was? "Did you think of that?"

"Naturally. But that was a risk I was prepared to take."

Julia shoved wet curls out of her eyes. "*You* were prepared to take? What makes you think you had any right to play with my life?"

"You belong to me," he insisted yet again. "If

you were too stupid or stubborn to realize it, then you deserved whatever happened."

"If you couldn't have her, no one could," Finn said. Unfortunately, he'd seen that mind-set before.

The professor nodded, as if the idea was perfectly rational. "Indeed."

"By the time you get out of prison, you're going to forget what a woman is," Finn said. "I'm going to make sure the DAs here and back in California throw the book at you. We're talking stalking, kidnapping, assault with a deadly weapon —"

"It's an air gun," Graham sniffed. "I would think any law enforcement officer worth his salt should be able to tell the difference."

"Sure I can. It's a Webley Nemesis. I suppose you thought you were being cute, choosing a model named for the Greek goddess of retribution."

"It seemed appropriate," Graham agreed. "Under the circumstances."

Finn shook his head and cursed softly. "You're also looking at attempted murder of a police officer, along with a shitload of other possible charges, including littering since there are pellets all over the cemetery."

"You know, you could save two states a lot of money by just feeding the bastard to the gators," Jack suggested.

"That's not such a bad idea." Finn rubbed his jaw.

"You wouldn't dare." Graham's tone lacked conviction and for the first time, his situation seemed to hit home.

"Want to bet?"

"You're an FBI Special Agent. You can't just assassinate someone."

"Relax, Sheffield. I'm not going to kill you. But only because you're not worth the trouble it'd cause me." He reached into the pocket of his wet jeans, dug out his car keys, and tossed them to Jack. "Why don't you put this guy in the Suburban and we can take him to the state cops in Baton Rouge?"

"Works for me," Jack said. Finn knew his brother had made the right decision to get out of the DEA after the near-fatal shooting that had taken the life of his partner, along with a lot of other innocent people. But it was obvious that Jack was enjoying playing cops and robbers again.

Finn took Julia aside. Excitement over for now, the others went back into the house, giving them some privacy. "I noticed you didn't exactly jump in and beg me not to shoot him," he said as they watched Jack walk Sheffield toward the SUV.

"That's because I wasn't worried. You promised me you wouldn't resort to unnecessary violence. And you're a good man who takes your oath to uphold justice seriously."

Despite the seriousness of what had happened, Finn felt himself smiling. "This from the woman who thinks cops are lower than pond scum."

"I may have been a little misguided about that."

"May have been?"

"All right. I was wrong. It's obvious that you and your brother are two of the good guys." Graham was now in the back seat of the Suburban. "Why are you taking him all the way to Baton Rouge? Doesn't Blue Bayou have a jail?"

"Sure. But since the department currently consists of one grandmotherly dispatcher, who sits behind the desk and crochets afghans, a deputy on the long side of seventy, and another fresh out of college who's as green as new grass, the jail's mostly being used as a place for drunks to sleep it off. Oh, and last month Jack and Dani's daughter Holly had a sleepover in the cells."

"Well, that does it. You have no right to make any more cracks against life on the commune, since a slumber party in a jail is more off-the-wall than anything my parents ever came up with."

"It was all Jack's idea. He's pretty much reformed since he and Dani got back together, but there's still a streak of bad boy in him."

"Lucky Dani."

"Jack's the lucky one. Fortunately, he knows it."

"That's nice." She'd always been a sucker for a love story. Which was probably partly how she'd ended up on a soap.

As the rain began to pick up again, they stood there, Julia looking up at Finn, him looking down at her. They were drenched to the skin but neither noticed. She felt the heat rise and wouldn't have been surprised if they'd been engulfed in clouds of steam.

"I don't suppose, after all you've been through, that you'd feel like going into New Orleans tonight?" he asked.

In all honesty, she'd rather take a long hot bubble bath to wash the swamp from her hair and skin, and then spend the night in bed with him. But then it occurred to her that Finn was a very traditional man. Perhaps he was taking her out for a night on the town to tell her, on her last night in Blue Bayou, how much he loved her. To tell her he couldn't live without her. Maybe even, she thought with a secret thrill, to propose.

"I'd love that," she agreed as heady anticipation sang like a siren's song in her blood.

The bathtub might not be true to the antebellum period, but it was wonderfully hedonistic. Julia soaked for a long time in the perfumed water, breathing in the fresh, fragrant sea mist scent of candles and luxuriating as the Jacuzzi jets bubbled away her aches and pains.

Not wanting to keep Finn waiting when he and Jack got back from Baton Rouge, she finally forced herself to abandon the bliss of the tub and was sitting at a skirted dressing table, putting on her makeup, while her mother perched on the edge of the antique bed.

Having packed only that one outrageously bare Amanda cocktail dress she'd worn to the parish council welcome party and casual clothes, Julia had been trying to figure out what she was going to wear for what might turn out to be the most important night of her life, when Dani had offered to lend her a dress she'd brought home from Hawaii. Made of gleaming white silk ablaze with scarlet poppies, it was a dress made for celebration. For seduction. It was hanging on the back of the closet door, a colorful promise of the night to come.

"I love him, Mama," Julia said.

"I know darling," Peace said gently. Julia had been grateful when Dani had insisted her parents spend the night at Beau Soleil so they could all have some time together before Julia left the country. "I was fairly sure when we talked on the phone while your father and I were still in Coldwater Cove. It was obvious the moment I saw you."

"Well, it sure wasn't obvious to me."

"Perhaps you were in denial, since Finn's so different from all those men you'd tried to love."

"Perhaps," Julia allowed. Deciding to forgo blush since her cheeks were already flushed with the heat of the bath and anticipation, she smoothed some taupe shadow on her eyelids.

"But it certainly hit home when I realized I might never see him again."

The idea had struck, while she'd been stumbling through the swamp, with such a clarion ring of certainty, she'd been amazed that she hadn't seen it coming. "I've been trying to tell myself that the only reason I responded to Finn so strongly was because he was an FBI Special Agent."

"Because Finn was an agent, you automatically saw him as an enemy?"

"I felt that way at the time." Now she realized that she'd needed to dislike him because the alternative of such a strong initial reaction would have been to fall in love with him. Which she'd gone ahead and done.

"I'd hoped we taught you more tolerance," Peace chided softly.

"It wasn't just me," Julia muttered. She took a sip of the herbal tea her mother had brewed. "Finn wasn't exactly flattering toward any of us."

"Nor your father toward him," Peace admitted. "Believe me, you would not have wanted to be in the bus with Freedom on the drive down here. Fortunately, they seem to have found a common ground in their love for you."

"Do you really think Finn loves me?"

"Absolutely." Julia would have felt more positive about her mother's declaration if it hadn't been accompanied by such a serious expression. "But I'm not that sure he's ready to accept the idea yet. And he's an incredibly stubborn man. Which is another thing he has in common with your father.

"It wasn't easy convincing Freedom that he was not going to ruin my life by taking me away from my wealthy, pampered, lonely existence. Of course he was also trying to protect his own heart, afraid I'd run back to Daddy at the first little problem." She took a blue stone from a small box. "This is the same love-enhancer stone I used to help your father see the light. It's been waiting all these years for you and Finn."

Although she didn't quite believe in magic spells and potions, Julia could have sworn her palm warmed when she held the lapis lazuli in her hand.

She'd just finished dressing when Dani came into the bedroom. "Wow," she said. "My poor brother-in-law is a goner."

"It's the dress. It's wonderful." Julia twirled on strappy red sandals with ice pick heels, causing the short skirt to flare around her thighs. The halter top dipped below the waist in back; and crystal earrings brushed her bare shoulders.

"The dress is gorgeous, and it fits as if it was designed with you in mind. If you're planning to entice Finn into proposing, you're definitely wearing the right ammunition."

"Is it that obvious?"

"Only to a woman who's been there recently." Dani exchanged a smile with Peace, who was beaming with maternal benevolence. "I'm so pleased for you and Finn. He's a good man. Strong, solid, steady. What you see is what you get."

"Not always," Julia murmured.

Dani nodded, seeming pleased with that assessment. "So he's let you in."

"A little. He's not an easy nut to crack."

"No, I imagine he wouldn't be. I also imagine the effort will be well worth it, in the long run. I hope you don't mind me telling you that there were times I wished I could fall in love with him."

"But you couldn't."

"No. Oh, I dearly love Finn, but it's the same way I do Nate. As brothers. My heart's always belonged to Jack."

"You're a lucky woman."

"Boy, do I know that. Though Jack sure didn't make it easy. But I suppose anything — or anyone — worth having is worth a little effort."

The front door slammed. "Hey, Mom," a young voice called out. "Guess what me and Holly did while you were gone."

"I'll be downstairs in a second, darling." Dani's smile touched her eyes, revealing gold flecks in the soft hazel. "Looks as if the honeymoon's over; it's time to return to real life. I'm so glad to have met you, Julia. We'll have to make sure we have lots more time to visit when you return to Blue Bayou."

"I'd like that. Oh, and I hate to argue, when you've so generously given up your room and lent me this drop-dead gorgeous dress, but I think you're wrong about something."

Dani lifted a blond brow. "Oh?"

"I'd say your honeymoon's not likely to ever be over."

"What a lovely thing to say. I'm going to have to thank Finn for the gift of such a wonderful sister." Dani hugged her, exchanged another smile with Peace, then left the room.

"Holly and *I*," Julia heard her correcting her son as she went down the curving staircase to the first floor. "Come into the kitchen and we can make some fudge while you catch me up on everything."

"Holly's got a boyfriend . . ."

"I do not," a teenage girl's voice countered. "We're just friends."

The conversation faded as the kitchen door closed behind the family trio. Julia had been too focused on her career these past years to really think about children. But now that she was in love, she definitely wanted to have children with Finn. Someday.

There was no point in rushing things, she reminded herself. After all, Finn hadn't even broached the L word, except for that evening she'd talked him into going shopping, and he'd seemed appalled at the idea. She hoped that would all change tonight.

Thirty minutes later, Julia was growing impatient. How long did it take to drive into Baton Rouge and back?

Leaving her packing, she wandered out into the garden outside the ballroom. The long Southern day was finally drawing to a close; the perfume of roses and jasmine hung seductively on the still air.

She'd bent to sniff an unfurled scarlet rose when she realized she was no longer alone. She turned, the welcome smile fading on her face when it wasn't Finn, but one of the local movie crew. The snug T-shirt hugging a muscled chest read *Louisiana Lighting Lights Up Your Life*.

"Hello," she said, a little surprised. She'd thought everyone had packed up and left.

"Hey, Miz Summers." His voice was friendly, molasses thick with the sound of the South. "I didn't mean to bother you."

"You're not. I was just enjoying the sunset."

"Sure is a nice one," he said agreeably. "And this is a real pretty place to spend it." He gestured toward the rose she'd been smelling. "That'd look awfully nice in your hair. Go real well with your dress. Want me to cut it for you?"

"Oh, that's not necessary." She'd already taken Dani and Jack's bedroom; she wouldn't feel right about raiding their garden.

"No problem." He whipped a knife out of his pocket and moved toward her.

30

"Damn, that sure as hell felt good," Jack said as he and Finn returned from Baton Rouge.

"Yeah. Not as good as putting my fist through the guy's face, but it's nice to know he's going to be spending a lot of years as a guest of the state."

"Maybe he can start a little theater group in Angola," Jack suggested. "That actor and his brother were something, weren't they?"

They'd been caught by a state trooper as they'd been racing for the Texas border. *"Dumb and Dumber,"* Finn agreed. "But the older one looked like he could be dangerous."

"Julia was smart to escape. Beauty and brains are a great combination." Jack grinned. "And I should know, having an exceptional woman of my own."

"Dani would have to be exceptional to put up with you. And yeah, Julia's pretty damn special, too."

"I sorta figured that out, since it'd take more than a drop-dead gorgeous face to bring my big brother down. So, are you gonna pop the question tonight?"

"No."

Jack shot him a surprised look. "Why not? It's obvious you're crazy about her. It's just as obvious she thinks you hung the moon. You're both single, unattached, available. And let's not forget she's leaving for Kathmandu in the morning."

"Which is only one of the reasons why I'm not going to ask her to marry me."

"Excuse me if I've got things a little confused. I'm still running on Hawaii time and probably a bit jet-lagged, not to mention worn out from days of hot, steamy sex with my bride on every private beach we could find.

"But while Nepal is admittedly not right around the corner, it's still on this planet and planes do fly there. Besides, it's not like she's going to be moving to the place permanently."

"It wouldn't work out."

"Christ, and Mom always thought you were the smart one. How do you figure that?"

"My life is with the Bureau. In D.C. Hers is in Los Angeles."

"Big deal. So get yourself transferred. I've no idea why you'd want to stay in the Bureau after the past few years, especially after what that Jansen woman did to you, but the FBI does have a field office in L.A. Or maybe you could just set up housekeeping somewhere in the middle."

"Like here?"

Jack shrugged. "It's a nice little town. A good place to raise a family."

"In the first place, I can't transfer to L.A. because I've got to track down Lawson. In the second place, I doubt the newest Bond Girl is real eager to start having kids."

"No reason to hurry," Jack said easily. "Have you even talked to her about it?"

"Hell, no."

"Then you have no way of knowing, do you?"

"We're too different."

"*Mais* yeah, you are. You're a man; she's a woman. It's what keeps life interesting, *cher.*"

"She's rich."

"So am I. Probably a lot richer than her. And you're still willing to put up with me as a brother."

"I don't have any choice. You're family. I'm stuck with you. Besides, it's different when the woman has the money."

"Bullshit. I loved Dani when she was rich, I loved her when she was poor, thanks to that lying son of a bitch she let her daddy talk her into marrying, and I love her like crazy now. Money doesn't have a damn thing to do with it. Never knew you to be a quitter, you. Aren't you the one who was always tellin' Nate and me that obstacles were just opportunities in disguise?"

"That's what Dad used to say."

"And he was right," Jack said as they pulled up in front of Beau Soleil. "The woman loves you, Finn, which is amazing, when you stop to think that she's one of the most gorgeous, soon-to-be famous females on the planet, and not only do you lack my smoldering dark good looks or Nate's boyish sex appeal, you can be a real pain in the ass sometimes."

"Thanks."

"If a brother won't be honest with you, who will? Don't let her walk away. Not without giving it your best shot. Because believe me, you could end up spending years regretting it."

Finn knew that Jack was speaking from personal experience. It had taken more than a dozen years for him and Dani to find their way back to Blue Bayou and each other. "I'm taking her out to dinner."

"That's a start. You goin' dancing, too?"

"Yeah. I figured we might."

"Good." He nodded approvingly. "Women like that. Not only is it the closest a guy can get to a female without gettin' horizontal, if you pop the question on the dance floor, she's less likely to turn you down, bein' how it's more public and all."

"I told you, I'm not popping any question. I'm in no position to get married, what with Lawson on the loose again."

"Nobody says you have to go to the altar tomorrow," Jack pointed out. "The idea is to make things official before she goes off to Kathmandu, meets some guy who isn't afraid of commitment, and gives up on you."

"I'm not afraid of commitment." It was Nate who'd rather go skinny-dipping in a bayou filled with hungry gators than allow himself to be tied down. "But I don't have any right to ask any woman to put her life on hold for however long it takes me to track Lawson down."

"I'm bettin' she'd be willing to wait."

"Maybe. But I don't want to force the issue and put her on the spot. Especially since we agreed going in to keep things casual."

"If you fight crime with the same speed, I'm amazed you ever get anyone behind bars."

"Good point. I sure as hell took too long with Lawson."

Jack grimaced. "Hell, that's not what I meant."

"I know." Finn sighed. "It's just proving real hard to put behind me. Especially now that the sick son of a bitch is on the loose again."

"You can't say the guy isn't providing you with job security."

"Yeah." The thought of resuming the hunt that had gobbled up his entire life for so long was goddamn depressing.

In a rotten mood for a guy in love, Finn went up to Jack and Dani's room, irritated to find Julia gone.

"She's in the garden off the ballroom," Dani told him. "At least she was, last I saw her."

Determined to make the most of their time together, Finn vowed to put Lawson out of his mind. At least for tonight.

Until he entered the country garden and saw the object of all his vexation chatting easily with Julia, who seemed unaware of the fact that the Brad Pitt look-alike holding that rose out to her was one of the most infamous murderers since Jack the Ripper.

Julia could not understand what was happening. One moment she was chatting pleasantly with the friendly lighting tech who'd cut a rose for her, the next she was being pulled against his chest, the glittering blade of a knife held against her throat.

"Hello, Special Agent Callahan," the man holding her drawled. "Fancy meeting you here."

"Funny. That's what I was about to say to you." Finn determinedly kept his voice calm even as banshees screeched in his head.

"It's such a small world, isn't it?" Ronald Lawson said pleasantly, as if they'd merely met in Beau Soleil's fragrant garden for an evening chat.

"And getting smaller by the moment. How about you let the lady go?"

"Surely you jest. And don't go making any heroic moves, Callahan. Or I'll slice her fragrant white throat."

Finn's remarkably calm eyes met Julia's. "How are you doing?"

Following his example, she struggled against rising hysteria. "I've had better days."

"Haven't we all," he murmured. "It's going to be all right."

Because it was Finn, Julia believed him. "I know."

"So it's true what they said on *Entertainment Tonight* about this being your woman?" Lawson asked.

"Yeah. And you harm one hair on her head and you're a dead man."

"Is that any way to talk to someone who's gone to so much trouble to come visit you?" Lawson's arm tightened around her; Julia fought the dizzying vertigo that was accompanied by a metallic taste of fear and forced herself to stay still. If she allowed herself to so much as tremble, she could die. "Besides, you're not exactly in a position to be making demands now, are you, Special Agent?"

"Let her go, Lawson. She doesn't have anything to do with this. It's between you and me."

"Just like old times. But there's one important difference now."

"And what's that?"

"Before, you didn't have any real weakness. Indeed, there were times when I wondered if you were even human, the way you kept doggedly tracking me, day and night, week after week, month after month. Bringing me down was all you appeared to cared about."

"It was."

"But now there's something else. Someone else. Which is what's going to make my revenge all the sweeter. When I first decided to escape, I was interested in only two things. Being free. And killing you. But now I've decided to let you live."

"That's real big of you."

"Thank you. I rather think so, as well. Unfortunately, you may not be so appreciative after you've watched what I have in mind for your girlfriend."

"Let her go," Finn repeated.

"Why would I want to do that? It's not as if I've anything to lose. I'm already under indictment for all those other killings."

"The reason you don't want to do it, is that whatever sick tortures you could possibly conceive will pale in comparison to what I'll do to you."

"You'll have to catch me first." The sly smirk in Lawson's voice turned Julia's stomach. "Besides, you'd never do anything outside the law. You're Mr. Black and White, go-by-the-book, law-and-order Special Agent."

"I'm not a Special Agent anymore."

"Of course you're not. And I'm not one of the country's Most Ten Wanted."

"It's true." Finn held up a broad hand. "I'm just going for my wallet here. So, don't go getting upset or jumpy or anything."

"I'm not at all upset. Actually, I'm almost giddy with anticipation."

Finn pulled his wallet from his jeans and flipped it open. "See. No shield."

Lawson's eyes narrowed. "Mary Hart didn't say anything about your quitting the FBI."

"Obviously she doesn't have the latest scoop, which isn't all that surprising, since *Entertain-*

ment Tonight isn't exactly investigative hard news. So, is that how you knew where to find me?"

"It was quite serendipitous, actually. When I was taken to the infirmary for a heart irregularity, one of the nurses had the television on. Imagine my surprise when your ugly face showed up on the screen."

"There's not much that surprises me these days, but I'll admit I wouldn't have expected you to get away with that old infirmary escape ploy," Finn said dryly.

"You've always underestimated me, Callahan. The same way my attorneys did. They actually believed I was insane."

"I never thought that."

"No." Julia realized that she had fallen into the hands of pure evil. "You always understood that my proclivities were merely a lifestyle choice. My new attorney didn't believe me mad, either. She understood how I'd been framed by a desperate FBI that was under pressure to make an arrest."

"You weren't framed. You tortured those women for no other reason than your own amusement. Then when they were no longer entertaining, you killed them You know it, I know it, and if she'd had half a brain, your attorney would have known it, too."

"Well, the bitch doesn't know anything now."

"You killed her." Finn's tone was flat. Unsurprised.

Lawson shrugged. "She'd served her purpose by getting me moved to the infirmary. Once I was out of the hospital prison ward, she was superfluous baggage. It was a shame, really."

"That she had to die?"

"No. Her death was predetermined from the start. The pity was that I didn't have time to do it right, to play with her, watch her beg. One snap of the neck and she was gone. It was like stepping on a roach."

Julia had meant to keep her mouth shut, but that cold disregard for a life, for a woman who'd foolishly made a fatal mistake, drew a soft moan from between her lips.

"I'd conceived a much nicer time for us," he assured Julia. He touched his lips to the corner of her tightly set mouth without taking his eyes from Finn. Her skin crawled. "Unfortunately, it looks as if I'm going to have to alter my plans. Again."

"You're not a stupid guy, Lawson. You've got to realize you'll never get away with this," Finn warned. "So why don't you just put that knife down and we'll end this right now. Before it gets deadly."

"Haven't you ever heard of suicide by police? The way I see it, my options are beginning to narrow. I can take your slut with me as a hostage, but she'd only slow me down. Though I would so enjoy knowing that you'd have to live the rest of your life with the idea that you put her in harm's way in the first place."

"Just let her go," Finn said doggedly.

"I could get this over with quickly," Lawson mused aloud. "If I slashed her throat, you'd have to shoot me. Which would make it a win-win situation for both of us. You'd get your man — again — and I'd avoid years lingering on death row followed by an immoral, state-supported murder, where the small-minded people who could never conceive a brilliant widespread crime spree like the one I pulled off, would take my life as easily as they might put down a rabid dog —"

"Good comparison."

"Well, well."

Julia's blood, already ice, chilled several degrees colder when Ronald Lawson actually chuckled like the monster he was. "It appears I misjudged you in one respect, Special Agent."

"What's that?" Finn asked with the rigid self-control that had frustrated her from day one, but which she'd learned to respect. The same control that she knew would allow her to escape this nightmare.

"I never would have taken you for a man with a sense of humor, even a dark one. Particularly at a time like this. Here's a little test for you, Callahan. Let's see if you still have the speed you did when you were a running back. Why don't you try to stop me before she dies?"

Julia felt the warning prick right below her earlobe, followed by a warm trickle of blood.

Fighting panic, she looked at Finn, whose icy

blue eyes counseled her to remain still. Ceding control wasn't easy, but Julia trusted him with her life. Then she felt another prick of the glittering steel blade beneath her jaw.

"You should have paid more attention to your history classes, Lawson." Finn's words were directed at the killer, but his eyes were on Julia's. "You would have learned about the fate of a certain Captain Farragut of the Union army, who made the mistake of overstepping his bounds. Of taking more than was offered to him."

With the synergy of mind they'd seemed to share, Julia recognized what Finn was referring to: they were going to act out the scene she'd played with Shane. But this time the bullets in the gun were going to be real.

"Farragut was a sick son of a bitch who got off on abusing his power," Finn continued conversationally. "Sometimes he traveled with Sherman, other times he went on ahead as a scout, or came in behind as a one-man looting machine. He saw the spoils of war as his just reward for preserving the union. He also had a personal plan that could have come right out your playbook, Lawson. Rather than slaughter all the women prisoners, he'd turn them over to his troops for a bit of entertainment. For some reason, those men felt empowered by rape and plunder."

"I can certainly identify with that."

"I'm sure you can. But Farragut made his

mistake by going after the wrong woman. Just like you've done today."

Now she read in his eyes. Trusting him implicitly, Julia allowed her rubbery knees to sag, going limp as she'd been taught in self-defense class.

Lawson cursed as the sudden dead weight pulled him off balance.

There was a swoosh of air as the silvery slash of the knife just missed her face.

In a blur of speed, Finn pulled his pistol from the back of his jeans. The shot rang out, sharp and loud enough to silence the cicadas. In a half crouch, the gun in both hands, he looked just like James Bond to Julia's shell-shocked senses.

Dark crimson blood bloomed across the front of Lawson's shirt. His eyes were wide with surprise and fury. But he wasn't dead.

"Drop the knife," Finn ordered.

Instead, the killer's fingers tightened on the handle.

Blood began trailing from beneath Lawson's shirt sleeve, trickled over his hand, and dripped from the blade of the knife.

The knife clattered to the crushed-shell path that wound through the roses.

"You wouldn't shoot an unarmed man," Lawson said.

"You sure about that, are you?" Finn's lips twisted in a half smile that was both grim and challenging.

"You play by the rules, Special Agent. That's your fatal flaw. Because some of us make our own rules." Julia's breath backed up in her lungs as he pulled an ugly pistol from behind *his* back.

Another shot shattered the soft, darkening evening.

Lawson stiffened, then fell face first to the ground, like an oak tree surrendering to the ax.

When Finn held out his arms to Julia, she flew into them.

"It's okay, baby." He pulled her tight against his chest, as if he'd never let her go. As she clung back, Julia hoped he never would.

31

After what seemed like forever, the FBI Special Agents who'd been dispatched from the Baton Rouge field office finally left Beau Soleil. The medical examiner had taken away Lawson's body, and Dani was already planning how she was going to change the garden she'd so recently planted, to rid it of the killer's presence.

"God," Julia said in a long, weary sigh when they were finally alone. "I feel as if I've landed in a road company production of the *Perils of Pauline*."

"It's all over now," Finn assured her.

"Thanks to you."

"No. That fiasco in the garden was my fault. Lawson never would have come here if it hadn't been for me."

"You know, you're really not responsible for everything that happens in the universe," she said mildly. "Besides, it's all over. And, though I would never wish for anyone to die, I think it worked out for the best, because that horrid evil man will never be able to hurt anyone again."

After a brief silence, Finn said, "I know I promised to take you into the city, and I will, if you still want, but —"

"I'd rather be alone with you. Back at the camp."

"Great minds," he said. "How long will it take you to pack?"

She glanced over at the open suitcase on the bed. The one she'd begun to pack while waiting for him to return from Baton Rouge. "I'm almost done."

"Good. I figured if we take your stuff with us, in the morning we can just leave for the airport from there."

"What if I don't want to leave?"

"Seems to me you don't have much choice. You made a deal, sugar. That studio's expecting Carma Sutra to show up in Nepal ready to go to work. And I'm going back to D.C."

She hated that he sounded so reasonable, when she was feeling anything but. Hated the way the warm, open-hearted sexy male she'd come to love was fading away right in front of her eyes. In his place was that unnaturally calm, rigidly controlled FBI Special Agent she now knew he played as a part, much the same way she'd played the unrelentingly amoral Amanda.

"We have, as Nate would say, passed a good time, you and me," he said. "But the time's come to move on. Neither one of us made any promises."

"Of course we did." Impending heartbreak warred with good old-fashioned anger in her breast. To keep from weeping, Julia concentrated on the latter. "We may not have said the words out loud, but we made promises. With our bodies. And our hearts."

"Just because you sleep with someone doesn't mean you're pledging to spend the rest of your life with them."

"That's all it was to you?" She couldn't — wouldn't — believe it. "You just were sleeping with me?"

"We said no strings," Finn reminded her.

"Maybe we both lied," she dared to suggest. "Without meaning to."

He cursed, softly, without heat. Sighed like a man carrying a heavy burden. "It wouldn't work."

"Why not?"

"We live in different worlds. I'm beer and boiled shrimp. You're champagne and caviar."

"You don't drink," she reminded him. "I've never liked caviar, and champagne makes me sneeze. And on top of all that, your snobbery's showing through again if you're going to hold my career against me."

"Are you saying the new Bond Girl would be happy being the wife of an FBI agent?"

"Are you proposing? Or is that a hypothetical question?"

He looked up at the ceiling as if seeking strength — or divine intervention — and made a sound somewhere between a curse and a groan. His expression, when he returned his gaze to hers, was not encouraging.

"Look, you're talking to a guy who spent

three years tracking down a serial killer. You were right about Lawson being in my mind. I ate, slept, and lived the bastard. He was all I thought about. All I cared about."

"He's dead."

"You think he's the only one out there? My work's too demanding, too all-consuming to allow for emotional involvement."

"Whether you want to admit it or not, Callahan, you're already emotionally involved. Besides, we've been through this before. Being an FBI agent is what you do. Not who you are."

"There's no difference."

"If that were true, it'd be the most purely pitiful thing I ever heard. We may come from different backgrounds, and you might have chosen to be a cop, while I became an actor, but deep down inside, where it really matters, we're more alike than either of us ever could have imagined."

She looked up at him earnestly. "I love you, Finn Callahan. I didn't plan for it to happen, and if anyone had ever told me I'd fall in love with a bossy, oversized —"

"I sure didn't hear you complaining about my size the other night when you were screaming my name into the pillow to keep from waking up the entire inn."

"Arrogant," she muttered. "But it does suggest there's some hope for you, that you can make a joke at a time like this. As bad as that one was."

"It's either laugh or shoot myself."

Julia was trying not to think about Finn shooting anyone. The scene with Lawson was still too fresh in her mind. "I know you're not a coward," she tried again. "I can't understand why you won't admit you love me."

"Hell, yes, I do!"

"You don't have to shout."

"I'm not shouting." But he did lower his voice several decibels. "Of course I love you, dammit," he shot back. "Okay? Are you satisfied? Happy now?"

"Let's just say I'm a bit less unhappy than I was a minute ago. But less happy than I would be if you seemed at all pleased with the idea."

"Look." He scraped his palm over his short-cropped hair. "I love you. You know it, I know it, I'll bet every damn person in south Louisiana knows it. Hell, even Lawson spotted it right off. But sometimes love just isn't enough."

"And sometimes it's all you need. Do you think it was easy for me, realizing I'd fallen in love with a man whose work could get him killed? Every time you walk out the door, I'll probably think back on that scene with Lawson and wonder if this is the day you don't come home to me. But dammit, if I can live with that, if I'm willing to love an FBI Special Agent, you can certainly put up with an actress for a wife and two ex-hippies for in-laws." There, she'd said it. She'd actually gone past love straight into marriage. And she wasn't the least bit sorry.

"Christ, you can be a stubborn, argumentative female."

"And you can be a rigid, obtuse male who can't recognize the best thing that ever happened to him when it's staring him right in the face."

"You *are* the best thing that's ever happened to me, which is why I'm probably going to spend the rest of my life kicking myself. But I'm trying to do the right thing here."

"The stupid thing." She blew out a breath as she realized she wasn't going to get anywhere tonight. His mind was made up, his size thirteen feet set in stone. Oh, Julia had no doubt that she could, with time, change his mind. Eventually. But since he seemed unwilling or unable to budge at the moment, she was wasting precious time.

"You think you're doing the right thing, but what you're really doing is making a huge mistake."

"It wouldn't be my first."

"No. And lucky for you, I'm not going to let it be your last. But meanwhile, time's flying, Callahan. Surely you can think of a better way to pass what little we have left."

Julia was relieved when Finn at least let her win that argument.

Each lost in private thoughts, wrestling with "what ifs," neither spoke much on the drive out to the camp.

"Just tell me one thing," she asked as they entered the cozy cabin.

"What?" he asked cautiously.

"When you knew you loved me."

"I don't know, for sure. I kept telling myself that I didn't want you. That you weren't my type. That a man would be a fool to get tangled up with a woman like you."

She arched a brow. "A woman like me?"

"It's a compliment," he said, wondering what it was about this woman that could so easily turn his brains to grit and tangle his damn tongue.

"You thought I was Amanda."

"Yeah, and you didn't do anything to change my mind about that in the beginning. Then Margot said you were one and the same —"

"Margot? You were discussing us with Margot Madison?"

"You," he said. "I was discussing *you* with her." Hell, why didn't someone just give him a goddamn shovel so he could dig this hole he was burying himself in a little deeper? "There wasn't an *us* yet. It was the night of the welcome party."

"The night you informed me that your tastes were too selective for a woman like me. And that if I was expecting to ease small-town boredom by having hot sex with my bodyguard every night, I was going to be disappointed."

"Damn, you've got a memory," he complained.

"It comes naturally. Sort of like your rotten attitude." She folded her arms. "So, what did Margot tell you about me?"

"That you and Amanda were pretty much the same character."

"I see. And you believed that."

"Yes. No." He rubbed the back of his neck where a boulder-size knot of tension had settled. "Hell, I don't know. Maybe in the beginning. But not later. That's when I started making promises to myself. That I wouldn't allow myself to touch you, even when every fiber in my body wanted you so badly, I was spending twenty-four hours a day aching from it."

"Good." She nodded her satisfaction, clearly not willing to let him off the hook anytime soon. "What other promises did you make?"

"That I wouldn't make love to you. That I wouldn't let it get serious, that I could keep it casual. That I wouldn't want you more than I wanted to take my next breath. Wouldn't need you more than I needed to breathe."

"Well." She blew out a short, surprised breath. Then her eyes narrowed suspiciously. And, he thought, a little dangerously. "Did you have your brother write that for you?"

"Hell, no. I haven't had Jack write me lines since I was sixteen and wanted to ask Mary Jo McCarthy to the Spring Fling."

"You had a twelve-year-old write your pickup lines?"

"Hey, he happens to have been a prodigy. But even Jack couldn't put down on paper a tenth of how I feel about you."

"Well," she repeated, mollified. "Why don't you tell me, then? In your own words?"

Julia watched him draw in another deep breath, and her heart went out to him. But she held her ground.

"I love you. More than I ever thought I would love any woman. More than I wanted to." He smoothed his hands over her bare shoulders, down her arms, then back up again. "I doubt if there's a minute in the day that I don't want you. Or a fleeting second during the night that I don't want to reach for you."

The emotions he kept so tightly locked inside him poured out, swamping her. How could he not see? she wondered as she tilted her head, parting her lips, inviting him to deepen the kiss, which he did, degree by weakening degree, until she felt herself going limp.

"I want you now." Her head fell back as he trailed his lips down her neck. "Then I'll want you again." His teeth nipped at her earlobe while his hands moved cleverly, tenderly over her breasts. "All night long."

"Yes." She lifted her hands to his shoulders and allowed herself to sink even more deeply into the tantalizing warmth. "Yes." Not wanting to ruin their last night together by arguing, she surrendered without hesitation. Without regret. "And yes."

True to his word, Finn made love to her all night long, hot flashes of devastating heat that had her bucking on the fragrant mattress, nails digging into his bare back, her own hot skin slick with passion.

Although she never would have imagined it that afternoon she entered the terminal and saw him standing there, looking so huge, so formidable, they fit together perfectly, their bodies attuned to each other even after the smoke clouded their minds and flames scorched their senses. As if determined to claim her, to brand her as his own before he sent her away, Finn abandoned control and allowed the primitive, possessive male to break free.

His greed was dark, thrilling, almost violent as he took her ruthlessly to peak after devastating peak. She'd never before dreamed that need could be so driving, so turbulent. Never dared dream that she'd so willingly lose herself in anyone, or that helplessness with a person you trusted implicitly with your body, your heart, your life, could give birth to its own special strength.

A crimson harvest moon sailed across a midnight sky as they plundered, all speed and heat and force, until finally, just before dawn, hands gentled, lips turned tender. The pace slowed. Sweetened. When he slipped into her, smoothly, silkily, Julia opened for him, taking him as fully as he'd taken her.

Later she lay nestled in his arms, her cheek

against his chest, cozy as a kitten and feeling just as boneless. "You've ruined me, Special Agent."

He idly brushed some damp spiral curls away from her face. "Should I apologize?"

"Of course not." She pressed her lips against his cooling flesh. "It's just that it could never be the same with any other man. Ever again." He felt her smile. "So, I guess you're stuck with me."

Finally surrendering to the events of the past eighteen hours, she drifted off. Gathering her close, not wanting to lose a moment, Finn watched her sleep as the pale shimmers of silver light signaled the dawning of a new day. The day he'd once been so looking forward to. The day he'd send her away.

32

"You realize, of course, that you're an idiot."

Finn blinked against the burst of sun that came flooding into the room as the window shade snapped up. "Jesus." He rubbed the heels of his hands against his burning eyes, vaguely surprised that there was a part of his body that could still feel pain, when he'd been working so hard around the clock to numb it. "What the hell do you think you're doing?"

"Sorry," Nate said, his easy tone dripping with insincerity. "We figured you might like knowing that it's nearly noon."

"So?" Finn reached down and picked the Jack Daniel's off the floor to pour himself another drink. Then frowned when he realized the bottle was empty. No problem; like any good former Eagle Scout, he'd prepared for this contingency.

"So, drinking by yourself is a good way to get into trouble." About this, Jack was definitely the voice of experience of the three Callahan brothers. "Drinking before noon shows you're already there. And sinking fast."

"This from the man who singlehandedly nearly turned Blue Bayou dry by drinking up all the booze in the parish when he came back home." Finn stood up, swayed as the bourbon swam in his gut and head, and sat heavily back down again.

"True. Fortunately, the love of a good woman turned me around. You might want to give it a try sometime."

"It's too late." God, what he'd give for a drink. Wondering what his chances were of talking either of his brothers into getting the backup bottle from the kitchen cupboard, Finn ran his tongue around fuzzy teeth that had been numb for the past eight days. At least he thought it had been eight days. It had been hard to tell with the hurricane shutters closed and the shades down. Which had been just the way Finn liked it. "I fucked things up. Big time."

He felt something wet push its way beneath his hand and didn't have to open his eyes to know it was Jack's oversized mutt's nose. The dog had gotten the name Turnip, because one day this past spring, she'd just turned up in Blue Bayou. The same way Julia had. But the dog had stayed and she'd gone.

"So unfuck them," Nate advised. "It's only been ten days."

"Ten?" Obviously he'd lost two somewhere in one of those bottles.

"Yeah. Ten. Which is not exactly a lifetime."

"It just seems that way in idiot years," Jack said. "This is something else I'm an expert on. Time doesn't stop just 'cause you shut down, *cher*. The old world jus' keeps on a turning. It

425

took me thirteen years to get Danielle back. That what you plannin' to do? Wait thirteen years?"

"I figured I should give Julia some time." He said what he'd been reminding himself of ever since he'd watched her plane turn into a little silver speck in the sky, then disappear out over the water.

"Time to find herself another guy?"

"Time to make sure she knows what she wants."

"Yeah, the woman seemed real indecisive," Nate drawled.

"Besides, this movie is a big deal for her." Liking this excuse, Finn nodded slowly, gravely, wishing he hadn't when the rock pile that he'd been building stone by stone, drink by drink, shifted, causing a few boulders to come crashing down behind eyes that felt like burning coals. "I don't want to distract her."

"Remind me to stop by Holy Assumption and tell Father Benoit to call the pope and ring the bells," Nate said. "Because Blue Bayou's just got itself a brand new martyr buckin' for sainthood."

"Saint Finn," Jack piled on. "Has a nice ring to it."

"So, I take it the reason you two came all the way out here was to tell jokes?"

Jack held up the empty bottle. "This isn't any joke, Finn."

"I know." Finn cursed. "Hell, I don't see how

you did it. Bein' a drunk isn't a whole lot of laughs."

"Spend enough time unconscious and you don't notice."

"Obviously I've been underachieving." He rubbed his jaw and tried to remember when he'd last shaved. About three days ago, he decided. When he'd put the razor away after damn near cutting his throat. "I'm going to have to crawl, aren't I?"

"Remember that old eight ball I had when I was a kid?" Nate asked.

"Sure. You believed those messages like they were God speaking to you from a burning bush."

"It hit things pretty much on the money most of the time," Nate said. "It told me I was going to lose my virginity to Misty Montgomery. And I did, two days later."

"I always figured that said a lot more about Misty's reputation than any magic in some dime store toy," Finn said. "Weren't many guys Misty didn't play hide and seek with beneath those bleachers."

"We're getting off track. The thing is, if I still had that sucker and asked, is my big brother gonna have to grovel to Julia, it'd probably answer that signs definitely point to yes."

"Groveling's definitely in the cards," Jack seconded his brother's appraisal. "Lucky thing you've been probably gettin' a lot of practice down on your knees worshiping at the porcelain altar since you decided to take up drinking."

The throwing up had been worse than the jackhammers in his head. Finn might have been wrong about a lot of things in his life, but sticking to RC Cola hadn't been one of them.

"Jesus, you're a million laughs. Maybe you ought to start writing comedy instead of thrillers."

"Might as well. Seein' I've got me a clown for a brother."

Finn glared at him. Jack crossed arms which were pretty damn big for a guy who spent most of his days at a computer keyboard, and stared right back.

"If you two are going to start pounding on each other, I'm leaving," Nate threatened. "Because if I hang around, I'll get dragged into the damn thing and there's no way I'm gonna risk getting my pretty face broken." He flashed a quick grin. "Hey, maybe I'll go to Nepal and see if I can talk a certain sexy red-haired Bond Girl into changing her mind and goin' for the handsome brother."

Finn snarled. Then lunged.

Nate might have been able to dodge the attack if it hadn't been for Turnip, who, always wanting to be right in the middle of things, got in his way. He landed sprawled on the floor, facedown.

When blood began gushing from his nose, Nate roared in outrage. Then grabbed his brother around the ankles and yanked him down.

Finn hit the wood. "Goddammit," he growled, "you never would have been able to pull that off if I wasn't plowed."

Jack stayed on the sidelines, watching the flailing fists and swinging elbows as they rolled around the camp floor uncharacteristically littered with old newspapers, fast food bags and underwear. Turnip was jumping happily around them, tail wagging to beat the band.

Obviously it must be true what they said about marriage and fatherhood settling a guy down, Jack mused, as Nate connected with a surprisingly strong left hook. There'd been a time, not all that long ago, when he would have swung the first fist, been the first on the pile. Now he was just content to play spectator. Until a crunch of bone on bone made him flinch.

"Okay, that's the bell." He grabbed his brothers by the shirt collars and shoved them in opposite directions. "Get to your respective corners before someone gets hurt."

"That's the plan," Finn muttered.

"Christ, you're pathetic," Nate shot back. "Getting all liquored up because you're afraid of a woman."

Finn looked on the verge of beginning World War III, and Jack decided the time had come to get things moving toward their logical conclusion. "Okay, here's what we're going to do." He yanked Finn to his feet. "We're going to sober you up, then drive you into New Orleans and put you on a plane to Kathmandu, where you will grovel like a dog with its belly in a rut so the woman will agree to save you from a life of booze and despair, living beneath some bridge in a cardboard refrigerator box and gettin' mugged by bag ladies."

He shot a look at Nate, who'd pushed himself to his feet and was pressing the back of his hand against his nose in an attempt to stem the flowing blood.

Shit, Jack thought. He'd better get Finn out of here and on a plane quick, before the prettiest Callahan brother realized that his big brother had broken his nose.

"Give me a hand," he told Nate. "Since the water pressure's shit out here, which rules out a decent shower to sober our big brother up, it's time for a swim."

Finn was cursing a blue streak when they tossed him into the bayou with a mighty splash. Turnip, thinking this was some new game of fetch her master had invented, dove right in after him.

Although it took some doing, Finn found Julia's parents in San Antonio, at an arts festival at the Riverwalk. Peace greeted him warmly. Freedom did not.

"You broke my little girl's heart." The artist's booming voice drew a startled glance from a pretty blonde selling handcrafted candles in the next booth.

"I'm sorry." He'd never spoken truer words. "I didn't intend for that to happen."

"Road to hell's paved with so-called good intentions." Freedom glanced down at his wife. "I'm sorry."

She sighed. Resigned. "I know. A man's gotta do —"

"What a man's gotta do."

Thinking it was odd that this hippie artist was quoting John Wayne, Finn didn't see the fist coming straight at him until it was too late. Knowing it was deserved, he didn't try to get out of the way; just stood there and took it right on the chin.

"I'm sorry about that, man," Freedom said, rubbing his knuckles. "But you deserved it after making my baby girl cry."

"I can't argue with that," Finn said. "If Julia and I are lucky enough to have a daughter, I'd have to do the same thing if some guy hurt her."

"Are you saying she's pregnant?"

"Darling," Peace interjected, "that's not your concern."

"Of course it's my concern. I'm her father. I'm only looking out for her welfare."

"I do believe those are the same words my father used when he threatened to disown me if I left the house with a long-haired, pot-smoking, hippie draft dodger."

"Times change," Freedom said. "Fathers don't. So?" he asked Finn again. "Did you get our Julia pregnant?"

"No." Not yet. But the idea was unreasonably appealing. One of these days. After she'd gotten her movie career on firm footing.

"But you're going to marry her?"

"If she'll have me, sir. Freedom," Finn corrected when Freedom's eyes narrowed dangerously. He did not point out that the older man had never seen fit to marry Julia's mother. Still, he'd never seen two people more suited to one another. Except the woman he was determined to win back and him. "That's why I came here. I thought you should be the first to know."

"Isn't that sweet?" Peace said. "And don't worry, Finn dear, of course Julia will have you. You may have to grovel a bit, but you'll win her over." She took a small blue box out of an oversized woven bag.

Inside the box was a stone, much like the ones Julia lugged around.

"To enhance your powers of persuasion," Peace explained.

"Thanks." He didn't really buy into the magic rock theory, but as he left the Riverwalk, headed for the airport, Finn figured he needed all the help he could get.

33

Kathmandu was set in an emerald valley shaped like an oval bowl. The city, encircled by green terraced hills dotted by small clusters of red tiled-roof houses, temples and shrines, was the most exotic and fascinating showcase of cultures, art, and tradition Julia had ever witnessed. There hadn't been a day for the past two weeks that she hadn't wished Finn was there to share it with her.

She was sitting on a rock away from the others, drinking up the atmosphere during the lunch break, when she saw him walking up the dirt road toward her. At first she thought she was imagining things. That he was merely the product of wishful thinking, a mirage born from her nightly dreams of him.

Hope fluttered delicate wings in her heart. Because she wanted to run to him, to throw her arms around him, to kiss him and never let go, she forced herself to stay where she was.

"Perhaps you need to get a new atlas," she said. "Because you're a little off target. This isn't Washington, D.C."

"Tell me about it. It's not the easiest place to get to." Finn had given up trying to count how many means of transportation he'd taken, beginning with the jet out of New Orleans and ending with a taxi driver who'd bartered the mileage fare like a camel dealer, then refused to use the meter. And just maybe, fifty years from now, he might be able to laugh about the hour he'd spent packed onto a bus where the animals had outnumbered the humans.

"But well worth the effort," she suggested.

Because he wanted to go to her, to pull her into his arms and kiss her silly, Finn dipped his hands into the pockets of his jeans. "It really is gorgeous."

"Isn't it? There's a legend that says this entire valley was once covered by a lake until the Bodhisattva Manjushri raised his sword of wisdom and sliced a passage through the mountain walls, which drained the water and allowed for the first settlements."

He rocked back on his heels and looked out over the valley that seemed to exude its own energy force. "That's very interesting."

"I thought so . . . what are you doing here, Finn?"

"I came to see you. You look great, by the way. You're going to be the best Bond Girl on record."

"Thank you."

"Great outfit, too," he said, obviously stalling. "You remind me of Emma Peel. Or Catwoman. But better."

"What is it about men and catsuits?" she murmured.

"You could wear a burlap bag and you'd still be gorgeous."

This wasn't getting them anywhere. "Shouldn't you be back to work? Surely the FBI didn't extend your suspension time?"

"No. I took a leave of absence."

"I see. For how long?"

"Forever. I quit."

"I see." It was taking a huge effort to keep that polite, distant smile on her face. "What are you doing now? Besides traveling?"

"I went into business for myself. Actually, with my former boss. Turns out he was ready for a change, too. This way there'll be someone to share the work, which will give us both more free time. Jim and his wife have an empty nest, what with their kids in college, so they decided to take up golf together."

"That's nice." Personally, she'd never understood why anyone would want to spend a perfectly nice day chasing a little white ball around, but it was always nice to hear about a marriage that was still obviously so strong after many years. "So you'll be working as a professional bodyguard?" Even as she loathed the idea of him guarding any other woman's body, Julia had to admit he'd be perfect.

"No. Yours is the only body I ever wanted to guard." Her smile turned a bit more genuine as she realized they were, once again, thinking the same thing. "This is more along the lines of corporate security. There's a lot of need for it these days."

"I imagine there would be. So, I suppose you set up office in D.C."

"No. That was never my home. Just a place I kept my clothes."

"Blue Bayou?" That seemed a bit far-fetched.

"No. I've got an office in L.A."

"Oh." *Oh, God.* She pressed a hand against her chest, over her heart, which was pounding against her sternum. She was just getting so it didn't hurt all the time; Julia wasn't sure she could take him reopening the wound. "Any special reason that out of all the cities in the world, you chose that one?"

"Dammit, of course there is," he said in an unusual flare of temper. Then he cursed softly beneath his breath. Scrubbed a hand down his face. "Nate said you were going to make me grovel."

"It's no wonder Nate's so popular with the ladies," she said mildly. "Since he obviously knows a great deal about female behavior."

"He also has one helluva left hook."

"So I see." Because she couldn't just sit there like moss on a rock, while the man she loved was so close, so real, Julia stood up and touched her fingertips to his bruised cheek. His right eyelid was almost swollen closed. His chin. "Did Nate do all this damage?"

"Most of it. The chin's your father's right uppercut."

"My father *hit* you?"

"Yeah. But it's okay because I deserved it."

"Well, I'm not going to argue with that. But my parents are in San Antonio." She'd just talked to them last night. "What were you doing there?"

"Asking Freedom for his daughter's hand."

"What?" How could a man who seemed so rigid, so set in his ways, prove to be one surprise after another?

"I figured, after you told me the story about how he went to your mom's father, well, it sounded like a family tradition or something, and hell, I just wanted to try to do things right."

Of course he would. Julia was trying to think of something, anything, to say when he pulled a small box from his pocket, went down on one knee, and handed it to her.

Julia slowly opened it. "A tiger's eye?"

"Damn. Wrong box. That one's from your mother. To me. She said it'd help my powers of persuasion." He dug a little deeper and came up with a second one. This time when she opened the lid, Julia drew in a quick, sharp breath.

The stone was small, certainly nothing that would draw cameras on the red carpet on Emmy or Oscar night. But it sparkled like moonlight on ice and was set in an antique white gold setting.

"It was my mother's," Finn explained. "Since I was the oldest son, it came to me after she died. I wasn't sure I'd ever have use for it. Until you."

She took the ring from its bed of midnight blue satin and slipped it on her finger. "It fits."

"Obviously a sign."

"Or you had it sized."

"Well, I suppose that's one possibility."

Julia suspected he had. "You were so sure I'd say yes?"

"I was hoping." He stood up again, towering over her, hands jammed deep into his pockets. "I haven't eaten a decent meal since you left. I haven't slept, haven't been able to think straight, until I sobered up and managed to focus long enough to figure out what I wanted to do for a job, once I realized there was no way I wanted to go back to jumping political hoops and having my life eaten up with lowlife scum who aren't worth the bullets it takes to get rid of them."

"Sobered up?" One more revelation in a day of surprises. "But you don't drink."

"I did. For ten days. I thought it was eight, but Jack and Nate say ten. Since I was unconscious a lot of the time, I took their word for it."

"You got drunk because of me?"

"No. Because of me. Because I was stupid enough to stand by and let the best thing in my life get on a plane and go halfway around the world, without me telling her that I wanted to be the one she came home to. That I want to be the one she'll make babies with, if she wants them —"

"Oh, she definitely does."

"Good. Because I want to watch those kids grow up together. I want to get them a big stupid dog who'll shed all over the furniture and chew up your scripts. I want to build a swing set in the backyard and stay up all Christmas Eve night putting together Hot Wheels tracks and Barbie dream houses.

"I want to teach them the joy of growing with parents who love each other more with each passing day; a home like we were both lucky enough to have when we were kids. And I want to hold hands while we walk on the beach when we're both old and gray, watching our grandbabies run in the surf and collect sea-shells, and showing them the whale migration."

"That's quite a scenario," she murmured when he paused for a breath.

"There's a lot more, but it'll take at least the next fifty years to tell it. Hell, I haven't even gotten to the hot sex part yet." His voice was roughened with a depth of emotion she'd once mistakenly thought him incapable of. "I never thought I was a greedy man. But I want it all, Julia. I want everything. But I only want that, will only ever be able to have it, with you."

She felt the tears welling up in her eyes. "Jack didn't write that for you."

"Hell, no." He looked affronted she'd even think such a thing.

Julia drank in the bruised and battered face of the man she loved, the man who'd made love to her with such exquisite patience, the man who'd so heatedly ravished her their last night together in the cabin. The man who'd stubbornly sent her away, then made her wait for so many days for him to see the light. To realize they belonged together.

The man who'd gone down on one knee and opened himself up to her in a way she knew hadn't been easy for him.

"Well," he demanded. "Could you please just put me out of my misery and say yes, dammit?"

It might be petty of her, but Julia loved the frustration that was etched all over his rugged face. Then again, she loved everything about Finn Callahan.

Julia laughed as she flung her arms around his neck. "Yes, dammit."